NEW YOR

JANE S

THE WITCHES' HAMMER

"Spinetingling."
USA Today

"A riveting thriller."
Liz Smith

"Relentless pedal-to-the-floor action."
New York Daily News

"Exceptional, clever, creative, unique. . . . [Hitchcock]
manipulates threads of sex, murder, and deviltry."
BookPage

"A racing plot coupled with characters both fascinating and terrifying . . . keep the pages turning as the
reader descends ever further into a dangerous world."
Roanoke Times

"Startling suspense."
Cleveland Plain Dealer

"Powerfully told. . . . It delivers!"
Boston Globe

By Jane Stanton Hitchcock

ONE DANGEROUS LADY
SOCIAL CRIMES
TRICK OF THE EYE
THE WITCHES' HAMMER

JANE STANTON HITCHCOCK

THE WITCHES' HAMMER

HARPER

An Imprint of HarperCollinsPublishers

This book is a work of fiction. References to real people, events, establishments, organizations, or locales are intended only to provide a sense of authenticity, and are used fictitiously. All other characters, and all incidents and dialogue, are drawn from the author's imagination and are not to be construed as real.

HARPER

An Imprint of HarperCollins*Publishers*
10 East 53rd Street
New York, New York 10022-5299

Copyright © 1994 by Jane Stanton Hitchcock
ISBN: 978-0-06-128421-2

First Harper paperback printing: May 2008

HarperCollins® and Harper® are registered trademarks of Harper-Collins Publishers.

Printed in the United States of America

Visit Harper paperbacks on the World Wide Web at
www.harpercollins.com

10 9 8 7 6 5 4 3 2 1

For Arnold Cooper

In much wisdom is much grief: and he that increaseth knowledge increaseth sorrow.

Ecclesiastes 1:18

The *Malleus Maleficarum,* or *The Witches' Hammer*, is a lawbook published in 1486. It was accompanied by a papal bull, sanctifying it with supreme Church authority. For over two hundred years, the *Malleus* held sway over the courts in both Catholic and Protestant Christendom. Solidifying papal power, it was almost as popular as the Bible in its day and served as a basis for the Inquisition.

THE
WITCHES'
HAMMER

Chapter 1

It came as no surprise to those who knew him that my father, John O'Connell, named me for a character in a book. He called me Beatrice, after Dante's guide in *The Divine Comedy*. A surgeon by profession, my father loved books: They were the passion that shaped his life. His library of rare books and manuscripts was well known to those in the field. Over the years, he had assiduously cultivated what he called his "little garden of knowledge," using expert advice and his own shrewd instincts to form an eclectic but first-rate collection. Even at the beginning of his career, when some purchases were a financial strain on the family, my father could not resist a book that struck his fancy. Unlike most other collectors, who sell their finds or trade them up for rarer, more valuable ones, having bought a book, Dad never let it out of his possession. To him, books were friends; once acquired, they were his for life.

The man most instrumental in helping my father form his collection was Giuseppe Antonelli, a renowned Italian book dealer, who sold him some outstanding treasures over the years, including a Book of Hours illuminated by del Cherico, Niclaus Jenson's incunabulum of Pliny's *Historia naturalis*, printed on vellum, and a complete set of the *Divina commedia*, with illustrations, published in 1804 by the master printer Giambattista Bodoni.

Dad met Giuseppe Antonelli in Rome in 1964. He liked to recall the day he wandered into a tiny rare-book shop on the Via Monserrato, where a volume of Plutarch's *Lives* on display in the window caught his eye. He bought the book on the spot and entered into a lengthy discussion with the proprietor, who spoke perfect English with a light Italian accent.

"Giuseppe and I recognized each other immediately, like Rosicrucians," Dad would say later. "We both knew a bookman when we saw one."

In the ensuing years, the relationship between the two men evolved into something more than that of client and dealer. They forged a genuine friendship with each other, based upon their mutual appreciation and love of rare books. Whenever Signor Antonelli visited New York, he paid a call on us in our town house overlooking the East River on Beekman Place, a quiet neighborhood, well away from the bustle of city life. Our four-story brownstone is one of a number of old-fashioned houses on the charming tree-lined block. Sometimes Antonelli brought with him a parcel of wares he thought might be of interest to my father. Dad, in turn, took pleasure in showing Antonelli his recent acquisitions. On occasion, a curator in the field or another bookman was invited to dine with the two gentlemen. Afterward, I remember how they would sit in the library, drinking brandy, smoking cigars, trading book stories, until long past midnight.

Giuseppe Antonelli was a wiry little man. Angular cheekbones, a prominent nose, and meticulous grooming gave him a striking profile. His beady black eyes, sparkling with inquisitiveness, were forever darting about in search of an object or a person to pin with their penetrating gaze. My father, on the other hand, was big and stocky. His large features and gentle pale-blue eyes were dominated by a mane of white hair. A ready smile and a shambling, cozy appearance contributed to his aura of strength and intelligence.

Signor Antonelli always wore a starched white shirt, a pinstriped suit, cut in the English style, and highly polished black shoes. He sported a cane, the handle of which was a gold hawk's head with an elongated beak. The sculpted bird had red ruby eyes and I was a little frightened of it as a child. Antonelli presented a marked contrast to my Dad, whose clothes, casual or formal, never seemed to fit him.

Even in their manner, the two men could not have seemed more dissimilar. Antonelli maintained a somewhat stiff, formal edge, while my father was naturally outgoing and friendly. However, there was an underlying remoteness in them both, which I believe expressed itself in their obsessive love of books and the solitary life of reading.

In later years, Signor Antonelli, semiretired, made fewer visits to the United States. However, he and my father continued to correspond. A bachelor, Antonelli filled his days with his studies and the company of a few close friends, while Dad enjoyed the life of a family man. When my mother, Elizabeth, Dad's wife of thirty-seven years, had died, two years before, Signor Antonelli sent his friend an incunabulum of Latin meditations on the life of Christ as a remembrance. Dad was a surgeon and he took a rather dim view of religion and its supposed consolations, but he much appreciated his old friend's gesture.

In the wake of my mother's death Dad grew pretty depressed, rattling around alone in his big house. Neither his work nor his library seemed to fill the void created by her passing. I, too, missed my mother very much. My own marriage had ended in divorce the previous year and I found myself drifting closer to my father because we comforted one another greatly. Eventually, I gave up my apartment and moved back home with him. We said it was only temporary, but as the days drifted on the arrangement suited us so well that no effort was made to change it.

One day, my father announced that Signor Antonelli was coming to New York, after a four-year hiatus. As the day approached, I watched him anticipate his old friend's visit with growing impatience, and I was pretty sure that his agitation somehow involved a book. I hadn't seen him quite so jumpy since he'd discovered a copy of the rare and valuable Bay Psalm Book, one of the earliest examples of Colonial printing, at a rummage sale outside Boston over fifteen years earlier.

Dad was often secretive about the books he acquired, or was thinking of acquiring, particularly if they had an odd provenance. Mom had learned early in their marriage not to intrude upon his collector's mind, and she had taught me likewise. When he'd get into one of his moods, he'd retreat to his library after work and shut himself in for hours. During those periods, my mother, who had a wry streak, used to joke that Dad was "away with his mistresses" but that luckily for her, most of them were "several hundred years old."

A few days before Signor Antonelli was scheduled to arrive, my father spent increasingly more time alone in his favorite room. Insisting on early suppers, he didn't linger over his coffee, listen to classical music, or discuss the news of the day with me as he usually did. He excused himself from the table abruptly and retreated to his library for the rest of the night, the door always closed. When I asked him why he was being so secretive, he responded evasively.

I knew better than to press him. Encroaching old age and the recent sorrows of life had deepened and darkened all his moods, and I decided it was best to let this one simply run its course. I just went on about my own business, knowing that sooner or later he would tell me what was going on.

Finally, the day of Antonelli's visit came. I felt my father's spirits lift when the doorbell rang promptly at seven-thirty that evening and Signor Antonelli, still the dapper dresser, still sporting the same hawk's-head cane, walked through the front door.

"Giuseppe! Welcome, welcome!" Dad cried warmly, shaking hands with the gaunt old gentleman.

"My dear John, how good it is to see you! *É cara Beatrice*," he said with a stiff smile and I figured it was because he was a bit taken aback by my appearance. Well, I was older, after all, and I was never one to pay too much attention to my looks.

The last time he'd seen me, I was wearing my brown hair
pulled back into a ponytail and I still had a fairly girlish
face. But now my hair was shorter and I looked my thirty-
two years of age, if not older. I didn't wear any makeup or
bother much about clothes. I just wasn't all that interested
in my appearance. The only feature of mine that I quite
liked were my eyes, which were large and blue, like my
father's.

"Giuseppe, I can't tell you how much I've been looking
forward to your visit," Dad said as I led the two men upstairs. "You haven't changed a bit."

"Nor you, John."

"No? I feel old. We'll have a drink before dinner, shall
we?" he said, affectionately patting his old friend on the
back as they climbed the stairs in tandem.

In the living room, I fixed Dad and Signor Antonelli
scotches and poured myself a glass of white wine. I sat by
silently, listening to them as they entered into polite small
talk. I stared at Antonelli—who looked jaundiced and
juiceless, like a dried lemon of a man—casually wondering if he'd ever had a passionate relationship with anyone.
He seemed so self-contained and cerebral.

Signor Antonelli allowed as how New York had changed
for the worse since his last trip. He said his regular hotel was
under new management, which, not knowing him, took no
pains to accord him the special treatment he was used to.
Dad, in turn, spoke briefly of the escalating turmoil in the
world, touching upon the political situation here and abroad.
The four years between the two old friends quickly melted
away, however, and the conversation took a more personal
turn.

"John," Antonelli said, "please let me say again how
sorry I am about Elizabeth. She was a lovely person, very
simpatica. I remember her with great fondness."

"That's very kind of you, Giuseppe . . . Yes, it's god-
awfully lonely here without her. Thank God for Beatrice,"
my father said, beaming at me. "She's moved back in with

me for a while. Gave up her apartment to be with her old man, didn't you, hon? Taking care of your dad now."

I gave him a little smile.

"Ah, so you and your husband live here?" Signor Antonelli asked.

"No, actually . . . I'm divorced," I said.

"Oh, I am so sorry," Signor Antonelli said with an air of concern. "I never met your husband, but he looked like a fine fellow from the little wedding picture your mother so kindly sent me."

I recalled the small marriage ceremony, which had taken place in that very room over five years earlier, remembering it as the happiest day of my life. However, my thoughts quickly tumbled through the dissolution of the union and the painful breakup we had.

"It was for the best," I said. "Anyway, I was looking for another place when my mother died, and Daddy seemed so lonely here in this big old house that I thought, well, why not just move back in here for a while until things get a little more settled?"

"She's like the daughter who came for dinner. I can't get rid of her!" Dad joked.

"I couldn't very well leave you to rattle around here all by yourself," I said.

"She's a devoted daughter. She's here because she knows I need her."

"Children must be a great comfort in one's old age," Signor Antonelli said with a wistful sigh. "I do not regret never having married. But I do regret never having had a child."

"So what are you up to, Giuseppe? Enjoying your retirement?" my father asked.

"Well, as you know, John, in my profession, one never really retires. It is true I have sold my shop. But I continue to deal privately for a few very special clients, among them you, my dear friend." He toasted my father with his glass of scotch. "In fact, I am very, very anxious to see this mysterious book about which you have written to me."

"I haven't told Beatrice anything about it yet."

"Then it must be very mysterious indeed!" cried Antonelli with mock seriousness.

"Oh, you know Daddy. He's like that about his books sometimes. I'm used to it."

"Yeah, I've been pretty distracted for the last few days, haven't I, Bea? . . . But she understands me," he said with an affectionate wink.

Just then, the clock on the mantelpiece chimed eight.

"Come on, let's eat," my father said, putting down his glass decisively. "I'll tell you the whole story at dinner."

Signor Antonelli and I followed my Dad downstairs to the dining room, where the round table in front of the bay window facing the tiny back garden was set for supper. The men helped themselves to the cold buffet laid out on the sideboard while I lit the candles around the room.

"Please excuse our informality," Dad said, pouring his friend a glass of red wine. "I let the cook go when Liz died, so it's a little bit catch-as-catch-can."

"But this is delicious!" Antonelli exclaimed, forking in a bite of *vitello tonnato*. "Who made it?"

"I did," I said as I joined them at the table with a plate of food.

"You are a marvelous cook. This is just the sort of supper I like."

I was pleased. I enjoyed cooking for my father even though he seldom noticed the finer points of my efforts. Dad didn't care that much about food. "Fuel for the engine" is what he called it and, indeed, how he thought about even the tastiest delicacies.

"I must say, it is lovely to be in a proper house rather than an apartment. What one misses in a city is space." Antonelli said, looking out onto the enclosed garden, where twilight was descending. "It is so relaxing and comfortable here—not at all like being in New York."

"It's really too big for me now, even with Bea here. But I can't leave it on account of my library."

"Not just because of the library, Daddy. All your memories are here. You said so yourself. Mother's here."

"Yes, you're right. Liz loved this house. Anyway, it'd be hell to pack up all those years of living. I don't know what you're gonna do when your old man croaks, Bea."

"Daddy, please. I can't stand when you say things like that." It pained me greatly to think that one day I might be without him, the only family I had left.

"I'm leaving the library to Beatrice," he went on. "She'll decide what she wants to do with it."

"Signor Antonelli, you can see this is a subject I hate," I said. "But rest assured my father's library will remain intact. It will go to a public library or a university with my father's name on it, so people can know what a wonderful collector he is."

"With one little exception, of course," my father said.

"And what is that?" Signor Antonelli inquired.

"In fact, it's an incunabulum you sold me. The *Roman de la Rose*. She's always fancied it, haven't you, Bea?"

I nodded.

"Ah, the poem of courtly love," Antonelli said. "A very good choice." He looked more closely at me as if divining for the first time a romantic streak in me.

"Now, John," Antonelli continued, "when are you going to tell us about this mysterious book you have acquired?"

"Yes, Daddy. I'm longing to hear about it too."

My father leaned forward and cleared his throat. He folded his large hands in front of him, looking somber. I poured us all some more wine and Signor Antonelli and I sat back, making ourselves comfortable, prepared to listen to the story.

"About a year ago," my father began, "I performed an operation on a referral patient from Oklahoma City. The operation was a success. The man went back to Oklahoma, and I didn't give it any more thought until one day last month, when a package arrived with the following letter." He extracted a piece of white paper from the inside pocket of his jacket, unfolded it, and read aloud.

Dear Dr. O'Connell,

I haven't known how to properly thank you for all that you have done for me. I feel I've licked this damn cancer thing thanks to you, and I am forever in your debt. I learned from one of your associates at the hospital that you have a very great book collection. Well, here is something I think you will enjoy. I picked it up during the war and kept it as a souvenir of those terrible and wonderful times.

I don't know if the book is worth much, but its sentimental value is, for me, enormous because it represents a time in my life when I felt I was doing something good for my God and my country. There is no person I would wish to have it more than you, Dr. O'Connell, for I know it will be safe and properly cared for in your fine, capable hands—just as I have been. God bless you.

"Et cetera, et cetera."

He put down the letter and stared at it for a long moment, having grown somewhat emotional while reading. His eyes moist with tears, he folded it carefully and put it back in his jacket pocket. I leaned over and touched his arm reassuringly.

"A lovely sentiment," Signor Antonelli said.

"Yes, the letter's very fine, very appreciative," Dad said, taking a sip of wine. "The book, however, is an altogether different matter."

"Whatever do you mean, John?"

"You'll see," he replied, perturbed.

"Why? What kind of book is it?" I asked.

"I'm not sure."

Antonelli fidgeted with the corners of his linen place mat. "Perhaps I will know," he offered.

"That's exactly why I wrote to you, Giuseppe. Because if anybody's going to know what the hell this thing is, you will."

"Please—may we be allowed to view the book?" implored Antonelli.

"Sure, why not? Might as well get it over with." Throwing down his napkin, Dad rose from the table. "Let's go on up."

Ever mindful of decorum, Signor Antonelli folded his napkin precisely before following his host upstairs. I was so curious, I decided to join them before making the coffee. Reaching the second floor, Dad opened the thick mahogany doors at the entrance to the library. They swung apart to reveal the famous double-height room lined floor to ceiling with books of all sizes. He flicked a switch, which lit up a row of old-fashioned brass light fixtures mounted on the bookcases.

Signor Antonelli looked around, taking a deep breath, relishing the smell of old leather as if it were fresh country air. He seemed pleased to see that almost nothing in the room had changed and he remarked on it. The two large windows facing out onto the garden were still cloaked in heavy dark-green damask curtains, pulled shut to block out all light. The antique furniture was just as he remembered it, he said, grouped away from the walls so as not to impede the locating of any book. He once more admired the old Tiffany lamp on my father's desk, its domed stained-glass shade dripping azure and emerald leaves. He joked that the tall wooden library ladders, which slid on tracks across the vast bookcases, reminded him of the mild arthritis in his knees. He noted one new acquisition—a draftman's table, tilting upward, on which a copy of Dr. Johnson's *Dictionary of the English Language* was displayed.

As was his habit, my father checked the thermostat on the wall, making sure the temperature was just right. He then unlocked the top drawer of his desk and took out a small black leather-bound book, measuring about six inches in height, four inches in width, and an inch and a half in thickness.

"This is it," he said, practically throwing the unprepossessing-looking volume down on top of the desk, as if he couldn't wait to get it out of his hands.

Signor Antonelli and I stepped forward to look at it. The dealer reached into his breast pocket and extracted a pair of spectacles, put them on, and picked up the book in order to examine it more closely. Holding the volume close to his face, he sniffed at it and turned it around every which way, gingerly running his fingers along the binding and the top, fore, and bottom edges, which looked brownish in color, as if they had been singed. Then he put the book back down on the desk and opened it carefully, with a certain ceremony. On the first page, there was a single line of Latin text in dense black Gothic lettering, the capital letters of which were rubricated.

"'*Videmus nunc per speculum in aenigmate, tunc autem facie ad faciem,*'" he read aloud, more to himself than to us.

"What does it mean?" I asked.

"It is a quotation from Saint Paul," Antonelli replied reflectively. "It means, 'For now we see through a glass, darkly; but then face-to-face.'"

My father and I stood by while Signor Antonelli gave the work a thorough examination. As he turned one yellowing page after another, his eyes flickered with excitement. Periodically, he issued a little cry of delight or recognition or horror—I wasn't quite sure which. He paused over the center section, then continued on until he reached the last page. Finally, he closed the book and looked up.

"Well?" my father asked.

"Please—let us sit down," Antonelli replied.

Dad sat behind his desk. Signor Antonelli and I pulled up two chairs and faced him. I picked up the book and began perusing it as Antonelli spoke in a slow, measured voice.

"Well, my dear John, you have in your possession a grimoire."

My father nodded knowingly.

"What's that?" I asked.

"Very simply, my dear, it is a book of black magic," Antonelli said.

"I figured it was something like that," my father said. "Though, from the looks of it, I thought it might have been a work of pornography."

Antonelli smiled. "Very often, they are one and the same, John. It is written in French," he went on. "Printed on vellum, published in 1670. Its author signs himself 'Pape Honorius III,' but that is a spurious attribution. No pope wrote this. The illustrator is not mentioned. It was rebound sometime in the eighteenth century, I would say. The text is accompanied by a series of illustrative woodcuts, as you can see. It has no title page except for the date, written in Roman numerals, and the place, "*À Rome*"—a rather humorous location for such a work, no? What is particularly interesting is the quotation from Saint Paul at the beginning . . . The author was having a little joke, trying to make the reader think he was about to embark on a religious tract, when, in fact, he was about to dabble in the black arts."

As my father and Signor Antonelli continued their discussion about the book, I leafed through it. Page after page revealed the most macabre sensibility imaginable. Interspersed throughout the dense French text were occult signs and a series of gruesome woodcuts depicting bizarre sexual acts, frightening supernatural occurrences, and images of demonic animals and people. A particularly disturbing section at the center of the book highlighted a terrifying journey of death and resurrection.

The vignettes first showed a man and a woman coupling in a clearing in the woods. The woman disappears and the man is murdered by a priest, who stabs him through the head, heart, and groin with a sword, the hilt of which is an upside-down cross. Left to rot, the corpse is assaulted by lions. The beasts then carry the dismembered pieces to the center of a maze and bury them. The flesh rots away, leaving only bones. A full moon rises, and by its eerie light a sorcerer appears, holding a book. He draws a circle on the ground, marking it with crosses, the twelve signs of the zodiac, and seven occult symbols.

Stepping inside the circle, the sorcerer calls out strange words from the book. Soon the woman reappears and tries to seduce the sorcerer, to no avail. Protected by his magic circle, he is immune to her advances. Becoming infuriated, she turns into a succubus with fiery eyes, fangs, and a tail, her mouth dripping with blood. This hideous creature again tries to get at the sorcerer, but she cannot, for the magic circle protects him. The sorcerer continues with his incantations. Unable to harm him, the succubus departs. With that, the bones of the dead man are reassembled, and his skeleton arises from the center of the maze. The sorcerer lifts the book to the heavens in praise as the skeleton flies upward toward the moon.

I felt a strange pull in my gut as I looked at the woodcuts. I stared at the succubus with its bloody fangs, rolling eyes, and flicking tongue, its hair and breasts blowing wildly in an imaginary wind. Was this ghastly, sexually voracious being, depicted by the artist with such evident loathing, the aspect of women that men fear most?

My father looked at me. "What do you think of it, Bea?"

"Primitive, but compelling," I replied matter-of-factly.

"The woodcuts deal with the blackest magic there is— namely, necromancy, the raising of the dead," Antonelli said.

"It seems to me that the artist was quite terrified of women, judging from this image of the succubus."

"Surely, a succubus is not anyone's image of a woman, my dear child. A succubus is an image of evil."

"Yes, but choosing to personify evil as a woman is an interesting choice nonetheless."

"It is in keeping with the imagery of the time."

"Perhaps." I shrugged.

Antonelli and I stared at one another for a long moment. Then I closed the grimoire and put it back on the desk. My father picked it up and scolded it directly, as if it were a person.

"Well, we're going to have to give you a shelf all to yourself, you hear? To prevent you from contaminating my friends! Tell me, Giuseppe," he went on, "have you seen a lot of these things?"

"A few, yes. I have a client who is interested in such oddities, and occasionally I have located one for him. But they are extremely rare, and this one is in very good condition. Also, the illustrations make it particularly amusing."

"Amusing?" I raised my eyebrows.

"My dear Beatrice, one cannot take it all that seriously. Grimoires are a product of the medieval mind, which was full of superstition, as you know. These are people who believed the earth was flat, after all, and that one would sail off the edge of it."

"How about the Inquisition?" I said. "Not a very amusing time."

"Oh, but that was mainly politics, my dear."

"A shameful time," Dad said, lighting his pipe.

"And of course, it all seems rather ludicrous today," Signor Antonelli said. "Imagine the idea that there are such things as witches among us—real agents of the devil. And that if a poor unfortunate old woman goes to gather herbs in her garden, it is for nefarious purposes. Or if a husband loses his potency, it is because his wife has put a spell on him and she is a succubus. No, no, no—it is all a grim fairy tale, if you will excuse my little pun!" He laughed.

Antonelli picked up the book and examined it again.

"But you know, John," he said, "this client that I spoke of—the one who collects curiosities—I think he would really rather fancy this little orphan. May I contact him and ask him if he might be interested in purchasing it? He will pay you a good price."

I detected a sense of urgency beneath Signor Antonelli's apparently casual proposal. In fact, I sensed he was far more interested in this "curiosity" than he was letting on.

"Giuseppe, that's very kind of you. But you know my policy: once a book in my library, always a book in my library."

"Yes, of course, John. I understand. But I thought as you had not acquired it yourself, and it seems to disturb you in some way . . . In other words, it is not a work that you yourself purchased, merely a present, so—"

"Presents are even more precious to me," Dad interrupted. "I have a little section set aside for them. I still have that Nancy Drew mystery Bea gave me for my birthday years ago."

"And just when did I give you a Nancy Drew mystery for your birthday, Dad?"

"You were around nine or ten, I think." Then Dad addressed Signor Antonelli in that affectionate way parents have of telling stories about their children when they are present. "Her note said she thought I'd like it, and P.S., could she borrow it after I'd finished."

Antonelli smiled politely, but he seemed preoccupied.

"I give Bea a book every Christmas and birthday, don't I, darling? Greatest present you can give someone—a book."

I smiled, recalling all the works of literature my father had given me through the years, which I kept lined up neatly in the bookcase stretching the length of one wall in my bedroom. They were not valuable books, except for their contents: classics meant to be read and reread, plus the mysteries I so dearly loved—everyone from Poe to Highsmith.

I noticed that Signor Antonelli was growing increasingly edgy. He caught me looking at him and rose abruptly from his chair.

"I'm afraid you will have to excuse me," he said. "It is quite late for me with the difference of time. Will you forgive me if I bid you both good night?"

"Won't you stay for a little coffee, Giuseppe?" Dad said. "I'm sorry I didn't offer you any, but I was so anxious for you to see the book."

"No, no, I really must make my apologies. I am so pleased to have seen you, John, and Beatrice. And the book, of course, is really very, very interesting—a little treasure. I hope you will reconsider my offer, John."

My father shook his head in amusement. I knew he was thinking how persistence was one of the essential qualities for a good dealer. Dad and I walked Signor Antonelli downstairs, where I removed his hawk's-head cane from the umbrella stand near the front door.

"I remember being frightened of this cane when I was a little girl," I said, handing it to him.

"What once was an affectation has now become a necessity," Antonelli replied, leaning on the elegantly sinister stick.

"What's your schedule like, Giuseppe?" my father asked.

"I am here for a few days. I will call you tomorrow, John, if I may, and we will certainly meet again before I leave."

"And when do you have to go back?"

"I am not sure. It will depend on a few things. In any case, it was lovely to have seen you both, and *mille grazie* for a delightful evening."

"I'll be puttering around here all day if you want to just drop in." Dad opened the front door for his friend. "Please stop by if you have a chance. In any case, I look forward to hearing from you."

"I shall telephone you in the morning, John, when I am more certain of my plans."

"Sure, Giuseppe, whatever you like."

"Buona sera, then. *A domani."*

Signor Antonelli walked into the night.

"Be careful, Giuseppe!" my father called out. "This neighborhood isn't as safe as it used to be!"

"Do not worry! I shall take care!" the old man cried back.

Antonelli disappeared down the dark street, the tap-tap-tapping of his cane on the sidewalk fading in the distance.

"There's something he's not telling us, Daddy," I said.

"You think so? Like what?"

"I don't know. But did you see the way he was looking at the grimoire? Plus, he couldn't wait to get out of here."

"He was just tired, that's all. You know how jet lag suddenly hits you and, let's face it, we're none of us getting any younger. But Giuseppe's always been very straight with me."

"You mark my words. It's something about that book."

Dad smiled. "Always the little mystery lover. How about making us some coffee?"

I made a pot of the strong espresso we both loved, prepared a tray and took it upstairs, joining my father in the library where he was examining the grimoire. He put it down as I handed him a cup of espresso.

"Giuseppe looks older, don't you think? Even though I told him he didn't," he remarked, taking little sips of the strong coffee. "I shouldn't lie, but that's what comes of having kissed the Blarney Stone, I guess. Anyway, I'm glad to know what it is for sure. Loathsome things, grimoires. But interesting."

"Don't give it to him, Dad."

"You know me. I don't part with my friends, Bea—even if they're a bit unsavory."

"I wonder what it is about this book," I said, picking it up from the desk.

Dad poured himself another cup of espresso.

"It's probably worth a few bucks and he thinks he can make some money. He's a dealer, after all."

I reflected for a moment. "No, it's something else."

"Like what?"

"I don't know, but something . . ." I ran my fingers over the black leather cover, colorlessly tooled with the signs of the zodiac and occult symbols.

"Giuseppe's an honest guy. He's not about to cheat me. Don't forget, I've known him since before you were born, you little pip-squeak."

"Yes, well, I think he's going to try to get it away from you, Dad."

"I doubt it," Dad said nonchalantly. "He understands my policy about the library and respects it. Not that he doesn't occasionally try to buy books back from me—I won't say that. After all, he's sold me some great stuff over the years. But he knows I mean no when I say no. And he never pushes."

"He will this time. Want to make a bet? I bet he calls you about it tomorrow."

"Bet he doesn't."

"How much? A hundred dollars?"

"Ten dollars," Dad countered. "I'm not as rich as you are."

"Okay, ten. Ten dollars says he calls tomorrow and makes you some amazing offer for it."

I pointed an accusatory finger at him and he shook his head, chuckling.

"Don't laugh, Daddy. I have a very uneasy feeling about this little devil. There's something about it he's not telling us. I just know it. I feel it."

"Come here and sit down, Sherlock Holmes," he said, patting the couch.

I obeyed immediately, snuggling up against him just like I did when I was a little girl.

"You know, ever since you were small, you always loved a mystery," he said, stroking my hair.

"Did I? I suppose I was preparing myself for life."

"Is life a mystery to you, Bea, dear?"

"Sort of, I guess. I wish I had more of a purpose at the moment."

"I just hope you're not waiting for something that's never going to happen."

"I know . . . like Emma Bovary, ever searching for that sail on the horizon. Or John Marcher and his beast in the jungle. I feel that way sometimes, Dad. I really do. Like I'm waiting for something or someone to shape my existence. Do you know what I mean?"

"In a way. But I was lucky. I had a calling. I always knew I wanted to be a doctor, and that shaped my life right there."

"I wish I had a strong calling," I said.

"What about your novel? Have you abandoned that?"

"I work on it sometimes. I like researching better than writing. But I'll get back to it one of these days. I just wish—I don't know—I wish I had a clearer path ahead of me. Mom's death, the divorce—have all kind of thrown me for a loop. But I'll survive."

"You're pretty hard on yourself, you know? All your authors seem to write good books and win prizes based on your efforts, sweetheart."

I was a specialist in a little-known area of publishing in which writers hire people to do their historical and sociological research work for them. The job was fairly well paying, as people of my competence and academic background are in demand. I prided myself on the investigative work I'd done for several best-selling authors, two of whom had won National Book Awards for nonfiction.

Doing research had always given me the illusion of being up on things, in on things, without ever really having to test myself as a writer. I simply supplied the ammunition to soldiers at the front lines of their profession, those willing to risk savaging by the critics. "No guts, no glory," my father used to say in an effort to encourage me to branch out and write a book of my own.

"I was thinking I ought to go back to school and maybe get my PhD."

Dad cocked his head to one side. "Really? That sounds like a fine idea."

"Perennial student. That's me. Sometimes . . . I don't know. Sometimes I feel sort of like a failure."

He hugged me closer.

"You haven't failed, honey. You're too young to have failed."

"I failed at marriage."

"That wasn't a failure. That was just a setback, nothing to be ashamed of."

"Daddy, forgive me. But you're speaking from the vantage point of a distinguished career and happy marriage. You've had such a full, productive life."

"Well, you see, life takes on a different aspect when you confront death, day in, day out. As a surgeon, I've seen people die, and within minutes of their passing, their faces are almost unrecognizable, because the life force has simply gone out of them. In that moment, it all seems very simple: A spirit inhabits a body for a finite length of time and drifts on to somewhere else. There's no intended shape to existence, Bea. Life is only the moment at hand."

We sat in silence for a time. I thought back to the grimoire and the figure of the succubus.

"Some moments are too dangerous, I guess," I said after a time.

Dad looked at me askance. "What do you mean, Bea?"

"I'm not sure. But when I was looking at the grimoire, I thought . . ." I hesitated.

"What?"

"Oh, I don't know." I was loath to tell my father what had really crossed my mind, so I made light of the thought. "So you don't think I'm missing my moment?"

"I don't know, sweetheart. Much as I love having you here with me night, I can't help feeling you ought to get out more with people your own age and have some fun."

"I have fun with you."

"I mean with your friends."

"You're the most interesting, fun friend I have," I said.

"And you're a darling. But my little *Beatrice*," he said, pronouncing my name with an Italian accent, "I don't want you staying with me because you're frightened of going out on your own. I worry about you after I'm gone."

"I've asked you not to talk like that, Dad. You're not going anywhere."

"I'm sorry, but I think about it a lot, particularly now that you're divorced. By the way, any news of Stephen?"

The mere mention of my ex-husband's name always sent a little jolt of anxiety through me, perhaps because the way our relationship had ended left so many emotional loose ends. I leaned over and opened the cigarette box on the coffee table. It was empty.

"What'd you do with all the cigarettes, Dad?"

He narrowed his eyes. "You smoking again?"

"No— Well, maybe occasionally."

"Bea," he said disapprovingly. "You should see what I see in the hospital."

"I know. I'll quit. I will."

"Do you still think about him as much as you used to?"

"I don't know . . ." I got up and started pacing around the room. "But it's hopeless. He can resist anything except female temptation. You know how he is . . . was."

"Darlin', I know how men are."

I stopped and glared at him. "Not all men, Dad."

"Find me the one that isn't, and I'll give him a medal."

"You were never like that," I said confidently. My father lowered his eyes. "You know, when things were really bad with Stephen, I used to think of you and Mom and how great your marriage was. It's hard to explain, but it was knowing in the back of my mind that it's possible to have a good marriage that made me want something better for myself."

He looked up at me and said slowly, "You know, Bea, no marriage is a steady course. There are always storms along the way."

"I know that!" I said. "Depends on the type of storm, though. Some of them are too damn tough to get through."

"Look, if you really love someone, you can get through anything. Love has to be greater than the sum of its parts, or it can't survive."

I looked at him skeptically. "Daddy, you don't know the half of what happened between me and Stephen."

"No, I don't. And it's none of my business. But I do know what happens in relationships, Bea. They all have twists and turns in common. It's their nature."

"Yes, but you never betrayed Mommy the way Stephen betrayed me. I couldn't forgive him after that. I just couldn't. Oh, I don't want to talk about it!" I threw my hands up in the air in exasperation. "I'm sick of thinking about it. It's over. Finished! I'm moving on, as they say."

My father didn't comment right away, but he seemed to be thinking hard about something.

"Men are vain creatures, Bea," he said. "Some of us respond a little too easily to flattery. Women are better able to resist temptation, I think."

I scoffed at this notion. "Somehow I doubt you would ever have done to Mom what Stephen did to me."

"Well, I never would have left her, that's true. But you mustn't be too judgmental about people, Bea. They can't live up to it. They'll always disappoint you in the end if there's no forgiveness in your soul."

"I'll tell you one thing: I'd rather live alone for the rest of my life than put up with a man who was unfaithful to me. It's just too humiliating."

"Even if he was sorry and wanted desperately to come back?"

"Stephen was sorry and he desperately wanted to come back. But I don't think you ever get over something like that. Anyway, I didn't."

I felt a tear at the corner of my eye and swiped it off with the back of my hand. My father winced as I did this, as if it caused him pain. A rare intensity came over his face.

"Bea, darlin'," he said softly, "just as there's a lot I don't know about you and Stephen . . ." He paused and took a deep breath. I could almost see him making up his mind to tell me something. "There's a lot you don't know about your mother and me," he said at last.

"Like what, for instance?" I was genuinely curious.

"A lot. And I'm worried that you're going to spend your life adhering to a standard that . . ." His voice trailed off.

"That what?"

"Nothing . . . Just that your mother understood me. And I understood her. We loved each other very much, but more important, we were friends."

"Friends don't betray each other."

He shifted uncomfortably on the couch, edging away from me.

"That depends on what you mean by betrayal."

"Well, you were never unfaithful to Mom."

He lowered his eyes. The statement hung in the air.

"Daddy . . .?" I said hesitantly. "You were never unfaithful to Mom . . . were you?"

"Was I what?"

"Unfaithful to Mom?"

He avoided my gaze. "I guess I made some mistakes," he said at last.

I stared at my father in disbelief. I heard his words but couldn't quite comprehend them. "Wait! Are you saying you were unfaithful to Mom?"

He suddenly looked up at me with a pleading expression on his face.

"You betrayed her?" I said, incredulous.

"Betrayal is the wrong word. I loved your mother deeply. But I confess to one or two missteps. One in particular."

I felt my chest constrict. "What do you mean?"

"I once fell in love with someone else."

"Who?"

"A nurse at the hospital."

"You fell in love?"

"Well, I thought I did. But it passed after a time, and Liz understood."

I was at a loss for words.

"Your mother accepted me, Bea," he continued, looking hard into my eyes, searching for some understanding. "She accepted me the way I am, not the way she wanted me to be."

I rose from the couch, shaking my head in dismay, unable
to believe what my father had just confessed to me. I felt
as if all these years I'd idealized a lie, and the thought was
unbearable. I looked back at my father who was holding his
breath as if this were a turning point between us.

"What was she like?" I asked coldly.

Dad cleared his throat. "She was a younger woman.
Much younger than I was. A very decent and good person.
It was very difficult for both of us."

"And just when did all this happen?" I couldn't control
the edge in my voice.

"About, oh, thirteen, fourteen years ago."

"Really?" I said, thinking. "That was right around the
time Mom got sick, wasn't it?"

"One thing had nothing to do with the other, Bea."

"No?" I glared at him.

"Absolutely not!" he said firmly.

Feeling my anger rising, I just shook my head from side
to side, while my father sat immobile.

"So that's where I got it from," I said at last, with great
bitterness.

"What?"

"My attraction to bastards."

A look of shock froze his face. "Your mother didn't think
I was a bastard, Bea."

"Stephen was a bastard."

"Maybe. But I'm not Stephen."

"And I'm not my mother."

Dad slumped deeper into the couch, looking utterly
defeated. "I shouldn't have told you," he said at last.

"No. Probably not. It's better when people don't tell
each other the truth. I've learned that from experience.
Honesty is a greatly overrated virtue, as Miss Austen
said."

I left the room in a rage and returned moments later
with a cigarette. My father hadn't budged. I leaned on the
desk and faced him.

"I have to tell you, you and Mom are the last people in the world that I ever thought anything like this could happen to. Was I blind? Was that it? There must have been signs I just didn't see."

"Children sometimes put their parents up on pedestals. They don't want to see things."

"Yes, but they feel them, don't they? I must have felt something—some tension between you two that I didn't recognize. There must have been some climate that prepared me for the pain of my own marriage." I was full of rage and recriminations as I puffed anxiously on my cigarette.

"You shouldn't smoke," he said.

"I shouldn't do a lot of things . . . But what the hell?"

"Did you ever think of forgiving him, Bea?" my father asked after a time.

"Tell me, are you trying to justify your own behavior, Dad? Are women always supposed to forgive? Is that our role?"

He began twisting his wedding ring in circles, a nervous habit of his.

"Believe me, I'm not trying to justify anything to you, darlin'," he said without anger.

"So," I said, shifting my weight from one leg to the other. "You said you were unfaithful once or twice. Who was the other one?"

"A brief dalliance at the beginning of our marriage."

"A brief dalliance?" I said sarcastically. "Did Mom know about that?"

"Bea, it was all a long time ago."

"No, I'm curious. I'm really curious. You started this."

"All right, yes," he said. "She found out."

"You told her?"

"No. A friend told her."

"Some friend," I scoffed.

"It meant nothing. It was a kind of . . . I don't know . . . Look, your mother and I were married. We had you. We had a life together. I only told you this because—"

"And what about Mom?" I interrupted him. "Did she ever retaliate?"

"I . . . I don't know."

"I wonder."

"I don't want to know."

"Why not? Are you afraid?"

"Of what?" He cocked his head to one side.

"That her drives might have been just as ungovernable as yours?"

He paused for a moment and shook his head. "I should never have said anything. But I thought, if you go on thinking people are perfect—"

"I think people are far from perfect, Dad! I think most of us, with some rare exceptions, are pretty neurotic and generally guided by forces we don't understand. But I did think that you and Mom had something special."

"Bea, your mother and I did have something special. Very special indeed. We had you . . ."

"Oh, so are you saying you stayed married to Mom because of me?"

He sighed. "Partly . . . In the beginning maybe. It was a very strong connection I didn't want to break . . . Look, all of us are human beings and vulnerable, even you, darlin'. I'm afraid you're going to be so lonely if you hold people to such high standards."

"Are fidelity and loyalty such high standards?" I asked, stubbing out the cigarette.

"They're different things, Bea. You can have one without the other."

"Can you?"

A black wave had suddenly swept over me. My father got up to give me a conciliatory hug, but I waved him away.

"Bea, honey, please—please don't be so upset. I'm sorry for you, sweetheart. You don't know how sorry I am."

"Don't be sorry for me! I got out of a hypocritical marriage. Be sorry for yourself and for poor Mommy, God rest her soul. You sure put on a good show."

I picked up the grimoire and brandished it in front of him. "I love the way men portray us," I said angrily. "We're all witches and temptresses, creatures of the devil. Tell me what you criticize, and I'll tell you who you are. It's you guys who can't keep your pants on. And I bet you that Mom maybe did get sick because of what you did to her. You never know."

My father put his hand on his heart and took an inadvertent step back, looking utterly stricken. "My God, Bea. Don't ever say that!"

I was defiant and felt no pity. "Why? Because it might be true?"

"There's a lot you don't understand—"

"*Me?* What about you? You never stopped to think, did you? Mom counted on your love, and you betrayed her. You betrayed her just like Stephen betrayed me!"

With that bit of self-righteous rhetoric, I turned on my heel, stormed out of the library, and ran upstairs to my bedroom, slamming the door behind me. Leaning against the dresser, taking deep breaths, I wondered if my mother had experienced the same sense of loneliness and abandonment I'd known during my brief, tempestuous marriage. For me, my husband's infidelity had been the most damaging, ego-bruising treason imaginable. There was no hurt in my life to compare with it—perhaps because I had loved him so much and thought he loved me. I looked down at the bureau and stared at the idyllic photograph I'd taken of my mother and father on the beach years before. Feeling nothing but contempt now for the hypocrisy it seemed to represent, I turned it facedown.

A few moments later, I heard a soft knocking on the door.

"Bea . . ." I heard my father say.

I remained silent.

"Open up, will you, sweetheart?"

I refused to answer him.

"Come on, darlin', talk to your old man, please? . . . Please try to understand."

"Go away," I said softly.

He knocked again. I said nothing and after a minute or so, I heard my father retreating down the hall. I cracked open the door and watched him enter his bedroom at the end of the corridor. Stooped over, he looked old and weary, defeated. I felt too raw to say that I understood, to tell him that if my mother could have forgiven him, so should I. The self-righteous, indignant daughter wasn't ready to grant pity or charity. I wanted nothing more than to seethe over my failed marriage and the disappointments of my own life.

As I undressed for bed, I brooded about this newfound knowledge. My relationship with my ex-husband now seemed less like an unlucky choice and more like an inevitable extension of my parents' marriage, except theirs had lasted and mine had split apart. All night long I lay awake, filled with regret and rage, thinking how ironic it was that I'd always rued not marrying someone who was like my father. Well, now it turned out that I had married someone like my father. Only the main trait they had in common was one unbeknownst to me at the time—and it was one I despised.

The next morning I heard Dad stirring about in his room. My anger had pretty much passed but, I don't know, I just felt ornery for some reason. I'll let him stew awhile, then take him out for a nice dinner, I thought. As I passed his room, however, I raised my hand to knock on his door and tell him I loved him, because I did love him so very much. I don't know why I didn't knock, but I didn't. Instead, I lowered my hand, walked downstairs, and slipped quietly out of the house.

Chapter 2

That morning, I had an appointment in Harlem, to gather information for one of my writers who was working on a book about black and Hispanic immigrants. He was interested in what he called the "love boutiques" that were flourishing around the city and he'd put me in touch with a social worker named Luis Díaz. He told me that Díaz knew all about the little shops catering to those seeking power over romance through the charms of the cult of Santería.

I'd phoned Díaz earlier in the week to ask some general questions and to set up a meeting. He sounded quite knowledgeable. When I asked specifically about the love boutiques, he'd told me that most of the potions and powders sold in such establishments were ineffective and harmless.

"For five dollars, you can buy an amulet guaranteed to attract a mate," he explained, talking with a slight Hispanic accent. "For ten, you can get a powder and sprinkle it on your lover's food to make him faithful. Mostly they're kind of seedy places run by bodega owners who want to make a quick buck off the lovesick. But I'm going to take you somewhere special," he assured me. "A place of real power."

Being innately skeptical about such things, I'd initially dismissed Díaz's claim. But since I'd seen the grimoire, I was more intrigued with the concept of dark, mystical sexuality and with magic itself. I'd arranged to meet Díaz at nine a.m. in front of Sister Marleu's shop, near Second Avenue at 113th Street.

"How will I recognize you?" I'd asked him.

"I'll recognize you," Díaz said, and hung up.

Two things were on my mind as I left the house that morning: the argument with my father and the grimoire. Though they were seemingly unrelated, the knowledge of my father's infidelities and the horrific image of the book's female succubus kept preying on my mind, coiling around each other, inexorably linked. I tried hard to concentrate on other things as I boarded the uptown bus, but I felt an uncontrollable anger switching this way and that between my father and, to my surprise, myself.

I got off the bus at 125th Street and began walking. The neighborhood was a combination of vitality and poverty. Distant strains of rap and salsa music wafted through the air. A group of kids played on the sidewalk, splashing one another with water spewing from a broken fire hydrant. Delicious cooking smells from open windows mingled with a slight stench of garbage. I passed a homeless man camped inside the carcass of a stripped car and noticed a couple of syringes and a used condom discarded in the gutter. A few people loitering on the stoops of the old brownstones eyed me with passing interest as I made my way down the block.

A young couple was walking ahead of me, holding hands. The girl was light-skinned and blandly pretty. She wore the same type of uniform I'd worn when I attended Catholic school. The boy was wearing chinos and a sweater. His face was beautiful in the way that the faces of adolescent boys can be beautiful—that is to say, almost feminine—with a delicate nose and a full-lipped mouth. Gazing into each other's eyes, they looked dreamily romantic.

They stopped abruptly, and I stopped too. I watched as the girl suddenly grabbed the young man's head with both her hands and insinuated her tongue into his mouth. They kissed and fondled each other, oblivious to the life of the street. I confess I stood mesmerized, impaled on a blade of longing. I finally walked past them, unsure if what I was feeling was distaste or simple jealousy.

I came to a tiny storefront wedged between a dry cleaners and a convenience store. A short flight of steps led to the entrance below, the door of which was partially open. A reddish glow radiated from within. A hand-painted sign nailed above the doorway spelled out the name SISTER MARLEU in uneven red letters. As I peered down, wondering if I should wait for my contact on the street or venture into the shop, I felt a light tap on my shoulder. Whirling around, I found myself staring at a man who stood slightly too near me.

"Did I frighten you? Forgive me," he said in that low, lightly accented voice I recognized from my phone conversation. "I am Luis Díaz. Hello."

Díaz was an extraordinarily handsome young man of medium height, with a smooth, tan complexion and wavy black hair slicked back in long, comb-marked strands. His watery brown eyes were rimmed with thick black lashes. He was dressed in khaki pants and a brown shirt, open one button too many at the neck. His sleeves were rolled up, revealing the strong, well-articulated muscles of his arms. He moved gracefully, never taking his eyes off me, almost as if he were stalking me. His mouth was slightly crooked and did not seem kind, even when he smiled. There was something feral about him and I felt uneasy in his presence, yet attracted to him at the same time. He was like a sleek jungle cat I wanted to pet, even fearing he'd bite.

"This way," he said, heading down the stairs.

I followed him until we reached a curtain made of long strands of red plastic beads, which he parted with his hand so I could pass through.

"Don't be afraid," he said.

"I'm not."

When I walked inside the little shop, I found myself in a small space lit with red and white candles of all shapes and sizes. It was quite dazzling at first—much more powerful than electric light. When my eyes became accustomed to the brightness, I saw shelves and wooden stands upon which a variety of bottles, jars, and amulets glinted like jewels in the candlelight.

On a low pedestal at the far end of the room was a three-foot-tall plaster statue of a young woman surrounded by candles and robed in a white cloth tunic and a crimson velvet cape trimmed with gold. The angelic face of the figurine was saccharine with symmetrical features, like a cartoon. Perched atop her head was a gold filigree crown. In her right hand, she held a chalice encrusted with faceted red glass jewels; in her left, a wooden sword painted gold and silver. A small plaster tower completed the display. Amid the offerings of bead necklaces and other cheap jewelry strewn at the feet of the image was a glass of copper-colored liquid and a cigar.

"That's Santa Barbara, isn't it?" I said, walking over to take a closer look.

"So you know something about Santería."

"A little. I did some research before I came here. I was interested in how the African deities have mixed with Catholic saints and become dual personalities. Though the idols take on the physical aspects of the saints, they still possess the magic of the old Yoruba gods."

"Very good," Díaz said, seemingly impressed.

"She's wearing her colors, red and white. And there's the tower, her symbol."

Díaz took a step back and folded his arms across his chest, regarding me with some admiration, I thought. I went on.

"You make an offering to Santa Barbara if you want love or . . ." I hesitated, unable to recall the second reason.

"Revenge."

"That's right, revenge. So all these little trinkets are from people who want passion or revenge," I said, plucking one of the cheap necklaces out of the pile.

"Love or revenge," Díaz corrected me.

"Love, of course. What did I say?"

"Passion. You said passion or revenge."

"Well, perhaps they're one and the same."

"What? Passion and love, or love and revenge?" he said.

"You're teasing me." I laughed, twirling the necklace around my finger. "So what's in the glass?"

"Rum. The rum and the cigar are for Chango, her other aspect—the god of fire, thunder, and lightning."

"I wish I had something to offer her,'" I said absently, putting the necklace back.

"Why?" Díaz asked. "Are you after love or revenge, or both?"

Just then, a low, musical voice cried out from the opposite end of the room. "Welcome! Welcome to Sister *Marloo*."

I turned around. Sauntering toward me was a short, plump woman of indeterminate age, with skin the color of milk chocolate. She was wearing a long tented dress and intertwining necklaces made of red and white beads, which swayed from side to side as she walked. Gleaming jet-black hair, plaited in a hundred snakelike braids, gave her round, friendly face a certain ominousness.

"Sister, meet Beatrice O'Connell," Díaz said.

Sister Marleu stood motionless for a moment, appraising me with slow-moving eyes. She gripped my hand and held it for a long moment in both of hers. Her hands were hotter than normal, studded with rings. An inscrutable expression crept over her face.

Staring directly into my eyes, she said, "We know each other, don't we?" in a suggestive, singsong voice.

I returned her gaze, slightly more amused than intimidated, and said, "No, I don't think I've had the pleasure."

"Yes, yes," Sister Marleu insisted, squinting at me. "I know you. We know each other very well."

"Forgive me, but I don't think we've ever met."

"No, we have never met," Sister Marleu said in a sly tone. "But sisters know each other."

When I withdrew from the strange little woman's clasp,

she held her hands up to her nose and sniffed them as
if she were trying to divine traces of my scent. A perfor-
mance, I thought, but not a bad one. I glanced at Díaz,
who was regarding the proceedings with a bemused look
on his face.

"Why have you come to Sister Marleu?" she finally
asked.

I figured leveling with her was my wisest course of
action.

"I'm doing research for the writer Nathan Markham.
He's quite famous. He won a Pulitzer Prize several years
ago."

Sister Marleu seemed to look at me with interest. "Research? About what?"

"Love boutiques, such as this one. I wanted to know
something about Santería."

"That is the reason you have come to Sister?" she said in
an insinuating tone.

"Why, yes," I replied, nonplussed.

The woman shook her head in amusement. "And you
think that is the real reason?"

"Yes. What other reason could there be?"

I was kind of intrigued by the strong energy emanating
from her.

Sister Marleu cocked her head to one side and smiled.
I felt slightly disconcerted by that smile, which reminded
me of a crocodile.

"Mr. Díaz here said you'd be willing to help me," I said.

"Luis may want to help you himself," Sister Marleu said,
flashing Díaz a brilliant, toothy grin.

"I've already helped her, Sister. I've brought her to you,"
Díaz said.

At that, Sister Marleu let out a great big musical laugh.
Flinging her arms into the air, she cried, "Sister Marleu can
help you for sure! Sister Marleu helps everyone! What is it
that you seek?"

I pulled out my notebook, poised to write. "I'd like to

learn about Santería," I repeated. "I understand that drug dealers use it sometimes to keep their soldiers in line."

"Sometimes," Sister Marleu said.

"How do they do that?"

"Are you a drug dealer?"

"No." I laughed self-consciously.

"Then you have no business to know that."

"All right, then. Tell me about the potions you sell here. What are they made of? How much do they cost? Who are your customers? Who comes to consult you? That sort of thing."

Sister Marleu looked directly into my eyes and was silent.

"That is not what you need to know," she said at last.

"Well, it is for a start, I'm afraid."

"No." Sister Marleu shook her head. "You have trouble. Love trouble."

"Good guess. Who doesn't?" I said with a self-conscious little laugh. "Look, I don't want to buy anything, if that's what you mean. I just need some information."

"You need answers, yes. But first you must learn the right questions." Sister Marleu waved her hand impatiently. "You come back to see Sister when you've found them." She started walking away.

"Wait! Please!" I called after her. "I don't understand. I thought you'd agreed to talk to me. I thought Mr. Díaz had explained . . ."

Sister Marleu stopped walking, faced me, and stood with her hands on her hips. She paused for dramatic effect, then said, "He cannot give you Sister Marleu's answers. Maybe he can give you your questions."

I snapped my notebook shut and looked at Díaz. "Can you please help me out here?" I said, somewhat impatiently. He nodded slightly.

"Sister, I told Miss O'Connell that this was a place of power and that you were someone worth talking to."

Sister Marleu was growing irritable. "She does not want

to talk to me. She wants me to talk to her. I do not talk to those who do not talk to me first."

"Listen, I'm happy to talk to you," I interjected. "What do you want me to talk to you about?"

"Chango," Sister Marleu shot back.

"Hey, you're the expert," I said, figuring a flash of temper might be a smart journalistic move. "You know more about Chango than I do—I hope."

"That is right. I am the expert," Sister Marleu said with a throaty chuckle. "Chango is desire. Sister Marleu will only talk to your desire."

"I'm sorry, but my desire's on vacation at the moment," I said.

Sister Marleu narrowed her eyes. "Oh, no. I see a wolf." With that, the little woman turned on her heel and disappeared into the back room.

I looked at Díaz, shaking my head in amused dismay.

"Not too big on small talk, is she?" I said. Díaz smiled. "Seriously, is she always like this?"

"Not always. But sometimes."

"Well, now what? Know anyone else who can help me?"

"We're here. Why not take a look around?"

"Might as well, I suppose," I said with a shrug. I started wandering around the shop. "I suppose it's too much to ask what I'm looking at . . . or for." I picked up a vial filled with yucky brown liquid. "And just what do we think this charming substance is?"

"Drink it and find out. Your wolf may be thirsty," Díaz said.

"Oh, you bet," I said sarcastically, holding the small bottle up to a candle and examining the contents. "It's green when you hold it up to the light."

"Give it to me."

I handed Díaz the vial. He uncorked it and swallowed the filmy contents in one gulp. I looked at him incredulously.

"Ugh! I don't believe you did that! You have no idea what was in there. It looked revolting."

"Whatever it was, it's in me now. And you're right. It was revolting."

"It could be anything. Poison, for all you know."

He put the vial down. "We'll find out soon."

"I guess your wolf was real thirsty," I teased him.

"My wolf is always thirsty," he said with a grin.

I had no idea what to make of Díaz. For one thing, I couldn't figure out whether he was mocking me or flirting with me, or both. I scanned a few more shelves.

"Seriously, Mr. Díaz, what do you suppose she meant by that?"

"By what?"

"All that business about my wolf." I pronounced the word with humorous disdain. "And that she knew why I'd come here."

"That is Sister's way. She is a *santera*, you see."

"I thought a *santera* was a sorceress. But now I know— it's a pain in the ass. How the hell am I gonna get this research done?"

"Oh, don't underestimate Sister. She's the real thing. A great *santera*, and a *madrina* too."

"A *madrina*?"

"A godmother—someone who helps initiates."

"Maybe she saw me as an infidel, since I don't believe in any of this crap. Too bad. I really wanted to talk to her."

"You might not have liked what she had to say."

"Why not?"

"She only talks to people's other side."

"What do you mean?"

"Their other side, their hidden side. The side they don't show. The side they may not even know they have. She talks to that side and makes it talk to her."

"I'm sorry to disappoint you, but some of us are pretty straightforward," I said.

"Some are, yes . . . but not you."

"Me? I'm very straightforward. Too straightforward for my own good, in fact. If you ask me, people like her just want to make you think they have power. A lot of posturing and acting to sway the weak mind."

"Are you feeling weak in the mind?"

I sighed in mock exasperation, resting my hand on my hip. He was definitely flirting with me, but in a light, rather charming way. I kind of liked it.

"I have a logical mind, Mr. Díaz. And my logical mind tells me that Sister Marleu, or whatever she calls herself, is a con artist with a good scam going."

"You didn't feel her magic? Honestly?"

"I don't believe in magic."

"Some of the most logical minds in the world have believed in magic."

"The psychological power of magic, maybe. But there is no actual power. Magic doesn't exist."

"For a smart girl, you don't know very much," Díaz said.

"All right—now you be honest. Have you ever seen any real magic?"

"Maybe." He edged closer to me.

"Are you a believer, Mr. Díaz?"

"Luis."

"Luis. Are you?"

"I am a believer, yes."

"Really? Do you believe in Santería? Do you believe that having drunk that potion, you'll become more potent or whatever it's supposed to do for you?"

"Is that what you think it was supposed to do for me?"

"What?"

"Make me more potent?"

"I don't know." I was kind of wearying of the verbal sparring. "I just said that because it's probably a love potion, and that's what love potions are supposed to do, aren't they?"

"Be careful. Your other side is jumping out."

I groaned. "Oh, give me a break, will you? It was just a passing comment. I have one side, and you're looking at it."

A smile crept over Díaz's face. "And a very nice side it is too . . . So what is it you think Sister saw in you, Beatrice?"

"Stupidity for ever coming here" I said flatly.

I meandered around the shop again and picked up a bean-shaped brown amulet attached to a string of wooden beads. As I absently ran my fingers over the rough-edged little charm, Díaz approached me from behind and insinuated his body against mine. My first instinct was to move away, but I didn't. I don't know why. I just stood there as he edged closer.

"A very nice side," he said.

I felt his warm, musky breath on the back of my neck. I breathed in deeply. Smell was a potent aphrodisiac—above looks, personality, everything. And Díaz smelled delicious.

He reached down and lightly touched the back of my hand with his fingers. We stroked the charm together. Then Díaz pressed down hard on my hand and the little bean cut into my palm.

"Ow," I said softly, turning to confront him.

We were face-to-face. I felt rather light-headed.

"You're hurting me," I said weakly.

"I'm sorry."

He gently squeezed his hand around mine.

"I know what she saw in you, Beatrice," he said. "And so do you."

"What?"

"Hunger."

"No."

"Yes."

Díaz put his hands up to my hair and I flinched. "Hold still," he said, laughing.

Ever so delicately, he started pulling out the bobby pins securing my bun. My hair fell to my shoulders.

"Magic!" he exclaimed, his eyes lighting up.

We stared at each other for a long moment. Díaz leaned forward and kissed me gently on the lips.

"Don't . . ." I breathed through the kiss. But I was unable to pull myself away.

When his kiss grew more insistent, I broke free, feeling extremely embarrassed. I could tell I was flushed. I steadied myself against one of the counters.

"Are you all right?" he said.

"I feel a bit dizzy."

"I'm sorry."

"No, you're not."

Díaz picked up the amulet and shook it.

"Listen, it's got something inside it. Listen . . . the wolf is hungry, hungry, hungry . . ." he said, rhythmically shaking the amulet around his head. His words were like an incantation, punctuated by the soft hiss of the rattle.

"Quit it . . . please?"

Díaz smiled. He put the trinket back on the table and walked to the front of the shop.

"My apartment isn't far from here," he said, holding out his hand to me.

I hesitated, although I was definitely considering it.

"I'm not sure. I've never done anything like this."

"Good."

"Why good?"

"Because first times are memorable. Trust me to be your guide. Like they say, when the student is ready, the master will come. Trust me, Beatrice."

I was both attracted and repelled by Díaz's raw sensuality and, indeed, by my own desire. I stood paralyzed for a long moment. Finally, Díaz strode over to me and grabbed my hand. I offered no resistance as he led me out of the shop onto the noisy summer street. We started walking together. I was unsure and a little unsteady. Díaz seemed confident, even a little macho as he led me down the glittering blocks.

Nothing in my background had prepared me for this type of encounter. The danger of it, the recklessness of it, struck me with full force as I climbed the dark stairs to Díaz's tenement apartment. Unlocking the door and swinging it open, Díaz put his arm around my waist, cementing me to his side as he led me inside. He slammed the door shut with his foot and, jamming me up against the wall, began kissing me all over. I squeezed my eyes shut, shocked by my impulsiveness and my own desire.

Díaz rose to his feet and led me into the bedroom, where a single small window faced out onto an alley devoid of sunlight. The only furniture was a lamp, a tattered chair, and an unmade bed. As Díaz pulled me down to the mattress, I shuddered, for I understood this to be the very moment that all the safeguards of my sheltered upbringing had conspired to prevent. My prim, privileged, upper-middle-class background of private girls' schools, genteel vacations, and carefully orchestrated meetings with "the right sort of boys" was meant to protect me from just such an anonymous sexual encounter, which might, if I was unlucky, lead to disease, violence, or even death.

Yet, in that moment I realized that I'd been brought up to remain forever shielded from a certain corner of myself. Here was an experience destined to reveal a darker aspect of my nature. I wondered briefly if my father's confession was in some way propelling me forward.

What the hell, I thought. I didn't care. I took a deep breath and surrendered to the wildness of it, and the danger.

It was getting dark when Díaz and I emerged from his building. We walked to the corner side by side without looking at each other and stood waiting for a taxi.

"Your blouse is torn," Díaz observed.

I ran my fingers along the frayed seam on the shoulder, remembering the moment when it had occurred. Embarrassed by the memory of my own passion, I started to put on my sweater. Díaz tried to help me, but I pulled away, hugging the sweater close around me to hide the tear.

"Are you okay?" he asked.

"I don't know," I answered in a barely audible voice.

"You haven't done anything wrong."

I remember looking up at him and asking, "Then why do I feel as if I have?"

"Because you've just met your wolf," Díaz said with a smile, putting his arms around me.

"You?" I said.

"No, *you*," he answered with a little smile. "And she frightens you."

I shrugged him away. "That wasn't me," I said.

"It's part of you."

My mouth was quivering, but I didn't want him to see me cry.

"You have nothing to be ashamed of."

"But I am ashamed." I started to weep. "I'm so ashamed. I feel wretched."

"No, no," Díaz said, kissing my tears away.

"You don't understand. It's not what you think. It's not about me."

"What is it about?"

"My father. I've been a fool, Luis—such a fool. I didn't understand how powerful sexual attraction could be. I . . ." My voice trailed off.

"You've only been asleep. And now Sleeping Beauty has awakened. Don't be ashamed of that. But there's no going back now. Call me if you need me. I'm here."

In the taxi on my way home, I couldn't get Díaz or his words out of my mind: "Sleeping Beauty has awakened . . . There's no going back." I pulled the compact out of my bag but kept it cupped in my hand, afraid to look in it, fearing what it would reflect. As the cab weaved its way through the traffic, I slowly raised the small round mirror to my face and studied my face. Something about me had changed, but only I would see it, I thought. I suddenly understood that the powers of darkness—whether manifested by the harmless little charms of Santería or by more potent rituals—could not be so easily dismissed as the vestiges of bygone, unenlightened societies and less sophisticated minds, as Signor Antonelli had implied. In fact, they were just beneath the surface of modern life because they stemmed, in part, from human sexuality and the human response to it.

It was a very curious thing, but as I looked at myself, the fury I'd felt toward my father completely vanished. In fact, I was desperately ashamed for having been so judgmental. Who was I to condemn anyone for the way he or she reconciled the paradoxes of the heart? Least of all my dear father, who was such a loving, caring man. I now understood his longing and his sacrifice.

I could barely sit still as the taxi lurched toward my house. I was anxious to get home and beg my father's forgiveness, to apologize to him for my stupid anger over his infidelity. The only thing I wanted now was to remove the wedge between us, particularly at this time, when we were all the family either of us had in the world. We were alike, he and I, in more ways than I could possibly have imagined before that afternoon.

I asked the cabbie to let me out a couple of blocks from the house, so I could get some fresh air. It was a chilly evening and I pulled my sweater close around me as I walked down the darkening street toward home. Rounding the corner, I saw three police cars parked outside our house, their lights flashing. A small crowd had gathered on the sidewalk. I made my way through the knot of onlookers craning their necks to see what was going on. Ducking under a yellow tape cordoning off the area, I was stopped by a young officer standing guard at the door.

"Sorry, lady, you'll have to stay back," he said, motioning me away.

"But I live here!" I cried, feeling a growing sense of panic in the pit of my stomach.

His expression changed to one of concern. "What's your name?"

"Beatrice O'Connell. This is my house. What's happened? What's going on?"

Without answering, he let me pass. I ran up the steps to the front door and barged into the foyer where I saw several more men, most of them in police uniforms, but some in plain clothes, all of them looking grim and purposeful. Barely acknowledging me, they seemed to be going about some work I didn't yet understand. I approached an officer.

"Excuse me," I said, trying to remain calm. "I live here. Will somebody please tell me what's going on? Where's my father?"

"You the daughter?" he said.

"Yes."

"Frank!" the officer cried out, never taking his eyes off me.

"Yo!" I heard a voice call down from upstairs.

"The daughter's here!"

A balding, heavyset man in a rumpled gray suit appeared at the top of the stairs. He stopped for a moment.

"Miss O'Connell?" he said softly.

"Please—what's happened? Where's my Dad?"

He trotted downstairs and introduced himself to me.

"I'm Detective Monahan," he said, shaking my hand somberly.

"Beatrice O'Connell." I could barely breathe.

He led me into the dining room and helped me to a chair. He sat down beside me. "Miss O'Connell . . ." he began hesitantly. "It's my painful duty to inform you that your father . . . Your father is dead."

The simple sentence unfurled like a big black flag in front of my eyes. Unable or unwilling to grasp its full meaning at first, I just felt cold and leaden.

"Wait—no, no!" I heard myself say. "There's been a mistake!"

"I'm sorry, Miss O'Connell. I'm so sorry. He was shot in an apparent robbery attempt."

"Shot! Oh my God . . . my God . . . !"

Hot tears sprang into my eyes and I began to reel.

"Burke!" the detective cried as he rose to steady me. "A glass of water! Quick!"

I felt a terrible dizziness, followed by a blast of air that gathered force and shot up through my body, straight out the top of my skull. That's all I remember until the moment when I was on my back looking up at four strangers, who were staring down at me as if they were peering into a well.

"Where's my father? I want to see my father!" I said, struggling to get up. It was too much of an effort. I fell back down again. I felt a rough hand stroking my forehead. It was Detective Monahan.

"Where's is he!" I cried.

"Just take it easy, Miss O'Connell," he said. "Take it real easy, now."

It was at that moment I realized this wasn't a nightmare I was going to wake up from. It was real. My father was dead . . . Shot . . . Shot dead.

Detective Monahan helped me back to the chair. I was weak and nauseous. It was the first time I'd ever fainted.

"Where is he?" I asked.

"Upstairs."

"Take me to him."

"Give yourself a minute. Here—drink this." The detective handed me the glass of water, but I pushed it aside.

"I want to go now."

Monahan led me upstairs to the library. The door was closed.

"I should warn you—" he said.

"Please," I said, shrugging his hand off my arm. "Let me go."

Chapter 3

Detective Monahan opened the library door, allowing me to pass in front of him. The room looked like a battlefield. Precious books covered the floor like stiff little soldiers, their spines broken, covers detached, pages torn. The locked, gold-grated cases in which the most valuable manuscripts were kept had been pried open, their priceless contents carelessly strewn in every direction. The drawers of my father's desk were scattered on the floor. A spidery blob of black ink from an overturned inkwell stained the Persian carpet. The Tiffany lampshade was in smithereens. Shards of the delicate glass crunched beneath my shoes as I proceeded slowly through the wreckage. The once orderly, elegant "little garden of knowledge" was in ruins.

There were people at work in the room—taking photographs, dusting for fingerprints, hunting for evidence—but I was hardly aware of their presence. My concentration was focused on the far end of the library where my father's body lay on the floor in front of the curtained window. Throbbing with dread, I walked toward him, like I was walking a plank. One by one, the people stopped what they were doing in order to watch me. Detective Monahan followed at a courteous distance.

I stared down at my father's body, hardly recognizing the man at my feet. Dried blood bearded his ashen cheeks and streaked his white hair. His right eye had been shot clean out, leaving a deep hole caked with black blood. The left eye was glazed and lifeless under a drooping lid.

His tongue peeked out from the corner of his mouth. He looked like a broken mannequin—his torso twisted, his legs zigzagged one on top of the other, his arms extended in a macabre gesture of welcome, as if he had been mowed down in the middle of an embrace. A urine stain had seeped through the front of his trousers.

In the room's deepening silence, I stood over this grim spectacle in a trance for I don't know how long. Then my knees seemed to give way and I sank down in front of his body and heard myself let out a wail of grief.

"Oh, Daddy, Daddy, Daddy!" I cried, rocking back and forth with my hands clasped in front of me.

Finally, I looked back at Detective Monahan, who was standing behind me and asked, "Can I touch him?"

He nodded and I tentatively touched my father's maimed face and stroked his hair with the tips of my fingers. My tears dropped down and mingled with his blood. I leaned over and kissed his cheek, allowing my lips to linger on his cold flesh.

"Forgive me, Daddy . . . Please forgive me," I whispered. "I love you . . . I love you. Forgive me . . ."

I finally stumbled to my feet, aided by Detective Monahan, who supported me as I rose. He led me to the couch and sat me down, signaling the workers in the room to go on about their business.

"Are you all right?" he asked.

"I can't believe it," I wept. "I just can't believe it. Who would do this to my father? He was the sweetest, dearest, kindest man. He was so good. He was. He really was. Who did this terrible thing?"

"We're going to try and find out," Monahan said, handing me a tissue. "Do you feel up to answering some questions, Miss O'Connell?"

"If it will help you." I blew my nose and wiped away the tears. Monahan extracted a small notebook and a pencil from his jacket pocket and began a gentle interrogation.

"Where were you today, Miss O'Connell?"

The question stung me and I hesitated. "I was up in Harlem, doing research."

"Were you with anybody?"

"Yes," I said, feeling myself flush. "A social worker named Luis Díaz."

"You were with him all day?"

"Yes." I lowered my eyes.

"You'll tell us where we can get in touch with him, of course."

I nodded as the detective jotted down notes.

"Did your father have any enemies that you know of?"

"No! Everyone loved him, I told you. He was a doctor. A surgeon. A healer. Who could have wanted to harm him? Who?"

I broke down again. Monahan waited patiently for me to recover. He continued to question me, but sometimes his words blurred in my mind and lost their meaning altogether, as if he'd lapsed into a foreign language. I couldn't help glancing over at my father's body, half expecting him to jump up, take off that hideous mask, and announce it was all a joke.

Presently, the plump old housekeeper, Nellie Riley, entered the room. She had to be supported by an officer. Nellie's kind, open face, usually as fresh as a colleen's despite her years, looked as if it had been trampled. Her rat-red eyes, quivering lips, and tear-glazed cheeks formed a picture of anguish. I sprang from the couch to embrace the stricken woman.

"Oh, Miss Beatrice!" she cried. "Forgive me, forgive me. I didn't know, I didn't know!"

Clinging hard, Nellie buried her head in my chest and sobbed inconsolably.

"It's all right, Nellie, dear. It's all right," I said, patting the old woman's head.

"It was Miss Riley here who found your father and telephoned us," Monahan said.

"Oh, Nellie, how awful for you," I said.

"I didn't understand," the housekeeper said, a dazed expression on her face. "You must believe me. I didn't know!"

"I believe you, Nellie, dear. How could you have known?" I said, believing the old woman to be in a state of shock.

"Please, Miss Beatrice, you mustn't blame me." She looked at me with fear in her eyes.

"Blame you? Of course I don't blame you, Nellie."

As I hugged the old woman close, two men hoisted my father's body onto a gurney and covered it with a sheet. Locked together in anguish, Nellie and I watched the corpse being wheeled out of the room. Nellie shrank back and blessed herself as the body passed by her. I tried to say a silent prayer, but the words turned to ashes in my mouth as I asked myself what kind of God could have let this happen to such a good and decent man.

After the body was gone, Detective Monahan continued to question me and Nellie. Nellie kept begging me to forgive her. She was clearly overwrought and I persuaded Monahan to let her have a sedative. After that, the detective sent her home, accompanied by an officer.

"She's taking it harder than I am, I said grimly when Nellie had gone.

"I think we must give her a few days to recover," Monahan said.

I looked at him blankly. "Recover? We'll never recover from this. Never."

The police left late in the evening. Monahan requested that when I was feeling up to it, I should go through all the rooms of the ransacked house and list anything I found missing. He posted a guard at the door for the night.

"I'll be back in the morning, around nine," he assured me. "Make sure you lock all the doors and put the alarm on." He paused at the door. "Oh, and Miss O'Connell. Allow me to say again how deeply sorry I am."

"Thank you," I mumbled, closing the door behind him.

Alone at last, I felt the full weight of the day descending upon me like a shroud. Sinking to the floor, I curled myself into a ball and wept for some time. When finally I managed to pull myself together and head upstairs, it was past midnight. Leaden-legged from grief and exhaustion, I gripped the banister to steady myself as I proceeded one slow step at a time.

I went to my bedroom, undressed, and got into the shower. I washed my hair and scrubbed myself, desperate to expunge the memory of Luis Díaz, who, despite all my efforts, remained a constant specter behind the cataclysmic event of the day.

Thoughts of Díaz spawned a wave of guilt over my father's death. Could I have saved him had I returned home earlier? Was his death somehow a consequence of my lustful misdeed? Or, worse, of my having wished my father ill the night before because of a force I was just now beginning to understand myself? Try as I might to dispel it, the connection between my own reckless passion and my father's murder was now firmly established in my mind.

I took a sedative and tried to sleep. It was no use. I cursed myself over and over, as my father's last words to me echoed in my mind: "Talk to your old man, please? . . . Please try to understand."

If only I had understood! As long as I lived, I would never eradicate the image of that dear, good man trudging down the hall to his room, without the comfort of my forgiveness. I forgave him now. I forgave him everything and wanted to beg his forgiveness for having been so hard and close-minded. But he would never know how I felt and this was almost as unbearable as the death itself.

Unable to sleep, I got out of bed and went downstairs to the library. The house was dark and still. Switching on the lights, I gazed once more at the wreckage in that grand room and walked over to the spot near the window where my father had been slain. I stared at the crude tape outline of his body on the floor—a cartoon of a fallen man. I knelt down and touched the space inside the jagged enclosure as if it were hallowed ground.

"Daddy," I said, folding my hands in prayer and bowing my head. "Forgive me for not understanding you. I understand you now . . . I understand. And I'll find out who did this to you and avenge you. I swear it."

I whispered the Lord's Prayer, and when I'd finished, I blessed myself, "in the name of the Father, the Son, and the Holy Ghost. Amen." Choked with tears, I rose to my feet. It was at that precise moment in the stillness of the night that I realized the full weight of being all alone in the world.

In my experience, work is the only remedy for self-pity. The thing to do now was to get my father's library back in order. That would not only be a fitting tribute to his memory, but it would help me get through my abject grief. I wandered around the wreckage, wondering how anyone could have mistreated such treasures? For what purpose?

I began by gathering up the undamaged books, one at a time, and replacing them in their appropriate shelves. At first, the task seemed daunting. But as I lingered over my father's favorite volumes—stroking their bindings, reading snippets of their contents—I experienced a sense of comfort. In handling the little "friends" my father had so dearly loved, I felt close to him again.

I worked through the night, occasionally stopping to stare at the spot where my father had been shot. My efforts proved therapeutic. The hours flew by. Before I knew it, it was morning. I cracked open the heavy damask curtains that protected the books from the light and stared out at a hazy golden dawn.

Having taken a cursory inventory, I found nothing missing—none of the most valuable books, not even the two priceless Book of Hours. One thing seemed certain: Whoever had done this terrible thing hadn't been after any precious volumes.

I was on my way to check the silver and my mother's

jewelry, which was stashed away in my bedroom, when a thought suddenly occurred to me: the grimoire. Where was the grimoire?

Running back to the library, I began a frantic search for the mysterious little book. No luck. I raced upstairs to my father's room, thinking perhaps he'd taken it up there. But no. I went through the rest of the house, looking in all the rooms. Though they'd been ransacked, nothing appeared to be stolen—not the silver, the jewelry, or any other valuable object. But the grimoire was nowhere to be found.

My heart was pounding. I sat down in the library and tried to calm myself down. One thought kept whirling through my mind. If the grimoire was the only thing missing, then Signor Antonelli must have had a hand in my father's death. With that, I telephoned the old book dealer's hotel, only to find that he had checked out the previous afternoon. I then tried to get in touch with Detective Monahan, but it was early and he wasn't in his office yet. I got dressed, made breakfast, and had a look at the morning papers, anxiously awaiting Monahan's arrival at nine.

My father's murder was a shocking event in our quiet, affluent neighborhood. The tabloid headlines screamed the news: TOP SURGEON BRUTALLY SLAIN . . . SOCIETY DOC SHOT . . . MURDER ON BEEKMAN PLACE.

The *New York Times* offered a sedate description of the crime, along with an obituary of my father, a large part of which was devoted to his book collection. The account mentioned that he had won a Bronze Star for bravery during World War II and detailed his pioneering efforts in the field of thoracic surgery. The last line, which read, "Dr. O'Connell is survived by a daughter, Beatrice," made me start crying again.

I was in the kitchen, poring over the newspapers, when Monahan rang the doorbell. I ran to admit him, barely able to contain myself.

"I think I know who might have been involved in my

father's murder!" I said breathlessly as he entered the house.

Monahan told me in a kindly way to calm down, but as I led him into the library, I couldn't stop talking. In a fast patter, I described the meeting between Giuseppe Antonelli and my father two days before, when Antonelli came for dinner and my father showed him the grimoire.

"You say that's the only book missing?" Monahan asked me.

"Yes, as far as I can tell."

"And what kind of book did you say it was?"

"A grimoire."

"What's that?"

"A book of black magic."

Monahan raised his eyebrows. He asked me to spell it and jotted down the word in his notebook.

"So you think there's a connection?"

"I certainly do. Don't you?" I said impatiently. "Signor Antonelli was fascinated by the book. He offered to buy it from my father. He told us he had a client who collected them. An 'oddity,' he called it. Naturally, Daddy refused to sell it to him."

"Why?" Monahan looked puzzled.

"That's—that was my father's policy. He would never part with a single book in his library. Once he acquired a book, it was his for life. He wasn't like a normal collector who trades up. Those books were his friends. Oh God, I wish he'd made an exception with this one!"

"Run that by me again," Monahan said rather thickly, I thought. "Why, exactly, do you think your father's murder is connected with this book?"

"I told you—it's the only thing missing. In a house full of treasures—not even counting my mother's jewelry, the silver, all the valuable bric-a-brac , the televisions, my computer. Anything an ordinary thief might want is all here. Everything's here—except that damn grimoire."

"Uh-huh. Interesting . . ."

I wanted to shake Monahan. He was so plodding and dense.

"Look, I called Antonelli's hotel early this morning. He checked out yesterday afternoon."

Even this revelation had no impact. He stared at me dully.

"Any chance your father could 'have put this, uh, grimoire somewhere else?"

"No! I checked his room. But it was here, in the library. He wouldn't have moved it. He didn't put books that were meant for the library anywhere else."

"You're sure?"

"I'm positive!" I snapped, losing my patience. "I know my father."

"Have you looked around?"

"I told you! I've been through all the rooms to see if anything else was missing. It's the only thing that's gone. Detective, forgive me, but why are you refusing to see this as an important clue?"

"Maybe you should check again."

I sighed in exasperation. It was like talking to a wall.

"All right, I'll check again. But I bet you anything I won't find it. That's what whoever killed my father was after. I know it. I feel it. Antonelli was desperate to have it. I told that to my father at the time. You've got to get hold of Antonelli. I'm not saying he killed him, but he may know who did. But he's probably back in Rome by now."

"Tell me, how old a man is this Antonelli?" Monahan asked.

"Around my father's age, I guess. In his seventies. Why?"

"Nothing. I'm just trying to get the picture. And he's a book dealer, you say?"

"Yes, yes. He's a book dealer. He's sold things to my father for years. If he is in Rome, can you extradite him?"

"Hold on, just hold on," Monahan said evenly. "I'm trying to get the facts here. And you say this book isn't as valuable as the others?"

"God, no. There are Book of Hours that are worth a fortune. But there was something about that grimoire—something he wasn't telling us. It didn't have anything to do with money."

"If he didn't tell you, how do you know?"

"I was there, okay? I saw the guy drooling over the damn thing. I even made a bet with Daddy that Antonelli was going to call him back and offer him some astronomical amount of money for it. Look, if you don't want to do something about this, then I will."

"Please, Miss O'Connell, I know you're upset. Let me ask you something. Did Antonelli call him back the next day?"

"Well, I don't know, because . . ." I hesitated.

"Because . . .?"

"Because I wasn't here. I never saw my father again." I swallowed hard and felt my eyes brim with tears.

Monahan offered me a tissue.

"I'm going to call the hotel and find out exactly what time he checked out," he said.

"Yesterday, they said. Yesterday afternoon."

"I'll get on this, Miss O'Connell. Don't you worry."

I wondered if Monahan was just being patronizing. He pulled a Danish wrapped in plastic from his pocket.

"Breakfast," he said, holding up the unappetizing-looking sweet roll.

I gazed into his weary eyes. He seemed to me like a man who had stopped expecting very much from life, who stubbornly, with cheerless resignation, made do with whatever came his way.

"So do you think I'm right, Detective?"

"I think it deserves to be looked into."

"How will you track him down in Rome?"

"Don't worry. If it's necessary, we'll do it."

"But it is necessary!" I cried. "Don't you see? That damn book is the only thing missing, and Antonelli wanted it. Put two and two together, okay? Forgive me, Detective, but you don't exactly have to be Sherlock Holmes to figure it out."

"Do you know his address in Rome?" Monahan mumbled with his mouth half full.

"I know his old address. I'm sure he can be located."

An officer came into the room. "Hey, Frank, there's a guy downstairs wants to see Miss O'Connell."

"Did you get a shot at the name?" Monahan said sarcastically.

"Some Italian name. Monelli or—"

"Antonelli?" Monahan interrupted him.

"Yeah, that's it."

Monahan and I just looked at each other. The hint of a smile crossed his lips.

"Send him up," Monahan said. The officer left the room. "Saves us a trip to Rome," he said. "Too bad."

I have to say I felt a bit sheepish. "Well, I know he's involved," I said defensively.

"Innocent until proven guilty, remember?"

"In this case, it's the other way around. I don't trust him."

Presently, the officer ushered Signor Antonelli into the library. The old Italian froze for a moment, surveying the wreckage.

"*Dio mio!*" he cried out, gesticulating with his hands. "What have they done to this beautiful place? I am reading the newspapers this morning and I cannot believe it. My dear old friend—shot! How is it possible? *É cara Beatrice . . .*" He walked toward me, arms outstretched.

I rose from the couch and let the old man embrace me, keeping my hands at my sides and showing him no warmth.

"Signor Antonelli," I said coldly, "this is Detective Monahan, the officer in charge of the investigation."

"Giuseppe Antonelli." The dealer bowed slightly as the two men shook hands.

"Monahan. Please sit down."

Signor Antonelli propped himself up stiffly on a chair opposite the couch. He shook his head, saying, "Only the day before yesterday, I was sitting here in this room with John. And now—"

"Mr. Antonelli, I have to ask you a few questions," Monahan interrupted.

"*Certo.* I am here to help you in any way I can." He smiled sympathetically at me, but I just looked away.

"Where were you between the hours of twelve and four yesterday afternoon?"

"Yesterday? I had lunch with an old friend."

"Who?"

"Father Morton from Saint Xavier's Church."

"Father Morton!" Monahan said with great respect.

"Do you know him?"

"Everybody knows Father Morton. He's one of the city's fixtures."

"Yes, well, we had much to discuss. We have not seen one another in several years—not since my last visit to New York."

"And you were with him until when, sir?" I noticed Monahan was calling Antonelli sir now that he knew of his association with the revered priest.

"It was close to four-thirty," Antonelli said.

As I studied Antonelli closely, Monahan glanced over at me as if to say, "There goes your theory."

"And Father Morton will verify that?" Monahan asked.

"I am sure that he will."

"Just a couple more questions, Mr. Antonelli. Miss O'Connell here says you were interested in a book Dr. O'Connell showed you."

The old dealer paused as if he had to think for a moment.

"Ah yes, of course—the grimoire. It completely slipped my mind."

"Wasn't that the reason for your trip to New York?" I asked him.

58 Jane Stanton Hitchcock

"No, no, my dear. I had other things to do as well."

"You wanna tell me a little about this book?" Monahan asked.

"I will tell you what I know," Antonelli said with a hollow smile. "John had written to me about a special book, wishing very much that I would come over to have a look at it. I was not about to make a trip just for that. But as I have said, I had some other business here, with Father Morton among others. So the night before last, I came here for dinner, and John showed me the grimoire. Beatrice was here. We all examined it together."

As he spoke, I studied his face, searching for a sign of guilt. However, I couldn't help thinking that he seemed genuinely distraught and without guile.

"I understand from Miss O'Connell that you became very interested in it once you saw it," Monahan said.

Antonelli shrugged. "Yes . . . well, it is a rare thing, very interesting to certain collectors."

"And you offered to buy it from him?"

"No, not exactly. What I said was, I have a client who collects these oddities. I thought I would telephone him and ask him if it would be of interest to him."

"Uh-huh. And who might he be?" Monahan was poised to make a note.

Antonelli demurred. "I'm afraid I cannot say. My client prefers to remain anonymous."

"So did you?"

"Did I what?"

"Telephone him?"

"Yes. As a matter of fact, I did."

"And was he interested?" Monahan inquired.

"Very much so. He authorized me to make John quite a sizable offer for it."

"And . . . ?"

"And I did—even though I told my client it would probably be useless."

"Why?"

"Because, as Beatrice will tell you, it was her father's policy never to sell a book that entered his library. When John said no, he meant no. And he had said no the previous evening. Still, in this case, as the book was a gift, and as he didn't seem to care very much for it, I saw no harm in presenting the offer. Particularly as it was an extremely generous one."

"How much, if I may ask?"

"Fifty thousand dollars."

Monahan seemed impressed. "And what did Dr. O'Connell say to that?"

"Exactly what I thought he would say: no. He declined very politely. You see, Detective Monahan, John O'Connell with his books was like a father with his children," Signor Antonelli said with apparent fondness. "He would not give them up for anything."

"And what time did you speak to him to make this offer?"

"I telephoned him from my hotel at about, oh, about eleven o'clock yesterday morning."

"You checked out of your hotel," I interjected, unable to contain myself any longer.

Antonelli looked startled by my accusatory tone. "Yes, my dear," he replied evenly. "I believe I told you and John that I was extremely disappointed with the service in my old hotel, because it had changed management. I checked out and went to another."

"Which one?" Monahan asked.

"I am at the Carlyle. On Seventy-sixth Street."

I had to admit that Signor Antonelli's explanation seemed entirely plausible. And, more than that, his manner was relaxed, if sad. He didn't act like a guilty man.

"Okay, so when you spoke to Dr. O'Connell, did you set up another meeting with him?" Monahan asked.

"Yes. I promised I would come by this morning and say good-bye. Then at breakfast I read in the newspaper that my dear friend was shot to death." Antonelli wiped away an invisible tear with the back of his hand. "Forgive me, but I still cannot believe it. Beatrice, my dear, is there anything I can do for you? I was going to go back to Rome today, but I am delighted to stay longer if you would like."

I looked him straight in the eye. "Do you still want the grimoire?"

He perked up immediately. "Well, yes, of course. Do you wish to sell it?"

I paused for effect, in order to gauge the look of expectation on Antonelli's face.

"I don't have it," I said at last. "It's been stolen."

The old man's eyes widened. "Really?"

I didn't quite believe his astonishment.

"That surprise you?" I asked him.

He cleared his throat. "So many treasures . . . What else has been taken?"

"Nothing. Just the grimoire," I said, pinning him with a fierce gaze.

"But how extraordinary."

"Why?" Monahan asked.

"My dear fellow," Signor Antonelli replied condescendingly. "If you knew anything about books, you would not ask that."

"So educate me."

"Rare and interesting as the grimoire is, it has not nearly the value of some of the other books in this library. Either the thief took it merely because he fancied it, or because he mistakenly thought it was worth more than it is."

"Fifty thousand dollars ain't hay," Monahan pointed out.

"Ah, no—but that is for a special client, whom the thief could not possibly know. Intrinsically, the grimoire is not worth much more than two, maybe three thousand dollars— as compared to the Books of Hours, which are worth many hundred thousands, perhaps even millions."

"Miss O'Connell mentioned that."

"In any case," Antonelli continued, "if the thief tries to sell it, I shall surely hear about it. My client in Italy is the largest collector of such books. All of them come to his attention sooner or later."

"Oh, come on. Tell us the name of this mysterious client of yours," Monahan said.

"As I have told you." Antonelli smiled, holding a finger up in protest. "Like a priest or a lawyer or even a psychoanalyst, I am not at liberty to divulge the names of my clients. Otherwise they would not remain my clients for very long. But rest assured, he is a serious collector."

"I don't doubt it," Monahan said, acknowledging the old gentleman's courtliness. "I assume you have no objections if I call Father Morton?"

"No, none at all. But surely I am not a suspect?"

"You are until you ain't, as they say."

"In that case, Father Morton will certainly confirm everything I have told you."

"Please don't leave the city until you hear from me."

"Of course not . . . Am I free to go now?"

Monahan nodded. Signor Antonelli reached inside his breast pocket and pulled out a slim gold case, from which he extracted two calling cards, handing one to me and one to Detective Monahan.

"Please, both of you, do not hesitate to get in touch with me if I may be of the slightest service."

I glanced at the elegant white card, on which Giuseppe Antonelli's name and his address in Rome were embossed in black.

"My dear, dear Beatrice," he said, rising from his chair. "I cannot begin to express my sorrow at your loss. Your father was a great man. I will miss him more than I can say. My only consolation is that I shall probably be joining him shortly, for I am getting old and rather fed up with life."

I accompanied the old gentleman downstairs. At the door, I allowed him to take my hands in his, even though I still didn't trust him.

"If you should find yourself in need of a sympathetic ear, please go and see my old friend Father Morton. He is a very

fine priest, and he will help you. You may trust him." He
kissed me on both cheeks.

I walked back up to the library.

"So I was wrong," I said to Monahan, who was just finishing up his Danish.

"Looks that way," he said, licking a finger. "Father Morton's
a pretty impressive alibi. Nice card." Monahan flicked its pristine edge before inserting it into his notebook.

"Now what?" I asked glumly, feeling let down that my
hunch about Signor Antonelli had proved fruitless.

"Now I go and question people in the neighborhood,
to see if anybody saw anything or anyone. We wait for the
results of the forensic tests and the autopsy. And maybe
we get lucky. Miss O'Connell, I'm going to ask you to give
me your father's address book and his diary and a list
of the people who knew him best—like the doctors he
worked with. And here's my card," he said. "Not as elegant
as your friend's, but it's got my direct line at the precinct.
I'll give you my cell." He jotted down the number on the
back. "You can call me anytime. I'll be in touch if there's
any news."

Chapter 4

Detective Monahan departed, leaving behind a forensic team to search the house for clues. Nellie called to say that she was sick with grief. I gave her the day off and took the telephone off the hook to avoid condolence calls and inquiries from reporters. I shut myself inside the library and continued the work I'd started the night before. I had a little system now. I stacked the volumes in separate piles according to the amount of damage they'd incurred.

As I worked, I pictured some of my happiest childhood moments with my parents—the Christmas Eves, when I was permitted to taste my father's famous eggnog and stay up late to trim the tree with the exquisite antique ornaments my mother had collected from all over the world; the Easter Sundays, when Mom and I dyed eggs for Daddy to hide all over the house—except in the library, which he said was "no place for little search bunnies"; Thanksgiving and Saint Paddy's Day, as my father called it, when he would take me to Fifth Avenue to view the parade, hoisting me up on his shoulders so I could see over the crowd; the school nights when I'd sneak down to the library after my mother had tucked me into bed and make my father read to me until I fell asleep and he carried me back upstairs in his arms.

I'd been happy, sheltered, and coddled by two adoring parents, or so I'd told myself until the failure of my marriage stained the idyllic landscape of childhood. But somehow I'd managed to shrug it off, explaining my divorce as a bad choice of a man rather than my own inadequacy as a mate.

Now, however, in the wake of the revelation about my

father and another woman, I began to excavate the terrain
of daily life with my parents more closely. I wondered if
my mother's apparent piety had been nothing more than a
mask for disappointment. Had my father's long retreats to
his library been a simple need to get away from the family
for a while, or was it an expression of impatience with a
false front?

I dug up some more disquieting moments—the slamming of doors late at night and then, in the morning, awak-
ing to find my father asleep in the guest room. I recalled
my father's brief, but violent, outbursts of temper for no
apparent cause. He would stalk off, leaving my mother
with a pinched expression on her face and the eternal sigh
of "Jesus, Mary, and Joseph" under her breath.

There were the dinners when my parents hardly said a
word to each other and I sat quietly between them, worried that they were angry at each other or, worse, at me. I'd
grown up with the feeling that I somehow had to amuse
my parents and their friends with my intelligence in order to allay the tension that existed in the house when we
were all together. But whatever I did never seemed to be
enough. They were always setting new standards for me,
and I never felt wholly approved of.

Sometimes silence reigned for days in the house—my
father reading obsessively and my mother sitting in her
bedroom, addressing envelopes and organizing benefits
for ever more prestigious Catholic charities. From a very
young age, I was acutely aware of my mother's social ambitions, which required the appearance, if not necessarily
the reality, of a family life that was stage-set perfect. She
was the star, my Dad and I supporting players.

I remembered my mother's snide, disparaging remarks
about her friends' husbands and then, later, about the
various boyfriends I brought home. It was as if she secretly
viewed all men with disdain and suspicion. And though
my mother had smiled through my wedding to Stephen,
I knew that she deeply disapproved of the maverick re-

porter who was not Catholic and who was slightly offbeat, with his liberal views and his strong attraction to danger.

"I don't trust him," my mother had told me on the eve of my wedding. And much to my chagrin, Stephen had proved my mother right.

I knew, too, that my parents had secrets from me, though I never could have guessed the existence of another woman. But I was just now beginning to fathom the deeper secret my mother kept: Elizabeth O'Connell— staunch Catholic, pillar of the community, good mother, and exemplary hostess—disliked sex, feared men, and was angry at herself and at me, her daughter, for being female, like herself.

By four o'clock, I was exhausted, both emotionally and physically. By that time, everyone had left the house and I dragged myself upstairs to my bedroom, where I lay down and fell asleep instantaneously.

Sometime later, I became aware that the front doorbell was ringing. I glanced groggily at my watch. It was nearly seven. A marked stillness gripped the air. I looked out my bedroom window. The sky had turned dark and silvery, as if a storm was coming. I leaned over to see if I could catch a glimpse of whoever was calling on me at this hour. The person was obscured from view by the lintel. The doorbell rang again. I smoothed my rumpled clothes, raked my fingers through my hair, and ran downstairs.

Looking through the peephole in the front door, I saw the face of a man I didn't recognize. A little jolt of fear coursed through me. I kept the chain on and cracked the door open.

"Who is it?" I asked warily.

"Simon Lovelock," the stranger replied.

"What do you want?"

"I have an appointment with Dr. O'Connell," the man said in a refined but raspy voice.

My heart skipped a beat. Who is this person who doesn't know my father's dead? I wondered. The stranger fished inside his trousers and extracted a ragged business card, which he slipped through the crack in the door. It read simply, SIMON LOVELOCK/LOVELOCK RARE BOOKS. An address and telephone number were underneath.

I examined the card, then peered out at him again. Thin and of medium height, he had straight lips, an aquiline nose, and a long, somber face, the color of aged vellum. His black hair was flecked with silver strands and his dark eyes, full of inquiry, sparkled with intelligence. Dressed in black from head to foot, he looked slightly shabby but presentable. I noticed that the collar of his jacket was fraying around the edges. He took a final drag of the cigarette he was puffing on nervously and flicked the butt away.

"What business do you have with Dr. O'Connell?" I asked him.

"I don't know," the stranger said, squinting at me through the crack.

"What do you mean, you don't know?"

"He telephoned me yesterday to set up an appointment. I told him I wouldn't be able to meet him until six-thirty, because my shop stays open until six. I'm sorry if I'm a bit late, but the subway was delayed."

Distant thunder rumbled through the air, then faded. It was beginning to drizzle. Mr. Lovelock hovered closer to the door.

"Uh—is he in, please?" he said, brushing raindrops from his head.

"No." I was testing him.

"Oh. Well, if you'd be so kind as to give him my card. He can call me tomorrow if he wants to set up a more convenient time." He started to walk away. Then, as if he'd had an afterthought, he turned and said, "Please tell him how much I'm looking forward to meeting him, won't you?"

I didn't answer. I was trying to assess the situation. Why, I wondered, had my father made an appointment with a book dealer, of all people? I closed the door and watched him through the peephole. Lovelock lit another cigarette and started down the street, pulling his collar up around his neck and hugging himself, an effort at protection from the steadily increasing rain. I felt a wave of pity for the stranger, but mainly, I wanted to satisfy my curiosity, so I ignored caution and flung open the front door to call him back.

"Mr. Lovelock, wait!"

Lovelock turned around and stared at me, a perplexed expression on his face.

"Won't you come inside, please?" I said, beckoning to him. "At least until it stops raining?"

"With pleasure!" he replied. Trotting up the front steps, he hastened inside the door. "It's getting nasty out there." He took a handkerchief from his pocket and brushed the rain off his head and shoulders.

He smiled at me, revealing a row of even but slightly tobacco-stained teeth. His smile immediately lightened the dour aspects of his face, lending him a soft, sweet expression.

"I'm Beatrice O'Connell," I said, extending my hand to him. "Dr. O'Connell's daughter."

Lovelock lowered his eyes. "I'm honored to meet you," he said, shaking my hand with a tepid grip.

"My father won't be keeping his appointment with you," I said, steeling myself for what I'd have to tell him next.

Lovelock raised his trim black eyebrows and cocked his head to one side. He seemed disappointed. "Why not?"

"My father is dead," I said simply. The words felt like ashes in my throat.

"Dead?" he repeated.

"Yes. He was shot yesterday afternoon during a robbery attempt, here in this house," I told him in a halting voice.

Lovelock blinked a couple of times, as if he were trying to digest the news. "Dear God, how terrible!"

"It's been in all the newspapers. I'm surprised you didn't see it."

"I'm afraid I don't keep up with the newspapers," Lovelock

replied apologetically. "I had no idea . . . Please forgive my intrusion . . . I'm so sorry . . . so very, very sorry."

"Thank you." I was touched by his genuine response.

"I think perhaps I should be going." The news seemed to embarrass him somehow and he fumbled for the door-knob.

"No, please. Please stay," I said. "At least until the rain lets up a little."

"Well, if you're quite sure . . ."

"Come into the kitchen, won't you? We could both use a cup of tea, don't you think?"

"Well . . ." He hesitated. "If you're sure I'm not intruding . . . ?"

"Follow me."

"Very kind of you . . . Very kind indeed."

Lovelock seemed a sympathetic person, and further-more, I was anxious to find out why my father had sum-moned him. I led him down the hall into the kitchen.

"Let me ask you something," I said, filling the kettle with tap water. "Do you remember what time it was when my father called you yesterday?"

Lovelock nervously kneaded the lobe of his right ear with his fingers and thought for a moment. "I think it was a little after twelve noon . . . Yes. It was about twelve-fifteen. I was just going to lunch."

Twelve-fifteen, I thought. In other words, very shortly before his murder.

"And you don't have any idea what it was he wanted to see you about?"

"No, not really . . . Well, I assume it was about a book. That's my business."

"But he didn't say what book it was?"

Lovelock shook his head. "No, I'm afraid not."

We lapsed into a brief silence, which was interrupted by the whistle of the kettle.

I prepared the tea.

"Do you take milk, sugar?" I asked him.

"Just plain, thanks."

I handed him a cup. Lovelock took a few sips, savoring the smoky blend.

"Ah, that's grand. Thank you," he said.

"You say you didn't know my father?"

"No. I never had the privilege."

"Do you have any idea how he got your name?"

"I'm afraid not."

"Why did you agree to come here?" I asked.

"Well, I didn't know your father personally, but I knew of him, of course. Most people in the trade know the name O'Connell."

I got up and fetched a copy of *The New York Times* for Lovelock to see. I sipped my tea as he studied my father's obituary, shaking his head as he read.

"Oh, dear God . . . dear God . . ." he kept muttering. When he'd finished, he looked up and gazed at me with real compassion. "A terrible thing . . . terrible. And they haven't caught the culprit?"

"Not yet. But they will—or I will."

"What a world." He sighed ruefully, putting the paper down.

We sat silently for a moment, drinking our tea and listening to the steady patter of the rain. I tried to avoid looking at my father's picture in the paper because I knew it would make me cry. But I caught a glimpse of the staid studio portrait the paper had used and I broke down.

"I'm sorry. Forgive me," I said, wiping my tears with a napkin.

" 'Heaven knows we need never be ashamed of our tears, for they are rain upon the blinding dust of earth . . .' " he said kindly.

"That's lovely."

"Mr. Dickens . . . He could always turn a phrase."

"When I was a little girl and I cried, I used to say I was raining," I told him, forcing a wan smile. "Tell me, Mr. Lovelock, have you ever wished that you could take back the last moments you had with someone and see them one more time?"

"Not only the last ones," he said with a sad smile. He looked away. His obvious pain discouraged further inquiry. "Perhaps I should be going."

"Please have some more tea," I urged him. I liked his quiet manner.

"Oh, thanks . . ." he replied gratefully.

I refilled his cup.

"I think the rain's stopped," he said, clearing his throat.

Partially on impulse and partially because I felt him to be a kindred spirit in grief, I asked Lovelock if he cared to see my father's library before he left. His sad face lit up with delight, as if he'd been given a present.

"Are you sure?" he said eagerly. "I wouldn't want to intrude."

"I'm sure," I said firmly, rising from the table. "However, I must warn you—the room's been ransacked. I've been trying to straighten it up, but it's still in a mess. It's difficult to explain," I said as I led him upstairs, "but it makes me feel close to my father to show his library to someone who'll appreciate it."

We reached the landing. "Prepare yourself for a shock," I said, facing Lovelock, before I swung open the heavy mahogany doors.

Lovelock gasped in horror at the terrible disarray of the great room. "Jesus!" he cried. "What in the name of God has happened here?"

"This is where—where he was shot."

We both entered the room slowly. The look of horror on Lovelock's face quickly melted into one of sorrow. He knelt down and picked up a book, cradling it in his hands, stroking it as if it were a wounded animal.

"Oh, dear, dear, dear," he said, addressing the tattered volume. "You poor little thing. Who did this to you?"

As I witnessed Lovelock's tenderness and concern for the bruised book, I was reminded of my father, who would have viewed the desecration of his precious library as an act of attempted mass murder. "He loved his books so much," I said. "They were his friends."

Lovelock got up, still holding the book. "This can be mended," he said.

"It can . . . I can't."

"No," he replied softly. "But the old adage about time, you know."

I handed him another book—the *Roman de la Rose*.

"This is my favorite book in this library," I said. "It was the only one I wanted out of my father's whole collection."

"Oh, she's a lovely little thing" he said, examining it. "But see here, she's been very badly wounded. She will certainly split apart if she's not tended to shortly—see?" He pointed to the spine, which was dangerously cracked.

"Yes, I know."

"I'd be honored to repair it for you," he offered. "I do some bookbinding in my spare time."

"That's very kind of you. Perhaps you'll let me think about it."

"Oh, of course," he said, flushing with embarrassment. "I just thought that, well, she's such a pretty little volume, and she doesn't need very much—just some stitching and gluing. But I don't mean to impose."

"No, please—you're very kind to offer."

"I'd like to do something," he said, surveying the wreckage.

His eye was suddenly arrested by the tape outline of my father's slain body on the floor at the far end of the room. He walked over to it. I followed close behind him. When we reached the spot, we both stood in silence, looking down at the jagged tape.

"That's where it happened," I said after a time. There were still dark vestiges of blood on the wood floor.

Lovelock lit a cigarette. "Oh, forgive me. I hope it's all right if I smoke in here," he said as an afterthought.

"Of course; go right ahead. I do myself sometimes."

He exhaled a long plume of smoke, offering me a cigarette from the crumpled pack. I declined.

"Do they have any idea who did it, or why?" he asked me.

"No."

I was anxious to get away from the spot.

"I need a drink," I said. "Will you join me in a glass of brandy?"

"With pleasure."

I went down the hall to the living room and brought us back two snifters filled with my father's good brandy. When I entered the library, Lovelock was perched on the couch, perusing the exquisite 16th century French Book of Hours, which he had laid on the coffee table.

"Well, the motive certainly couldn't have been robbery," he said, looking up at me. "This volume is priceless."

"I'm not so sure. There's one book I can't find."

I handed him a glass of brandy and sat down beside him. Lovelock popped another cigarette into his mouth, lighting it with the burning butt of the one he'd just smoked.

"Nothing could be more valuable than this." He indicated the tome in front of him. "What artistry!" With the tips of his fingers, he touched the outline of a delicately painted white lamb in a circle of gold leaf in the center of the large page. "The sweetness of it . . ." he said. "The beauty of faith and, well, the horrors of it never cease to amaze me."

"The book that I can't find is a grimoire. Do you know what that is?"

Lovelock cocked his head to one side and smiled. "Indeed I do," he said, perking up. "In fact, I happen to specialize in occult books."

"Ah!" I cried. "That's it, then. That's why my father wanted to see you."

Lovelock narrowed his eyes. "That's not the type of thing I'd have imagined your father would go in for, judging from what I see of the collection. It's rather a unique field, and I know just about everyone in it."

"It was a present from a patient. He'd just been sent it, only about three weeks ago. It was a terrifying thing. I saw it."

"You saw it? Can you tell me about it?"

I described the book. I have a researcher's memory for detail. I told him about the pornographic woodcuts and the vivid section on necromancy. Lovelock listened attentively. Then, almost as an afterthought, I mentioned the Latin inscription at the beginning.

"Do you remember what it was?" he asked me.

I don't think it was my imagination, but when I said the words, *"Videmus nunc per speculum in aenigmate, tunc autem facie ad faciem,"* it seemed to me that his eyes flickered with alarm.

He paused for a long moment, then murmured, "Sounds interesting," as if he didn't really mean it.

"Tell me, would something like that be of enormous value?"

Lovelock heaved a sigh. "Oh, it's difficult to say really. I'd have to see it. In monetary terms, it isn't worth anything like some of the other books here. Tell me, did anyone else have a look at it?"

"Just Signor Antonelli, an Italian book dealer my father's dealt with for years."

"Giuseppe Antonelli?"

"Yes! You know him?"

Lovelock hesitated. "Again, by reputation only. He lives in Rome."

"Right. He's an old friend of my father's."

"Is he?"

"He was fascinated with it."

"Was he indeed?"

I detected something ominous in Lovelock's tone.

"Look, between us, Mr. Lovelock, I don't trust Signor Antonelli. I never really warmed to him, and last night, when I discovered the grimoire was missing, I thought maybe . . ."

"What?"

"I thought maybe he was involved."

"Ah . . . But now you don't?"

"I don't know. I honestly don't know," I said thoughtfully. "He came over here this morning. And he seemed genuinely upset. If he is involved, he should win an Academy Award. So I sort of changed my mind. But still . . . he was just fixated on the grimoire when he saw it. He immediately offered to buy it. Said he had a client who collected things like that. But of course, Daddy wouldn't sell it to him."

"No? Why not?"

"My father would never part with a single book in his library. He was famous for that. If you'd known him, you'd have understood. Parting with a book would have been like parting with a friend. But I bet Daddy ten dollars that Signor Antonelli would call him again and make another offer."

"And did he?"

"As a matter of fact, he did. He told me and the detective in charge of the case that his client authorized him to pay fifty thousand dollars for it. But apparently my father turned him down."

"And the grimoire—you're sure it's gone?"

"Oh, it's gone, all right. I've checked every book here. It's just disappeared. As I said, it's the only thing missing. I'll tell you a secret. I tried to trick Signor Antonelli when he was here this morning. I asked him if he still wanted it. He leapt at the idea, so I knew he hadn't taken it. Unless that was an act too."

"So you believe that whoever killed your father took it?"

"I can't think of another explanation for its disappearance, can you? Maybe whoever killed my father just took the grimoire because it's so bizarre. That was Antonelli's theory, anyway. Like you, he said that anyone who knew anything about books wouldn't have bothered with it. There are so many other things to take. On the other hand, a person who commits murder might like something like that. You know, something dealing with the occult. What do you think, Mr. Lovelock?"

"Oh, I think it's just as well to let sleeping dogs lie," he said.

"What do you mean?"

"Nothing . . . I really should be going."

"Obviously, my father wanted you to have a look at it, or he wouldn't have called you. From what I've described, do you think it's worth anything?"

"Again, I'd have to see it."

"Ballpark figure?"

"It all depends on the buyer. It's a different sort of market."

"What do you mean?"

Lovelock shifted uncomfortably in his seat. "Well, there are people who take grimoires quite literally," he said.

"You mean they believe in them—believe in black magic?"

"Uh—yes. You might say that."

"And what would the book I've described to you be worth to a believer? Roughly."

"In monetary terms—oh, say, two to three thousand dollars."

"And in other terms?" I pressed him.

"A true believer might think it priceless."

"Might pay anything for it?"

"Yes."

I pinned him with my eyes. "Might kill for it?"

"Might," he said somberly.

I sank back in my chair and contemplated this thought.

"Listen, Mr. Lovelock, if you think there's a connection between my father's death and this book—"

He raised his hand in protest. "I never said that!"

"Not in so many words, no. But I can see it in your eyes. You know there's a connection, don't you?"

"I know no such thing."

"I don't know you, but I have a feeling you're a kind man."

Lovelock lowered his eyes.

"I loved my father very much, and I want—I need—to find out who did this. Can you understand that?" He nodded. I went on. "This world of occult books is fairly small, you say. Specialized. You said you knew nearly everybody in the field, or know of them. Do you have any idea—any hunch—who might have done this?"

Lovelock puffed nervously on his cigarette. The smoke drifted over his face. He seemed to me to be in the throes of a decision. He waited before he answered, then spoke in a measured tone of voice.

"I'd like to help you, Miss O'Connell. Honestly, I would. But . . ."

"But?" I said anxiously.

"I cannot get involved."

"You have a suspicion, don't you? What's the matter? Are you afraid?"

"It's not a question of that."

"What is it a question of? Please—please, Mr. Lovelock, help me."

"I—I have to go," he stammered. "I'm sorry." With that he rose abruptly and started for the hall.

"Wait!" I cried, hurrying after him. "I apologize if I've upset you. But I have to know what you know."

Lovelock walked downstairs and paused at the front door. He looked at me sympathetically. "It would be a different thing if you actually had the grimoire," he said.

"Why?"

"It just would. Don't ask me to explain."

"But I *am* asking you."

"I can't say any more. Really I can't." He put on his coat and opened the front door.

"Can I at least come and talk to you some more?"

"My shop is open from ten to six. You would be most welcome."

He stepped outside. The rain had let up, but there was still a misty drizzle in the air.

"You're sure Antonelli knows you don't have the grimoire?" he asked.

"Yes—positive. What? What? Tell me what you're thinking. Please, I beg you."

"I'm not thinking anything," he said with a dismissive wave of his hand. "It's late. Thank you for showing me the library and for the tea and brandy. It was very nice to meet you, Miss O'Connell. I wish it could have been under happier circumstances."

"Would you like to borrow an umbrella?"

"You're very kind, but I'll be fine, thanks."

I bid him a reluctant good night.

"Good night," he said.

Lovelock started to walk away, then stopped abruptly. Wheeling around, he stood poised on the steps, clasping the railing to steady himself. He looked up at me.

"Forget about the grimoire, Miss O'Connell," he said, his eyes sparkling and intense.

"I can't, Mr. Lovelock. You know I can't. That's like telling me to forget about my father's murder."

"You must try to understand that some things are better left alone."

With that, Lovelock turned away, raising his collar to shield himself from the rain. I watched him as he hunched over and scurried down the block, a lone black figure fading into the twilight. I closed the door behind him, swearing on the soul of my father that I would somehow learn what this odd man knew.

Chapter 5

Two weeks later, a memorial was held for my father at Saint Thomas More's, a small church tucked away in the middle of a block of apartment buildings on Manhattan's Upper East Side. Despite his aversion to organized religion, I wanted him to have a Catholic service. It was really more for me and his friends, I guess. But I did recall my father's oft-spoken words that the Catholic Church, for all its political problems, "christens, marries, and buries people better than any other institution."

Organ music by Bach and Mozart, Daddy's favorite composers, played softly as well over three hundred mourners filed into the pretty little church to pay their last respects. A huge black-and-white photograph of my father in his younger days, mounted on pasteboard, was placed on a pedestal to the right side of the altar.

Monsignor Regan, a stocky, white-haired cleric, conducted the solemn mass with immense dignity and obvious compassion. Nellie and I sat side by side in the front pew, holding hands, as the monsignor spoke of death being, in some sense, a joyous time, a transition from this earth to the glorious world of life everlasting through Jesus Christ. I think Nellie took more comfort in this than I did. I was more my father's daughter.

However, as the service progressed, to my surprise, I became caught up in the wonder and beauty of the ceremony—the blessing of the cup and the wafer, the soft rhythm of the priest's voice as he recited the moving liturgy, the pungent fumes from the censer. Monsignor Regan's touching humility and devotion soothed me in an unexpected way. I'd tried to follow my father's scientific rationalist's path but had always known in my heart that human beings need more than a mere logical explanation can provide, particularly in moments of grief. The memorial provided that intangible comfort of faith. The kindly prelate renewed my respect for the the Church, and I was grateful.

During the eulogies, by six of my father's colleagues and friends, I reflected on many things. Disparate images of my father swept across my mind in the pastel colors of memory— his quirky facial expressions as he read aloud to me in front of a blazing fire in the library on cold winter nights, his strong arms holding me tight in the rough, bracing waters of the Atlantic, where he taught me to swim during long, lazy summers in East Hampton, his slow, loping gait, the sadness behind his eyes, his animation when he talked about books.

Daddy hated television, calling it "the scourge of the modern age." Determined to instill an appreciation and reverence for the written word in me, he rarely allowed me to watch it. I smiled to myself, remembering how my schoolmates used to tease me for never being up on the latest shows. But now I was indebted to him, for I'd learned to love books as he did; they were my lasting friends.

Toward the end of the ceremony, my mind took a darker turn, to the day of my graduation from Barnard College, when I saw my father reach out affectionately for my mother's hand, whereupon my mother abruptly turned away. This fleeting rebuff had struck me as odd at the time, but I denied its importance until this moment. Now, in the wake of my father's recent admission, I realized that the encounter had taken place around the time he said he fell in love with the nurse at the hospital.

Was my father's gesture toward my mother an attempt at reconciliation or an expression of guilt—or both? Did my mother know of his infatuation? Was she expressing her anger toward him, or was this strictly brought-up Catholic girl simply uncomfortable with displays of affection?

In contrast to my father, who barely concealed his contempt for the Church, my mother had always been deeply religious. Her faith made her seem kind, but passive, as if she viewed life as something to be accepted rather than challenged. To be honest, I'd never quite been able to get a grip on my mother, who, wrapped in the mantle of a conviction that everything was God's will, seemed oddly untouched by experience. I was more my father's daughter and I wondered if my parents' clash of beliefs had led to the breakdown of their marriage and my father's need for another woman. But their marriage had lasted. So in the end, perhaps, their opposing views had bonded them together in some strange way.

My mind then jumped to Stephen, my ex-husband. I hadn't heard a word from him since my father's death, and his silence plagued me. I thought the least he could have done was called. Was he consciously staying away, or did he just not know what had happened? I found myself hoping to see him among the mourners when I left the church. But I doubted he was there. I was convinced I would have sensed his presence, for I still felt deeply connected to him, even after all this time. My mind drifted back to the baby we almost had—and with that terrible thought, the loss of my father crashed down on me harder than ever.

I almost cried out, but I managed to control myself—unlike a certain day I vividly remembered. Thoughts of Luis Díaz and scenes of the afternoon we spent together now zigzagged through my mind. I was ashamed that my sorrow was polluted by past desire. But somehow, it was a crazy jumble, all connected.

The service concluded, I dried my tears and stood outside the church with Monsignor Regan, accepting condolences from friends and my father's colleagues. I knew most of the people there, and a small receiving line formed spontaneously in front of me and the monsignor. Presently, a heavyset priest with a round, friendly face marched up to me, wiping his brow from the heat.

"Beatrice," he said to me, extending his hand in a forth-right manner. "I'm Father Morton, Giuseppe Antonelli's friend."

I was slightly taken aback to see him there since he didn't really know my father.

"Giuseppe asked me to come and pay my respects on his behalf. I'm deeply sorry for your loss. I hope you will feel free to come and visit me at Saint Xavier's at any time. Or if you wish, I can call on you."

At that moment, Nellie walked up beside me with a look of awe on her face. I introduced her to Father Morton, who smiled and said a few comforting words to the old housekeeper before moving on.

"That was Father Morton," Nellie whispered excitedly to me. "It's an honor he came here."

"Do you know him?"

"Oh, no, not personally," Nellie said with marked reverence. "Will you be wanting me for anything this afternoon, Miss Beatrice?"

I told her to take the day off. Nellie left the church mumbling numerous God bless yous and other things I couldn't hear. I was afraid my father's death had unhinged the dear woman a bit.

When the crowd thinned, I walked down the block to hail a taxi. I was tired and anxious to get home. I was standing on the corner looking for a cab when I felt a light tap on my arm. Turning around, I saw a pretty, middle-aged woman standing in front of me. She was a little shorter than I was, and pleasantly plump. The starched white collar of her simple brown dress had wilted from the heat.

"Miss O'Connell, my name is Mary O'Shaunessy. I was a friend of your father's. I just wanted to express my deepest sympathy to you. Dr. O'Connell was a very great man." I could see she was nervous. Her little speech sounded rehearsed. I also saw the wet handkerchief she was carrying.

I thanked her and asked her how she knew my father.

"I was a nurse at the hospital. I assisted him on many occasions. He was a remarkable surgeon. He had God-given hands—the hands of an angel."

As she spoke, I looked at her more closely and noticed a striking physical similarity between her and my mother in my mother's younger days.

"You were a friend of my father's?" I asked, probing the woman's face.

She lowered her eyes. "Yes," she replied shyly. "That's all I wanted to say. I'm sorry to disturb you."

I had a pretty good idea who she was.

"No, no," I said. "You're not disturbing me. Miss O'Shaunessy, is it?"

"Mary, please."

"Mary," I repeated softly. "Mary, you knew my father very well, didn't you?"

She lifted her eyes to mine and flushed with embarrassment. "Quite well, yes."

I paused. "You were the one, weren't you?"

Her eyes widened. "I . . . I don't know what you mean."

"My father told me everything before he died," I said.

"Everything?"

"You're the one he fell in love with, aren't you?"

She looked away, seemingly at a loss for words.

"Please. It's all right. I don't blame you. And I don't blame him. I just wish I could have told him that before he died. I'd give anything for him to know that I understand and that I love him." I started to cry.

Mary O'Shaunessy touched my arm. "He loved you," she said with great feeling. "He loved you more than anything else in the world."

"I was so judgmental," I said through my tears. "Please forgive me, Mary. Somehow, if you forgive me, it would be like him forgiving me, in a way."

"There's nothing to forgive. Your father and I—we loved each other very much. But we knew that it could never be."

"Why? If you loved each other . . . ?"

"Because of who he was. He had a deep sense of loyalty to you and your mother. It was just a moment when he needed to recapture his youth. But you and Liz were his history. He always told me he could never leave you both, and I accepted that. It was enough to be with him for whatever time he allowed me. He was the greatest man I ever knew."

"Tell me something . . . did my mother make him give you up?"

"Oh, no. Quite the contrary . . . Your mother offered him his freedom, even though the idea of divorce was against everything she believed in. She was a kind and generous woman. And she wanted what was best for him. I don't know if I could have done what she did . . ." She paused, as if the memory haunted her. "It was when he saw the great sacrifice your mother was willing to make for him that he gave me up voluntarily. I think he realized then how much he loved her and how much she loved him—how much they meant to each other."

"My mother became ill around that time, with a heart condition. Did you know about that?"

"Beatrice, I don't know if I should tell you this . . . I don't know if your father would have wanted me to, but . . ."

"What? Please, you must tell me."

"Your mother was ill for a long time before your father and I . . ."

"No, she wasn't," I interrupted.

"She was but they kept it from you. In a way, your mother welcomed your father's relationship with me. Things were very difficult for her. It's just that . . . well, no one expected that we would fall in love."

I took a moment to digest this news. "You mean my mother knew about you and my father for a long time?"

"That was my understanding."

"And did you ever meet my mother?"

"I met her once when she came to visit your father at the hospital. We shook hands and she smiled at me . . . She knew."

"My God, I had no idea any of this was going on."

"Your father wanted to protect you. They both did. We all did."

"After he gave you up, did you ever see him again?"

She shook her head sadly. "No . . . I left the hospital and moved up to Hartford. We spoke on the phone once or twice, but it was only to say hello, see how the other was getting on. I'm married now," she said, trying to be more cheerful. "To a doctor. I have stepchildren but no children of my own."

"I'm sorry."

"Please, don't be. Your father was the love of my life, Beatrice. I wouldn't have traded one second with him for anything in the world. Few people had what I had with him, and I'm very grateful. I couldn't believe it when I read about . . ." Her voice trailed off. "And—forgive me, but I just had to meet you, Beatrice. I've seen your pictures, of course. But I had to meet his only child, even after all these years."

I was profoundly moved and I reached out to Mary O'Shaunessy and hugged her close. "Thank you, Mary," I said. "You have no idea what this has meant to me."

"Beatrice. If there's anything I can ever do . . ."

"You've done it. I feel as if my father sent you to me."

"Yes," Mary O'Shaunessy said with conviction. "I feel that too . . . Well, I'll be going now. I have to catch my train."

"God be with you, Mary O'Shaunessy," I said to myself as the woman turned the corner and disappeared from sight.

After the memorial service, I experienced successive waves of grief. I missed my father very much. I had such a different picture of my parents now. And this new picture of them gave me an insight into myself. I reflected on my touching encounter with Mary O'Shaunessy, wondering if I should have taken Stephen back when he'd begged my forgiveness. I thought how different my life might have been had my father followed his heart and left my mother and me. For the first time, I was able to see how rigid and intolerant

I'd been during the course of my marriage. I kept wishing I could go back in time and do things differently.

The business of death helped to alleviate the pain. My father's will left me everything—the house, a modest portfolio of securities, and the magnificent book collection, which, with the one exception of the *Roman de la Rose*, I intended to donate to a university within the year. My father had wanted to be cremated and I followed his wishes. His ashes rested in a small silver urn on the library mantelpiece.

Putting aside my researching jobs, I concentrated my efforts on getting the house straightened up and the library back in order. I farmed out the most damaged volumes to my father's regular bookbinders, an elderly couple on Lexington Avenue. I saved the *Roman de la Rose* for Mr. Lovelock to repair. His visit continued to prey on my mind, and I figured I could use the little incunabulum as an excuse to get in touch with him again.

Detective Monahan's visits to the house tapered off. He seemed curiously inept and I didn't hold out much hope that he would find my father's murderer, despite his assurances to me that he'd taken a "personal interest" in the case.

"We're going to find this man," he promised me.

But no one in the neighborhood seemed to have heard or seen anything unusual on the day of my father's death. His murder was beginning to look more and more like a random break-in that had ended in gratuitous violence.

Signor Antonelli telephoned me from Rome a few times to find out how I was getting on. I told him I was grateful Father Morton had attended the memorial service on his behalf and that I'd entered a period of mourning and reflection, staying close to home, accepting only a very few invitations from close friends. He urged me to seek out Father Morton if I needed counseling. I politely assured him that I would, though I had no intention of doing so. I was still suspicious of Antonelli, particularly because at the end of each of our conversations he would ask me, as an apparent afterthought, if I had found the grimoire. I would tell him no and he would say something like, "Well, never mind," or words to that effect. I can't explain it, but his continued interest in that book made me wary. I was unable to shake a feeling of dread.

Meanwhile, I had other things to occupy me. Nellie was becoming a problem. The grieving housekeeper missed work continually, saying she had to go to church and pray. I felt ill at ease alone in the house all the time. The sweet memories it harbored were poisoned by the murder. I couldn't strike the image of my father's body from my mind. My most innocuous daydreams would suddenly mutate into terrifying reruns of the crime. I locked my bedroom door at night. I lay awake for hours, listening to the creaks and cracks of the house, fearing intruders. Even the gentle ticking of the old grandfather clock on the stairs sounded like an ominous heartbeat. What had once been a secure home now seemed a place of evil, of moving shadows and dark corners.

Finally, the situation finally became intolerable. I reached a painful decision: I decided to sell the house. I telephoned several real estate brokers and arranged for them to come and see it. A couple of days after the house was appraised and officially on the market, I received a call from Father Morton.

"I wonder if you remember me, Beatrice," he said in the sonorous voice of an orator.

"Yes, of course I do, Father," I replied. "You came to my father's memorial on behalf of Signor Antonelli. It was very kind of you."

"The reason I'm calling is because I've just spoken to Giuseppe, and he tells me that you're very serious about donating your father's library to a nonprofit institution."

"Yes?" I said warily.

"I have a proposition I would like to make to you. Would you consider coming down to Saint Xavier's to discuss it with me?"

"Father Morton, I'm sure Signor Antonelli has told you that my father wasn't very religious. I'm really thinking more in terms of a university or a library."

"Yes, yes, my dear. I understand that. But I think what I am offering you will fit that criterion. From what Giuseppe tells me about you and your father, his books might be happy with us," he said. "We never met your father, but we know he was serious about the preservation and dissemination of knowledge, and so are we."

Father Morton was charmingly insistent, and I thought that perhaps he could be helpful, after all. With the house now on the market, I realized, somewhat to my own surprise, that I was ready to think about placing my father's library in caring hands. And the old cleric sounded caring. He seemed concerned about the great books my father had amassed over the years so I agreed to the meeting.

Having made the appointment with Father Morton, I decided to take the *Roman de la Rose* down to Simon Lovelock, as his shop, on West Fourth Street, was in the neighborhood of Saint Xavier's.

The incunabulum in hand, I headed downtown in the subway early the next day. The summer heat was rising as I got off at Astor Place and walked over to Fifth Avenue. Seeing the old church looming up ahead, its dark stone spires piercing the morning sunshine, I stopped, momentarily struck by its uplifting beauty.

I went around the back to the rectory, whose architecture was in keeping with the Gothic style of the church. Entering, I found myself in a stark white reception room. The sounds of the outside world melted away as I closed the great oak door behind me. A prim-looking elderly woman, wearing a white blouse and a black skirt, with a pencil spearing the tight bun near the nape of her neck, was sitting bolt upright at a desk, typing on a computer. She looked up and squinted at me through a pair of horn-rimmed glasses.

"Miss O'Connell?"

"Yes."

"Father Morton is expecting you. Just one moment, please," she said crisply. She picked up the receiver of an intercom. "Miss O'Connell is here, Father," she announced, then put down the phone. "Be seated, won't you? Father Morton will be with you in a moment." She resumed working.

I sat down on a long wooden bench resembling a pew—the only other piece of furniture in the room. Looking around, I noticed a romantic oval portrait of the Virgin Mary, carved out of ivory, hanging alone on a slim space of wall between the front door and the window. The words *Defensores Fidei* were engraved on an ivory ribbon at the bottom.

A few moments later, the intercom buzzed.

"You may go in now," the secretary said, nodding at an inner door.

Father Morton's office was a striking contrast to the reception area. A large, wood-paneled room with carved moldings, it had crisscrossing mahogany beams supporting the high ceiling. Two stunning tapestries, both depicting the unicorn, the symbol of the Virgin Mary, faced each other on opposite walls. The heavy oak furniture was upholstered in red velvet. Two picture windows curtained in thick blue velvet faced out onto a lush back garden.

Father Morton, a fat, pink man with thinning white hair and a ready grin, was seated behind a large, ornately carved desk at the far end of the room. He was holding a pair of binoculars.

"Beatrice, my child, welcome," he said, rising. "I was just doing a little spying on the birds."

Putting down the binoculars, he strode across the room. Little beads of sweat dotted his forehead. His black priest's garb was wilted from the humidity. I noticed that his bulk did not interfere with a marked agility. He clasped my hand enthusiastically. His palm was clammy.

"How very, very good of you to come. Have a seat and make yourself comfortable," he commanded in a deep, robust voice—effective in sermons, I imagined.

Sitting on one of the two chairs across from his desk, I

crossed my legs, placing the brown paper bag containing the *Roman de la Rose* under the pocketbook in my lap.

Father Morton returned to his desk and collapsed into the large leather chair, dabbing his brow with an oversized white cotton handkerchief.

"I'm afraid these humid summer days are the very devil to a man my size," he said. "I'll have Maddy bring us some iced tea, shall I?"

"Sounds great. Thanks."

Father Morton picked up the receiver of an advanced telephone system, which looked incongruous in the nineteenth-century decor. I was struck by a medieval gauntlet on his desk fashioned out of steel mesh and attached to an iron cuff. It looked like a severed hand.

"Maddy, be so kind as to bring us some iced tea with lots of ice." Father Morton put down the phone and addressed himself to the object of my attention. "Marvelous thing, that, isn't it? It was worn by Frederick the Second during the sixth crusade, in twelve twenty-eight—the same year Francis of Assisi was canonized," he said.

"There's a wonderful book on arms and armor in my father's collection. The Germans always made the best armor. As my father liked to say: 'Even then they knew.'"

Father Morton chuckled. "See over there." He pointed to the far corner of the room, in which a full suit of armor was displayed.

"God, that looks uncomfortable," I said. "Actually, I've always had this theory that if women could have peed from the saddle of a horse, the history of the world would have been different."

The minute I said this, I flushed with embarrassment. Like Poe's Imp of the Perverse, it had just popped out of my mouth before I knew it. Father Morton's eyes widened, and I clapped my hand to my mouth to stifle a sheepish giggle.

"Oh, dear—I don't know what made me say that."

He gave me a tolerant smile. "It's an interesting hypothesis. Very of the moment."

"I must say, this is quite a spectacular place," I said, relaxing into my chair. "One doesn't think of the Church as being so rich these days."

"Saint Xavier's is fortunate to have the support of many generous friends. Beatrice, may I say what a lovely memorial service I thought that was."

"Thank you very much for coming."

"Well, Giuseppe has spoken so fondly of you and your dear father over the years. And again, let me express my condolences."

"That's very kind of you. Do you mind if I smoke?" Talk of death always made me anxious.

"No, no. Go right ahead. I'm a slave to the after-dinner cigar myself." He pushed forward the large glass ashtray on his desk.

"Have you known Signor Antonelli a long time?" I inquired as I lit the cigarette.

"I've known Giuseppe for, oh, let's see now . . . We became friends when I was a student in Rome, so that would be nearly forty years ago . . . My, has it been that long?" he reflected. "Yes, yes, it has. Forty years! The wink of an eye, and yet a lifetime."

As he spoke, I studied his ruddy face more closely. His features were large and fleshy. The fold of his double chin partially obscured his white clerical collar band. He had a nervous habit of occasionally licking his lips, which, combined with his easy and ingratiating manner, reminded me of a friendly hound.

Father Morton folded his thick hands on the desk and looked at me intently. "Your father's death must have been a terrible shock for you, you poor child."

"To say the least."

"I could hardly believe it myself. A terrible tragedy."

"Yes, it was—is." I took a long drag.

"Giuseppe told me the library was torn apart. Was there much damage?"

"Nothing that can't be repaired, I hope. I've got his regular bookbinders working on some of the volumes now. It'll take some time."

"Yes, a terrible tragedy from all points of view," he reiterated. "And how are you getting on?"

"Well, up and down—you know."

"That's to be expected, of course."

"So I'm told," I said without conviction. "You mentioned on the telephone that you wanted to talk about my father's library?" I nervously rubbed the tip of the cigarette in the ashtray.

"Yes." Father Morton leaned back and, looking thoughtful, pressed his palms together as if in prayer. "You mentioned you wished to donate it intact to a nonprofit institution."

"That's my plan. I'm considering several places at the moment. I'm under a certain amount of pressure because I've put the house up for sale."

"Have you indeed?" Father Morton said with interest. "Why is that?"

"It's too big, for one thing. And frankly, it's just too difficult for me to stay there now—with what's happened."

"Yes, I can well understand that." He sighed, then cleared his throat. "I don't know whether or not Giuseppe has told you, but I'm affiliated with a foundation—the Duarte Institute. Do you know it?"

I shook my head. "I'm afraid not."

"It's an interesting place, specializing in philosophical studies. It supports students and researchers around the world. We have a magnificent property in upstate New York, with several buildings on it. One of them is a library, housing several extremely valuable book collections. There's space for expansion, and what I was wondering is if you would consider donating your father's library to us. We would like nothing better than to memorialize him in a suitable manner."

"As I told you on the phone, my father wasn't very religious."

"I'm aware of that. But as I said, the institute is dedicated to philosophical studies. It's nondenominational."

"And your connection with it is . . ."

"Purely as an interested party. I'm one of the governors. I wear many hats."

"Well, look, Father Morton, I don't know what to say. I'd be glad to take a look at any literature you have on it," I said politely, but patently unconvinced.

"Better still, you must come up one day and visit. It's a fascinating place. These tapestries were woven there." Father Morton pointed to the unicorn tapestries on the wall.

"Really? They look so authentic."

"We have a crafts program where we instruct students in the old ways of doing things."

"Well, they're wonderful."

"In fact, the Duarte Institute is a little haven from the modern world. You'll see what I mean when you go up there."

"Perhaps when I have a little more time." I shifted in my chair and the *Roman de la Rose* slipped out of its bag and dropped to the floor.

As I bent down to pick it up, Father Morton rose slightly from his chair and peered over the edge of his desk.

"What is that book you have there?" he said with sudden interest.

"This?" I held up the little incunabulum. "It's from my father's library. I'm taking it to be repaired."

"May I see it?" Father Morton said eagerly.

I was just about to give it to him, when there was a knock at the door.

"Enter!" Father Morton cried, obviously irritated at the interruption.

The secretary came in, carrying two glasses of iced tea on a small silver tray. She placed it on the desk.

"Father, don't forget the bishop at eleven," she said, and closed the door behind her.

"Help yourself." As I reached for a glass, the cleric said, "You were going to show me your book," and extended his hand.

"Please be careful," I cautioned him as I handed him the little volume. "It's about to fall apart."

"The *Roman de la Rose*," he said, sounding strangely disappointed. He gave it a cursory look. "From your father's library?"

"Yes. It's the only thing I'm keeping."

Father Morton handed back the book, then picked up his iced tea and proceeded to drink it down in one long swallow.

"Ah!" he said, licking his lips. "Forgive me, but I can't abide this heat . . . Tell me," he asked nonchalantly, "did you ever find that grimoire?"

I paused in mid-sip and looked up. "Who told you about the grimoire?"

"Giuseppe . . . Why? Shouldn't he have? Is it a secret?" Father Morton said innocently.

"No. I just wonder why he'd bother telling you about it."

"Well, I'm an amateur bibliophile. Giuseppe and I often discuss books. He said it was a fascinating little thing. He was going on and on about it."

"I see."

"So—has it turned up?"

"No."

"You've looked for it?"

"Yes."

"Everywhere in the house?"

"Pretty much."

"Perhaps it's in a safety-deposit box?"

"No, I've looked there too. It was obviously stolen."

"Well, if it does turn up—"

"I doubt if it's going to," I interrupted him. He was far too interested in the little book.

"Well, if it does, I'd love to see it."

"Apparently, so would everyone else."

"Who else?" he asked, narrowing his eyes.

My suspicions now aroused, I was not about to mention Mr. Lovelock.

"Well, Signor Antonelli and his secret client," I said. "You must know about his secret client if you've been a friend of his for so many years."

"Ah, yes. He's told me he has someone who collects occult books."

"He's very mysterious about it." I set my glass of tea on the tray. "Perhaps that secret client is you, Father," I said forcing a smile.

Father Morton burst out laughing. "Not exactly my line—the occult—would you say?"

"Do you have any idea who it is?"

"Giuseppe's client? Heavens, no. Giuseppe's a tomb about such things. He'd never tell me. I doubt he'd tell anyone. You have to be discreet in his trade."

"I suppose so."

"You're a bit suspicious of me, aren't you?" he said playfully.

"Why no," I said, lying. "I just find all this interest in the grimoire a little disconcerting . . . Particularly as everything bad happened after it came into our lives."

"Things are bound to upset you more now, dear," he said solicitously.

"Maybe." I shrugged.

"You know what I've found to be very helpful after one has experienced a great loss?"

"What's that?"

"Going to a museum."

His response took me aback. Having expected some sort of religious homily or the like, I was pleasantly surprised.

"Why a museum, particularly?" I asked, cocking my head to one side.

"Stepping out into the world a little at a time, at your own pace, in a soothing environment that promotes contemplation and reflection, is good for the soul in trying times. Museums offer us a silent sense of history and beauty, and in so doing, they tell us we are not alone in our struggle to understand what this life is all about." He paused. "And, of course, there's always the Church."

Oh-oh, here it comes, I thought.

"Well, I'm willing to try a museum, but I'm afraid I've inherited my father's skepticism about the Church."

Father Morton sank back in his chair. "You and so many others," he said ruefully.

"I did find some comfort in the memorial service, though. I like Monsignor Regan very much."

"Yes, a good man," Father Morton said. "Rather progressive in his views . . . Of course, one needn't go to church to believe in God and find comfort in faith. The Church doesn't exist in a building or a mass or a sermon. The Church is the totality of one's faith."

"And what if one doesn't have any faith?"

"Oh, everyone has faith in something, I find, don't you? Even if it's not in God. It's been my experience that if you take the kernel of that faith—whatever it is, however inconsequential it seems—and you try and apply it to something larger than yourself, eventually you come around to God."

"Really? How so?"

"Well, I'll give you an example. What is it that you have the most faith in?"

"Books," I replied without hesitation.

"A good answer. You definitely are your father's daughter. Now, may I ask what way you have faith in them?"

"They're sources of knowledge and comfort and imagination," I replied, as if the answer were obvious.

"All right, then, let's take this faith you have in books. What does it consist of? The power to restore and invigorate you; the power to know another person's mind, another universe, perhaps. But what is that mind? What is that universe? And who created it? And why do you want to connect with it? 'Only connect,' as E. M. Forster said. You see, that little silver thread of connection to the world, which in your case starts with a book and in someone else's may start with painting a picture or having a child or just getting a square meal—that little silver thread of connection can stretch all the way to heaven, if you let it."

"My mother used to say that faith was like a gift: You can't buy it, you can't work for it; it just comes."

"Oh, I think you can work for it a little. After all, if I didn't, I'd be out of a job," he said with a wink.

"Good point." I glanced at my watch, an action that Father Morton pretended to ignore.

"I believe that when the mind opens fully, it receives God, like a flower opening itself to the sun."

"I wish it were that simple," I sighed, rising from my chair. "I'm sorry, Father, but I'm late. I should go."

He escorted me to the door. "Life needn't be such a lonely business," he said.

"Unfortunately, it feels just that way at the moment."

Father Morton took my hand as we reached the door.

"Beatrice, if you need me, you know where to find me. Don't hesitate to call. And please, do think seriously about my proposal regarding your father's library."

Father Morton gave me a little wave as I left, to which I responded self-consciously by inclining my head slightly. I felt his eyes on me as I walked away. I didn't trust him despite all his elegant words, and he knew it.

Outside in the open air, I took a deep breath, experiencing a great sense of relief to be out of that splendid but stifling rectory. The interview had left me wary and disconcerted. I was suspicious of Father Morton. He wears his kindness as a disguise, I thought, under which he's hiding something sinister. What was he really after? Not simply my father's collection, that's for sure. And why all the interest in the grimoire?

Tightly clutching the little incunabulum in my hand, I made my way through the sunny, tree-lined streets of the Village, dogged by apprehension.

Chapter 6

Simon Lovelock's bookshop was located in a dilapidated building, above an abandoned storefront. A small sign near a separate entrance read, in black calligraphy, LOVELOCK RARE BOOKS, SECOND FLOOR. PLEASE RING. I pressed the black button beneath the sign several times, but got no response. I stepped backward, shading my eyes from the sun with my hand, and peered up at the large window with LOVELOCK RARE BOOKS painted in large black letters across the center. It looked dark inside. I tried the button again. There was still no answer. Just as I was about to give up, a sharp buzzer sounded, unlocking the shabby gray door.

I walked into a dingy, dimly lit corridor, at the end of which was a flight of stairs. A slim, dark figure loomed above, barely visible in the gloom.

"Come in, come in," the figure called down to me.

"Mr. Lovelock?" I said. "It's Beatrice O'Connell. Do you remember me?"

"Indeed I do, Miss O'Connell," Lovelock said, holding the door to his shop open for me. "Come up, please."

I walked up the flight of narrow steps, holding on to the rickety railing. Lovelock stood on the landing, dressed all in black, as he had been on our first meeting. His shirtsleeves were rolled up. A cigarette dangled from the corner of his mouth, and he squinted as the smoke occasionally curled into his eyes.

"I'm sorry I took so long to answer," he said as I reached the top. "But you caught me in the middle of a delicate operation. It's very, very nice to see you."

"I hope I'm not interrupting you," I said, following him into the little shop.

"No, no, no, please," he replied nervously. "But if you don't mind, I'll just go finish up what I'm doing, and then I'll be right with you, right with you." He smiled at me and I couldn't help noticing that his eyes lingered on my face. Then, flushing slightly, he seemed to catch himself. "Please feel free to have a look around. I won't be a moment."

Lovelock quickly retreated to a back room, leaving me in the front of the shop. The walls were covered with built-in bookcases filled with every imaginable size and shape of volume, some new, but most of them old and worn. A long wooden reading table surrounded by a few chairs was set up near the grimy picture window facing out onto the street. Though fairly cool, the atmosphere was musty. This place definitely needs a good airing, I thought as I browsed around.

The books appeared to be extremely well organized, despite a layer of dust on some of them. There were various sections, delineated by little white cards scotch-taped to the bookcases; the headings appeared to be written in the same hand as the sign downstairs. I perused the numerous volumes lined up neatly under a large array of alphabetically ordered topics ranging from Africa, Alchemy, America, Angels, Animism, Anti-Christ, Apparitions, Aquinas, Arabs, Arithmancy, Assassins, Astral World, Astrology, Atlantis . . . to Visions, Werewolves, West Indian Islands, Wild Women, Witchcraft, Yoga, Ziito, Zodiac, and Zoroaster.

Noting the appearance of Thomas Aquinas in this curious lineup, I speculated about the venerable saint's connection with the occult. I removed a secondhand copy of G. K. Chesterton's biography, St. Thomas Aquinas, published in 1933, and took it over to the reading table. I was leafing through it when I heard a loud crash and then a thump, coming from the back of the shop.

Grabbing the *Roman de la Rose*, I shot up from the table and hurried through the shop, and knocked on the back-room door. Receiving no answer, I opened the door and peered inside. Lovelock was down on all fours in front of a stack of overturned boxes, picking up a handful of instruments.

"Mr. Lovelock!" I cried. "Are you all right?"

"Fine, fine, thanks," he said, snaking his head around and seeming embarrassed. "Just clumsy, that's all."

"Can I help you?"

"No, no. All's well." He rose to his feet and dusted himself off.

Looking about, I recognized the trappings of a rudimentary bookbindery. In the middle of the cramped and cluttered space was a wooden paper press and a frosted-glass table lit from below. Vials of colored liquid dotted the shelves, and a damp, crinkly sheet of an old manuscript was clamped in a pair of clothespins suspended from strings stapled to the ceiling.

"Welcome to my little hospital," he said with some pride. "Every week I make a vow to clean it up, and every week it gets worse . . . just like life, eh? I s'pose I'll get around to it one of these days—like quitting smoking. I was just performing an operation on one of my more ancient patients."

"May I watch?" I asked.

"Be my guest, please . . . Sorry it's so crowded. If you stand there by the door, you won't be in the way. I'm trying to patch up this little fragment of Saint Augustine's *Confessions*. Thirteenth century."

Lovelock pointed to a withered leaf of parchment resting on top of the underlit glass table. The dense black Latin text was rubricated throughout, with touches of silver and gold on some of the lettering.

"It's beautiful," I said.

"Will be, will be. See this break?" He pointed to an ominous tear at the center. "This is the infection. If we're not careful, it will spread. He's a sad little man now, but wait . . ."

Crushing out his cigarette in a coffee tin filled with butts and ashes, Lovelock selected a sheet of new parchment from a thin stack lying on the one clean shelf in the cramped space. Comparing it to the original, he did not seem content with the choice and proceeded to try three more sheets, until he found one to match the color, thickness, and finish of the fragment almost exactly.

Centering the old leaf on the glass table, directly above the electric lights, he skillfully traced the outline of the tear and cut out a matching piece from the new parchment with a razor blade. His movements were precise and economical, like those of a skilled surgeon. He dipped a wooden stick, half the width of a tongue depressor, into a small glass vial nearby.

"What's that?" I inquired.

"A solution of gelatin and pure acid of vinegar," he replied slowly, concentrating hard as he applied the glutinous mixture to the fragment. "It's an excellent adhesive for this type of work."

He carefully glued the newly cut piece directly onto the ripped portion of the old page.

"There!" he said with evident satisfaction. "Now we'll let him dry on top of the lights, and then we'll press him. You won't be able to tell he was ever wounded. All healed!"

I was both amused and touched by his genuine concern. Having watched him perform the delicate task with such tenderness and sureness of hand, I was pleased to give him my treasured little book.

"Here," I said, handing it to him. "I'd like you to repair this for me."

"Ah, the *Roman de la Rose* . . . I'm honored. We'll take good care of you, my lady," he said, clearing a space for the volume on one of the less encumbered shelves.

"Where did you learn this art, Mr. Lovelock?"

"Oh, here and there," he said, lighting a new cigarette. "Patching parchment is relatively simple. It's when you get into the handmade paper that things become difficult. Like that old gentleman there."

He pointed to the still-damp sheet of paper hanging from the clothespins. "A rotting Pliny fragment. I had quite a time with him yesterday—transferring the text onto fresh paper. Luckily, the ink on these old pages is so durable, it doesn't run."

Lovelock pulled his black jacket from a thick nail on the back of the door and accompanied me to the front of the shop. "So—find anything that interests you?"

"Well, now that you mention it, I was wondering about the section on Saint Thomas Aquinas . . ."

"You mean, what's a nice saint like him doing in a place like this?" he said, grinning at me.

"I guess so." I laughed. "I'm interested in Aquinas because he appears in *The Divine Comedy* and I was named after Beatrice."

"Ah—a literary namesake. Well, he's quite a fascinating case, our 'Angelic Doctor,' as the Church refers to him. Historically, he's had his brush with the occult."

"No! Aquinas? The founding father of Catholic doctrine? I don't believe it."

"Oh, yes indeed." Lovelock's dark eyes glinted impishly beneath his bushy eyebrows. "His tutor was reputed to be a man called Albertus Magnus, a renowned alchemist. Magnus spent thirty years fabricating a man made entirely of brass, which he endowed with magical powers, one of which was the gift of speech. It was reported that Thomas, who had a horror of noise, dashed the effigy to pieces because it wouldn't stop talking!" He giggled, covering his mouth with his hand as if self-conscious about his slightly tobacco-stained teeth.

"Oh, please!"

"I'm only telling you the legend. And it was further said that Thomas himself, having learned certain alchemical powers from his master, made a small brass horse, which he buried under the road in front of his house. The effect of this was that no real horses would go near the place, no matter how hard they were spurred on by their riders, thus ensuring him total peace and quiet. This little legend, plus the fact that books on alchemy were once attributed to him, have gained him a place in my shop."

"Do you actually believe all that?" I asked warily.

"No, no, of course I don't. In fact, it's been proven that the magical books Thomas Aquinas supposedly authored were falsely attributed to him by those seeking to discredit his position in the Church. But the occult isn't about objective truth. It's about mystery, personal perception, and belief. The word itself, as you might know, comes from the Latin *occultus*, the past participle of *occulere*, to conceal. I make no claims for the veracity of what's in my stock. I simply present it as part of the literature of a fascinating subject, for those who are interested to enjoy."

"And just how did you become interested in all this, Mr. Lovelock?"

"Oh, that's a long story," he said evasively.

"Well, it's a great bookstore. But you should get someone to come in and dust it for you."

"It's all I can do to keep my little apartment upstairs clean. Anyway, I think dust adds to the atmosphere, so to speak."

"How long do you think it will take you to repair my book?"

"I'll examine her and let you know, if I may. It may not be for some time, if that's all right."

"I'm in no hurry." I scribbled my phone number on one of the shop's cards and handed it to him. "You can call me when it's ready."

He stuffed the card in his trouser pocket. "Would you care for some coffee, perhaps, or tea?"

"No, thanks. I should be going."

Lovelock seemed disappointed.

"You're getting on all right, I hope?" he asked, walking me toward the door.

"Oh, well, you know . . ."

"I'm sorry you had to come all the way down here. I would gladly have come to pick up the book."

"I was in the neighborhood, anyway," I said. "I was visiting Father Morton over at Saint Xavier's."

Lovelock stopped dead. "Father Morton?"

"Yes. Do you know him?"

"Of him," he said. "May I inquire why you were visiting with him?"

I noticed a marked agitation in his manner. "He wanted to discuss my father's library. Why?"

"How did you happen to come into contact with him, if I may ask?"

"He's very close to my father's friend Signor Antonelli, and he's affiliated with something called the Duarte Institute. He wants me to consider donating the library there."

"Does he indeed?"

"Yes. Why? What's the matter?"

"Oh, nothing, nothing . . ."

"Do you know about this place? Father Morton says it specializes in philosophical studies. I'd never heard of it. Have you?"

"Yes, I've heard of it," he said.

"Mr. Lovelock? What is it? What's the matter?"

"Nothing, nothing . . . Come. I don't want to keep you." He shook his head and continued toward the door.

I held my ground. "Wait a minute. I know there's something. Please tell me what you're thinking."

He hesitated. "Well, it's just that . . ."

"That what? What?"

"Well, I wouldn't trust him, if I were you," he said finally.

"Why not?"

"Just wouldn't, that's all. I really can't say any more."

"Look, I'm asking you. Please." A look passed between us.

"Was the library the only thing he wanted to discuss?" Lovelock said.

"Okay—to tell you the truth, I think the real reason he asked me down there was to see whether or not I'd found the grimoire."

"You haven't found it, have you?" he said with alarm.

"No."

Lovelock seemed relieved. "That's all right, then."

I grabbed his sleeve. "Look, what is it about that god-damn book?" I cried impatiently. "We've been through this before—that evening at the house. If you know some-thing, you have to tell me!"

Lovelock lowered his eyes and gazed at my hand. I let go of his sleeve.

"It's better not to get involved with that thing," he said. "Let's leave it at that."

"I don't want to leave it at that."

"Well, I'm afraid I do."

I sighed, seeing I wasn't going to get anything further from him. "I suppose we'll have to, then."

We reached the door.

"I'll call you about your little 'friend' in a day or so." Lovelock edged into the corridor, holding the door open for me to pass.

"Good-bye, Mr. Lovelock," I said, extending my hand.

Lovelock shook my hand and held it for a long moment, looking into my eyes. "Take care," he said with feeling.

"I will, thank you. I look forward to hearing from you."

I decided to walk home. Beekman Place was a long way from the Village, but I wanted some exercise, plus I wanted to think. As I walked, I mulled over my meeting with Father Morton. Why was Morton so interested in the grimoire and why was he pushing the Duarte Institute on me? I sensed that Lovelock didn't like him at all. Lovelock, who had seemed rather dry and introverted at our first meeting at the house, was growing on me. Just now, when he shook my hand and held it, he seemed stronger and a comforting, reassuring presence. But he knew something too—something he wasn't telling me. I imagined that if I got to know him better, he might eventually open up and tell me what exactly it was he knew.

When I arrived back at the house, envigorated after my

long walk, I heard stirring upstairs and I froze with fear. My first instinct was to run out of the house, but I didn't. Instead, I crept up the steps and followed the sounds. I was relieved and rather surprised to find Nellie bustling around the master bedroom. The old housekeeper was in the midst of packing up my father's clothes, putting them into shopping bags to give to Goodwill.

"Nellie!"

"Oh, Miss Beatrice, you startled me!" the old housekeeper cried, whirling around.

"And you nearly scared me half to death. I thought you were taking the week off."

"I wanted to come in to help you. Did you see Father Morton?"

"Yes, I did." I thought for a second. "I didn't tell you I was going to see him, did I?"

She hesitated. "No, but I saw him at the service and I thought he'd asked you to come see him."

"Oh . . . Well, I went."

"What do you think of him?"

"He seems quite nice," I said cautiously. I picked up the beige cashmere sweater I'd given my father for his birthday the year before. "Remember this, Nellie? How Daddy used to wear it even in the summer?"

"He loved that sweater because you gave it to him. He loved everything you gave him, Miss Beatrice."

"Well, I hope the next person who wears it will appreciate it."

I folded the sweater and put it into one of the shopping bags. "On second thought, I don't think I'll give it away." I took it out of the bag and slung it over my shoulders. "I like having it near me."

"I'm sure Father Morton was a comfort to you."

"Why are you so interested in him, Nellie?"

"Father Morton is a great man. A man of God. I go down to Saint Xavier's to hear his sermons. He's an inspiration. All my friends think so too."

Over the years I'd met some of Nellie's friends. They were a little network of Irish-Catholic working women who, like the old housekeeper, were all spinsters and devoutly religious.

"He says he has a place for Daddy's library."

"Well, you should listen to him then."

"You think I'm a little heathen, don't you, Nellie?" I said, teasing the old woman.

The old housekeeper sniffed. "Well, I wouldn't be so proud of it, if I were you. You take after your father, you do—God rest his soul. But if you ask me it was your blessed mother you should've taken after, Miss Beatrice. She was a saint, your mother—a real saint. She believed in the Church, she did."

For Nellie, the world was divided into only two types of people—saints and heathens—according to how much faith they had in Catholicism. Her impatience with my lack of religion always made me smile a bit, even though I pretended to take her reprimands seriously.

As we continued the packing, I realized that the more insignificant the article, the more I was affected by it. My father's toothbrush, an odd sock, his razor, a nail clipper, bifocals—all the things that he had used or worn day in, day out—these were the things that made me the most teary. I saved his watch, his pipe, his diplomas and citations, and the pile of old prescription pads he used for scrap paper, putting them into a separate box.

In the midst of our efforts, the doorbell rang. Nellie went downstairs to answer it. When she came back up to announce who it was, her face had a beatific expression that made me suspect that the caller was a member of the clergy. But I was wrong.

"You have a visitor."

"Who is it, Nellie? You know I don't want to see anyone."

"You'll be wanting to see this person," Nellie said with a grin, refusing to identify the caller.

Nellie had shown the mystery guest into the library. When I saw who it was, I froze for a moment, and not just because the man was standing on the exact spot where my father had been slain.

"Hello, Bea," he said softly.

"Stephen . . ." I whispered, swallowing hard.

He walked over and put his arms around me, holding me tight for a long time. "How's my girl?"

The sight of my ex-husband filled me with sorrow and regret. I just stood there, weeping like a fool. Stephen hadn't changed. He was still boyish-looking, dressed in his usual blue jeans, blazer, open shirt, and worn-out moccasins with no socks—an overgrown preppy. Like my father, he had a ready smile and an easy manner. And like my father too, he was adept at gaining people's confidence. Stephen, however, used his charm as a tool to extract information for whatever story he was working on. He offered me a tissue and I wiped my eyes.

"I just heard the news," he said. "I was away."

"Where were you?"

"Afghanistan."

"What were you doing there again?"

"A big piece on the poppy growers."

"Something safe for a change," I said.

"Listen, everything's a risk these days—including staying at home," he said pointedly.

Stephen viewed the world as an intricate lock he could pick through persistence. He was bright, inquisitive, and attracted to danger—a lethal combination in a husband. He was always on the move somewhere. During his career as a reporter, he covered the Kurdish revolt in northern Iraq, lived with the rebels in Afghanistan, and infiltrated an arms-smuggling ring in south Florida. Then he withdrew from the mind-numbing demands of newsweekly journalism to write books and long magazine pieces. He'd hired me to do some research for his prize-winning book on Islamic sectarianism and the ideological and tribal struggles of the Persian Gulf and Middle East. Soon after we met we fell in love.

"Let me look at you," Stephen said, studying my face. "Still gorgeous."

"Oh, I am not, and you know it," I said, pooh-poohing the idea. "But you, on the other hand, really haven't changed. Men are so lucky."

"Well, I have. But maybe not physically."

"So—how's life?"

"Come sit down and tell me what happened, Bea."

He led me to the sofa.

"What have you heard?" I asked him.

"That he was shot by a burglar."

"Yes . . . well, that's what they think. It was right over there. Right where you were standing."

"Do they have any make on the guy?"

"No."

"Any leads at all?"

"Nope," I said, absently biting at the corner of my finger-nail. His presence made me nervous.

'Who's been assigned to the case?"

"A Detective Frank Monahan. He seems competent, but he hasn't turned up anything yet."

Stephen stared at me. "You still mad at me?"

"Oh, it's so complicated." I sighed. "Just let me get used to seeing you again."

"Bea, I know what a blow this is for you. Believe me, I know how close you were to your dad. I loved him too, Bea. He was a terrific guy. Just a wonderful, wonderful man."

I swallowed hard, fighting back fresh tears. "So," I said in a quaky voice, "how've you been? What have you been up to, aside from trying to get yourself killed?"

"Here," he said, gently turning my face toward him. "I have something for you." He kissed me lightly on the mouth.

I just stared at him. "What'd you do that for?"

"Don't know. Just felt like it, I guess."

"We haven't seen each other in . . . God, what's it been? Two years?"

"You look a little thin."

"I'm just worn out, that's all. Grief is exhausting. This is the worst thing that's ever happened to me . . . Why did you come here?"

"Did you really think I wouldn't?"

"You weren't at the memorial."

"I told you. I was in Kabul. I just got back last night. A friend of mine left a message on my service. I rushed over here as soon as I could. Bea, I still love you. You know that, don't you?"

I buried my head in his chest and was silent for a time, hoping to experience the comfort I'd once felt in his arms.

"If you loved me so much, why did you leave me?"

"I didn't leave you. I made one horrible mistake and not a day goes by when I don't regret it. I was a shit. I admit it."

I pulled away. "Yeah, well, just because you say you're a shit doesn't mean you're not one."

Stephen chuckled. "I was scared of being married, I guess. Scared of having a family. Scared of being tied down. And I'm sorry. Really sorry. I was just scared, that's all."

"You're not scared of getting shot at."

"It's a quicker death," he said deadpan.

I couldn't help but smile. "Ha. Ha."

He raked his fingers through his hair. "I know how big you are on revenge, Bea. And if it makes you feel any better, you sure have gotten your revenge on me. Not a day goes by when I don't think about you and us and what might have been. I know you blame me for the miscarriage. But believe me, you can't blame me any more than I blame myself."

"Well, it's all in the past now," I said. "Like everything else—including my life."

"No self-pity, please. Not you. You were the one who was always warning me about feeling sorry for myself. What do you think your dad would think if he heard you talk like that?"

"He'd hate it."

"He sure as hell would." He looked at me intently. "I

don't suppose you could ever find it in your heart to forgive me, could you?"

Hearing my father's last words to me about forgiveness
echoing in my mind, I extracted myself from his arms, got
up, and paced around the room.

"You know what I found out?"

"What?"

"Daddy was unfaithful to Mom during their marriage. And at one point, he even fell in love with another
woman."

"You're kidding?" Stephen said with interest. "Who told
you that?"

"He did. The night before he died."

Stephen shook his head in disbelief. "Dr. John . . . Jesus
. . . I never would've suspected it."

"No. Me neither . . . And I was so hard on him, Stephen.
I felt so betrayed somehow, and I just hated him for it at
the time."

"I wonder what made him tell you."

"We were talking about you, in fact, and our marriage,
when he admitted it. He said he was worried about me,
worried that I was wasting my life because I had some notion that relationships had to be perfect. You know how
I always idealized my parents' marriage." Stephen rolled
his eyes slightly, as if to say he knew that only too well.
"And I think that finally he just decided to remove my rose-
colored glasses," I continued. "He did it as a kindness to
me, really. He took a big chance—and I threw it back in his
face. He always liked you, Stephen. You know he did."

"Did he tell you who he fell in love with?"

"He just said it was a nurse at the hospital and that
my mother understood. But then something amazing
happened."

"What?"

"I met her."

"How?"

"She came to the memorial, and after the service, she introduced herself to me. The minute she said she'd worked with my father at the hospital, I knew exactly who she was. And the most remarkable thing was that she looked just like Mom used to look when she was younger. Oh, Stephen, she was such a lovely woman. She told me that my father was the love of her life and that my mother had offered to give him up, but he wouldn't leave us . . . I feel like such a self-righteous fool. I'd give anything—anything in the world—to see Daddy again and tell him that I understand . . . Oh, well." I shook my head sadly. "That's life, isn't it? You don't get second chances."

"Sometimes you do. You could have given me one, for example."

"It was slightly different with us, wasn't it? We weren't exactly married for years before you ran off. And besides, I suspect my mother hated sex."

"You weren't so fond of it yourself."

I looked askance at him. "What a thing to say!"

"You weren't, Bea."

"What do you mean?"

"Well, you tolerated it. But I don't know how much you actually enjoyed it."

"Of course I enjoyed it. And if you felt that, why did you marry me?"

"I love you," he said simply. "Sex isn't everything, you know. And I thought after a while you'd—I don't know—kind of open up more."

"Open up?" I interrupted him.

"In the bedroom . . ."

"I see . . . And when I didn't, you looked elsewhere, is that it? It was my fault."

Stephen lowered his eyes. "No. I was an idiot."

"You didn't really give us a chance, you know."

"I know." He took my hand. "Not a day goes by when I don't think about what I threw away."

I thought for a moment, considering what he said instead of being angry about it. "Well, maybe I was at fault too.

God knows I didn't see myself clearly. So maybe you're right about what you say. Maybe I was afraid of sex."

"Sex does have a way of screwing things up. Everyone goes to their pathological battle stations . . . Let me ask you something, Bea," Stephen said after a time. "Do you think we could ever make a go of it again?"

"Oh God, I don't know. I don't know anything anymore . . . Except one thing," I said with sudden conviction. "I'm going to get the bastard who murdered my father if it takes me the rest of my life."

"Will you let me help you?"

I was touched by his offer. Also, I knew that Stephen's skills as a reporter would make him an invaluable aid.

"Aren't you working on something?"

"It can wait. This is so much more important."

"Well, I could really use some help. But tell me one thing first."

"What's that?"

"Are you seeing anyone?"

Stephen shook his head. "No."

I narrowed my eyes.

"Are you sure?" I said skeptically. "I've never known you not to be seeing someone."

Stephen cleared his throat, obviously on the spot.

"Well, I assume the real question is am I involved with anyone? And I am not involved with anyone, okay? Yeah, I see women, but there's no one special. I can promise you that."

I paused. "Has there been anyone special since me?"

"Why do you want to know?" he asked provocatively.

"I don't know. I just do, that's all."

Stephen heaved a sigh. "Not really, no."

I knew he wasn't being honest with me and I just kept staring at him without saying a word.

"Okay, okay," he conceded. "There was this reporter in Boston. But she and I broke up about a year and a half ago. I haven't seen her since."

"Why'd you break up?"

"You want the truth?"

"It would be a nice change."

"Very funny. The fact is she told me I was still in love with you," he said with a grim little laugh.

I perked up, wondering why this made me feel so happy.

"Really? *She* told *you*?"

"Right. How about you? What have you been up to in the romance department?"

Díaz flashed through my mind.

"Nothing. I'm not seeing anyone." I could tell from his expression that he didn't quite believe me either. "I'm not!"

Stephen just shook his head and smiled. "Oh, Bea, I know you so well. What are you not telling me? Never mind . . . I said I'd help you, and I mean it. So tell me what exactly happened?"

I took a deep breath and reviewed the whole story, starting with Signor Antonelli's visit. I told Stephen about the grimoire and Simon Lovelock and my disturbing encounter with Father Morton. When I mentioned the Duarte Institute, a quizzical look passed over his face.

"The Duarte Institute?" he said reflectively.

"You've heard of it?"

"Yeah, I'm just trying to think where. Somebody mentioned it to me just recently. I'll think of who it was . . . I will. Go on."

"I have a weird feeling about Father Morton. His ostensible reason for inviting me down to Saint Xavier's was to talk about donating my father's library to this place, but I think his real reason was to find out if I had that wicked little grimoire."

"So he knows about the grimoire through Antonelli?"

"Right. They're old friends."

"Yeah, well, you know: Catholicism—black magic. Flip sides of the same coin. As an intellectual, he's probably interested."

"Lovelock doesn't like him," I said.

"Did he say so?"

"He didn't have to. I could tell. I mentioned Father Morton's name, and he practically froze."

"Okay, but what do we know about Lovelock? He's a dealer in occult books. Talk about weird! If you ask me, the jury's out on Lovelock too."

"Oh, I rather like him. He's such a strange bird. I can't even tell how old he is. He's got one of those ageless faces. But there's something quite gentle and eccentric about him. He calls the books he repairs his 'patients' and refers to them as 'he' or 'she.' I'm inclined to trust him."

"I wish I could think of who it was who was telling me about the Duarte Institute," Stephen said, distracted.

"Well, I guess I'd better get back and help Nellie. We're packing up Daddy's things to send to Goodwill."

Stephen kissed me gently on the cheek. "There's a nice chaste kiss for you."

I gazed at him for a long moment, trying to gauge my feelings for him. I still felt something, though whether that something was residual anger, or attraction, or an odd combination of the two was anybody's guess. What I knew above all else was that Stephen could be invaluable in helping me solve my father's murder, and that was the most important thing in the world to me now. It took precedence over every other emotion.

I hugged him and said, "Thanks for coming over. It's good to see you. I'll be in touch."

"Give me another chance, will you, Bea? You won't be sorry this time. I promise."

I just smiled.

Chapter 7

"How's Mr. Stephen?" Nellie inquired as she and I continued packing up my father's effects.

"He's fine."

"You're happy he came, aren't you?"

"Maybe."

"He never changes. He's a good-looking boy."

"I think he's lost a little weight," I said.

"Pining away over you, no doubt. He still loves you, you know. And you love him."

"Nellie . . ." I warned her.

"You ought to marry him again and have a baby, Miss Beatrice. It's no good for you to be alone. You need a husband and a family. Your mother always said so, and your father said so too. We're none of us getting any younger, you know."

"Thanks for reminding me," I said with a laugh.

Having no relatives of her own, Nellie Riley had always attached herself to the families she worked for, freely offering her views on the conduct of their lives. This trait was both endearing and irritating. Nellie, a white-haired wisp of a woman in her sixties, never spoke much about her own life. All I knew about the housekeeper's past was that her parents had died when she was young and that she and an older brother had been raised by nuns in a Catholic orphanage outside Cork, Ireland. She loved the Catholic Church and was much indebted to it.

Her brother, the last of her family and a man she worshipped, had joined the Irish Guards when he was eighteen. He was

killed in a hunting accident at the age of twenty-one. Nellie
then left Ireland and traveled to the United States when she
was twenty-four to work as a housekeeper for a family in
New York.

I knew that my father's death must have been almost as
hard on poor Nellie as it had been on me. She now seemed
as if she had begun to accept it, however, as she accepted all
the sorrows of life, tucking it under the comforting blanket of
"God's will." Nellie had worked for us a little over seventeen
years, living in a small, rent-controlled apartment on Ninety-
third Street off Second Avenue. Daddy and I loved her dearly,
although he sometimes teased her about her rigid Catholicism. Nellie looked back nostalgically on the days of the Latin
mass, went to church every day, still ate fish on Friday, thought
Vatican II far too liberal, and feared for the souls of all non-
Catholics. She saw all world conflict as a religious war.

Nellie folded up the last of my father's shirts and stuffed
it into a shopping bag filled with his clothes. "There, that's
done," she said, with sad resignation. She looked at me as I
was rummaging through a pile of his suits. "Honestly, Miss
Beatrice, I don't know how you can stand to stay in this
house all by yourself."

"That's why I'm selling it, Nellie. Have you been through
all his suit pockets?"

"Indeed I have. You should move out now. There's
ghosts here. The banshees'll soon be wailing."

Nellie went into the bathroom and came back with the
wicker hamper, which was filled with my father's soiled
clothes. "Shall I wash these before we give them away, or
just let them go to Goodwill like this?"

"I think it would be nicer to wash them, don't you?"

"Huh!" Nellie sneered. "As if most of them would know
the difference, or care."

"Don't be such a snob, Nellie. Remember, 'But for the
grace of God . . .'"

"The grace of God comes with an honest day's work,"
Nellie retorted.

"Well, you don't have to do it today. Why don't you just leave it and go home? Tomorrow's plenty of time."

"Are you sure, Miss Beatrice? I would like to go to church this afternoon. I'm going to have another novena said for your father."

"You go on, then. I'll sort the laundry out."

Nellie paused at the bedroom door. "It was God's will, Miss Beatrice. You must believe that."

"Thank you, Nellie. I'll try."

When the old woman left, I wearily lifted up the large hamper and dumped the contents onto the floor. In doing so, I saw a flash of black in the clothing and heard a light thump. Digging through the heap of shirts, socks, and underwear, I retrieved the object and held it up in front of me. My hands were shaking. It was the grimoire.

"Oh my God," I said softly, staring at the book in disbelief.

Opening it, I found the letter from the patient who had sent it to my father, plus a ten-dollar bill, which meant Dad had hidden it after he'd spoken to Signor Antonelli. Here's the payment on my bet, I thought, fingering the money. I thumbed through the grimoire, page by page, trying to look at it objectively. The thought that my father might have been killed for this "curiosity," as Signor Antonelli had referred to it, seemed far-fetched. The crude woodcuts at the center of the book retained their disturbing power, however.

I studied them more closely—in particular, those depicting the transformation of a beautiful, enticing woman into a voracious and bloody succubus, images that had so arrested me when I first encountered them in my father's library. The metamorphosis seemed to me to be rather a cartoonish representation of dark female sexuality: Sexual Woman equals Woman the Temptress equals Woman the Devourer equals Evil Woman Incarnate.

The phone rang. It was Stephen, calling to check up on me. I didn't tell him I'd found the grimoire because—and

I know this is crazy—I was afraid someone might be tapping my phone. He was excited, I could tell.

"I have some news for you about Simon Lovelock," he said.

"What about him?"

"Fred Viner knows him."

"Who's Fred Viner?"

"You know, Viner Books? They're right around the corner from me, on Columbus."

"Oh, that place."

"I stopped by on my way home this evening. Fred's known Lovelock for years. Says he's a real character. A former Jesuit."

"Really? You mean he isn't anymore?"

"Fred says something happened. They either expelled him or he quit the order. He didn't know exactly. But you'll love this: Lovelock used to work in the Vatican Library."

I was very interested to hear this.

"That's how Fred first heard of him," Stephen went on. "Apparently, Lovelock was there for a number of years, in charge of publishing mega-expensive facsimiles of the Vatican's most famous books for the American and English markets. Books of Hours and illustrated Bibles—that kind of thing. Fred used to special-order them for a good customer of his. Anyway, the publications stopped for some copyright issues. Lovelock moved back to New York and opened his occult bookshop about six years ago. According to Fred, he's *the* man in the occult field—the dealer's dealer. That's probably why your dad got in touch with him. What do you think?"

"I think I have to talk to him some more," I said.

"Why don't we go down to his shop together tomorrow," Stephen suggested. "I'd like to meet him."

"Okay."

"I'll pick you up at ten."

"Fine."

"Bea? You all right?"

"Fine, yes," I said, debating whether or not to tell him what I had in my hands that very moment.

"You don't sound it."

"No, I'm fine. See you tomorrow."

I stayed up examining the grimoire until I fell asleep, exhausted.

The next morning, I paid closer attention to my appearance as I got dressed. I didn't want Stephen to think I was making a special effort for him, but I was. I fixed my hair the way I knew he liked it and put on a dress instead of my usual blouse and pants. When the doorbell rang, I was already on my way downstairs, grimoire in hand. Opening the door, I saw Stephen standing there, his face obscured by a bunch of straggly flowers.

"Madame, these are for you." He held out the ragged bouquet.

"Oh, weeds!" I exclaimed. "My favorite. How did you know?"

"Sorry, but it's all they had at the fruit stand. What's that?" he asked, noting the book in my hand.

"This is it," I said hesitantly. "The book I told you about. Come on, I want you to take a look at it."

Stephen followed me into the kitchen. He put the flowers down on the counter. I handed him the grimoire and searched for a vase in the cupboards.

"So this is the famous grimoire, eh?" he said, turning the book over in his hands. "Where was it?"

"In my father's hamper. He'd obviously put it there to hide it. There was a ten-dollar bill in it, which was the amount of our bet. So that means he hid it after Antonelli called him and asked to buy it again."

Sitting at the kitchen table, Stephen gave the grimoire a cursory look. "Too bad my French is so lousy," he said.

I arranged the flowers in a vase and made a pot of coffee.

"I studied at it last night," I said. "It's a strange thing. I think we should go and show it to Lovelock."

Stephen turned to the first page and read aloud.

" *'Videmus nunc per—'* How's your Latin?"

"It means, 'For now we see through a glass, darkly; but then face-to-face.' It's from Saint Paul. Signor Antonelli explained that it was probably a little joke of the author's, to make you think you were about to read a religious tract."

Stephen nodded. I poured us each a cup of coffee.

"Remember when we saw that Bergman film *Through a Glass Darkly* and you freaked out?" he asked.

"I did not freak out," I protested.

"Yes, you did. You said the helicopter looked like a spider, and then we went home and had what was possibly the best sex of our entire lives."

"According to you, that wouldn't have been difficult," I said.

"You're not going to let me off the hook about that, are you?"

"I just keep wondering if it's true."

"Why don't we find out?"

I rolled my eyes heavenward. There was still a spark between us, but I wanted to keep our relationship platonic for the moment.

"Stick to the grimoire, please."

"Can't we flirt a little?"

"Just turn the page, will you?"

"You smell good. What's the name of that perfume?"

"Eau Contraire," I replied deadpan.

"Very funny. 'Age cannot wither, nor custom stale her infinite sarcasm.'"

"Just turn the page," I said.

"Okay, okay . . . Now, let's see, what have we here?"

Stephen read aloud slowly from the Old French text in a fractured accent. " *'Gremoire du Pape Honorius avec un recueil des plus rares secrets. À Rome. MDCLXX.'* Well, that's not too difficult. Even I understand that. 'The grimoire of Pope Honorius with a something of the rarest secrets.'"

"Collection," I said. "*Recueil* means collection. Want some toast?"

"Thank you. 'With a collection of the rarest secrets. Rome, 1670.' Then there's this weird little design with a circle and a half-moon and a pentacle, some lions. Wonder what that means. Who knows? Okay. Moving on . . ."

Again, Stephen read aloud from the text in a halting voice. Finally, I looked over his shoulder and read aloud the opening paragraph of the text myself.

"'*Conftitutions du Pape Honorius le Grand, ou fe trouvent les conjurations fecrettes qu'il faut faire contre les Efprits de ténébres—*'"

"Translation, please," he said.

I ran my finger over the sentences, one by one.

"It's roughly this: 'Constitutions of Pope Honorius the Great, where one finds the secret conjurings which are necessary to use against the Spirits of Darkness . . . The Apostolic Throne'—I think that means throne—'to whom the keys of the Kingdom of Heaven have been given by these words of Jesus Christ to Saint Peter: "I give you the keys to the Kingdom of Heaven," the sole power to command the Prince of Darkness and his Angels, which, like the servants of their master, owe honor, glory, and obeisance, by the other words of Jesus Christ: "You will serve your only master"; by the power of the keys of the church you have been made the lord of hell.'"

"What's that supposed to mean?" Stephen asked. "That the pope's been made the lord of hell with the help of this book?"

"Who knows?" I shrugged. "And take a look at this." I showed him the woodcuts.

"Crude but effective," he said, looking them over. "Although I like my succubi a little more succulent."

I flung him a withering glance. He theatrically cleared his throat. "Moving right along . . ." he said, turning to the back of the book where the word *Table* was written in bold black type. A pair of grinning demons cavorted on the arms of the *T*. "Table . . . Table of contents, right? Oh, hell, you read," he said, handing me the book.

I took the book from him to read aloud. "Page one is the Constitution of Pope Honorius III. Page Two says: *'Bulle du meme Pape, ou fe trouvera la manière de donner á cet Ouvrage la force de contraindres les Efprits & les faire obéir.'* Roughly translated, that means: 'The Bull of the same Pope, which gives the work the power to invoke the spirits and make them obey.'"

"A papal bull—whaddaya know?" Stephen said, amused. "So, basically, it's kind of an evil parody of Church conventions."

"Looks like it. I wonder who Pope Honorius III was?"

"Probably some guy they didn't like."

"Skipping a bit," I went on, thumbing through the pages, "here we have a list of things: *'Conjuration universelle—* universal conjuring; *Conjurations des Demons*—conjuring of demons; *Conjurations des Mortes*—conjuring the dead; *Conjuration du Livre*—conjuring of the book—'"

"Wait," Stephen said. "What page is that?"

"Twenty-one."

"Read it."

I turned to page twenty-one and read the text aloud:

" *'Conjuration du Livre . . . je te conjure, Livre, d'etre utile & profitable à tous ceux qui to liront pour la reuffite de leurs affaires—'"*

"Quit showing off," Stephen said, irritated. "Let's save a little time here."

"You just hate that I can speak French and you can't, don't you?" I said playfully.

"Oui, Madame. Now, *donnez-moi un break* and read, please!"

I cleared my throat and assumed a mock serious air: "Okay. 'Conjuring of the Book . . . I conjure you, Book, to be useful and profitable to all who read you for the success of their affairs . . . I conjure you immediately by the virtue of the blood of Jesus Christ contained every day in the chalice to be useful to all who will read you. I exorcise you in the name of the Holy Trinity.'"

"That's it?"

Stephen sounded disappointed. "That's it."

"Back to the table of contents," he ordered.

I returned to the beginning of the book. "Here we have conjuring for the days of the week: Monday, Tuesday, Wednesday, et cetera."

"I guess a day without conjuring was like a day without sunshine for these folks."

"Stephen, you're not taking this at all seriously, are you?"

"No, I am," he said, straightening up. "I really am. Continue, please."

I turned the page. "Let's see, we have conjuring for sore throats, conjuring for headaches, conjuring for buried treasure—"

"Read that one," he interrupted.

I located the page and scanned the text. "Oh, you're going to love this! . . . 'Take the brain of a rooster, powder from the dust of a human grave—*c'est-à-dire,* the powder in the coffin itself—oil from nuts, and wax from a candle. Mix them all together and wrap them in a virgin parchment, in which the words *Trinitas, Omnipotens, Deus, Aeternus, Summum bonum infinitas, Amen* are written with the following caricature . . .' There's a little sketch here—look."

Stephen examined the odd drawing of a triangle, a pentacle, and an eye, unevenly juxtaposed in a circle. He shrugged. "Go on."

"'Burn the mixture, and prodigious things will be revealed to you. But caution: this may not be done by fearful people.'"

"Or intelligent people. Speaking of burning . . ." He sniffed the air.

"Christ!" I ran to the smoking toaster and removed the charred bread from the slots, muttering an apology.

"I think the devil is trying to tell us something," Stephen joked.

I poured us both more coffee and sat down again, perusing the book.

"Go back to the table of contents," Stephen said, sipping the strong brew.

"I'm just looking through it. There's nothing much more than some spells. Here's a spell to make a naked girl dance . . ."

"Really?" Stephen leaned in.

"Yes, here it is," I said, pointing it out to him. " '*Conjuration pour faire danser une fille nue.*' "

"Oh, read that one!" he cried.

Shaking my head in mild amusement, I glanced at him out of the corner of my eye, thinking what a teenager Stephen was at heart. He just couldn't help himself.

" 'Write on a virgin piece of parchment the first letter of the girl's name with the tooth of a wild beast dipped in bat's blood. Then wrap it around a stone which has been blessed and put the stone on top of a copy of a mass. Bury the stone under the door where the person will pass . . . *A peine aura-t-elle fait ce trajet, que vous la verrez entrer en fureur, fe desabillant toute nue, & dansera jusqu'á la mort, fi l'on n'oté pas le caractère, avec des grimaces & contorsions qui font plus de pitié que d'envie.*' I'm not quite sure what that means—something about seeing her entering in a fury, becoming naked, and dancing herself to death, and regarding her with more pity than envy."

"Right! Well, we get the gist of it. I tell you what. I'll get some parchment, a stone, and a bat. You strip naked, and we'll see if it works," he said with a big smile.

"You're not taking any of this seriously, are you?"

"Sure I am, sure I am! Aren't you? This is horrific stuff. Girls dancing naked, spells for sore throats and days of the week. I'm terrified," he said.

"But look at the woodcuts. They really are frightening. Look at the woman. First she's the beautiful temptress. Then she turns into a succubus. The evil seductress."

Stephen shrugged. "Sounds like life to me."

"Very funny. But you guys really do think about us like that, don't you? Sexual temptation equals evil. I mean, you don't like to admit it, but . . ."

"Seriously?"

"Yes, be serious for a change, Stephen," I said, growing impatient. "I'd appreciate it."

He straightened up, assuming an authoritative air. "Okay. The fact is you may be right. Men are children, as you have so often pointed out. Maybe we do have some cartoon notions about women. But frankly, that's all irrelevant. We're not examining the male psyche at the moment. We're trying to figure out why this goofy little grimoire of yours may be the key to something truly horrific. Am I right?"

I nodded.

"Now, I happen to think it's a pretty ridiculous little item," he went on. "However, in deference to the number of apparently intelligent people who seem to be interested in it, I'm willing to reserve judgment until I know more about it. And since neither of us is qualified to assess this thing properly, you know what I think?"

"What?"

"Lovelock's the man. Unless you want to call Signor Antonelli."

"God, no!" I cried. "I really don't trust him."

"Then we have to go with Lovelock."

"Yes, I think you're right. For one thing, we know my father called him, so obviously Daddy trusted him."

Stephen furrowed his brow. "And how do we know your father called him?"

"Because he came to the house. He said Daddy called him."

"That's what he *said* . . ." Stephen said ominously. "So we only have his word for it."

I took his point. "Well, I trust him. I think."

"He may well be trustworthy. But you know me, Bea. Everyone's guilty until proven innocent. The reporter's credo."

Chapter 8

We took a cab to Lovelock Rare Books. Stephen followed me into the run-down building. Simon Lovelock, dressed in black as usual, was waiting for us on the landing, just outside his shop. I looked up and bid him good morning. When we got to the top, I introduced him to Stephen.

"Stephen, I'd like you to meet Simon Lovelock. Mr. Lovelock, Stephen Carson."

The two men gave each other a wary handshake. Lovelock ushered us into the premises. The moment we entered, I knew that Stephen was intrigued by what he saw. The musty little bookstore obviously delighted him and he immediately began browsing around.

Mr. Lovelock looked at me with tired eyes and said, "I'm afraid I haven't had a chance to examine your little *Roman de la Rose* yet."

"Oh, I didn't come about that," I said.

"What may I do for you, then?"

"I'll get straight to the point, Mr. Lovelock. I found the grimoire."

Stephen, who was preoccupied with a book he'd taken from one of the shelves, glanced up. Lovelock betrayed no emotion, but he was silent for a long moment.

"Where?" Lovelock asked.

"In the house. My father had tossed it in the hamper with his dirty laundry. Looks like he was trying to hide it."

"We thought you might like to take a look at it," Stephen said.

Lovelock hesitated. "Do you have it here?"

"I do."

I opened my purse and extracted the grimoire, which I'd carefully wrapped in tissue paper. I handed it to Lovelock. He walked over to the long reading table by the window and sat down. Stephen and I followed him, watching him as he carefully unwrapped the book and pored over it for several minutes. When he'd finished, he looked up at us and motioned us to sit down with him.

"What is it, exactly, that you wish to know about it?" he asked.

"Everything. What's the deal with this goofy little book? Why's everyone so interested in it?" Stephen said, crossing his arms in front of him.

Lovelock winced. It was clear that he didn't appreciate Stephen's cavalier attitude. I knew from experience how abrupt Stephen could be and sensed his tough-guy approach wasn't going to work here, particularly as there seemed to be some friction between him and Lovelock already. I figured we wouldn't get anywhere like this so I leaned forward, folded my hands on the table, and looked him directly in the eye, remembering my father's old dictum: "You catch more flies with honey than with vinegar."

"Mr. Lovelock," I began in a conciliatory tone. "The day you came to see my father and I told you about the grimoire, you seemed hesitant, as if you wanted to tell me something about it but then decided not to. Then, the other day, when I saw you, you seemed disturbed that I'd been to see Father Morton and that he'd asked about the grimoire. I don't want to offend you or impose on you, but I get the feeling you know a lot more than you're letting on. Am I wrong?"

Lovelock held my gaze for a long moment, then squeezed his eyes shut, as if he were in pain.

"No," he said at last. "You're not wrong."

"Then please . . . I beg you . . . Tell us what you know." I glanced at Stephen, who just shrugged as if to say, good luck.

Lighting a cigarette from the crumpled pack he took out of his jacket pocket, Lovelock stared at me across the table through strings of blue smoke.

"All right. I will tell you some things. After that, you'll have to make your own decision about what to do."

He leaned toward us and spoke quietly, as if he were in danger of being overheard. His manner was solemn. "First of all, how much do you know about grimoires?"

"Nothing, really," I said. "Except what Signor Antonelli told me and my father."

"Then let me explain a little bit about them. A grimoire is essentially a textbook of black magic. The three most famous grimoires in existence are the *Grimorium Verum,* published in 1517, translated from the Hebrew and supposedly based on the Key of Solomon; the *Grand Grimoire,* edited by Antonia del Rabina, also supposedly based on the writings of King Solomon; and the *Grimoire of Pope Honorius III*—the heretical Pope—which purports to give papal sanction to sorcerers, conjurers, and necromancers."

"That's our grimoire, isn't it?" I interrupted.

Lovelock held up his long, thin hand. "Please let me finish. Aside from these three, there are many others. Their object is to invoke devils and demons and then to trick them—usually into finding buried treasure, which the practitioner will then use to fund good works. Before you can properly use a grimoire, you must fast and pray and practice the rites of the Church. That's why many of them have the appearance of being religious books in the opening pages. It's difficult for the rational mind to take them seriously, because they seem quite silly when you examine them."

"I'll say," Stephen said with a smirk.

"Make no mistake, however," Lovelock warned, flinging him a severe glance. "There are those who do take them seriously. Very seriously indeed."

"Who, for instance?" Stephen asked with a touch of belligerence.

"I'm coming to that," Lovelock assured him. "Recently, that is, within the past sixty years—since the Second World War, in fact—interest in grimoires has been growing steadily, along with interest in the occult in general. The important ones have been very difficult to find. Only one or two have come up at auction during the last ten years, but the prices have been so high, it's been impossible for ordinary dealers like myself to obtain them. Now, the rumor is—just so you know—that your friend Giuseppe Antonelli has cornered the market on them for a special client."

"Yes!" I cried. "He mentioned that mysterious special client to me and father the night we saw him."

Lovelock nodded. "Yes . . . I'm not surprised." He leaned back in his chair. "Let me tell you a little story . . . As you may know, when dealers can't afford to buy at auction, we must seek out private sources. About seven years ago, I heard about an important grimoire in a collection of rare books in France. I traveled to France to contact the man who was selling it. I was anxious to buy it . . . Unfortunately, I was too late." Lovelock paused.

"Someone already bought it?" I said.

"Not exactly. The owner of the grimoire had died under what I understood were rather cloudy circumstances, and the book had been stolen."

I shuddered and reflexively reached out for Stephen's arm. I noticed that Lovelock was slightly perturbed at my involuntary gesture, and for a moment, he grew distracted until Stephen urged him to continue.

"Please go on," Stephen said, obviously much more interested than at first.

Lovelock cleared his throat and continued, his eyes now darting between the two of us as he spoke.

"I didn't give it a great deal of thought until, oh, about three years later, when a friend of mine—an occult-book dealer named Jeffreys—came to me and told me a similar story. He'd gone to England to try to buy a grimoire from an old noble family, and when he got there, the owner had died and the grimoire had been stolen."

Now I couldn't help myself. I let out an inadvertent gasp, "My God!"

Lovelock acknowledged my concern with a solemn nod.

"Jeffreys and I did business together on and off," he went on. "One day, he called me up and told me he'd purchased a very important grimoire in Pennsylvania. He asked me if I would put it on consignment in my shop. As it was quite expensive, I told him I'd have to see it first. We made an appointment for a viewing. He never showed up."

"What happened?" Stephen asked.

"Apparently, his car went off a bridge. They didn't find him for a month."

"I guess we don't even have to ask about the grimoire," I said.

"Vanished, of course," Lovelock said. "At least it wasn't with the rest of his stock, some of which I bought. And there was no record of it in any of his inventory lists."

I swallowed hard. Lovelock took out a fresh cigarette, using the glowing tip of the old one to light it.

"So when my father called you and asked you to come and see him that day—"

"I had no idea what he wanted," Lovelock interrupted me. "But when I met you and you told me that he had been . . . murdered . . ." He hesitated before saying the word. "And you then told me that a grimoire was missing, I recognized the pattern."

"So what does it mean?" I asked. "Who's responsible?"

"I'm coming to that. Your grimoire," he went on, tapping the cover of the little black book on the table, "is one of the most important grimoires of all—if not *the* most important. In fact, it's a legend in the occult trade."

Stephen and I glanced at each other.

"Rumors have circulated about it for years," Lovelock continued. "I first heard about it when I was working in

Rome. I was told by a friend in a position to know that Pope Pius XII had been in possession of a grimoire. The book had been seen by several people and was described to me in detail by my friend. Sometime during the war, that grimoire disappeared."

"Yes!" I exclaimed. "This grimoire was sent to my father by a man in Oklahoma, who said he'd gotten it during the war. Here, look, I have his letter!"

I reached inside my purse, pulled out the letter, and extracted it from the envelope. I was so excited my hands were shaking as I handed it over to him. He scrutinized it carefully, holding it close to his face as Stephen and I looked on. I could hardly breathe. Finally, he handed it back to me, saying, "Yes, it's just as I thought."

"What? Tell us, please."

"This is it. This is the one."

"Yes, but can you tell us why? Why is this particular grimoire so important? Is it because it's more valuable or what?" I asked him.

"Well, there are two schools of thought on that," Lovelock said, opening the book. "It depends on what you believe."

"What do you mean?" Stephen asked.

"Those who sincerely believe in the occult think that the book contains Solomon's own long-lost spell for the most profound sorcery of all—namely, the raising of the dead, otherwise known as necromancy: *nekros* being the Greek word for dead, and *manteia* the word for divination," he added in the swift patter of a scholar. "Those who are more pragmatic and less magically minded, if you will, believe that it contains the key to a vast fortune."

"What fortune?" I asked him.

Lovelock took a puff of his cigarette. "Well, the common theory is that it harbors Jacques de Molay's coded map to the lost treasure of the Knights Templar, which, as you may know, was a great military and commercial organization in the Middle Ages."

"I knew about the military, but a great commercial organization . . . ? That's certainly an interesting way to refer to them," Stephen chided him.

"Well, yes, the crusades and all that," Lovelock said dismissively. "Basically, however, they were a huge commercial enterprise, with branches in most of Western Europe. Christianity was big business in those days."

"In *those* days?" Stephen interjected, raising his eyebrows.

Lovelock smiled. "Point taken . . . Anyway, Jacques de Molay was the Grand Master of the order in the early fourteenth century," Lovelock went on. "He was in charge of the organization's treasury, to which all the knights contributed every year. It constituted a vast fortune, which the Templars used to propagate their faith and work. De Molay, however, had two extremely dangerous and powerful enemies: Philip IV of France, who was jealous of the Templars' power and wealth, and Pope Clement V, who feared them as a competitive force. Clement was anxious to bring them under the jurisdiction of the Church, so he and King Philip conspired to bring down de Molay and thus dilute the Templars' power. De Molay was denounced by the Inquisition. He was arrested, accused of heresy, tortured, and eventually burned at the stake in Paris. His followers in France and in virtually every other country where the Templars were active were rounded up, tortured, and killed. Their individual fortunes were confiscated, divided up, and sent in equal measure to King Philip and Pope Clement. Before de Molay died, however, he managed to send orders to have the great treasure of the Knights Templar hidden. For centuries, that treasure has been the subject of legend."

"And you're saying there are people who believe it still exists intact?" Stephen asked with a definite air of skepticism.

"You may laugh, but just remember, the *Iliad* was believed to be a work of fiction until Schliemann took it seriously and discovered Troy. And Machu Picchu was only a legend until Hiram Bingham stumbled on it. Just because a notion is fantastic doesn't mean it isn't true. These ancient legends are, perhaps, often more valid than one imagines."

"So let me get this straight," Stephen said, shifting in his seat. "This grimoire is meant to contain a map to the treasure of the Knights Templar."

"That's what they say. And if you look at the woodcuts closely, you will see the inverted sword as a recurrent theme. That is the symbol of the Knights Templar. Their gravestones are marked with it and only it—no names."

Stephen picked up the book and turned to the woodcuts. "Okay, I see it . . . Here it is." He pointed out an upside down sword to me. "And here it is again."

"As I said, it recurs throughout," Lovelock said.

"Is there only one copy of such a famous book?" I asked.

"No, but there are very few," Lovelock said. "And in any case, no two grimoires are ever exactly alike. The binders made sure of that. They would often insert pages or keep pages out, or else add words by hand to the printed text here and there, so that each grimoire would be unique. Yours happens to be the only Honorius III grimoire with the quotation from Saint Paul up front. That is the immediate clue that it contains a secret code of some sort."

"'For now we see through a glass, darkly; but then face-to-face . . .'" I said softly.

"So," Lovelock continued, "now that you know its history, what are you going to do with it?"

"Wait." I held up my hand. "What about the first reason—the spell? Are there people who really believe in raising the dead?"

"Certainly," Lovelock replied.

"Come on, Bea," Stephen said.

"Wait, Stephen . . . Do you, Mr. Lovelock?" I asked. "Do you believe in it?"

Lovelock paused. "Oh, you know, 'There are more things in heaven and earth . . .' as the Bard said. I don't dismiss it as a possibility." He paused and took a long drag on his cigarette. "But may I be presumptuous and say that you're both missing the point—as nearly everyone who thinks about this book does."

"What do you mean?" I asked him.

"Yeah, what do you mean?" Stephen repeated.

Lovelock spoke slowly and with great seriousness. "The real question here isn't whether this particular grimoire contains a magic spell or a map for the treasure of the Knights Templar, or even whether men have been killed for it."

"What's the real question, then?" I asked.

"The real question is this: What was the pope doing with a book of black magic?"

A deep chill went through me. Even skeptical Stephen cocked his head to one side with interest. Lovelock continued to puff on his cigarette. The smoke drifted up his thin pale face and faded into the air.

"Well," Stephen said after a time, "let's face it, the history of the Catholic Church is intertwined with black magic. Obviously, it was in his collection."

"Still, it's a rather odd thing for the pope who is, after all, the spiritual leader of the Catholic Church, and God's word on earth, to have, isn't it? A grimoire—a manual of the Enemy?"

"The Enemy?" I asked.

"The Enemy," Lovelock repeated firmly. "Grimoires are supposedly the work of the devil, God's enemy on earth. The Church has spent more than a thousand years ferreting out such books, not to mention their authors. It has always sought to destroy such nefarious works and their devotees and practitioners. As Mr. Carson pointed out, there's a profound relationship between the Church and black magic. You have, I take it, heard of the Inquisition?"

"But that was centuries ago," I said.

"Was it?" Lovelock retorted.

"Granted, there have been witch-hunts through the ages in many forms," Stephen said.

"And what makes you think that this age is different from all the others?" Lovelock interrupted. "Do you really think there's no more evil left in the world?"

"Yes, of course there is," I said. "But civilized people don't think of evil in the same way."

"No? And how do civilized people think of evil?" Lovelock stared at me.

"Well," I said, growing uncomfortable, "evil is more of a concept than a reality now. I mean terrorism is evil, certain people are what you might call evil. But evil itself isn't viewed as a real presence like it was in, say, the Dark Ages. You can't reduce things to such black-and-white terms as good and evil anymore."

"Can't you?" Lovelock asked.

"What Bea means, I think," Stephen said, interjecting, "is that things that were once considered evil are now viewed as, well, different ways of thought and alternative lifestyles, to use the vernacular. Isn't that what you mean, Bea?"

I nodded. "Right. Life's much too complex these days. There's no such thing as good and evil per se."

Lovelock smirked. "Oh, isn't there? Perhaps not to you. One tends to forget the soul in this chaotic age of telecommunications and mass media. But make no mistake. Daily life presents a perilous spiritual journey even today. And the only real purpose of the Church is to save souls—to make it possible for each person to attain eternal life after death. Churchmen view themselves as soldiers in an ongoing war, the war against God's sworn enemy on earth."

"Sworn enemy?" I said grimly.

"Satan," Lovelock said matter-of-factly.

"But surely, for most people, Satan is just a kind of metaphor now," I said.

Lovelock seemed irritated. "*Metaphor?* Metaphor, you

say? No, no, Miss O'Connell . . . Satan is no metaphor. He's as tangible as this table," he said, knocking the wood top. "The struggle between God and Satan for the souls of humankind is no metaphor, but a war as bloody and destructive as any ever fought on the face of this planet. And," he added, "many feel that we are losing that war. There is evil everywhere."

"Exactly what kind of evil do you fear?" Stephen inquired.

"What I fear is irrelevant," Lovelock snapped. "But as far as the Church is concerned . . . ? Witches are a great evil, for one thing. I would say the Church fears witches."

"Witches, eh?" I exclaimed. "Are we sure that the Church's view of witches isn't just a euphemism for feminism?"

Lovelock gave me a questioning look. "What do you mean?"

"Well, witches no longer have the same connotation as they once did, let's face it. People openly practice witchcraft today . . . Wicca . . . It's a choice, a religion of sorts. But it's not viewed as evil anymore—except, perhaps, by those who view women's rights as evil," I said with a little laugh.

Lovelock shook his head wearily. "If you really believe that, then you are sorely mistaken. There are real witches, and there is real witchcraft. And for many in the Church, evil exists just as it did all those centuries ago. Time in that particular realm is frozen. The war for the souls of men is still going on full force between God and his fallen angel."

Lovelock's conviction was palpable. I was impressed by his fervor on the subject. Stephen, who seemed edgy, asked Lovelock if he could bum one of his cigarettes.

"Of course—forgive me," Lovelock said, handing Stephen the ragged pack. "It's so unfashionable to smoke these days, I never think of offering one to anybody."

It was a brand Stephen didn't recognize. "What kind are these?" he asked, turning the filterless cigarette around in his hand.

"The cheapest kind, I'm afraid," Lovelock apologized.

"They're generic. I buy them by the gross. Smoking as much as I do, I'd be bankrupt if I bought good cigarettes. Sorry."

"That's fine by me. I can't tell the difference, anyway," Stephen said. "So, Mr. Lovelock in your view, what was Pius XII doing with a grimoire?"

"I wonder," Lovelock mused.

"You must have some theory," I said.

"I do." Lovelock nodded. He paused for a moment, then asked, "Are you aware that the Vatican Library is supposed to have a huge collection of pornography?"

"Yeah, I've heard that," Stephen said.

"Well, I haven't." I was amazed.

"They don't admit to it—not publicly, at any rate," Stephen went on. "But it's there. Isn't that right, Mr. Lovelock?"

"That's quite right. In fact, I myself have seen part of it. The eighteenth century was a particularly fertile time for such works."

"That's some collection for the Catholic Church to have, isn't it?" I said with a snicker. "Particularly since they don't allow priests to marry."

"Celibacy has its limits. Several popes didn't practice that particular discipline as rigorously as one might have hoped, and even fathered children in the time they held the office. But that's not why I mentioned it. I mentioned it because it's my belief that the Vatican had, at one time, another kind of collection they never admitted to."

"What kind of collection?" I asked.

Lovelock's eyes sparkled. "A collection dealing with black magic and the black arts," he said.

I glanced at Stephen who didn't even notice. He was now staring at Lovelock in rapt attention.

"When you think about it, it stands to reason, doesn't it?" Lovelock continued. "Don't forget, the Church has spent centuries ferreting out and confiscating such books in order to burn them. But I have good reason to believe that these works were never burned. Or that if they were, copies were made and hidden."

"But why?" Stephen asked. "Why would they bother?"

Lovelock smiled. "Tell me, would Wellington have destroyed Napoleon's charts and maps had he captured them? Would Roosevelt or Churchill have burned Hitler's secret papers? On the contrary. Enemy documents, should they come into one's possession, are carefully preserved and studied."

"So you're saying that the Catholic Church treats grimoires like enemy documents?" Stephen asked.

"They certainly did at one time," Lovelock replied.

"Isn't that a little far-fetched?" I said.

"Extreme is the word I would use, Miss O'Connell," Lovelock said. "It betrays an extreme point of view about the nature of evil in the world."

"Okay, so the Church has a collection of books of black magic. So what?" Stephen pressed.

Lovelock shook his head. "What if these books are taken seriously by serious men?"

"What if they are?" Stephen asked, seemingly uncomprehending.

"I don't think you realize the full implications of that, Mr. Carson. After all, if you take a disease seriously, don't you try to cure it—or at least fight it?" Lovelock asked.

"Yes . . . " Stephen said warily.

Lovelock looked at Stephen as if he now expected him to make the connection.

"And do you agree with me that the antidote to cancer is very often as deadly as the disease itself?" Lovelock said. "In trying to cure the cancer, a doctor may wind up killing the patient."

"I don't understand what you're getting at either," I said, impatient with his cat-and-mouse game.

Lovelock cleared his throat and spoke in a more forthright manner.

"Let me put it this way then: The men who take these

books seriously are as dangerous to their fellow human beings as the very evil they are purporting to fight. For they have taken it upon themselves to be the judges, juries, and executioners of all those whom they believe to be a threat to the sovereignty of the Church. They believe in fighting fire with fire."

"But who are these men?" I asked. "And who takes them seriously?"

"You might think of taking them quite seriously yourself, Miss O'Connell," Lovelock said.

"Are you saying that these men, whoever they are, killed my father?"

Lovelock was silent for a long moment, then: "Or, perhaps, had him killed."

I winced. "My God."

Stephen patted my hand. "Mr. Lovelock, you seem to know much more than you're telling us. And yet, by the way you're telling us, you want us to know that you know more."

Lovelock said nothing, regarding Stephen with impassive eyes.

"All right, what do you know about Father Morton, for example?"

"He's the priest of Saint Xavier's," Lovelock said noncommittally.

"The last time I was here, you told me not to trust him," I said, still agitated. "Is he one of your 'serious men'?"

"And what about this Duarte Institute? You must know about that," Stephen said.

"They want my father's library. Remember, I told you?"

Lovelock glanced at his watch. "I'm afraid I have an appointment."

"No—wait a minute, please. What is that institute, exactly?" Stephen asked.

Lovelock hesitated. Then he said softly, "It's an evil place. You must stay away from it."

"Evil? In what way?" I asked him.

Lovelock closed his eyes and rubbed the bridge of his nose. "Just stay away, that's all."

I said: "Do you think Father Morton is involved in my father's murder?"

Lovelock got up from the table and began pacing back and forth, his head lowered, as if he were deep in thought.

"I don't think either of you realizes exactly what it is you're up against," he said at last. "You're dealing with extremely dangerous people."

Stephen said flippantly, "Yeah, we're beginning to get the picture."

Lovelock whirled around and faced them. "No!" he said angrily. "You have no idea. Absolutely no idea!"

I was taken aback by his flash of temper, a sudden lick of fire out of nowhere. We were all silent for moment, then I pleaded with him: "Why won't you tell us what you know, Mr. Lovelock? Please."

Stephen, who was more impatient, said, "Come on, Lovelock. What's the story with Morton and this Duarte Institute?"

Lovelock took a deep breath in order to calm himself.

"I'll tell you this," he said at last. "What they say they are, and what they are in fact, are two very different things."

"What do they say they are?" Stephen asked.

"An institute for philosophical studies, I believe," he said with evident contempt.

"And what are they really?" I asked.

Lovelock hesitated. "I can't tell you any more than that," he said with some anguish in his voice. "I'm not a disinterested party. I'm sorry."

"Does that mean you're involved with them?" Stephen asked, trying to fathom Lovelock's reaction.

Lovelock glared at him and remained silent.

"Mr. Lovelock, I beg of you. If you believe they had something to do with my father's murder, you must please tell us what you know. Please!"

"That's all I care to say," Lovelock replied coldly. "I'm afraid I have to ask you to go. I have an appointment."

I stood up and glared at him. "What are you so afraid of?"

"You're right. I am afraid," he said, holding my gaze. "But it's not just fear, believe me. Think of your own father and how much he meant to you. Then think of me."

"What do you mean?"

"I cannot express it to you in any other way, except to say that the bonds of family are ones we can never free ourselves from, no matter how hard we try. Perhaps one day you will understand."

I felt a sudden rush of sympathy for him. He seemed so lonely standing there, this pale, gaunt man surrounded by musty books.

"Won't you please help us, Mr. Lovelock?" I begged him.

Lovelock shook his head. "I've helped you all I can for the moment. I've told you a great deal more than I should have."

"Come on, Bea," Stephen said abruptly. "Let's go."

Reluctantly, I picked up the grimoire and put it back in my purse. I somehow felt that if Stephen hadn't been there, he might have told me more. But for now, it was no use trying to pry anything more out of him. As we were leaving, Lovelock stopped us.

"Miss O'Connell, a word of advice," he said to me. "Don't let Father Morton find out you have the grimoire unless you plan to give it to him."

"Why not?"

"Because if he knows you have it, he will certainly get it from you—one way or another."

"He won't find out unless you tell him," I said.

"Me? Me tell Father Morton!" Lovelock laughed so hard he began to cough. His hacking bordered on a kind of hysteria. "Oh, forgive me, forgive me," he said at last, wiping tears of laughter from his eyes. He cleared his throat. "I'm sorry. It's just that the idea is so preposterous. Well, anyway," he went on, taking out a handkerchief and wiping his eyes. "Please be careful."

As Stephen and I walked downstairs, Lovelock hovered close to the door of his shop like a black shadow, watching us. As we reached the ground floor, he called after us.

"I'll do this for you. If you find out more things, and you want to check your facts, you know where to find me."

When we hit the pavement outside, Stephen exploded with irritation. "Who the fuck does he think he is—Deep Throat?"

"I think he's frightened, Stephen. Really frightened. You can feel it. And what was all that business about the bonds of family?"

"Bullshit, that's what. He's on some sort of weird power trip. I've seen it before on stories. You interview these guys who want to make you think they know the secret of life just so they can feel important. The hell with him. We don't need him." He put his arm around me and hugged me tight. "I think we ought to go up and pay this infamous Duarte Institute a little visit ourselves."

"But Lovelock told us to stay away," I said.

"All the more reason to go."

Chapter 9

"Beatrice, my dear, I'm delighted you called," Father Morton said on the telephone. "When were you contemplating a visit to our little institute?"

"Well, as soon as possible," I said, eyeing Stephen through the open doorway; he was listening in on the extension in the hall.

"No time like the present. How about Saturday? We can drive up there together if you like," Morton suggested.

"Saturday sounds fine but I've made arrangements to drive up with a friend of mine, if you don't mind."

"A friend? What friend?"

"Stephen Carson. Actually, he's my ex-husband."

"I see." Father Morton sounded hesitant.

"Is that a problem?"

"No, no, not at all. I'm pleased he can join us. It takes about two hours to drive up. What time do you think you might arrive?"

"Oh, say, around . . ." I looked at Stephen, who held up ten fingers and then one. "Around eleven o'clock, if that's okay?"

"That's lovely, lovely—in time for a little tour before lunch. When you get to Milbern, just go through the town and follow the signs. You can't miss us. And besides, everyone knows where we are, if you should get lost."

"Thank you, Father Morton. See you Saturday."

"Yes, Saturday, God willing," the priest said brightly.

I hung up the phone wondering just how much God had to do with any of this.

* * *

Stephen picked me up in a rental car on Saturday morning at nine A.M. We headed north up the Taconic Parkway to the town of Milbern, near Poughkeepsie. It was a scenic drive, and Milbern was a picturesque little village with a white clapboard church at one end, a red-brick courthouse at the other, and neat little shops and houses tucked in between. Grand old oak trees shaded the town square and the atmosphere resonated with small-town tranquility. I was struck by the comforting clarity of rural life.

"What a pretty place . . . It's so peaceful," I remarked as we drove through the town.

"Yeah, too peaceful," Stephen said. "Like Sherlock Holmes, I don't trust the country. Give me the big bad city any old day."

We reached the end of the main street, and there, as Father Morton had said, was a small hand-painted sign with an arrow pointing straight ahead. It read: THE DUARTE INSTI-TUTE. Leaving town on a wooded country road, we followed several like signs until we reached an almost imperceptible break in the foliage.

"Slow down," I said, having been warned that the ultimate sign was not easy to see. I spotted it. "There! The Duarte Institute. Turn here."

Stephen turned left onto a narrow dirt road leading into the dense pine forest. About a mile later, the trees thinned and the winding road became a wide, gleaming white gravel driveway leading to the entrance of what looked like a sprawling farm. A high wooden fence surrounded the property. Not far beyond it was a nineteenth-century wooden barn, standing massive and solemn against the radiant blue midmorning sky. A proud golden rooster weather vane was perched atop its sloping copper roof, keeping vigil over the horses and cattle grazing in their separate pastures. The long open fields were surrounded by verdant woodlands stretching to the horizon.

We pulled up to a locked metal gate, which clicked

open and swung back slowly, allowing us to pass through.

"Electric eye," Stephen commented.

Driving down through the fields into the surrounding forest once more, we found ourselves traveling along more tended grounds. Tucked into the woods and along the side of the road were weatherworn examples of the stonemason's art—low walls, fountains, benches, and small classical statues of Pan and other sylvan creatures peeking out of the foliage here and there. We crossed over an arched stone bridge spanning a small stream, drove past what appeared to be some abandoned kennels, and came upon a fork in the road. A painted sign nailed to a tree read: TO THE INSTITUTE, with an arrow pointing to the left, and TO THE COTTAGES, with an arrow pointing right.

Just as Stephen was about to turn right, a figure in the distance caught my eye.

"Wait! Stop!" I cried.

Stephen jammed his foot on the brake.

"What?"

"You see that man walking over there—just beyond those trees?" I pointed in the direction of the cottages.

Stephen craned his neck in order to peer out the passenger-side window. "No," he said at last. "I don't see anything."

"He's gone now," I said. "He was wearing a soutane."

"What's a soutane?"

"One of those long black old-fashioned cassocks that Roman Catholic priests used to wear. They still wear them in Europe sometimes . . . He looked like something out of another century," I said pensively.

Stephen stepped on the accelerator.

"We've got to get a move on. Father Morton's going to wonder what the hell happened to us."

"Hell being the operative word, I suspect," I said, with a wink.

Presently, we pulled into a circular driveway in front of a

huge Palladian-style villa made of limestone, shaded by giant elms and maples. Father Morton was standing in front
of the grand double-door entrance, looking at his watch.
As we got out of the car, he waved and started down the
wide crescent-shaped steps to greet us.

"Welcome, welcome, children!" he said, clasping my
hand. His hands felt clammy.

"Hello, Father Morton. I'm so sorry we're late," I said.

"Not to worry, as they say in England."

Stephen Shook hands firmly with the portly priest.

"Mr. Carson, very nice to meet you. How nice that
you've both remained on such friendly terms," Father
Morton said.

The remark was so personal and unexpected that I was
slightly embarrassed by it. Stephen and I exchanged a
glance.

"Now, if you'll both come inside," Father Morton continued. "I'll take you on a little tour. Then we'll have a bite of
lunch. How does that suit you?"

We followed Father Morton up the steps.

"Tell me, Mr. Carson—"

"Call me Steve, please."

"Steve, tell me, how much do you know about the institute?" Father Morton said, pausing midstep and pinning
Stephen with a cool gaze.

"Nothing, really. Just that you want Bea to donate her
dad's library here."

"Oh, I thought being a reporter you might have looked
us up."

"How did you know I'm a reporter?" Stephen asked.

"When Beatrice told me you'd be accompanying her, I
did a little research on you," he said, continuing on up the
steps. "You've had a fascinating career. And what a brave
young man you are too."

Stephen, who was immune to flattery and, indeed, suspicious of it, said, "So tell us about the institute."

"Basically, we are a nondenominational institute for

philosophical studies. Scholars come here from around the world to avail themselves of the materials we are fortunate enough to have at our disposal."

"And what materials are those?" Stephen asked.

Father Morton continued talking as he led the way. "Over the years, we have acquired many outstanding book collections, like your father's, Beatrice. And we keep them and care for them here in our library, which we will visit, for the benefit of visiting scholars and other interested parties—students, researchers, whomever . . . We call this the Bungalow," he said, pushing open the large double doors.

We walked into a large foyer, which was painted white and starkly furnished. There were no decorations except a square bronze plaque over the empty fireplace. On it was a head cast in relief, and the inscription INIGO DUARTE, 1880–1968.

"It was built in 1914 by the daughter of the man who built the original estate," Father Morton went on. "We've converted it into administrative offices."

He escorted us to a large reception desk, behind which a pockmarked young man wearing a black suit and tie stood stiffly at attention.

"This is where our visiting scholars register," Father Morton said. "Even though we are about preserving the knowledge of the past, we are also very high-tech," he said with an amused inflection as he pointed to a computer. "So, for example, when the scholar is assigned a room, he fills out a card listing his main areas of interest. We feed that information into this computer and then we are able to supply him with a list of the books and materials that we have pertaining to his subject. It speeds everything up, you see, so that by the time he goes down to the library, he knows exactly what's available and what to ask for."

As Father Morton was speaking, I noticed the pale young man behind the desk staring at me intently. When our eyes met, he flushed and quickly looked away as if embarrassed that I'd caught him.

"How many scholars are here?" Stephen asked.

"We can only accommodate twenty at the moment. But we're in the process of expanding our facilities. Let's take your car, and we'll go for a quick tour of the property, shall we? Inform Central," Father Morton said to the young man behind the desk.

I chuckled and said, "That sounds very spylike, Father Morton."

"Well, it's just that we have quite an elaborate security system here because of the value of the books and because the property is so large. We have to protect ourselves."

"How big is it?" I said.

"Over three thousand acres. It's just like a little island," Father Morton replied. "It's a rather interesting story, the story of this estate. I'll tell it to you on the way."

We walked outside to the car. Stephen got behind the wheel and Father Morton took the front passenger seat. I sat in the back.

"Just go around the driveway and follow that road to the left," Father Morton said, sitting sideways so that he could address both of us as we drove along.

"This entire estate was built in the nineteenth century by a German immigrant named Wilhelm Dieter. He invented some sort of gas valve that made him a millionaire, and he bought this property around 1880. He imported stone-masons from Italy to indulge his fantasies."

"Yes, we saw a lot of stonework coming in," I mentioned.

"He certainly kept them all extremely busy. He built a number of houses on the property, along with kennels, barns, a riding stable, and several greenhouses. Even a bowling alley. There are so many fountains and bridges and little follies all over you can't count them. Plus there are extensive root cellars underneath the ground. Thanks to Dieter, the town of Milbern has a large Italian community to this day, many of them descended from the original masons.

"Anyway, his daughter inherited the estate when he died in 1912, and she built the Bungalow—the building we were just in. Dieter, as you will see, had rather heavy-handed taste, and his daughter apparently couldn't abide living in his old house. So she had it boarded up and built one of her own. In the thirties, she went bankrupt and was forced to sell the property to a Texas oilman by the name of Walters. He hardly ever used it, and it became very run-down. Then, just after the war, Inigo Duarte happened to be visiting in this area, and he heard about the property. It was exactly what he was looking for to start his insti-tute. Fortunately, he was able to arrange its purchase through friends who believed in his work. Of course, there have been improvements over the years. We try and keep things up to date."

Just as Father Morton said this, we passed a large satel-lite dish nesting in the middle of a wildflower field. Ste-phen glanced at me in the rearview mirror.

"Who exactly is this guy Inigo Duarte?" Stephen asked.

"A great humanitarian and religious scholar."

"That's funny. I've never heard of him," Stephen said.

"Me neither," I concurred.

"He was a very shy and retiring man—not a self-promoter. But the force of his ideas is unstoppable."

"And what exactly are his ideas?"

Father Morton laughed. "I can see why you're a good reporter, Steve. You're like the proverbial terrier with a bone. I'll give you some literature when you leave and you can have a look."

"So how do scholars apply to come here?" Stephen asked.

"We only work through referrals," Father Morton said firmly. "A scholar must be recommended by someone who has been here or by a member of the board . . . Take a right just up here, if you will," he said, pointing with his beefy hand.

We turned into a driveway, at the end of which was an

ugly stone cottage. Stephen pulled up to the entrance and stopped the car.

"Dieter built this for the gatekeeper. You can see what I mean about his taste," Father Morton said.

"Tales of Hoffmann meets Stonehenge," I said, looking at the strange house built of huge cobblestones, with ornate wooden eaves.

Father Morton smiled. "I'll have to remember that." He hauled himself out of the car. "We've converted it into workrooms. Come and see."

The cottage had been gutted inside and divided into three spacious rooms. In the first room were several large wooden hand looms.

"You remember the tapestries in my office, Beatrice?" Father Morton said. "Both were woven right here."

"By whom?" I asked, noting the absence of any workers.

"We have special courses for those who are interested in learning the old ways of doing things . . . This may amuse you," he said, leading us into the second room. "We make all our own soap and candles."

Stephen and I looked around at the large vats filled with tallow and an array of metal candle and soap molds hanging from hooks on the walls.

"So many arts and crafts get lost over time," Father Morton went on. "Such a pity. You see, the Duarte Institute is interested in preserving many forms of past knowledge, not just the knowledge that is contained in books."

"Interesting," I said, absently fingering some loose wicks lying on a worktable.

"And here is our smithy," Father Morton said, leading us into the final room. "We shoe the horses here and mend tack. We even make some rudimentary farm implements and cooking utensils, as an exercise. Many of our scholars come here to watch or to participate. They enjoy getting a small sense of what life was once like."

Something caught my eye near the cold forge. I bent down to pick it up.

"What sort of farm implement is this?" I asked, holding up an iron shackle attached to a chain.

Father Morton squinted in the dim light. "Oh, a hobble for the animals, I suppose," he said indifferently. "Let's move on, shall we? I want to show you the library before we go to lunch."

We got into the car and headed down the road once more, until we reached a large clearing. There, on the right, elevated on a little hill, was a fussy Queen Anne Revival house with pointy turrets, elaborate moldings, and stained-glass windows overlooking a large formal garden, at the center of which was a round classical marble fountain spewing dainty jets of water into the air.

"This was Wilhelm Dieter's residence back in the 1880s," Father Morton said as we parked in the lot on the side of the house. "It has over fifty rooms. It is now our library."

"I can see why his daughter hated it," I declared, looking up at the ersatz castle.

We climbed the front steps to the entrance. "Yes, it's certainly a monstrosity, but extremely useful for our purposes—all those rooms, you see. We use the old servants' quarters as cubicles for the scholars. We had quite a time restoring it," Father Morton said.

The entrance hall of the house was paneled in pale mahogany. Another ascetic-looking young man dressed in black suit and black tie sat behind a desk at the far end. Father Morton nodded to him in passing and then led us up a flight of stairs. Each of the rooms we entered was lined from floor to ceiling with books. Some had long tables in the center and comfortable chairs for reading. Sometimes a plaque on the wall commemorated the donor of the collection on display. Other rooms were simply filled with a selection of books, all duly numbered and cataloged in the conventional Dewey decimal system. All the windows were sealed and locked.

We climbed up another flight of stairs. On the landing,

Father Morton pointed to a long corridor with doors on either side.

"Here are the cubicles I mentioned," he said. "They're the old servants' rooms."

We walked down the hall and reached a much larger room, outfitted with rows of chairs and desks.

"And here is our scriptorium, where the scholars are allowed to examine some of the more fragile works—the ones that cannot be checked out for the night."

"Where are all these scholars?" I asked, regarding the empty room.

"Oh, around and about, I imagine."

"I thought I saw a priest walking in the woods as we drove up."

"Did you?" Father Morton said with interest.

"He looked like he was wearing a soutane," I said.

"That's quite possible. We have visitors from all over the world."

"Priests?" I asked.

"A few," he said, leading us back down the hall.

Stephen grabbed hold of my hand and squeezed it tight, giving me a look that warned me not to pursue that line of inquiry. We continued on in silence.

After our tour of the upstairs, Father Morton took us down into the basement. There, amid the pipes and the climate-control system, were computers, scanners, and printers.

"And this is the heart of the institute," Father Morton announced with pride. "Every book, every incunabulum, folio, and fragment, is scanned here and entered into the computers, along with its history and when it was acquired."

"Very organized," Stephen said admiringly.

"Yes, well, as I said, the Duarte Institute likes to keep up with the latest technology."

I noticed a black door at the far end of the basement. A large sign on it read: DANGER—NO ADMITTANCE. "What's behind that door?" I asked.

"Just the generator and the boiler," Father Morton said. "Come, please."

We walked back upstairs to the main hall. Just as we were leaving, I noticed a book in a glass case on one side of the room.

"What's this?" I said, walking toward it.

Father Morton sidled up behind me. "Ah, that is the pride and joy of our collection. It is an original edition of the *Malleus Maleficarum—The Witches' Hammer*—a magnificent fifteenth-century work by two Dominican monks, Jakob Sprenger and Heinrich Kramer. It's one of only two in the United States. Do you know it?"

I knew of the *Malleus*, but had never actually read it. When Stephen asked what it was, an almost beatific look suffused Morton's jowly face. "The *Malleus* is the single most authoritative study of witchcraft ever written: a thorough examination of witches and their nefarious practices, as well as a practical guide to hunting them down and ridding the earth of them."

I read aloud the small gold plaque on the front of the case. "THE MALLEUS MALEFICARUM—GIFT OF DESMOND DOUGHERTY." I tried to catch Stephen's eye, but he was focused on the case and its contents. "Who's Desmond Dougherty?" I asked Father Morton.

"He is a member of our board of directors, a very great book collector and scholar. Your father's collection—if you decide it should have a home here—would occupy the room next to Mr. Dougherty's collection upstairs. That is not, if I may say so, undistinguished company."

Father Morton took us to lunch in a pristine white dining room in the back of the Bungalow. A large picture window framed a dramatic view of sloping hills and a distant pine forest. We dined alone at a long refectory table. Seated on wooden benches, we were served by a grim-looking older woman in a black dress.

"And what are you working on at present, Stephen?"

Father Morton said, helping himself to a hefty portion of boiled beef and cabbage.

"Oh, this and that," Stephen said noncommittally.

Father Morton stiffened slightly. "I must remind you that all of this is off the record, as I believe you reporters say."

Stephen cocked his head to one side. "And why is that?"

"Because we don't encourage publicity."

"Oh? Why not? This is such a fascinating place," Stephen said with that double edge in his voice that I knew so well.

Father Morton smiled unctiously. "Because, well, no offense, of course, but some reporters have a way of twisting facts—pardon me for saying so. There was a man from the *New York Times* up here a few months ago who wanted to do a story on us. I'm afraid we gave him short shrift. We are a scholarly institution, you see, and we don't think it's necessary for the world to know about us—not yet, at any rate."

I could see Stephen's eyes lighting up.

"Tell me, Father Morton, who pays for all this?" Stephen asked.

"Private contributions. We have a few extremely generous benefactors, I'm pleased to say—people who feel that the preservation of the past's great knowledge through books is man's key to understanding the future."

"And woman's," I added.

"Of course," Father Morton said, acknowledging me with a perfunctory little nod.

We continued to chat amicably about other topics. Father Morton punctuated his worldly conversation with some amusing little anecdotes, pointedly steering clear of any more talk about the institute. Nevertheless, halfway through the Spartan meal, I began to feel very uneasy in the bleak surroundings, and I longed for the lunch to end. As the waitress passed a dessert of cut fruit in a glass bowl,

Father Morton said absently, "Beatrice, my dear, I understand your house is on the market."

"Yes. How did you know?" I said, spearing a fresh slice of orange.

"I think I saw an advertisement for it in some magazine or other. I hope that means we may have a decision about your father's library shortly?"

I'm working on it." I gave him a tepid smile.

"The grimoire, I take it, has never turned up?" he asked, trying to sound nonchalant.

"No." I glanced at Stephen. "Tell me, Father, do you have any grimoires up here?" I asked him.

"Oh, no, most certainly not . . . Although we almost acquired a collection of witchcraft once. But the board members felt it wasn't a useful addition to our canon. It tends to attract the wrong sorts of people, you know."

After lunch, Father Morton escorted us to the car.

"Feels like rain." He looked up at the gathering clouds. Just as I was about to get in, the old cleric took my right hand in both of his and held it. "Well, Beatrice dear, I hope you enjoyed your day and that you'll think seriously of donating your father's library to us. We'll take excellent care of it, I can promise you that."

"I'll think seriously about it. Thank you for everything. It's been very enlightening," I said, gently extracting my hand.

"Well," he smiled, "I hope we've answered some of your questions . . . Drive carefully. Thanks again for coming to see us."

As soon as we'd driven off the property, I sat back and let out a huge sigh of relief. "Thank God that's over!" I said.

"Quite some spread they have there," Stephen said.

"I know. And there's something so sinister about it, don't you think?"

Stephen didn't answer. He seemed distracted. Then, as

if a light had gone on inside his head, he slapped his hand on the steering wheel.

"Bea, I got it! You remember I said someone had told me about the Duarte Institute and I couldn't think who it was?"

"Yeah?"

"The reporter from the *Times* that Father Morton mentioned at lunch . . . That's my friend Cap Goldman. He's the religion editor. We had dinner together a few months ago and he said something about it in passing. That's where I heard about it."

"Can we go see him?"

"You bet we can . . . By the way, where the hell are all these scholars he was talking about? There's hardly a soul in the whole effing place."

"And how about that so-called farm implement?" I said derisively. "It looked like a handcuff to me, unless those cows have very dainty ankles . . . What a day!"

"Well, I'm glad we went up there. And, hey, if by some miracle they actually are on the level, maybe your father's library would be well served."

"Stephen, they're *not* on the level. You can feel it."

"No, you're right. He's a helluva salesman, though, old Father Morton. Cap will have an interesting take on it, I assure you. I'll call him tonight."

"Thanks for coming with me. I dread to think what I would have felt like going there alone."

Stephen reached over and patted my hand. "We got through it, Babe. It's over."

I stared out the car window at the passing scenery and said softly, "Really? I have an awful feeling it's just beginning."

Chapter 10

T he next morning, Stephen took me to the *New York Times* to meet Cap Goldman. A security guard handed us identity badges and directed us to a bank of elevators.

We rode up to the newsroom. Cap Goldman, a beefy, bespectacled man in bow tie and suspenders, his shirtsleeves rolled up, was sitting at the computer in his cubicle.

"Hey, Steve," he said in a harried voice, rising to greet us. "How're you?"

"Good. You?"

"Oh, you know. Plugging along. Trying to manage a byline and a life at the same time."

"Bea, Cap . . . Cap, Bea," Stephen said, introducing us in his typical offhand way. Cap shook my hand with marked feeling.

"Pleased to meet you. I'm very sorry about your dad."

"Thank you."

"Sit, sit . . . This is what happens when there's anarchy in the world, right?" He pointed to his desk, littered with clippings from various publications with headlines like: POPE'S SEX STAND HAS 'EM HOT & BOTHERED; CATHOLICS TORN ON STRICT NEW EDICT; WAKE-UP CALL: THE RELIGIOUS RIGHT; RATTLING THE POPE'S ROOST; CARDINAL VOWS TO CLEAN UP DISSIDENTS; CHRISTIAN CONSERVATIVES COUNTING HUNDREDS OF GAINS IN LOCAL VOTES; FATHER SHAMEFUL: A PRIEST'S CONFESSION.

"So what can I do for you?" Cap said, punching a key on his computer with a flourish. "I'm on deadline, so I'm afraid we gotta make it quick."

"The Duarte Institute. What's the deal?"

"Oh, them. Jesus." He took off his glasses and rubbed the bridge of his nose.

"What do you mean?" Stephen said.

"Tough story."

"In what way?"

"Something's goin' on up there, but I can't quite figure out what. Let me ask you guys a question first. Why are you so interested?"

"Because the pastor of Saint Xavier's wants me to donate my father's library to it," I said.

"Morton?"

"Yes."

"Figures. He's on the board. Well, they've got one hell of a spread up there."

"You can say that again. We were up there visiting yesterday," I said.

"The two of you?" Cap asked.

"Yeah, why?" Stephen said.

Cap chuckled. "Jees, I hope you didn't tell 'em what you do for a living. They're totally paranoid about reporters. Not that paranoia's bad. Paranoids are the only ones who notice anything these days."

"Morton already knew. He checked me out," Stephen said.

"No kidding. Well, all I can say is, if I were you two, I'd steer very clear."

"Why, Cap? What's with this place?" Stephen said.

"Okay, look, I've been working on this story off and on for about six months. It's a bitch. There's a lot of rumors flying around, but I can't pin anything down. They bill themselves as an educational and charitable society— an 'Institute for Philosophical Studies,' quote, unquote. They're named after a guy called Inigo Duarte—I'll get to him later. That property they have up in Milbern is worth a fortune. So where are they getting the money? Well, it sure ain't from weaving tapestries and making soap."

"They say they have big contributors who are interested in preserving books or some such bullshit," Stephen said.

"Father Morton told us people from all over the world go there to study," I added.

"Study what is the question. That's what I'm trying to find out," Cap said. "And they're so goddamn secretive."

"Not so secretive. He invited me up there, after all," I said.

"Sure. You have something they want. That collection of your dad's is worth a fortune. They've got books up the wazoo. But I guarantee you, you didn't see anything they didn't want you to see. They pretend it's fucking Colonial Williamsburg, but if you ask me, it's closer to Salem."

"What makes you say that?"

"A hunch—well, a little more than a hunch actually. I have a source. It's complicated and I just can't get into the whole thing right now, but it's a little scary, if true."

"So who's Duarte?" Stephen asked.

"Oh, well, now he is a fascinating character. He was from a very humble family in Spain. Born around 1880. He became a priest, then a kind of éminence grise, very close to Pius XII. Only a handful of people ever knew about him."

"He was a priest?" I asked. "I thought the institute was supposed to be nondenominational."

"Inconsistency number nine hundred and eighty-four," Cap said, shaking his head. "These guys are something else."

"Remember how much my father hated Pope Pius?" I said to Stephen. "Dad always said if that coward had threatened to excommunicate any Catholic who supported the Nazis, there wouldn't have been a war. I think that was when he turned off religion completely."

"Okay, so Duarte founded this very right-wing secret society within the Church in the late twenties—something called Defensores Fidei—" Cap went on.

"Shit!" Stephen cried. "You're fucking kidding me!"

I was startled by his reaction.

"That's why I mentioned them to you, Steve. Because you did that thing in South America."

"Defensores Fidei. Jesus!" Stephen said.

"I take it you know what I'm talking about," Cap said.

"I sure as hell do."

"Wait a second," I said. "In Father Morton's outer office, he's got a carved ivory Madonna with Defensores Fidei written underneath it. I noticed it when I was waiting to see him. I was going to ask him what it meant, and I forgot. So what's Defensores Fidei?"

"It means Defenders of the Faith. And Father Morton, the old devil, is involved in it up to his eyeballs, if you want my opinion," Cap said. "What he is and what he *says* he is are two different things. I think the guy's a hard-nosed reactionary."

"Who are these people?" I asked impatiently.

"I'll explain everything later, Bea," Stephen said. "So Cap, what's with them?"

Cap exhaled fiercely. "A whole bunch of stuff. We're talking tip of the iceberg here. Unfortunately, I can't go into it right now: as I said, I'm on deadline. But, I'd be damn wary of the Duarte Institute. I'm convinced it's a cover, but I can't prove it."

"When's your story coming out?" Stephen asked.

"How about never? I can't corroborate my information. Morton's got friends in very high places."

"Cap, can I see your notes?" Stephen asked.

"Sure. Let me see if I can dig 'em up. They're at home. Also, I'm gonna send you a book that will interest you."

"What book?" I asked.

"It's a lulu, believe me. It defies description. I won't even attempt to tell you about it. I'll just send it to you, you read it and we'll discuss it afterward, okay?"

"It's not a grimoire, is it?" I said.

"No; it's a historical document. They sell facsimiles of it up at the institute, because they have one of the original copies on display."

"The *Malleus Maleficarum*," I said.

"That's it!" Cap said. "You know it?"

"We saw it when we were up there. It's in a display case."

"Yup, they're real proud of it . . . Only one of two copies in America and all that shit. But have you ever read it?"

"No," I said. It was one of those books I'd always been meaning to read.

"Fasten your seat belt," he warned me. "I'm surprised they didn't try to foist a copy on you. . Although it's probably smart of them, because after you read it, you ain't donating nothing to that place—not even comic books."

"I can't wait," I said.

"Look, I'm going away tomorrow on vacation. I'll try to get everything to you before I go, Steve, but if not, we'll have a drink when I get back, and I'll give the stuff to you then."

"Can't you get stuff to me now? This is urgent." Stephen wrote his address and fax number on a piece of paper and handed it to Cap.

"I'll try. Listen, you guys, I gotta get back to work. Duty calls." Cap escorted us to the elevators. "And if you find out anything I can use, let me know, will you?"

"You bet," Stephen said.

"So what's Defensores Fidei?" I asked Stephen as we walked.

"What's the Inquisition? Defensores Fidei is one of those scary secret societies . . . Want an ice?"

"Sure."

Stephen stopped at the little stand near the curb and ordered two raspberry ices. The vendor poured thick red syrup over a ball of crushed ice in a paper cup.

"I remembered your favorite flavor, right?" Stephen said, handing me my treat.

"Right. So how do you know about them?" I asked as we strolled up Eighth Avenue.

"My drug-dealer book—you know, the one I always wanted to do? One of my informants in Chile told me about a Jesuit mission they wiped out down there. Then they got the head of the national police to kill the investigation. They're all tied in with the drug trade. That's how they get a lot of their money."

"So the big contributors to the Duarte Institute may be drug dealers?" I asked incredulously.

"It's possible."

"Why would they bother to wipe out a Jesuit mission in Chile?"

"Eliminating the competition. It's a real ecclesiastical power struggle. I like the Jesuits—some of them, anyway. But they're miles too liberal for Defensores Fidei."

"But if everybody knows this, then—"

"No proof," Stephen interrupted. "And lots of fear. These guys are fucking princes of darkness."

I shook my head in mild amusement. "Stephen, you think the world is one big conspiracy, don't you?"

"It is." He gobbled down his ice in three swallows, crumpled the cup, and threw it into the gutter.

"Litterbug," I said, nudging him in the ribs.

"These people hate women, gays, minorities, activists—basically anyone who doesn't agree with the sovereignty of a Catholic, white, male-dominated society. They're 'Today the church, tomorrow the world' types. Tons of fun."

"So what is it they really want?"

"The Middle Ages. They don't believe in the present. They believe in the past. They think we should go backwards—*way* backwards. Since they operate a lot in South America, I suspect they want to control governments and possibly some of the drug trade through the Church. Anyway, that's part of what I've been working on. Small-world department."

"And what does the Church say about all this?"

"Listen, the Church has a lot to answer for these days.

Talk about a cover-up. What about the sex abuse? But I have to say in the Church's defense, these guys are definitely not in the mainstream. They're fanatics. The Church is just an alibi for their craziness. I wonder if the pope even knows they exist. They're operating under a cover."

"You mean the Duarte Institute."

"Apparently so."

"Stephen, the United States isn't a third-world Catholic country. What do you think they're planning to do here?"

He shrugged. "As Cap said, no one really knows what they're up to and you can't get people to go on the record. But he's right. They're definitely up to something. It's a sticky web, and I think it's growing."

"Hey, look at this," Stephen said, stopping in front of one of the seedy pornographic cinemas along the avenue. Laughing, he pointed to a big color poster of a movie entitled *The Witches of Dick's Wick*. Three buxom young women, dressed in black lingerie and witches' hats, were coiled around a virile, vacant-looking young man wearing only a jacket, shirt, and tie. He had an enormous erection, most of which was hidden by the thatch of an upside-down broom.

"You think John Updike knows about this?" I asked.

Stephen guffawed. "Maybe we should go inside and do a review for him. You want to?"

I eyed him. "What? See a pornographic movie?"

"Yeah," he said.

"Not particularly."

"Why not?"

"I don't know. They don't interest me that much."

"I'd kind of like to," he said.

"Come on, Stephen, it's the middle of the day." I tugged his arm but he resisted.

"So what? It looks amusing," he said.

"No. Come on, let's go. Those places are too raunchy—not to mention unsanitary."

"Okay," he said. "If you feel threatened . . ."

"I don't feel threatened. I just don't feel like seeing this movie . . ." He started to walk on. "Oh, okay!" I said, giving in. "If you really want to."

Elated, Stephen shoved his hand in his pocket and pulled out a twenty-dollar bill.

"Two, please," he said to the cashier.

"Show's already started," the man said in a monotone.

"Good. I hope it's nearly over," I muttered as Stephen swiped up the two tickets.

He grabbed my hand and we went inside. Several male patrons were scattered throughout the theater—no women, no couples. A rancid odor permeated the atmosphere, and many of the seats were broken and fraying at the seams.

"Notice they don't sell popcorn," I said as we sat down.

The grainy-looking, amateurishly shot movie consisted mainly of women dressed as witches, wearing heavy, macabre makeup, going down on a hapless young man with an extraordinarily oversized penis. Intermittently, the women fondled one another—sucking each other's breasts and licking each other—all for his delectation. Though perpetually aroused, the young man seemed curiously bored by this display.

"Great plot line." I yawned conspicuously.

"Okay, I'm ready to go," Stephen said, obviously bored himself.

"I feel like I need a bath," I announced, as we came back out into the daylight.

"You're right. Not great."

The movie had a depressing effect on us both and we walked in silence for a long time.

"You think we could ever get together again?" he said finally.

"Odd you should ask me that after seeing that movie," I said.

"Why?"

"I don't know. Men and women are just so different

when it comes to sex, that's all. I know it's not fashionable to say that, but it's true."

"Yeah, you gals aren't big on the anonymous encounter."

"Oh, I don't know about that," I said, thinking of Luis Díaz.

Stephen bridled a bit. "You don't, huh? You'd never just sleep with someone you met for five minutes."

"Why wouldn't I?"

"Because you just said that was the difference between men and women."

"I didn't say that. What I said was that men and women are different when it comes to sex."

"Well, different how?" Stephen pressed me.

"Women need more of a fantasy."

"Yeah, but you still wouldn't just pick someone up off the street. I know you," Stephen said.

"Not as well as you think."

Stephen stopped and grabbed my arm. He looked into my eyes. "Have you ever done something like that?"

I narrowed my eyes. "Why? Would you be jealous?"

"I'd be fucking amazed," he said. "Have you?" I didn't say a word, but he still knew me well enough to know I was hiding something. An incredulous smile crept over his face. "Jesus . . . Don't tell me . . . Who was he?"

"Just a guy," I said, walking on.

Stephen stood his ground and stared after me, shaking his head in amused disbelief.

"Come on!" I called after him.

He caught up to me. "Who was he?" he demanded.

"Just this guy. I told you. I'm never going to see him again."

"But you, you what . . . ? You met him on the street and just went to bed with him?"

"Something like that."

"Bea! Are you out of your mind?"

"It wasn't exactly like that, okay? I kind of knew him. I mean, I knew who he was."

Stephen kept shaking his head over and over. He raked his hand through his hair. His mild amusement was quickly curdling into anger. "Jesus . . . Bea, you are the last person on God's earth . . . Did he wear any protection?"

"That's it! I'm not saying anything more about it, okay?"

"Fuck." He shoved his hands into his pocket and lowered his head.

We walked on in silence.

"Why do you care so much?" I asked him after a time.

"I don't know . . . I just do."

"You're not jealous, are you?"

"Maybe . . . You could have been killed, for Chrissakes. You could be infected with AIDS or something . . ."

"I'm not, don't worry."

"How the hell could you do something so stupid?"

"Don't get sanctimonious with me . . . Talk about stupidity . . . How could you have slept with that slut and ruined our marriage?" I said with a mordant little chuckle.

"There were problems in our marriage. I never felt you really enjoyed sex."

"So you said . . . Well, maybe I didn't. Maybe I was just like my mother."

"Your mother didn't enjoy sex?"

"I don't think so. I think she was threatened by it . . . God, Stephen, I just can't stop thinking about my father and the fight we had before he died."

"It doesn't matter. He knew you loved him."

"But it does, Stephen, it does. Because it was right after that fight, the very next day, that I slept with this guy. And afterward I understood something about my parents' marriage and my own feelings about sex and everything . . . I was going home to beg my father's forgiveness for being such a little self-righteous prig . . . And he was dead. The last image I have of him is walking down that hall, all alone, looking so old and frail and lonely. I wanted to call out to him and tell him how much I loved him, but something stopped me—some horrible, perverse, mean streak just stopped me dead. I blamed him for things that were my own damn fault."

Stephen put his arm around me.

"He loved you, and you loved him. And he knew that, no matter what happened."

"I miss him," I said, growing tearful.

"Of course you do."

"I used to wonder what would have happened if you hadn't met that girl. We probably would have wound up like my parents, in an arid marriage, with a child . . . Who knows?"

"Bea, I'd give anything to undo what I did to you. But I can't."

We walked on in silence. I thought about my father and then about Simon Lovelock and what an odd duck he was.

"So I want to know who this guy is," Stephen said.

"Forget it, will you? God, I'm sorry I told you . . . You think Lovelock's a witch?"

Stephen chuckled. "Where'd that come from?"

"No, seriously . . . Do you think he might be a male witch?"

"Lovelock the warlock, you mean? He could be. Why not? He owns an occult bookstore. Who do you think buys that crap, after all? God knows he must come into contact with them."

"Do you think he really believes in black magic?"

"On some level, sure. If he didn't, he'd be sort of like a teetotaling wine merchant."

"I like the idea of a former Jesuit being a witch, don't you? It has a nice symmetry to it. And, for that matter, what the hell *was* Pope Pius XII doing with a grimoire? And the fact that he thinks the Vatican has or had a collection of black magic."

"Seriously, Bea . . . ? Do you think we could ever make a go of it again?"

"I don't know. Maybe when all this is over. I'm too confused right now."

"Okay!" Stephen said decisively. "Screw romance. Time for action. We're going back to my apartment." I looked at him warily. "No, I'm not trying to seduce you. We're going to approach this case systematically, like I do a story, okay?"

"Okay."

Stephen's studio apartment, on West Seventy-third Street, was pretty much as I remembered it—bare-floored, sparsely furnished, cluttered with books, stacks of old newspapers, file boxes, a computer, laser printer, fax machine, and eccentric souvenirs he'd acquired on his travels. A writer's lair. He'd refused to give it up when we got married, saying he needed to keep it for an office. It was rent controlled so it seemed like a good idea until I caught him using it as a love nest.

"Don't you have a cleaning lady? Look at this place. You're not a teenager anymore," I said, picking up a dirty shirt from the floor.

"All men are teenagers at heart."

"But they don't have to live like one," I said, looking around, disgusted with the mess.

"Give me a break. I've been away."

He rinsed out a couple of glasses from the pile of dirty dishes in the sink, got out a bottle of white wine from the refrigerator, and poured two glasses and handed me one.

"Never lacking for spirits," I said, toasting him.

"Okay, come on over here," he said, beckoning me to his desk.

Stephen sat down on the swivel chair in front of his desk and turned on his computer. I stood behind him, watching as I sipped my wine.

"We're going to create a file," Stephen said, turning toward me. "What do you want to call it?"

I thought for a second. "'Black Magic.'"

"'Black Magic' it is," he said, pecking at the keyboard.

"So right now, what we're going to do is put down a bunch of headings. Let's see—we have O'Connell, grimoire, Antonelli, Lovelock, Father Morton, the Duarte Institute."

Stephen typed in the names in capital letters on separate lines, leaving a large space under each one.

"You know the name of the guy who sent your father the grimoire?" he said.

"I have his letter in the grimoire," I said. "I'll get it."

He gave me an incredulous look. "Don't tell me you're carrying that thing around with you?"

"I didn't want to leave it in the house. It's too valuable."

"Yeah, well so are you," he said.

I took the book out of my purse and extracted the letter.

"Schroeder," I said, reading the letterhead. "His address and telephone number are here too."

Stephen added the name to the list.

"It's hard to believe people may have been killed for this little monster," I said, staring at it with distaste. "I feel like it's going to fly out of my hand or something. What are we going to do with it?"

"Give it here. Hang on to the letter, though."

I handed the book to him, and he slipped it into the bottom tray of his printer, under the legal-size pages he never used.

"Will it be safe there?"

"Safe as anywhere," he said.

"Now what?"

"Now we do a kind of shorthand, stream-of-consciousness thing under each heading. For example, we take the heading 'Grimoire,' and under it we put: 'Legend in occult trade. Lovelock info: said to contain spell to raise dead and/or map for Knights Templar treasure. Belonged to Pius XII? Part of occult collection once belonging to Vatican? Lost during WWII. Sent to Dr. O'Connell by Schroeder, former patient. Related to O'Connell's death? Interested parties: Antonelli says he deals for private client. Who? Father Morton? Other? . . .'"

Stephen continued typing. I drew up a chair and supplied him with relevant information about each subject.

"Under 'Father Morton' put 'Defensores Fidei,' 'Lavish offices,' and 'Wants to see grimoire,'" I said.

"Why 'Lavish offices'?"

"I don't know. You said this was stream-of-consciousness and his offices are lavish. Put down 'Medieval gauntlet on desk.'"

Stephen looked at me quizzically. "He has a medieval gauntlet on his desk?"

"Yes; it's very striking."

"I'll bet," he said, adding my observations to the list.

We went through each category, bouncing ideas and impressions off each other. When we'd finished, Stephen saved the file and printed two copies. He handed one to me. I studied it carefully.

"You see," Stephen said, pointing out the paucity of information under the headings 'Duarte Institute' and 'Schroeder.' Now we know where we have to concentrate our efforts."

"How are we going to check them out?"

"Google the Duarte Institute for starters."

Nothing showed up on Google or Wikipedia.

"They weren't kidding about a low profile," Stephen said.

"Now what?" I asked.

"I'm a database junkie. I subscribe to several of these services." He punched in another internet address and fed the home page his password. Then he typed in: "Tax-exempt educational foundations." The screen registered the information and took him to another page. He typed in the words "Duarte Institute, Milbern, NY."

Another few seconds passed. Then lines of text started scrolling across the white field.

"Here they be," Stephen said with satisfaction.

I leaned closer to the screen, looking at the seven-man board of directors.

"Hey, see your pals Father Morton and Giuseppe Antonelli right at the top of the list? And get a load of those other names, will you? Pretty amazing, huh? Bart Winslow, the chairman of Fidelity Bank. Chuck Kraus, the congressman. George Cahill, the senior partner of Keegan and Goddard, the law firm. Phil Burgoyne, the right-wing talk-show host. And Desmond Dougherty, the guy who donated the book . . ." Stephen leaned back in his chair. "I'll tell you one thing, though. This is some heavy-duty board for such an obscure little institute. And a strange collection of people. Eclectic, to say the least."

"So what do you make of it?"

"I don't make anything of it yet," Stephen said, continuing to study the data. "It was incorporated in 1966 in Milbern. Here's a brief description of its purpose." He read aloud: "'An institution dedicated to all branches of philosophical studies—metaphysics, logic, epistemology, aesthetics—but particularly as applied to the branch of ethics.'" He paused. "Ethics, eh? Whose ethics, I wonder?" He went on. "Then it's all pretty standard stuff . . . Okay . . . I think the next step is go and see this guy Schroeder. What exactly do we know about him?"

"Just that he was my father's patient and he sent him the grimoire as a present for saving his life. He knew Dad was a collector."

"He sent him a very strange book."

"I'm going to go see him."

"Not alone. You don't know anything about this guy. I'll go with you."

"No. You could be finding out other stuff here. I want to go alone. I have to learn to be alone now."

The truth is, I'd always been a little afraid of life because I feared death. Ironically now that I was in the proximity of real violence, I felt less fearful—defiant even.

Chapter 11

I called Mr. Schroeder in Oklahoma that evening and he
agreed to see me as soon as I wished. I was on a plane the
next day. During the flight, I thought a lot about Stephen,
how I felt about him, and mainly how grateful I was to have
him spurring me on and directing my efforts. Stephen was a
good reporter, renowned for his tenacity as well as his talent
for ferreting out a good story. His compulsion to dig deeper
and harder had led him to rich soil beneath old, raked-over
stories on many occasions. I admired his bird-dog instinct
for gathering intelligence, and thought that even his slight
paranoia, which slanted his view of the world toward cover-
ups and conspiracies, could be useful to me now. My father's
murder was my sole preoccupation, my obsession.

After a brief stopover in Dallas, the plane landed in
Oklahoma City at twelve-thirty, slightly ahead of schedule.
There were no taxis at the airport, but I found a car service
to take me to Mr. Schroeder's house, wait for me there, then
take me back to the airport in time for the flight back to
New York.

It was a gray, sultry day. The black car made its way out
of the airport toward the city. I settled back on the warm
vinyl upholstery and gazed aimlessly out the window.

"What parts are ya from?" the driver asked me after a
time.

"New York."

"City?"

"Yes."

"Never been there. Wanta go, though. M'wife's scared

to. She thinks we'll get killed." He laughed. "I keep tellin' her don't believe everythin' you read. Whadda you think? Think we should go?"

"Yes, why not?" I replied absently. I was hardly listening.

"Folks get killed 'round here often enough. But that doesn't seem to bother her none. A minister shot his wife and kids over in Enid just the other day. I guess the God business ain't goin' so good these days." He snickered.

The driver rattled on. I paid little attention. I stared out the car window, struck by the flat, jangly landscape of neon signs, fast-food chains, gas stations, movie complexes, furniture marts, and shopping malls, absently wondering where all the students of urban planning went after they got their degrees.

The car gradually worked its way through the long, dismal blocks of commercial enterprise to a residential area. Here, at last, were quiet, tree-lined streets and neat, patio-backed houses with their all-weather barbecue grills, flower-bordered driveways, and tidy aprons of lawn. The driver slowed down for a group of children who were running and giggling as they took turns dousing one another with a garden hose. Here, I thought, was an innocent version of inner-city life, where kids play in front of the homeless on drug-infested streets, cooling themselves down with water from fire hydrants.

"This here's Eighteenth Street," the driver announced. "What address did you say?" He squinted at the numbers on the houses.

I rechecked my piece of paper. "It's 3141 . . . There's 3147 . . . Should be coming up . . ."

I spotted 3141 in slanted gold numbers on the side of a black mailbox up ahead. Beneath it, just before one of the uniform driveways, a white sign was struck upright in the ground. The name SCHROEDER appeared in neat black capital letters surrounded by a small scene of a hunter aiming his gun at flying ducks.

"There it is," I said.

We pulled into the driveway. I got out of the car and asked the driver to wait. I climbed a small flight of slate steps, glancing at the American flag planted to the right of the front door. There was no doorbell. I was about to lift the brass eagle knocker when the door opened. A man with white crew-cut hair and a ruddy complexion, built like a fireplug, stood very erect just inside the entrance. He had a military bearing that made him look taller than he was. He wore cowboy boots, a navy blue sports shirt buttoned to the top, and well-ironed khaki pants with razor creases dead center down each leg.

"Miss O'Connell—Hank Schroeder," he said in a crisp voice. "You're right on time." We shook hands. Schroeder's grip was firm.

"Mr. Schroeder . . . I appreciate your seeing me. The driver will wait, if that's okay."

"Fine, fine. Come in. Had your lunch?" Schroeder asked.

"No."

"Good. The wife's fixin' some sandwiches. You look just like your dad, you know that?"

"Some people say so."

"Wonderful man, your dad. Wonderful man."

"Thank you. He was," I said softly with a catch in my throat. Using the past tense about my father still made me a little teary.

I followed Schroeder into the house, which was quite chilly due to the central air-conditioning. It was a spacious, immaculate place, filled with reproduction Early American furniture and colorful braided rag rugs. The finial at the tip of the staircase banister was another brass eagle. Schroeder pointed out some things he was particularly proud of.

"I got these plates on a trip to Winterthur with my first wife," he said, indicating a pair of decorative Chinese Export saucers. "And this chair is an antique reproduction of one from Mount Vernon."

I was always amused by oxymorons like "antique reproduction," "fresh frozen," and "authentic copy."

Schroeder then showed me into a pine-paneled den. Two sleek gray muskets hung above the stone fireplace. The furniture was all brown leather. On the floor was a navy shag rug. He led me over to a glass case in one corner of the room. Lined with pale blue velvet, it displayed World War II souvenirs, including a Nazi helmet, a Walther PPK pistol, and an SS dagger. He lifted the top and reached inside.

"I took this little bugger off a dead officer outside Rome," he said, picking up an Iron Cross with an oak-leaf cluster and holding it out to me. "One thing positive you can say about those bastard Krauts is that they had a damn fine sense of design."

I gave the medal a cursory look. Artifacts of that kind held little interest for me. Schroeder replaced it carefully inside the vitrine.

"The book I sent your father used to live right there," he said, pointing to a slightly depressed and darker patch of velvet on the right-hand side of the case.

I glanced around the rest of the room, which was very neat and orderly. The built-in bookcases were filled with volumes on oil and engineering.

"What do you do, Mr. Schroeder?"

"I'm a seismic engineer."

"What's that?"

"We use seismic surveying gear to find oil. I used to work for Schlumberger. Know what this is?" he asked, pointing to a strange-looking metal object on one of the lower bookshelves. I shook my head.

"It's a drill bit from the first well I ever spudded in. See here." With his finger, he traced the words etched into the brass plate on which it was mounted: DAISY MAE.

"Why Daisy Mae?"

"You remember the character from Li'l Abner?"

"Sure," I said.

"That's what we called the well. You see, your first well's kinda like your first girlfriend, if you get my drift." He smiled. "Oil's been good to me. Now I'm retired, of course. Just relaxing and enjoying life, thanks to your dad. How is he, by the way? I never heard from him about the book. I guess he got it all right."

I looked him straight in the eye. "Mr. Schroeder, my father is dead."

Schroeder's face darkened. "Oh Lord," he said with real sadness. "I'm damn sorry to hear that."

"That's what I need to talk to you about. May we sit down?"

"Sure, sure. Sit. Susie'll be in soon with the lunch."

I made myself comfortable on one of the two leather couches flanking the fireplace. Schroeder sat down opposite me. He offered me some peanuts from a small bowl on the coffee table between us. I declined. Schroeder munched on a few while he listened attentively.

"About a month ago, my father was shot and killed in his library by an intruder."

Schroeder winced. "Shot . . . Jesus," he said, under his breath.

"At first, nothing appeared to be stolen. But then I discovered that the book you'd sent him was missing."

"No kidding."

"No kidding, Mr. Schroeder. Out of all the books in his collection, that's the only one that's gone."

"I don't know what to say. I'm just real sorry about all this." He squinted at me. "So you think maybe the book had something to do with it?"

"I'm not sure. That's what I'm trying to find out. That's why I came out here to see you. I need to know everything you can tell me about that book—how you got it, where you got it, everything you know about it. Everything."

"I see."

"You were fond of my father, weren't you?"

"Oh, I sure was," Schroeder said with great feeling. "I'm convinced if it hadn't been for John O'Connell, I wouldn't be here today. Look, I wanna show you something."

Schroeder pulled his sport shirt up out of his pants and bared his chest, revealing a long scar.

"That's what your daddy did for me," he said proudly. "And I thank him and the good Lord I'm alive today to show it to you. So—anything I can do. Anything at all. It's a damn shame."

"Thank you." I was touched by his evident concern.

"Thing is, though," he continued as he tucked his shirt back in, "I don't know what all I can tell you about that book that's gonna help you."

"You said you got it during the war. How?"

"Well, now, that is kind of an interesting story."

"You mind if I take notes?"

"Be my guest."

I pulled out a small notebook and pen from my purse. "How, exactly, did you come across it?"

Schroeder leaned forward and took a pipe from a round rack on the coffee table. Tamping in some tobacco from the tin nearby, he lit it and sat back reflectively.

"In August of '44, I was in Rome. We'd just gotten there. I was a captain in G-2. One of our patrols spotted a priest wandering around in a field at dusk, waving a flashlight at the sky—a pretty unpriestlike thing to be doing, especially when there was a plane circling overhead. So they picked him up, and sure enough, he was no priest but a German officer. They brought him back to corps HQ, and I was in charge of his interrogation. All he had on him were some forged identity papers and that book I sent your dad."

"Did he tell you anything about it?"

"The book? No. I mean, he said it was something he'd picked up as a souvenir. Of course, we thought it contained a code of some sort, so we went over it with a fine-tooth comb. Translated it, tested it for invisible ink—all the usual stuff. In the end, we couldn't find anything, so we just confiscated it."

"Did you know what it was? Did you know it was a grimoire?"

"A what?"

"A grimoire. A book of black magic."

Schroeder chuckled. "We knew it was a spooky little devil, all right. Didn't know there was a particular name for it. I got a kick outta some of the illustrations. But far as we could tell, it had no military implications."

"Didn't you wonder what he was doing with it?"

"Well, to tell you the honest truth, we thought he was up to other things."

"What things?"

"Well, we had to find out what he was doing there, number one."

"And did you find out?"

"Eventually. But we had a helluva time."

"In what way?"

"He was a tough bird. Didn't wanna talk at first. We interrogated him for a long time, and he gave us a song and dance about this and that. But after we kinda bent the rules of the Geneva Convention a little bit, he opened up."

"What do you mean, you bent the rules?"

Schroeder took short puffs on his pipe. The aroma of sweet tobacco filled the room. "Little lady, you don't want to know, and I sure as hell ain't gonna tell you. However, I will say that our friend the fake priest never looked at a car battery in quite the same way again," he said with a grim smile.

Just then, a squat, olive-skinned young woman with American Indian features appeared at the doorway. Her jet black hair was pulled back in a long ponytail, fastened with a silver barrette. She was wearing white jeans and an unbuttoned man's shirt, under which was a T-shirt and a string of turquoise beads. Not pretty but exotic-looking, she had a dull expression on her face.

"Lunch is ready," she said in a soft voice. "Shall I bring it in?"

Schroeder beckoned to her. "C'mon in for a second,

Susie. I want you to meet Miss O'Connell, Dr. O'Connell's daughter."

I stood up to greet her.

"This is my wife, Susie. Susie, go on over and shake hands with Miss O'Connell. Go on," he urged her, as if she were a child—and indeed, she looked young enough to be his granddaughter.

The young woman walked across the room with lowered eyes, giving me a limp, perfunctory handshake and an embarrassed "Hi."

"Very nice to meet you," I said.

The shy young woman nodded without saying anything.

"What would you like to drink with your lunch?" Schroeder asked. "I take milk."

"Just some water, thanks," I replied.

"Okay, hon. You can bring in the lunch now."

The young woman quickly turned around and went out of the room.

"She's a registered nurse," Schroeder said. "I met her in the hospital. Took care of me during my convalescence. She's a full-blooded Osage. Grew up on a reservation, oh, 'bout ninety miles from here. A man needs a pretty young girl around when he gets older, to take care of him. I was married before, of course. For thirty-eight years. Thirty-eight wonderful years. Four kids. My wife died, God bless her. Susie's younger than my youngest daughter, but they all seem to get along fine.

"How long have you been married?"

"Ten months. It was hard for some of my friends to understand it. But you see, we're both grateful to each other in a certain way. She takes good care of me, and I give her a nice home. She doesn't talk very much, which is fine with me. I just don't have the energy to start up a brand-new life with someone. I wanted someone quiet and capable, who doesn't complain. My first wife, Ginny, used to complain all the time, God rest her soul. I loved her, and I was used to it. But I don't think I could get used to it again."

I found his candor refreshing, figuring that was really what a lot of men wanted in the end: a quiet, uncomplaining nurse to take care of them. And in exchange, a man gave a woman a home, financial security, and protection from a harsh world.

A few moments later, Susie appeared again, carrying a tray. She laid the lunch out on the coffee table: a platter of tuna fish and peanut-butter-and-jelly sandwiches, a bowl of potato chips, and a creamy dip in a plastic container.

"Please help yourselves," she said, her face a mask of indifference.

Avoiding eye contact with me or her husband, she acted more like a servant than a wife. After giving us our drinks, she left the room.

"Isn't she going to join us?" I asked.

Schroeder shook his head. "Nah. She's kinda shy around people. So," Schroeder continued, biting into his peanut-butter-and-jelly sandwich, "where were we?"

"The car battery," I said, picking up a tuna fish sandwich.

"Oh, right. So anyway, he loosened up after that."

"What did you find out?"

"His reason for being in Rome."

"Which was?"

"He gave up the six guys in an agent network he was servicing. He'd been flown in to pay them off and set up communications with them."

"And who were they?"

Schroeder chuckled. "You sure know how to ask questions. Let's see now . . ." He leaned back and ticked off the list on his fingers. "Uh—two were in the carabinieri, one was with the railroad, another was with the phone company. There was a priest inside the Vatican. I forget who the other guy was."

"Inside the Vatican?" I said excitedly. "Do you remember the priest's name?"

"No; sorry."

"But he was definitely inside the Vatican? So it's possible your prisoner did see the pope."

Schroeder looked at me quizzically. "The pope?"

"Yes. You see, I think that book you sent my father was given to this man by the pope."

Schroeder seemed interested but skeptical. "Uh-huh . . . What makes you think that?"

"I've been told by someone who's in a position to know."

Schroeder shrugged. "I somehow doubt it."

"Why?"

"Because this man was simply a courier. It was a pretty big deal, getting to see the pope—even if you were a Nazi," he said with disdain.

"Yes, I'm sure. But you see, I think that was the real reason for his trip to Rome. Or, at least, an important one."

"What?"

"Seeing the pope and getting that book."

Schroeder sipped his milk thoughtfully. "You do, huh? Lemme ask you something. Why would the pope be giving this guy a book? Not to mention that particular book."

"I don't know. That's what I'm trying to find out."

"That book was strange—to say the least," Schroeder said, wiping a half-moon of milk from his upper lip with a paper napkin.

"But you never found out what he was doing with it?"

"At that point, it didn't matter."

"It didn't matter?" I said incredulously.

Schroeder looked at me sympathetically, as if I couldn't possibly get what war was about. "I told you. We had the book, and there was nothing in it. He told us it was a souvenir, and there was nothing to make us think it wasn't. And more important, we had him and we knew what he was doing. We got it out of him."

"I think he fooled you into thinking he was there for those other reasons, Mr. Schroeder. I think those reasons were a decoy."

"Oh, I doubt if he fooled us," Schroeder said with a sigh. "See, war's an impossible thing to imagine. You have to be in one to get the picture. It's like walking into a loony bin. That's the only way I can describe it. You may walk in there sane, but after a while you begin to lose it, pure and simple. You get something in your mind—an objective—and you go for that objective. You don't think much about anything else. I saw two of my best friends in the world buy it right in front of me. I still, to this day, don't know why it was them and not me . . ." He paused, staring into space for a moment.

"I don't think you really understand," he continued. "My concentration was on who his contacts were in Rome. We'd just occupied the city, and we were in a precarious situation, as everyone is in wartime—to put it mildly. You got subversives all over, just waiting to blow you up or foul up your communications. You got to find out who they are, weed 'em out, and get rid of 'em. That was my main objective here. I wasn't interested in any old book."

"You didn't think the book was odd and that it might have been a code for something?"

"I told you we did," he said, growing mildly impatient. "But we checked it out thoroughly, and that did not appear to be the case. But even if it was, it didn't matter in the end. My job was to get names outta him that would lead to arrests. And he gave those names to us, and we made the necessary arrests. Arrested everyone. All except the priest. We decided we couldn't touch him."

I thought for a moment. "May I ask you why you kept the book, Mr. Schroeder?"

"For a souvenir. As you can see, I kept a lotta souvenirs." He gestured toward the case. "No one else wanted it."

"Did he say where he got it?"

"Nope. Musta picked it up in a bookstore, I guess."

I was frustrated. "Can you tell me anything else about him? Anything at all?"

"His name and the name of the town he came from, 'cause that's all he'd tell us for the first few hours of questioning."

"Yes?" I said anxiously.

"Erich von Nordhausen, from Hamburg."

I asked him to spell it for me and printed the name in large capitals in my notebook.

"Von—that means he was noble," I said.

"There wasn't anything noble about that Nazi bastard."

"I just meant he was from a noble family. Do you know what became of him?"

"Well, after we finished with him, we handed him over to the MPs, and I guess they would've taken him to a POW camp and held him till the end of the war."

"Do you think there's any way to find out what happened to him?"

Schroeder shook his head. "That'd be real hard. We took hundreds of thousands of prisoners, you know. Unless you've got a contact in Hamburg who could track him down. Who knows? He might still be around. He wasn't much older than me, I don't think, and I'm still here . . . well, barely." He gave a mordant little laugh. "You're not eating your sandwich."

"I guess I'm not very hungry."

"Chips?" he said, offering me the bowl.

"No, thanks."

"They're good with this dip," he said, helping himself. "Thousand Island."

"Look, Mr. Schroeder, I don't mean to keep pressing you, but I don't think you got the whole truth out of this man."

"How do you mean?" he said through a crunchy mouthful of potato chips.

"It's true, I don't know anything about war and wartime. But I don't think he came to Rome just to contact agents. I have a feeling the real reason he came to Rome was to get that book."

Schroeder washed the chips down with the last of the milk and wiped his mouth and sighed. "So you have said . . . And I guess anything's possible in a war. But I'd say it's water under the bridge now, wouldn't you? What the hell difference does it make?"

"I suspect it made a great deal of difference to my father," I said with an air of defiance.

Schroeder was taken up short. "I'm sorry. Maybe you're right. I mean, who knows?"

I got up from the couch and began walking around. "Are you sure there's nothing else you can tell me?"

"'Fraid not."

"Mr. Schroeder, did anyone else know you had this book?"

"No . . . Well, my wife when she was alive."

I noticed his answer didn't bode well for Susie.

"And why did you send it to my father?"

"Well, as I explained in my letter, I knew your daddy was a book collector, and I thought he might like to have it. He talked about his collection some, and I figured he'd appreciate it."

"I knew. I knew it was evil," said a voice at the other end of the room.

We both turned and saw Susie standing at the door, her dark eyes glistening. The young woman, who had seemed so nondescript and flat to me at first, suddenly came into relief, gathering intensity as she spoke.

"I told him to get rid of it," Susie went on, her voice slightly twangy. "I told him it was bad luck."

Schroeder chuckled. "Yeah, she did."

"What made you think that?" I asked.

"I felt it. I felt it was a dangerous thing and that whoever had it was in danger."

Schroeder waved his hand dismissively. "Susie's just superstitious."

"I'm not superstitious. I know when a thing is evil, that's all," she said. "I told him to burn it. Didn't I tell you to burn it?"

Schroeder nodded sheepishly. "She did. But I don't burn books. Nazis burn books."

"My people understand about magic," Susie said. "We're more interested in the things you can't see."

The comment struck me deeply, and I felt a sudden empathy with the young woman.

"My father was like you, Mr. Schroeder," I said. "Pragmatic and principled. He was interested in the book from a collector's point of view. I don't think he attached much significance to it beyond that. But I'm afraid I have to agree with your wife. There was a palpable evil about that book. I felt it the moment I saw it. It confused me, because I don't believe in black magic."

"Magic is magic," Susie said.

Schroeder shook his head. "I don't know . . . All I know was that the guy was in Rome to contact German agents. And he gave those names up to us and we made the necessary arrests. I didn't think twice about the book—except as a souvenir of war," he said defensively.

"War," Susie said grimly. "All men love war."

"Now looka here," Schroeder protested. "We don't love it. But it's necessary sometimes. You have to fight for what you believe in."

"Or what other people believe in," Susie said.

"Yeah, well, you shouldn't be so smug. Wasn't it Leon Trotsky who said, 'You may not be interested in war, but war is interested in you'? And if women ran the planet, things wouldn't be any different, lemme tell ya."

"Maybe, maybe not." Susie shrugged.

"Look, Mr. Schroeder, I absolutely need to contact that courier, Erich von Nordhausen."

Schroeder leaned back and sighed. "I think it's like looking for a needle in a haystack. But I s'pose you could try."

"How would I go about it?"

"If you know someone in Germany, you might try tracking him down through the army pension records. That's one way. 'Course, he was from Hamburg, so maybe you could just try looking up his name in the phone book. Who knows? You might get lucky."

Susie squinted. "If I was you, I'd leave it alone," she said.

"That's impossible." I glanced at my watch. "Oh God, it's nearly two-thirty. I should be going." I got up to leave. "Thank you for lunch and for all your help."

Schroeder and his wife saw me to the door. I walked to the car.

"Good luck to you," Schroeder said, waving good-bye.

"Thanks. I'll need it."

As the driver started the engine, I glanced back at the house. Schroeder had gone inside, but Susie was on the front steps, staring at me. The young woman extended her right arm, making a graceful sign with her hand, which I interpreted as an Indian blessing. I nodded my thanks and we locked eyes in a kind of understanding as the car pulled out of the driveway.

Chapter 12

The trip to Oklahoma had been useful. I had a name: Erich von Nordhausen. If I could just find him . . . It was a long shot—a very long shot after all these years—but at least it was something to give me hope. On the return flight, I thought about my career as a literary pack animal. Now I had my own story to research. And it was not only the most important story of my life, but perhaps a very important story on its own.

The taxi dropped me off at home. At first, I felt nervous entering my house, which felt so big and dark and silent in the night. But I made a conscious effort to steel myself against fear, telling myself that my father was watching over me. "Take it one step at a time," he always urged me in his kind, easy-going way. "Don't jump to terrible conclusions."

I had a fitful night's sleep and the next morning, the phone rang bright and early, waking me up. I figured it was Stephen. But when I heard the deep, jovial voice at the other end of the line, I felt a jolt of fear.

"Beatrice! Father Morton here . . . How are you today?"

"Fine, thank you, Father, and you?" I said warily.

"Very well, thanks. I didn't wake you, did I?"

"No," I lied.

"Everything going all right? Keeping yourself busy, are you, dear?"

"Yes . . . Trying to get things in order."

"Ah, but you mustn't work too hard. You must take some time off, relax, take a little trip somewhere to refresh the spirit. Have you taken a little trip anywhere?"

I suddenly had the chilling feeling that Father Morton knew very well I'd been out to Oklahoma.

"Um . . . Is there something you wanted, Father?" I said, stonewalling him.

"As a matter of fact, there is, dear. I'm calling to see if you'd given any more thought to my little proposition regarding your father's library," he said.

"Oh, yes. I have. Um, I'll give you a call back later in the week, if I may," I said.

"Of course, my dear. But don't forget us now, will you?"

"No. I won't forget you."

"God bless you, dear," Father Morton said. "I look forward to hearing from you soon."

When I hung up, I was absolutely sure he'd been spying on me. I called Stephen immediately and arranged to meet him later that morning.

Stephen was waiting for me in the neighborhood coffee shop, a bright little spot decorated in the style of a 1940's luncheonette. Two short-order cooks in white aprons were busy filling orders behind the long pink Formica counter. Bacon sizzling on the griddle smelled delicious. The café was crowded with customers glued to their morning papers. Stephen waved to me from a booth at the far corner. As I sat down opposite him, I noticed a thick manila envelope on the table.

"What's that?" I asked him.

"Cap's notes. How was your trip?"

"Fascinating. I found out the whole story of how Schroeder got the grimoire. And the name of the courier he got it from. Erich von Nordhausen."

"Great. I found out a few things myself." Stephen pointed to the envelope.

"Anything interesting?"

"Extremely. Let's order first. I'm hungry," he said, looking over the menu.

A tired-looking waitress with stringy blond hair and a

pencil stuck behind her ear sauntered over to our table, pad in hand. I ordered tea and toast. Stephen ordered a double stack of pancakes, sausages, a large fresh orange juice, and coffee. I looked at him askance, and said, "I forgot how much you eat."

"What did Schroeder have to say?"

I took out my notes and filled him in on all that the retired engineer had told me about the grimoire.

"So, basically, Schroeder didn't think the book was at all important."

"No. He told me they examined it and found nothing."

"And he had no idea why this von Nordhausen guy had it or where it might have come from?"

"Von Nordhausen convinced him it was a souvenir—nothing more. But of course, I think he fooled them with all that bullshit about enemy agents. Don't forget, he was disguised as a priest when they picked him up, and he even admitted that one of the agents he'd been sent to contact was a real priest inside the Vatican. So there is a definite connection with the pope."

"Lovelock's theory may be correct," Stephen said thoughtfully.

"Assuming the pope did have a book of black magic, why was he sending it by courier to Germany? Why did the Nazis want it? And why do people still want it?"

"We've definitely got to try and track down von Nordhausen," Stephen said.

"Schroeder says we could try the Hamburg phone book or the army pension records," I said. "But after all these years, it's a real long shot."

The waitress finally arrived with our orders. Stephen put my notes aside. He poured a river of maple syrup on the large stack of pancakes and smeared on extra butter. I looked at him enviously as I dotted my dry toast with a stingy portion of marmalade.

"How in heaven's name you stay in shape . . ." I said incredulously, watching him dig in.

"I'll go to the German consulate," he said, ignoring me. "They may be able to help us. Still, I bet he's dead by now. Just tell me again—why did Schroeder send the book to your father?"

"He said it was a thank-you present because he knew my father collected books. But I told you, I think the real reason is that his new wife wanted him to get rid of it. She thought it was evil and bad luck. She wasn't kidding."

"Yeah, well, I think the bad luck part came when your dad showed it to Antonelli. If you ask me, Antonelli's the key."

"What makes you say that?"

"Think about it. Antonelli's the link between your dad and Father Morton."

"He called me again this morning. Woke me up."

Stephen bristled. "Morton? What'd he want?"

"To see how I was getting along and if I'd made any decision about my father's library. He asked me if I'd taken any trips. I think he's having me watched."

"Unfortunately, you may be right. We've got to be careful. If he's mixed up with Defensores Fidei, he could be a very bad guy. He and Antonelli both."

I paused, staring into space. "I wish to God Schroeder had never sent that book to my father."

"You can't think about that, honey. What's done is done."

"I miss him so much."

"I know." Stephen reached for my hand across the table and squeezed it tight. "I love you, Bea."

I didn't reply. Stephen went on: "Do you think after . . . ? I mean, when we get things straightened out . . . Do you think we could get back together?"

I pulled my hand away and lowered my eyes. "I just don't know. I'm sorry. I just need some time."

"Sure . . . I understand. Listen, I'm the one who screwed up originally, so you're entitled to exact some revenge."

"Hey, I'm not trying to exact any revenge, Stephen. It doesn't have anything to do with you."

"That's the problem . . ." He took a deep breath. "Okay,

down to business. Something's definitely going on, even if it's not between us," he snickered.

He opened the manila envelope, took out a handful of newspaper articles, and handed them to me. "Here. Take a look at these."

I sifted through the articles, some of which were years old. They all had to with women who had disappeared in the East Coast area and had headlines like: UTICA REPORTER FEARED DEAD . . . GLENN FALLS MOTHER OF THREE DISAPPEARS FROM SHOPPING MALL . . . HELENA ROBERTS SKIPS TOWN.

I paused and thought for a moment. "Helena Roberts. Where do I know that name from?"

"She was involved in that lesbian adoption case in Pennsylvania a couple of years ago. There are several articles there about it."

"Oh, right," I said, vaguely recalling the story.

"She vanished before the case could come to trial. Take a look at this one." Stephen handed me another clipping.

I read the headline aloud: "'NEW YORK COUNCILWOMAN MISSING.' That happened last year," I said, noting the date.

"Read it."

I scanned the article. "'Police are seeking information on the whereabouts of Pat Slivka, a member of the Elmhurst City Council . . . Ms. Slivka disappeared from her home in Elmhurst sometime on Tuesday night and has not been seen since. Her husband reported her missing to the police the following morning,' et cetera, et cetera. 'During her campaign, Ms. Slivka described herself as a "humanist" as opposed to a "feminist." She was elected to the City Council by a narrow margin after a bitter fight where she infuriated conservative groups by her pro-choice stance on abortion. She is currently backing legislation that would end restrictions on gay and lesbian marriages . . . Police have yet to turn up any clues in her disappearance, and foul play has not been ruled out.'"

"The missing Utica reporter was someone called Tina Brand, who was a staunch advocate of affirmative action and minority rights," Stephen said. "That happened about six months ago. She's cute. Look at her picture."

I glanced at the grainy news photo of an attractive black woman in her mid-forties.

"The latest one is Patricia Hall, the 'Glenn Falls Mother of Three.' She was abducted a couple of weeks ago from a shopping mall."

"And what's her story?"

"It's unclear from the article. But obviously there must be a connection, because here she is in Cap's clippings."

"It just says she vanished, but it doesn't say anything about her," I said, reading the small story. "Wait—'active in school politics,' it says."

"That's kind of amorphous, but it's the most recent episode, so we're going to take a little trip to Glenn Falls today and snoop around. I got the name of the reporter who wrote the piece. He's willing to talk to us."

"Great. Where's Glenn Falls?"

"Connecticut. Near New Haven."

I continued to peruse the articles. "So the common thread here is that they're all women activists and they've all disappeared."

"Exactly right. And this," he said, pulling out a large paperback book, "is a copy of the book Cap mentioned—the one they sell up at the institute. The one he said we'd have to read to believe."

"Ah, yes, the *Malleus*," I said.

He handed it to me. The book had a scarlet cover, with the title printed in black. A pair of medieval woodcuts flanked the names of the two authors. One was of a witch with hair of orange flames, riding backward on a ferocious beast, grasping its crooked tail. The other was of a witch being burned at the stake, with a long green tongue curling lasciviously from her mouth.

I read the cover: "The *Malleus Maleficarum* by Heinrich Kramer and Jakob Sprenger . . . Reminds me of the woodcuts in the grimoire."

"Cap's made some notes on the inside back cover. Have a look," he said.

I turned to the back and examined the black ink scrawls. "Doctors and reporters always have the most appalling handwriting," I observed. "What's this at the top?"

"D-I," Stephen said.

"Duarte Institute?"

"Yeah. Here he lists the board of directors. See? 'B-O-D' and then the names: Phil Burgoyne, George Cahill, Chuck Kraus, Father Morton, Giuseppe Antonelli, Bart Winslow, and the elusive Desmond Dougherty. Then underneath are the names of the women in the articles I showed you."

I raised my eyebrows. "He didn't say anything more about it?"

"I didn't get a chance to talk to him before he left. He just sent me this package, with a note saying he looked forward to seeing us when he got back from his vacation."

I examined the list. "What's this word after the names of the members of the board? "Pre . . . something?"

"'*Presenter.*' See, it says: 'Phil Burgoyne—Presenter . . . George Cahill—Presenter . . . Chuck Kraus—Presenter,' et cetera. Father Morton and Signor Antonelli both seem to be presenters."

"What could that mean?"

"I have no idea. Must be some shorthand of Cap's."

"What do you suppose they're presenting?"

"Beats the hell out of me. I tried calling Cap, but he'd already left."

"Can't we get in touch with him?"

"He's fishing up in Canada. No phone, no email. He wants some peace."

"Shit. Look here—there's something else after Dougherty's name. The initials 'G.I.' What do you suppose 'G.I.' means?"

"Well, it usually means Government Issue or General Issue. G.I. Joe?"

"So could it be an army thing?"

"I doubt it. It must stand for something else."

"Like what?"

Stephen shook his head. "No idea."

"G . . . I . . ." I said, mulling the letters over in my mind. "Gift something? . . . If all the others are Presenters, then maybe the *G* stands for Gift or Giving. Maybe it stands for Grimoire."

"Maybe."

"*Grimoire Iniquitous* . . . And all these women are some-how connected with the Duarte Institute?"

"I don't know. Looks that way, though."

I flipped through the pages. "I look forward to finally reading it. So what now?"

"Now I have another cup of coffee. Then we drive to Glenn Falls."

The day was overcast and the lulling rhythm of the car made me reflective. I stared out at the industrial landscape as we sped along.

"Some women's lives are so bleak," I said to Stephen.

"Some men's lives are pretty bleak too," he countered.

"I know. But there's a certain sense of doom connected to being a woman."

"How about just being a person?" Stephen said with a chuckle.

"The whole system grinds women down," I said.

"I got news for you, baby—the system grinds us all down. That's what it's there for. Anyway, what brought this up?"

"I was just thinking of Schroeder and his new wife . . . I mean, there he is, an ancient widower, happily ensconced, starting life all over again with a young, healthy partner less than half his age. Now, I ask you, what are the odds of a widow, a woman in her eighties or nineties, say, like Schro-eder, starting over again with a man—not to mention a man young enough to be her grandson? Schroeder's wife is going to take care of him until he dies, just like a nurse. In fact, she *was* a nurse. And yet, when she gets old, if she doesn't have any kids, chances are she won't have anyone to take care of her—unless he leaves her well off financially."

"We die younger. That's your revenge."

"Yeah, well in some countries we're nothing but chattel."

"Listen, when you gals have your turn—and you will one day—you'll screw it up just as badly as we have, trust me."

"That is not possible," I said with a grim little laugh.

We drove in silence for a while. I thumbed through the clippings. One in particular interested me.

"Hey, Stephen, listen to this: 'Pat Slivka rose to prominence in her community defending a fourteen-year-old girl who was gang-raped, became pregnant, and . . . then was denied an abortion by her parents, who are Catholic.' Jesus. What is it with the Catholic Church and women?"

"You ought to know. You're a Catholic."

"Was. Technically, I'm excommunicated because I divorced you. Not that I was too upset. I don't trust any institution where I can't get the top job."

Stephen laughed. "Now, if you ask me, I think I'd make a pretty good priest."

"You couldn't remain celibate for five minutes," I said, scoffing at the idea.

"Maybe not, but I'd be great in the confessional. Demonstrate a real reporter's gift for drawing people out."

I looked at him askance. "I think you've got the confessional confused with analysis, dear," I said, patting him affectionately on the knee.

"Want to move that hand up a little higher, please?"

"Concentrate on the road, you dog."

Stephen glanced over at me. "You like us being together again, Bea?"

"Don't start," I said, closing my eyes. "Why do you suppose these women have disappeared, Stephen? Are they linked, I wonder? . . . And why does your friend Cap think they're connected to the Duarte Institute? I hate that place."

"Well, that's exactly what we're here to try and find out," he said, heading for the exit.

Chapter 13

We arrived in Glenn Falls just after noon. It was a gray, run-down little industrial town, built up in the nineteenth century to make parts for the gun factories of southern Connecticut. Several of the shops on the long, wide main street were closed and boarded up. Others had signs in their windows proclaiming sales and drastic price cuts on all merchandise. There was little traffic on the street. A listless feeling pervaded the atmosphere. We cruised around the town, searching for the bar where Stephen had arranged to meet his contact. Joe's Place was a dingy little joint paneled in dark wood. It smelled of beer and cigarettes. A vintage jukebox was playing a Frank Sinatra tune. Stephen approached the bartender, who was polishing glasses behind a long bar.

"What can I do you for?" the man said cheerlessly.

"You know a guy called Dick Ramsey?"

"Hey, Ramsey!" the bartender called to a balding middle-aged man in a brown suit, sitting in a wooden booth reading a newspaper and sipping beer. "You got company."

The man looked up over his bifocals and squinted, then waved us over. He had a pasty face, with dark circles under his eyes. His jacket was open, his shirt unbuttoned, his tie slack around the collar, like a noose.

"Mr. Ramsey? Steve Carson. This is my friend Beatrice O'Connell."

The three of us shook hands. Ramsey had a flaccid grip.

"Have a seat," Ramsey said. "You folks want a beer or something?"

"Sure," Stephen said.

"Joe! Two more beers!"

"I like that Joe's Place really has a Joe," I said, edging my way into the cramped booth.

Stephen and I sat facing Dick Ramsey, who removed his glasses and began cleaning them with a red paper napkin.

"You found your way up here all right, I guess," he said.

"Yeah," Stephen replied. "It's a nice, scenic drive."

"Oh, scenic's the word," Ramsey said sarcastically, folding his glasses and sticking them into the breast pocket of his jacket. "So—what brings you folks up to scenic Glenn Falls? You mentioned something about the Patricia Hall case on the phone."

I opened the manila envelope, pulled out the clipping headlined GLENN FALLS MOTHER OF THREE DISAPPEARS FROM SHOPPING MALL and handed it to Ramsey.

"You wrote this story for the *Glenn Falls Gazette*, right?" Stephen said.

Ramsey glanced at the article. "Yeah. That's the old by-line."

"Has there been any follow-up on this? Did you ever find out what happened to her?" I asked.

"Nope. It's just like I say there. She was last seen over at Parsons Mall, about a quarter of a mile outside of town. It was around—oh—what'd I say in the article?" He referred to the clipping. "Eight-thirty in the evening, yeah. A clerk at the Kmart remembered waiting on her. She never made it home. Her car was found in the mall, so the police figured she was abducted."

"Mr. Ramsey—"

"Call me Dick."

"Dick, did you know Patricia Hall?"

"Know her? No. Saw her around. Knew who she was. This is a small town."

"Do you have any theories about what happened to her?"

Ramsey drew himself up and cleared his throat, as though he relished being asked his opinion. "There's been some speculation that she might have run off with someone. Supposedly, her marriage wasn't any too hot. But I don't buy it."

"Why not?" I asked.

"The kids. She has three kids. Women don't just run out on three kids, as a rule. And they're still youngsters. People say she was a good mom. It's pretty unlikely she'd fly the coop with those chicks at home."

"So what happened?" Stephen asked.

"Hard to say. The Halls aren't rich, so kidnapping seems improbable. Anyway, there was never a ransom note."

"What does Mr. Hall do?"

"He owns a small lumberyard. If you ask me, it was probably some sort of a sex thing, most likely. Rape murder. She was an attractive gal. Or just a straight murder, maybe. Something like that. I'm sure they'll find her body eventually."

He was very matter-of-fact about the case. A little too matter-of-fact for my taste. The bartender brought over a small tray of beers and handed them out. Stephen took a long sip.

"Do we know anything else about her? Your article mentioned she was active in school politics," Stephen said.

"To put it mildly," Ramsey went on, "Patricia was a flaming liberal."

I glanced at Stephen. "A flaming liberal?" I said, amused.

"Yeah, you know the type. The ones who like to stir the pot."

"In what way did she stir the pot?" I inquired.

"Pushing a lot of stuff the folks up here just don't go for."

"Like what sort of stuff?" Stephen asked.

"Oh, like, uh, you know—the kinda things they're into these days. She wanted to distribute condoms in the classrooms and make sex education mandatory for the kids. She was a big proponent of the 'alternative lifestyle' business that's going on up here now. I guess it's going on everywhere. And then there was the stopping-the-prayers-in-the-public-school bit. She also demonstrated against the closing of the abortion clinic. She was into all that. A real little shit-stirrer."

Ramsey caught the look that passed between me and Stephen and quickly added, "Hey! I'm not passing any judgments here. I'm a just a lowly reporter—a 'just the facts, ma'am' kinda guy. But she was poking her nose into some hornets' nests—particularly the school."

He licked off a mustache of beer foam and cleared his throat.

I gave him a thin smile and kept staring at him. Ramsey shifted uncomfortably on the banquette and looked sheepish.

"Okay," he said. "You want to know the rumor?"

"That would be great," I said.

"Well, supposedly she was sleeping with the head of the school board. There was a big stink about it even before she disappeared."

"What kind of stink?" Stephen asked.

"Findlay's wife—Findlay's the head of the board—his wife, Midge, was going around saying that Patricia Hall was a witch. Plus something else that rhymes with witch," he said with a little laugh.

"So where were Mr. and Mrs. Findlay when she disappeared?" I asked.

"Good for you. Actually, the police checked up on them . . . One of the first things . . . They both had solid alibis. Camping trip with the kids . . . They weren't suspects, either of them."

"I'm curious, what did Ms. Hall look like?" I asked.

"Jees, a good-looking woman in an offbeat kinda way. Long, blond hair. Nice features. Good figure. She wore one of those Egyptian things around her neck. She wasn't from here, originally. I think she was from up in Vermont somewhere. She made pottery and sold it out of her house. I guess she was kind of a neo-hippie. It's a pretty cold case now. The police don't have any leads as far as I know. My personal opinion is that some stranger got her. Wrong place, wrong time. It happens, unfortunately. That's about all I can tell you, I'm afraid. Sorry."

The three of us sat in silence for a moment, sipping our beers. The illuminated Budweiser sign above the bar buzzed and flickered.

"So, tell us, have you ever heard of something called the Duarte Institute?" Stephen asked after a time.

Ramsey thought for a moment. "Nope. Can't say as I have."

"How about a man named Desmond Dougherty?"

Ramsey shook his head. "Why? Should I of?"

"No," Stephen said. "I was just wondering. And you've been a reporter here for how long?"

"Oh, Jees, going on twenty years. The *Gazette*'s a good little paper. We're not going to win any Pulitzers, but we keep everybody informed."

"Well, listen, Mr. Ramsey, thanks for your time," Stephen said, starting to rise.

"Dick. Call me Dick . . . You hardly touched your beer," Ramsey said to me.

"I'm not thirsty."

"May I?" Ramsey said.

"Be my guest."

Ramsey drained my glass.

"Are people still interested in the case?" I asked as we got up to leave.

"Not really." Ramsey wiped his mouth with the back of his hand. "People have more important things to think about right now—like getting jobs."

"The beers are on me," Stephen said, walking over to pay the bartender.

"Thanks," Ramsey replied. "What's all this about? How come you all are so interested in this case?"

"Well, it's always interesting when a person just vanishes into thin air, isn't it?" I said.

"You bet. But Glenn Falls is kinda out of the way for you folks, isn't it? How'd you happen to see the *Gazette*?"

"We have a friend who cut out the story," Stephen said.

"You're a reporter, right?" Ramsey asked.

"Yes, but I'm not writing about this case, don't worry."

"Level with me—you folks haven't heard anything, have you? You don't have any new information, do you?"

"No," Stephen said. "We were just interested in the background of the case, that's all."

"We wanted to know a little bit about Patricia Hall— who she was, what she was up to," I added.

"Uh-huh," Ramsey said. "Well, now you know. And if you do find something out, I'd sure appreciate your letting me in on the loop. And I'll do the same for you," he said with a weary air.

"We'll keep you posted," Stephen said.

As we got into the car, Stephen turned to me and said, "I doubt that guy's gonna find any sweet young thing to take care of him in his old age."

"Don't bet on it," I said.

Before we left Glenn Falls, we took a swing by Parsons Mall to view the scene of the crime. It had three vast parking lots and rows of stores, most of which were vacant.

"Well, it certainly wouldn't be hard to be abducted from here," I observed. "At night, when it's dark, someone could just hit you over the head, drag you into a car, and no one would notice."

"Yeah, but what's interesting is the type of women who've disappeared."

"What do you mean?"

"Well, women who were all socially and sexually active. For a lot of people, that kind of woman is threatening."

"So Cap may be onto something really interesting?"

"I think he thinks he is . . . We just have to wait until he gets back from his vacation."

"Maybe the *Malleus* will give us a clue," I said.

"I hope something will," Stephen said, stepping on the accelerator. "In the meantime, let's try and hunt up your courier, von Nordhausen. I think that's the next logical step."

Chapter 14

T he next day, Stephen went to the German consulate while I settled down on my father's worn leather
sofa with the *Malleus*. I read the foreword, which not only
praised the book as "one of the most effective and invigorat-
ing works in the vast canon of writings on witchcraft," but
also as "a book for the present age, full of logic, clarity, and
insight into the judicial system, even today." It was signed,
Desmond Dougherty.

I couldn't wait to tell Stephen that Dougherty had
written the foreword. I eagerly dove into the book that
Dougherty had solemnly proclaimed as "a work for all
eternity."

Mildly intrigued at first, I soon became utterly fascinated. I took notes, copying passages, often wondering if
this book was for real. It purported to be a lawbook dealing with the trials and punishments of witches. However,
in fairly short order, the word *witch* and *woman* became
synonymous. Parts of it were so stunning, I nearly burst
out laughing. But other parts were nothing short of dazzling, incandescent misogyny.

Random Notes from the *Malleus Maleficarum*, by Heinrich
Kramer and Jakob Sprenger:

> The first part, treating of the three necessary
> concomitants of witchcraft, which are the devil, a
> witch, and the permission of almighty
> GOD

PART I

Question I

Here beginneth auspiciously the first part of this work. Question the First.

Whether the belief that there are such beings as witches is so essential a part of the Catholic faith that obstinately to maintain the opposite opinion manifestly savours of heresy ...

Question VI

Why it is that Women are chiefly addicted to evil superstitions ...

Therefore let us now chiefly consider women; and first, why this kind of perfidy is found more in so fragile a sex than in men. And our inquiry will first be general, as to the general conditions of women; secondly, particular, as to which sort of women are found to be given to superstition and witchcraft ...

Now the wickedness of women is spoken of in Ecclesiasticus XXV: "I had rather dwell with a lion and a dragon than to keep house with a wicked woman" ... All wickedness is but little to the wickedness of a woman. Wherefore S. John Chrysostom says on the text, It is not good to marry: What else is woman but a foe to friendship, an unescapable punishment, a necessary evil, a natural temptation, a desirable calamity, a domestic danger, a delectable detriment, an evil of nature, painted with fair colours!

When a woman thinks alone, she thinks evil.

Wherefore in many vituperations that we read against women, the word woman is used to mean the lust of the flesh.

As it is said: I have found a woman more bitter than death, and a good woman subject to carnal lust.

For as regards intellect, or the understanding of spiritual things, they [women] seem to be of a different nature from men; a fact which is vouched for by the logic of the authorities, backed by various examples from the Scriptures. And it should be noted that there was a defect in the formation of the first woman, since she was formed from a bent rib, that is, a rib of the breast, which is bent as it were in a contrary direction to man. And since through this defect she is an imperfect animal, she always deceives. For Cato says: "When a woman weeps, she labours to deceive a man. Therefore a wicked woman is by her nature quicker to waver in her faith, and consequently quicker to abjure the faith, which is the root of witchcraft."

And as to her other mental quality, that is, her natural will; when she hates someone whom she formerly loved, then she seethes with anger and impatience in her whole soul, just as the tides of the sea are always heaving and boiling.

Can he be called a free man whose wife governs him, imposes on him, orders him and forbids him to do what he wishes, so that he cannot and dare not deny her anything that she asks?

Let us consider another property of hers, the voice. For as she is a liar by nature, so in her speech she stings while she delights us.

Let us also consider her gait, posture, and habit, in which is vanity of vanities. There is no man in the world who studies so hard to please the good God as even an ordinary woman studies by her vanities to please men.

She is more bitter than death because bodily death is an open and terrible enemy, but woman is a wheedling and secret enemy.

All witchcraft comes from carnal lust, which is in women insatiable.

Three general vices appear to have special dominion

over wicked women, namely, infidelity, ambition, and lust ... Since of these three vices the last chiefly predominates, women being insatiable, etc.

Is it a Catholic view to maintain that witches can infect the minds of men with an inordinate love of strange women, and so inflame their hearts that by no shame or punishment, by no words or actions, can they be forced to desist from such love; and that similarly they can stir up such hatred between married couples that they are unable in any way to perform the procreant functions of marriage; so that, indeed, in the untimely silence of night, they cover great distances in search of mistresses and irregular lovers?

Serpents are more subject to magic spells than other animals ... It is the same in the case of a woman, for the devil can so darken her understanding that she considers her husband so loathsome that not for all the world would she allow him to lie with her. Later he wishes to find the reason why more men than women are bewitched in respect of that action; and he says that such obstruction generally occurs in the seminal duct, or in an inability in the matter of erection, which can more easily happen to men; and therefore more men than women are bewitched.

When the member is in no way stirred, and can never perform the act of coition, this is a sign of frigidity of nature; but when it is stirred and becomes erect but yet cannot perform, it is a sign of witchcraft.

And note, further, that the Canon speaks of loose lovers who, to save their mistresses from shame, use contraceptives, such as potions, or herbs that contravene nature, without any help from devils. And such penitents are to be punished as homicides. But witches who do such things by witchcraft are by law punishable by the extreme penalty.

Wherefore the Catholic Doctors make the following distinction, that impotence caused by witchcraft is either temporary or permanent. And if it is temporary, then it does not annul the marriage. Moreover, it is presumed to be temporary if they are able to be healed of the impediment within three years from their cohabitation, having taken all possible pains, either through the sacraments of the Church, or through other remedies, to be cured . . . Much is noted there concerning impotence by Hostiensis, and Godfrey, and the Doctors and Theologians.

Question IX

Whether Witches may work some Prestidigitatory Illusion so that the Male Organ appears to be entirely removed and separate from the Body.

There is no doubt that certain witches can do marvellous things with regard to male organs, for this agrees with what has been seen and heard by many, and with the general account of what has been known concerning that member through the senses of sight and touch.

Peter's member has been taken off, and he does not know whether it is by witchcraft or in some other way by the devil's power, with the permission of God. Are there any ways of determining or distinguishing between these? First, that those to whom such things most commonly happen are adulterers or fornicators. For when they fail to respond to the demand of their mistress, or if they wish to desert them and attach themselves to other women, then their mistress, out of vengeance, causes such a thing to happen, or through some other power causes their members to be taken off.

I closed the book, unable to decide whether this fifteenth century "establishment" view of women was more shocking or amusing. The book's magisterial language made the vile nuggets of misogyny oddly palatable—rendering them seemingly quaint and harmless, something out of the distant past.

The most disturbing thing about it was, in fact, the modern foreword written by Desmond Dougherty. There was no condemnation of the text. Dougherty deemed the book to be, "an impartial and scrupulously reasoned account," an astonishing accolade given the nature of the work and its horrifying place in human history. Was this serious commentary? Or was he having us on?

I figured the one person who might be able to shed some light on this odd subject was Simon Lovelock. I immediately telephoned him in his shop and asked if I could come down and take him to a very late lunch. He agreed, suggesting a restaurant on Spring Street, not far from his bookstore.

I arrived at the restaurant with the *Malleus* tucked under my arm in a paper bag. It felt like contraband. The little café Lovelock had chosen was light and airy, with white walls, a gray-and-white tile floor, and plants hanging from the ceiling in terracotta pots. I spotted the black-garbed Lovelock sitting at a small round table in the corner, directly under a dripping fern. He looked like a raven in a spring garden, expectant and alert.

He seemed different somehow, more scrubbed and combed, as if he'd made a special effort. I detected the light scent of cologne. He stood up to greet me and one of the plant's delicate tendrils caught his hair. For a moment he appeared unsure whether to brush it aside or shake my hand. He finally stuck his hand out to greet me. He was a shy, rather awkward man and there was something very touching about him. He motioned me to sit down and I made myself as comfortable as possible on the slat-back wooden chair facing him.

"Thanks so much for seeing me on such short notice, Mr. Lovelock. I really appreciate it."

He nodded and cleared his throat. "This is my summer lunch spot," he said. "In winter, I prefer a rather cramped little restaurant right around the corner from me with no natural light. In winter I tend to gravitate toward dark places. I can't think why that is."

"Hibernation," I said.

Lovelock thought for a moment, as if he were giving my flip comment some weight. "Very possibly."

"I was kidding."

"Oh." He smiled, and I noticed that his teeth were cleaner.

"Are you hungry?" he asked me.

"I am."

He handed me the small menu card. "This restaurant specializes in what I call hippie gourmet food. Most things come with brown rice, and if you're not careful, you'll order something with a flower on it. Nasturtiums make me ill. Do they you?"

"I don't think I've ever had one."

"I suggest the grilled vegetable sandwich, or any of their sandwiches, really, provided you like sandwiches, of course. I have the vegetable one every day."

"I'm in your hands, Mr. Lovelock."

He shifted uncomfortably in his chair. "And what to drink?" he continued. "They have something called a jam fizz, which is just crushed raspberries, sugar, and soda water. It's really quite refreshing. Anyway, I like it."

"Sounds great."

A waiter who obviously knew Lovelock came over to the table and took our order. "Grilled vegetable sandwich, right?" the young man said.

"Two. And two fizzes, please . . ." The waiter left and Lovelock turned his attention to me. "Well, now, I was delighted that you called because I felt our last meeting was extremely unsatisfactory."

"I've found out quite a lot since then, Mr. Lovelock—"

"Simon, please," he said eagerly.

"Simon . . . You said I could come to you and ask you questions."

"I meant that. I want very much to help you, but as I told you, I'm in a difficult position."

"Yes, I understand." I slid the book out of the paper bag and handed it to him across the table. "Will you tell me everything you know about this book?"

"Ah," he said with a sigh. "So you've discovered the *Malleus*, have you?"

"Well, I finally read most of it. And quite a revelation it is."

"It's not that well known, you know. It should be a staple of women's studies and law courses. But people think it's just a relic of the past . . . They can't see it as being of any interest today . . . Where did you get this copy?"

"From a friend of Stephen's, a reporter. He got it from the Duarte Institute." Lovelock winced at that name. "They have an edition up there and they sell facsimiles of it."

He narrowed his eyes. "How do you know that?"

"I saw it."

"You *saw* it?"

"Yes, I . . . We went up there—Stephen and I."

Lovelock flushed with concern. "You went up to the Duarte Institute? Even though I warned you not to?"

"Stephen wanted to see it. And I thought it was important."

He lowered his head and took a couple of deep breaths, as if trying to compose himself. Finally, he looked up at me.

"Who took you around?" he asked.

"Father Morton."

"No one else?"

"No. Why?"

He leaned in toward me. "Beatrice—may I call you Beatrice?"

"Yes, of course."

"Beatrice, you must promise me—promise me—that you will never, ever go up there again."

"Why not?"

"Just promise me, will you?" he said with urgency.

"Okay. I promise. But what's the big deal? It's just sort of a scholarly Colonial Williamsburg, isn't it?"

He shook his head in perturbed amusement. "No, it's not. Believe me, it's definitely not."

"Tell me about it, then."

"Let's get back to the *Malleus*, shall we?" he said, obviously agitated. He turned the book over in his hands, thumbing through the pages. "In its day, it was widely read, second only to the Bible. It solidified the Church's power and was used as a basis for the Inquisition. What you have here is the most comprehensive edition. It's got Pope Innocent the Eighth's 1484 bull in it. You see, here it is."

He turned the book around and showed me the page. I glanced at it and when I looked up, he was staring at me with an odd look on his face.

"You're staring at me," I said.

"Am I? Yes, I am . . . Well . . ." he began as if he were trying to get up his courage. "In fact, I was going to telephone you."

"Oh? About what?"

"But I didn't think it was correct somehow."

"What were you going to telephone me about?"

"Nothing . . . Just telephone you . . . Like people telephone each other, you know. When they want to . . . to telephone each other."

"Oh . . . Oh, I see." His awkwardness made me smile.

"But I didn't."

"No, you didn't."

"No . . . Because you were with . . . your friend. So I just assumed that, um, he was your friend and that you two were . . . friends."

"Stephen is my ex-husband and we are friends, it's true. But just friends."

"Ah," he said, nodding with what I thought was some relief.

Lovelock smiled and stared at me for a long intense moment as if he were memorizing my face. I gave him a questioning look. Catching himself suddenly, his gaze dropped down to the book. He cleared his throat and got down to business.

"Well, literally translated, *Malleus Maleficarum* means *The Witches' Hammer*, or, as some prefer, *The Hammer of Witches*. It's a lawbook, telling exactly how to hunt, arrest, try, and execute witches. It was written by two fanatics—Heinrich

Kramer and Jakob Sprenger—and published around 1486:
Scholars generally accept that as the date. There were another
fourteen editions between 1487 and 1520, and, oh, another
sixteen or so between 1574 and 1669. These were printed by
presses in France, Germany, and Italy. So you see, the work
was very widespread, and its impact was incalculable . . . incalculable even today." He paused, seemingly lost in thought.

"Please go on," I urged him.

"Kramer was a German, born near Strasbourg. A Dominican prior who became an Inquisitor for the Tyrol and the
surrounding areas—Bohemia, Moravia, et cetera. Sprenger
was born in Basel, and early on he was recognized as a genius and a mystic. He also became a Dominican and was an
Inquisitor around Cologne, a very large district. By all accounts, he was saintly, and some chronicles of the day even
refer to him as 'Beatus.' He's buried in Strasbourg. Kramer
and Sprenger both wrote a great deal on their own. But the
Malleus, their masterwork, is a collaboration."

"Kramer and Sprenger sound like a vaudeville team," I
joked. "And as for their masterwork . . . I read parts of it this
morning. Forget witches. It's just this shimmering diatribe
against women."

"That it is. And a great deal more than that, I'm afraid,"
he said somberly. "It was a vastly influential book. No self-
respecting magistrate or judge of that day was without his
copy of the *Malleus*. It was the final and irrefutable authority on combating witchcraft, accepted and used by both
Catholics and Protestants as such. Not only did it tell them
about witches and their nature and how to discover them,
it outlined in detail how witches should be captured,
brought before a court, tried, and punished."

"A lawbook."

"*The* lawbook on witchcraft for over two centuries. People
really believed in witches, you see. And when people believe
something, they suspend logic. Emotion takes over. Religion,
love, hope, fear—all great opponents of logic."

"And hate."

"Hate is the worst," he said thoughtfully. "Witchcraft, of course, was always a tricky thing to prove. They invented degrees of it in order to legitimize it in an odd way. By refining it and parsing it, they made it seem a weighty thing, like the law itself. They had to give the law a worthy opponent. Witches fell into different categories. So, for example, the *Malleus* addresses the problem of how to deal with a witch who has confessed to heresy but is penitent." As he enumerated each offense, he ticked off the fingers of one hand with the other. ". . . Or a witch who has confessed to heresy but is *not* penitent. Or a witch who refuses to confess even though he or she has been convicted. Or a witch who has been accused of witchcraft by another witch. That last is a sticky one, to be sure. On and on like that, in the most minute detail. And then it outlines the various methods of punishment."

"Like burning at the stake," I said.

"The most extreme."

With that, our orders arrived, served by a waitress with purple hair, heavily made up eyes, and a nose ring.

"She'd definitely have been considered a witch," I whispered, when the young woman was out of earshot.

"Who knows? Maybe she is." I couldn't tell if he was joking.

Lovelock tucked his napkin up under his collar. He looked over the sandwich intently, then carefully removed the top slice of bread and placed it to one side of his plate. Next, he picked up his fork and began poking around the vegetables, careful to seek out only one variety at a time. He ate all of the carrots before he started on the zucchini, and all the zucchini before starting on the tomatoes, and on and on like that, down to the last bean sprout. Between bites of food, he took a tiny sip of the raspberry fizz concoction he'd recommended, then he dotted his lips with his napkin. All this was accomplished with speed and precision. Finally, he put down his fork and removed his napkin from his throat. With a little sigh of contentment, he leaned back in his chair and fumbled in his pocket for a smoke.

"That hit the spot," he said, starting to light up. I was just about to stop him when he said, "Ah, yes, I forgot. The smoking police," and put the cigarette away.

"Simon, may I ask you a question?"

"Certainly," he said.

"Why do you order a sandwich when you only eat the vegetables? Why don't you just order the vegetable platter?"

"I always like to see bread on my plate," he replied, as if that made perfect sense. "Bread is the staff of life, as they say."

"They have a bread basket," I said, nodding to it.

"You do things out of habit, not because they make sense. I like the familiarity of routine. Stuck in my ways, I am. Do you taste the dill in the vegetables?"

"Yes, it's delicious."

"Interesting herb, dill. In certain countries, it was believed to counteract the spells of witches."

"Simon, let me ask you something else. Do you believe in witches?"

He smiled enigmatically. "Let's get back to our friend the *Malleus* for the moment . . . You remember the papal bull I just showed you . . . ?"

"Yes."

"How much do you know about papal bulls?"

"Not much. Even though I'm a Catholic."

"Let me tell you a little bit about them, in that case. The term bull comes from the Latin word *bulla*, which means bubble. But in the vernacular, it came to mean a type of metal amulet. Gradually, it was associated with the lead seals used to authenticate papal documents. And by the end of the twelfth century, the word *bull* was used to describe the document itself." Lovelock smiled with delight. "I love the way certain words drift around in a language, don't you?"

He raised his long-fingered right hand, waving it gracefully back and forth through the air, as if he were conducting an orchestra. "They drift and drift and then—" His hand suddenly stopped. "Zap! They attach themselves like a barnacle to something seemingly unrelated to their original meaning. To think that the word for a mere bubble came to signify one of the weightiest and most important of Church instruments. Don't you find that amusing?"

"Very," I said, impressed. "You know so much about so many esoteric subjects, Simon."

He lowered his eyes and flushed slightly with embarrassment.

"Odd things interest me . . . Anyway," he went on, "of all the edicts issued from the Cancellaria, the bull was preeminent. A real papal bull is very different in both form and content from an encyclical or a decree, let's say, even though the latter are both sometimes described as bulls. Papal bulls were written in Latin, in an almost indecipherable Gothic script that was, interestingly, unpunctuated. They had seals on both sides—one depicting Saint Peter and Saint Paul, and the other either a likeness or else the name of the reigning pope.

"Now, the bull of Pope Innocent VIII, which accompanied the *Malleus* into the world, was written in the gravest possible language, giving the book enormous weight and prestige. Basically, it said that whoever defied the work would bring down the wrath of God and his Apostles on his own head."

"Simon," I said, mischievously. "You know what I think this book is really about. I mean, do you know what I think its deep psychological truth is?"

"Tell me."

"Man's fear of impotency," I said simply. "And, by implication, man's fear and loathing of all women. What do you think about that?"

I was baiting him slightly, but he didn't flinch, as I thought he might. In fact, he gave an appreciative little laugh.

"I think that's quite astute," he said. "But I also think it's a rather larger canvas than that."

I shook my head. "I don't think there is a larger canvas than the relationship between men and women. It's where everything starts, let's face it. That's the whole canvas, as far as I'm concerned. Everything else is just paint."

"Go on," he said with the amused, somewhat smug air of a professor to a student.

"In my opinion, *The Witches' Hammer* is a literal, as well as a literary, expression of man's primal fear of impotency. The authors use the generic term witch to describe evil people. But you and I both know, Simon, as would any intelligent reader, that for them, *witch* is really a euphemism for *woman*. Do you agree with that?"

"Perhaps."

"The book states over and over that women are an inferior, lustful, and depraved sex—which, of course, we are," I said with a wink in my voice. Lovelock smiled. I went on. "In many instances, the authors don't even bother to use the word *witch*. According to them, all women are basically evil to begin with. Original sin. And because of our weak minds and polluted bodies, we are more susceptible to becoming evil incarnate—that is, witches. Do you agree with that?"

Lovelock gave a solemn nod.

"And according to this book, what is the main power of witches?"

"I'm listening."

"To render men sexually dysfunctional. Either by making them impotent or else by making them so lustful that they have no control over their own desires. Then they have to resort to whoring, which, in the authors' view, isn't their fault. It's the fault of us lustful women. Listen to this."

I picked up the book, turned to a page I'd marked, and read aloud:

"'Question IX: Whether Witches may work some Prestidigitatory Illusion so that the Male Organ appears to be entirely removed and separate from the Body . . . And what, then, is to be thought of those witches who in this way sometimes collect male organs in great numbers, as many as twenty or thirty members together, and put them in a bird's nest, or shut them up in a box, where they move themselves like living members, and eat oats and corn, as has been seen by many and is a matter of common report?

For a certain man tells that, when he had lost his member, he approached a known witch to ask her to restore it to him. She told the afflicted man to climb a certain tree, and that he might take which he liked out of a nest in which there were several members. And when he tried to take a big one, the witch said: 'You must not take that one; adding, because it belonged to a parish priest.' How about that for a concept? This book is a virus which still lingers a little, let's face it. But what really got me is the foreword."

I read Dougherty's words aloud: "'A masterpiece . . . a scrupulously argued and convincing work, astonishing in its modernity . . . worthy of the attention of all mankind, even today.' Now that was written recently. And that's really scary."

We were silent for a long moment.

"There's a great deal in what you say," Lovelock said at last. "You've made an interesting connection."

"Want to hear something else interesting? The word *glamour* is used over and over. To 'cast a glamour' means to cast a spell. And who are associated with being glamorous even today? Women . . . Tell me something—why is this book a mere footnote in history?"

"That depends on whose history you're talking about."

I lowered my voice. "Simon, at our last meeting, you mentioned something about 'serious men who must be taken seriously.'"

"Yes," Lovelock said softly.

"Who are these men? And what the hell are they up to? This guy Desmond Dougherty, who wrote the foreword praising this as one of the great books of all time . . . He's on the board of directors of the Duarte Institute, where they sell the damn thing . . . Who is he anyway? And how does all this tie in with the grimoire? Because I just know it does somehow. Please, Simon, I really need your help here."

Lovelock paused. "I want to help you. I want to tell you so much, but . . ." he paused. Something held him back.

Leaning in closer, I pressed him. "Simon, you said that

if I found out things by myself I could ask you about them. Deep Throat, remember? Well, okay—on the back page of the book, you'll see some notes. Here, look—"

I opened the *Malleus* and pointed out Cap Goldman's notes to Lovelock, who gave them a cursory glance.

"That's a list of the board of directors of the Duarte Institute," I said. "Phil Burgoyne, George Cahill, Chuck Kraus, Father Morton, Giuseppe Antonelli, and Bart Winslow. I don't know much about the others, but God knows Phil Burgoyne is a major reactionary. I can't even listen to his goddamn talkshow. All these important men. And after each name, Goldman has scribbled the word *Presenter*, as you can see. Except after this guy Desmond Dougherty's name, where he's written simply the initials 'G.I.' Now, question: Is there anything in the *Malleus* that would explain the initials G.I. or explain what a "presenter" is?"

Again, Lovelock shifted uncomfortably in his seat. I knew he knew something and I knew he liked me. I put my hand on his.

"Please, Simon . . . Please tell me what all this means."

He stared down at my hand on his without moving a muscle. "I wish I could," he said at last. "But I'm not free to."

"Why not? Are you sworn to secrecy?"

"In a way."

"You're not one of them, are you?"

"No, God, no," he whispered, fervently shaking his head.

I squeezed his hand. "I believe you, Simon. I do. I also believe that these people are involved in kidnappings and heaven knows what else. You might want to think about just who it is you're protecting."

He stared at me intently and then said, with great emotion: "I'm protecting you."

"Me?"

"Please listen to me, Beatrice. You're getting too close. You must stop before it's too late. I can only be of value to you if I remain neutral—even though I'm not neutral. But I'm not holding back for the reasons you think I am. It's not because I don't want to tell you things—I do. But I can't.

I'm caught. I'm caught . . ." Tears welled up in his eyes. "You must believe me. I'd do anything for you—help you in any way I can. But the greatest help I can offer you now is to urge you to give up this search and stay away from the Duarte Institute. Never, *ever* go there again."

"What are you so frightened of, Simon?"

He bowed his head. "I can't say. Please don't ask me."

I withdrew my hand from his and we sat in silence for a long moment, listening to the bustle of the restaurant. Lovelock was obviously in deep conflict. I wanted to know more about him.

"Simon, where were you born?"

"Albany. Why do you ask?"

"Oh, I'm just curious about you, that's all. May I ask how old you are?"

"Fifty-one."

"Any brothers and sisters?"

"No."

"Parents still alive?"

Lovelock hesitated. "My . . . My father is, yes," he said with evident pain.

"Are you close to him?"

"I was at one time," he said, barely audible.

"And why did you leave the Jesuits?"

Lovelock shot me a fierce look. "How did you know I was a Jesuit?" he asked.

"A bookseller told Stephen about you."

He sighed. "Well, I suppose that wasn't too difficult to find out."

"I also know that you worked in the Vatican Library."

"I worked there, yes."

"So why did you leave the Jesuits?"

Lovelock sat motionless for a time. He was deep in thought and seemed a bit anxious. Finally, he said:

"I'm going to tell you something I've never told another soul. I don't quite know why I'm going to tell you, but I am. I would like you to know."

I held my breath. "Go on," I urged him.

He looked at me, eyes wide and weary, and said, "I once had an affair with a woman—someone I loved very deeply. She . . ." He paused and took a deep breath. "She took her own life."

"Oh God, Simon. I'm so sorry. I really am."

"Independent of the fact that I betrayed my order and went against my vow of celibacy," he said in a grave voice, "I could not, for many reasons and in all good conscience, find any consolation whatsoever in the Church. So I left."

"I see."

"You . . . You remind me of her," he said at last.

"I do?"

"You both have such interesting faces."

"Thank you . . . I guess," I said with a little smile.

"Oh, dear. Was that the wrong thing to say? I should have said you were pretty, shouldn't I? Women want to be told they're pretty."

"No. You said an honest thing. I like having an interesting face . . . I think."

His lingering gaze made me a trifle uncomfortable. It was as if he were trying to look through me and see his dead love.

"Who was she, Simon?"

He quickly looked away. "Never mind . . . You'll forgive me now if I go back to my shop," he said, rising from his chair. "The check's been taken care of."

"Thank you." I got up too.

As we walked outside into the sunshine, Lovelock put his hand on my arm to stop me. He turned to me, looked deep into my eyes, and said: "Beatrice, know one thing, and know it always. I will never let anything happen to you as long as I have a breath in me."

Before I could answer, he walked away abruptly. I watched him light a cigarette as he disappeared around the corner.

Chapter 15

I walked home, thinking a lot about Simon Lovelock and what a complex fellow he was. His personality was so different from his essence. Over the years, I'd made a study of personality versus essence. Personality was what confronted me when I was face-to-face with someone—their appearance, manner, conversation. Essence was what lingered after they were gone—that intangible impression that was often much truer and more lasting than any concrete trait. Very often the personality and the essence were in conflict.

Father Morton, for example, had an engaging personality. He was outgoing, intelligent, and a good conversationalist. Though I found him likable to talk to, he left behind a rancid essence. The more I thought about him, the more I mistrusted him. The same was true of Signor Antonelli—a charming and seductive man in person, but someone who left an icy wake.

Lovelock, on the other hand, had an eccentric, rather thorny personality, full of quirks and neuroses. But his essence was kind and comforting. The more I thought about him, the more I liked and trusted him. He reminded me of a courtly knight, who admired and protected women from a distance. He somehow embodied the delicate concept of *amour courtois* in the Middle Ages, first expressed by the lyric poetry of the troubadours and trouvères in the courts of France. I thought of the lai poems of Chrètien de Troyes, Henri d'Andeli, Jean Renart, Marie de France, and, of course, Guillaume de Lorris, who composed the first section of my beloved *Roman de la Rose*. These poets all described love as ennobling when directed toward a fine and virtuous cause. They chronicled lovers who won their ladies by feats of heroism, a strict code of worthy conduct, and, above all, patient hearts. In extolling the theme of chastity and contained passion as the highest forms of love, they idealized womankind and made her the catalyst for deeds of courage.

Lovelock's odd but kindly face flickered in my mind's eye like a candle in the mist. His personality was eccentric, but his essence was good and true.

Suddenly, my attention was caught by an arresting vignette. There, in the window of a little pleasure shop by the amusing name of "Come Now," was a female mannequin outfitted as a sexy witch. Wearing a black pointed witch's hat, a leather Merry Widow corset, black fishnet stockings, and black satin stiletto-heeled shoes, the dummy held up a riding crop which looked like a skinny broom, sprouting a long black tuft of hair at the top. A variety of vibrators, restraints, and other sex toys were strewn at her feet.

I was amused by the display. I thought of the authors of the dreaded *Malleus* and how they must be spinning in their graves knowing their worst nightmare had finally come to pass: Woman as witch, on exhibition for all to see—without reprisals.

I ran some errands, then went over to Stephen's. He opened the door holding a glass of wine. He looked gray with fatigue and smelled of alcohol.

"Hey, how're ya?" he said, giving me a perfunctory kiss on the cheek.

"Fine. But you look exhausted," I said, entering the dark little apartment.

"You'd be exhausted to if you'd been with the Krauts all day. I feel like Poland must have felt in 1939," he said. "Want some wine?"

"Sure, thanks."

"Where've you been?" he asked as he poured me a glass. "I thought you were staying here. I called you on your cell phone."

"Oh, I always forget to turn it on. I had lunch with Lovelock."

Stephen furrowed his brow. "How come? Did he call you?"

"No. I called him. I think I've figured out something crucial."

"What?" Stephen handed me a glass of wine and slumped down on the couch.

"You first," I said, raising my glass.

"Cheers," he responded wearily. "I've been in the sea of red tape all day. But the good news is, I think I've located von Nordhausen."

"You're kidding! Where is he?"

"Germany . . . Let me get my notes." He put down his glass, fished in his back pocket, and pulled out a ratty brown notepad. "Okay, so army pension records are restricted by a privacy act, so I couldn't find out anything about him through his war records. However . . ." he said, raising an instructive finger. "Being ever organized, the Germans have something called the *Einwohnermeldeamt,*" he said, reading in fractured German from his notes.

"The what?"

"Don't ask me to repeat it, okay? It's a city organization enforced by the police—or the *Bundeskriminalamt.* Basically, it works like this. Every German citizen must register a change of address within ten days or else face severe criminal penalties. The small village registration office is called the *Gemeindeamt.* The big city registration office is called the *Einwohn-*whatever I just told you. So after I found all this out, I got this guy at the consulate to actually call the *Einwohner-*whatever in Hamburg, to see if he could track down von Nordhausen."

"Just like that?"

Stephen raised his hand in protest. "Please don't say

'just like that.' It took the whole goddamn day for me to convince him to do it."

"At least he did it."

"Actually, he was a pretty amusing guy. He told me it's not a problem finding out who's registered where, 'ass long ass you don't vant to kill zem,' he said with a big wink."

"How does anyone know what you want to do with them once you find them?"

"Good point. Luckily, he wasn't as scrupulous as you. Although he did ask me four hundred million questions about why I wanted to locate the guy."

"And what did you tell him?"

"I said I got his name from a friend, that I was doing a story on the surviving veterans in Europe. Some bull like that. You know me—I can't wing it when I have to."

"Oh, yes, I know you," I said pointedly, thinking how often Stephen had lied to me in our marriage.

"Bea, I wish you would try not to *always* refer back to my egregious record. I admit, it was egregious, but I'm no longer like that, okay?"

"Go on. I'm listening."

"Okay," he continued. "To make a long and tedious story short: Erich von Nordhausen moved to London in 1957. He lives in Highgate, and here's his address and telephone number."

Stephen ripped a piece of paper out of his notebook and handed it to me.

"Twelve Delphinium Street," I said, reading the page. "But 1957? Christ, that's fifty years ago. Do you think he's still alive?"

"I'm coming to that. So I call the number in London, and a woman with one of those cheery English voices answers the phone. And I say, 'May I speak to Mr. von Nordhausen, please?' And there's a pause. So I say again, 'Is Mr. von Nordhausen there, please?' Another pause. Then click."

"Maybe you just had a wrong number."

"No. I don't think so. She wouldn't have hesitated after I asked for him the first time. And she hesitated—she really hesitated, like she was going to say something."

"It's a long shot."

"Long shots are all we've got here."

"So, let's go to London and check it out."

"My feelings exactly. Remember that cute little hotel off Sloane Street? We can stay there. Maybe have a second honeymoon? Or a date?" he said with a little laugh.

I felt a tiny tug of attraction as I looked at him sitting on the couch, all rumpled and cozy. He really was trying to help me and I was grateful, but still wary.

"I'll think about it. Now can I show you something? This was my day," I said, handing the *Malleus* to Stephen. "I read it and then I went to see Lovelock."

He read aloud from the text. "'Woman is a foe to friendship, an unescapable punishment, a necessary evil, a natural temptation, a desirable calamity, a domestic danger, a delectable detriment, an evil of nature, painted with fair colours!' Wow, well, they sure got you gals down pat," he said with a mischievous glance.

"Here, look at this," I said, finding the section. "Don't you love that witches steal men's members and put them in nests where they feed on oats and corn?"

"Oh, so that's where my member goes when it doesn't want to perform."

"And when exactly would that have been?" I teased him.

Stephen rolled his eyes. "Give me a break."

"Sorry . . . Anyway, we can laugh now," I said, taking the book away, "but believe it or not, that evil little sucker was the law of the land in all of Christendom for over two centuries. And, it's not just the authors talking here, you know. They reference the Bible, St. John Chrysostom, St. Augustine, and a lot of other important thinkers who all seemed to have hated and feared us. No surprise. But what really kind of freaks me out is the foreword, which was written, like, yesterday . . . Read that," I said.

Stephen read aloud. "'The *Malleus Maleficarum* is one of the greatest books ever written, for it makes manifest the eternal conflict between good and evil and is, therefore, a tribute and an inspiration to all men who seek the truth beyond the finite realities of this world.' The guy who wrote this is a wacko. So what?"

"Three guesses who that guy is, Stephen."

"Who?"

"Desmond Dougherty."

Stephen raised his eyebrows. "No kidding?"

"And if you ask me, they're doing more than selling it up there. I think they're teaching it. They may even be acting it out."

"Whoaaa . . . Let's not get crazy here."

"What about all these women disappearing? I mean, Cap—your friend—thinks there's a connection between them and the institute. Anyway, that's why I went to see Lovelock today."

"Another loon heard from!" Stephen laughed.

"He's not a loon. He's just eccentric."

"Eccentrics are loons with money."

"Seriously, I think he knows what's going on, but he won't tell me."

"No, naturally."

I knew Stephen had no patience for Lovelock.

"He thinks he's protecting me by not telling me," I said in Lovelock's defense. "However, he did say I was on the right track."

"He did?"

"Yes . . . And that Desmond Dougherty is a bad man . . . Want to hear something amazing? He told me the reason he left the Jesuits was because he had an affair with a woman and she killed herself."

"I always said you should have been a reporter. You get the damnedest things out of people. Well, we both had pretty interesting days," he said.

Stephen motioned me to come and sit by him. He

poured us each another glass of wine and we sat side by side in silence for a long time. I took a few sips of my drink and put it down. I put my head on his shoulder, inhaling the sweet scent of him.

"Thank you for helping me, Stephen."

Stephen put his glass down and before we both knew it, we were kissing. It wasn't the old electric passion I remembered, but something calmer and deeper—a sensuality born of shared experiences and deep disappointments and a new inkling of trust.

"Get into it," Stephen whispered as he caressed me. "Really get into it now . . . Just let yourself go."

I thought of the mannequin in the shop window and imagined myself dressed as that witch. I wanted to like sex more than I did. I wanted to be that woman Stephen was yearning for. But I was still afraid to really let go, as he put it.

Finally, Stephen took my hand and led me into the bedroom and we lay down on the bed. As he became more aggressive, I retreated. I closed my eyes, attempting to abandon myself to the touch of his skin and the shapes of our bodies. I tried to feel the passion I had felt with Díaz, but it was no use. I felt self-conscious and even a little fearful. The room was dark except for an aura of twilight around the drawn shades.

"Come on, fuck me," he whispered, grabbing my arms and pinning me under him.

The whole thing was pretty much of a disaster. I wanted so much to please him, but I don't know why, I just couldn't really respond. And Stephen couldn't really function. We kept on grappling with each other like two wet logs waiting for a magic spark. But nothing happened. Finally, he rolled off me and lay on his back, staring up at the ceiling.

"I . . . I'm sorry," he said.

"No, it's not you. It's me. You're right. I'm frightened of sex. That's all there is to it."

"What about that other guy?"

"That happened just after my father made his confession. I consider it an aberration."

"What are you so afraid of, Bea?"

"I wish I knew. If I had any inkling, maybe I wouldn't be so fearful."

"Well, my member wasn't being that cooperative either, in case you didn't notice. Wait! Did you steal it and put it in a nest?"

"Ha, ha," I said. "Shall we try again?"

We started kissing, but it was no use. Both of us were acting. Finally, we quit.

"I do love you, Bea, I do," he said after a time. "I don't quite understand why I couldn't . . . Probably had too much to drink."

"No, it's me. I don't enjoy myself. I feel somehow humiliated."

"I can't get over the fact that you slept with somebody else. And the way you did it. Without knowing the guy. A complete stranger."

"What if I'd never told you?"

He thought for a moment. "That probably would've been better. I wish you hadn't done it."

"What? Told you?"

"No, slept with him."

"Wait. Let me get this straight . . . It's okay for you to be unfaithful to me while we were married. But it's not okay for me to have sex once with a man after we're divorced and I don't think I'm ever going to see you again? You're kidding, right?"

"No."

"This is crazy."

"Maybe, but it's how I feel," he said, getting up. He put on his briefs and padded over to the chair in the corner and sat down, facing me.

"Are you saying you can't make love to me not because I'm not into it but because I had sex with another man? Is that what you're saying?" I asked him.

"This has never happened to me before," he said morosely. "I mean, I've never not been able to . . ." he hesitated, "do it," he said at last.

"Well, we haven't been together in a long time."

"That's not it. You've changed."

"I've changed? I have not! I wish."

"No, you have . . ."

"How exactly?"

"Well, how come you liked it with him?"

"I didn't really. I just tried to explain. It was just an isolated thing."

Stephen stared at me. "I can feel a difference."

I shook my head in exasperation. "Blame it on me. The women always get blamed, don't they? Just like in the *Malleus*. We steal your members. You have nothing to do with it," I said with a grim chuckle.

"Okay, it's just that I always kind of figured we'd get back together and be together . . . But now that you've been with someone else . . ."

"You want me to be perfectly honest?"

"Yeah."

"You were right. Sex repulses me. I think there's something truly horrible and frightening about it. I hate it. Just like my mother hated it."

"And when did you discover this?"

"You mean when did I admit it?"

We stared at one another. It was a deeper moment than any in our entire marriage.

"You'll understand if I go to London alone, right?" I said after a time.

"I guess so. But I don't want to end up being just friends with you, Bea. I'd really like to try and make a go of it again."

"Let me ask you something. Is it just possible you married me because I *wasn't* that fond of sex, not in spite of it?"

He furrowed his brow. "What do you mean?"

"I don't know. You tell me. Maybe you envisioned the mother of your children as this chaste and frigid being?"

"Madonna-whore . . . Puh-leeze!" he said shaking his head.

"I gave you a perfect excuse to be unfaithful."

"Maybe . . . Now let me ask *you* a question. Why did you marry *me*?"

"Well, I was crazy about you. You led this exciting life. You were a little dangerous, non-Catholic, and my mother didn't approve of you. I married you to escape everything I'd been brought up to believe."

"But you were in love with me, right?"

"I thought I was."

"But sex is a big part of love. It's like the shock absorber that gets you through the fights and the tough times. So are you sure you really loved me if you didn't really enjoy sex with me?" Stephen asked.

"I'm trying to be honest with you. Sex embarrasses me. I'm sure it's because of the way I was brought up and how my mother viewed it. I guess I thought of it as a duty, not a pleasure. But I did love you, Stephen. You know I did."

"Did," he said with a snicker. "So do you love me now, Bea?"

I couldn't really answer him because I didn't know myself.

"Look, I care for you very much and I'm so grateful to you for everything you're doing."

He shook his head. "I get it. But you're not *in* love with, right? Well, I'm in love with you, Bea. And I have a horrible feeling I always will be."

"Why is that a horrible feeling?" I said, teasing him.

"I meant futile . . . Let's go get some dinner."

Chapter 16

I thought about Stephen and Lovelock and Díaz on the flight to London—how different each man was and yet how each had had such a deep effect on my life of late. They were all intertwined in this macabre mystery of mine, the object of which was to find the person or persons who had murdered the first man in my life: my father. And in a curious way, each one of them reminded me of an aspect of my father. The adventurous Stephen, the scholarly Lovelock, the sensual Díaz. All together, perhaps, they formed his whole in my mind. I thought about what an anomaly the psyche is, how delicate and mutable on the one hand, yet tough and impervious to real change on the other. We seek to transform as we live, to grow with experience and understanding. And yet, the subconscious is an uncanny timekeeper, always pulling us back to old rhythms and patterns despite ourselves.

It was drizzling slightly when I got off the plane at Heathrow. A gray haze permeated the morning atmosphere. I changed some money and found a cab.

"Can you take me to Highgate?" I said, stepping into the black beetle taxi.

"Highgate. Right you are," the driver said in a bright Cockney accent. The meter clicked on.

"Nice flight?"

"Fine, thanks," I responded with a tired smile.

As we drove, I thumbed through the guidebook I'd purchased in New York. There was a long section devoted to Highgate Cemetery, where so many famous people were buried—everyone from Karl Marx to George Eliot to a fellow named Frederick William Lilly-white, the cricketer who, according to the guidebook, invented something called round arm bowling. Soon, however, I felt the effects of the long journey and as we sped along the M4, I dozed off.

Suddenly, I heard the driver say, "Now, whereabouts in Highgate, Miss?"

"Twelve Delphinium Street," I said.

Highgate looked to me like a fairly prosperous old sub-urb that had been preserved or restored through the ef-forts of history-conscious homeowners and civic groups. One side of the high street was interspersed with build-ings in the Elizabethan style. Little specialty shops lined the block—clothing boutiques, a chemist, butcher, bak-ery, greengrocer, and the like, along with several pubs and restaurants. A roundabout anchored the center of a wide road, where cars circled past a village green and a church.

Veering off to the right onto a narrow side street, the driver suddenly took a sharp left turn down a cobbled alley.

"Delphinium Street," he announced proudly, pointing up to a black-and-white street sign nailed to the corner house.

The driver and I both scanned the numbers on the doors as the taxi crept slowly down the block. We finally pulled up in front of a small, three-story pale-brick house. A sign hanging directly above the front door read SNACKS & TEAS in bold black lettering.

"Number twelve," the driver said with evident satis-faction.

I gathered up my carry-on bag and my purse, got out of the taxi, and paid the fare, tipping him generously.

"Oh, ta," he said in appreciation, then pulled away.

I stood in front of the little building fighting a rising tide of anxiety. After a few deep breaths, I threw back my shoulders and pulled down the handle of the glass-paned door. A bell tinkled as I entered. The tearoom was empty except for a weary-looking middle-aged man wearing a flannel shirt and blue jeans, sitting by himself at a table in the back, reading. He flung me a brief, annoyed glance as I entered, then called out at the top of his lungs:

"Katrine! Customer!"

I heard the muted squeals of children coming from a back room. The man returned to his book. I propped up my luggage on an empty chair and sat down at a table near the front of the café. It was a rather seedy little parlor, with yellow walls and fraying tieback curtains. The rickety wooden tables were draped in faded pink cloths, set with four thick cups, facedown in their saucers, and four folded napkins containing cheap silverware. Bud vases at the center of each table sprouted cheerless bouquets of daisies. The one bright note was the delicious aroma of baking bread that filled the air.

I picked up one of the soiled menu cards from the table. I wasn't that hungry but the selection of teas and cakes looked inviting. Soon, a plump and pretty woman appeared from the kitchen, followed by two young children, a boy and a girl. The children were giggling and dancing around her legs, much to her annoyance. "You're both going upstairs if you don't behave! Now go and sit with your father. Mummy's got work to do."

"Come here, monsters," the man at the rear of the shop cried out, motioning to the unruly pair.

The children obeyed. The woman walked over to my table.

"Please excuse the brood," she said with an exasperated smile. "You know what they're like."

She was wearing a loose-fitting sweater, a flour-dusted apron over a pair of khaki trousers, and thick brown orthopedic shoes. A wilted white lace cap, tilting toward the back of her head, was haphazardly pinned to tufts of her short blond hair. Her round face was open and friendly.

"Just one, are we?" she asked.

"Yes."

"What'll it be, then?" she said, clearing the other places. "We have fresh scones and some nice lemon cake, baked yesterday."

"Just some tea, please."

"China or Indian?"

"I don't care. You recommend something."

"Lapsang souchong's nice. Goes nicely with everything."

"Sounds fine."

"Any cakes? Scones? Toast? We make our own bread."

"No, thanks."

"Nothing else, then? You sure? Just got in from a trip or going on one?" she ventured, nodding to my suitcase.

"I just got in from New York."

"Ahh . . . What brings you to Highgate, then? Wait, don't tell me." She held up her hand. "The cemetery, right? That's why most tourists come here."

"Uh, no."

"Ahh . . . Friends here?"

"Um . . . Not exactly. Um, actually, I'd like to speak with the proprietor here, if that's possible."

The woman cocked her head and gave me a closer look.

"I'm the proprietor here. Well, my husband and I are. What can we do for you?"

I screwed up all my courage.

"I'm looking for a man named Erich von Nordhausen," I said, looking closely to see how she would react. Her friendly expression quickly evaporated and she looked away, as if embarrassed or frightened.

"There's no one here by that name," she said.

I knew she was lying. "Look, I don't know if I'm in the right place, okay? But we tracked him down to this address through a registration office in Hamburg. A friend of mine called here a couple of days ago and said that a woman answered the phone. When he asked for von

Nordhausen, she hesitated. Just tell me: Are you that woman?"

She stared at me coldly. "I can't help you," she said.

My fatigue and anxiety and sheer exasperation made me bolder than usual. I decided not to beat around the bush, but get straight to the point.

"Look, this is a matter of life and death. I've got to find this man. He could be very important in an investigation."

"No . . . I can't do anything for you," she said, starting to walk away.

I got up from the table and called after her. "You have children. You know how much family means. My father was murdered and I believe that this man can help me find out who killed him. Please, I'm begging you, please help me!"

She turned and looked at me. I must have presented a pathetic sight because her expression softened.

"Aaron!" she called out without turning around. "Come here, will you?"

Cautioning the children to stay seated, the man at the back of the room got up and walked over to our table. Slinging his arm around his wife's shoulder, he said, "What's the matter here?"

"She says she's looking for a man named von Nordhausen."

He and his wife exchanged a knowing glance. He pulled her in closer.

"We don't know anyone by that name," he said.

"Please. I just want to talk to him."

"Why?"

"I told your wife it's a matter of life and death and it's very urgent. Please, if you know where I can get in touch with him, I'll give you anything. Money, anything, just name your price."

The man shrugged and shook his head. "No. We've never heard of him, have we, Katrine?"

"No," the woman said hesitantly. She hung her head, unable to look at me.

"Look, I don't want anything from him except some information—" I pleaded.

The man narrowed his eyes. "What kind of information?" he asked.

"I can't tell you that. I have to speak with him directly."

The man shrugged. "We can't help you," he said.

"But you know him, don't you?" I said, staring at the woman. She looked at me. I could tell that she took pity on me.

"What if we do?" she said softly.

Her husband squeezed her tighter and shot her a dirty look.

"Can you get him a message for me?"

"No!" the man said emphatically.

"What message?" the woman asked as her husband yanked her closer.

"Tell him there's someone who needs to speak to him about the book—the grimoire. He'll understand."

A marked change swept over the couple. The woman visibly shuddered. The man's arm dropped to his side. He stood as still as stone, staring at me with a mixture of curiosity and fear. The three of us were silent for a long moment.

"Who are you?" he said at last in a low voice.

Sensing I had the upper hand now, I invited them both to sit down. They looked at one another and then each took a place at the table. I sat between them and leaned in, talking softly, even though there was no one else in the café.

"My name is Beatrice O'Connell," I began slowly. "My father was a surgeon and a book collector. A few months ago, a patient he'd operated on sent my father a strange little book in gratitude for saving his life. That book was a grimoire—a book of black magic—although I gather from the look on both your faces that you already know that."

They both nodded solemnly. I took a deep breath and resumed. I was tired and anxious. My mouth was dry.

"This patient wrote my father a letter, saying he'd picked up the book as a souvenir during the war. Shortly after my father received the book, he was—" I paused and swallowed hard, trying to gain control of my emotions.

"He was murdered," I went on. "And the book was stolen. It was the only one taken from my father's library of valuable books. So I knew it had a connection to his death. I tracked this patient down, the one who sent it to him, and he told me the story of how he happened to come by the book. He said he'd gotten it in Rome from a German courier, disguised as a priest. The courier was trying to escape when the Allies picked him up. They interrogated him, and he admitted he was a spy. He told them the grimoire was just a souvenir, and as they couldn't prove otherwise, they believed him. But I think he was lying. I'm convinced that the grimoire was his real reason for being in Rome. And I'm also convinced it's the reason my father was murdered. That courier's name was Erich von Nordhausen. I believe you both know exactly who he is and where I can find him. I've told you everything. The whole truth. Now will you please help me?"

The woman looked at her husband. He nodded slightly.

"Excuse us a minute, will you?" he said to me.

They got up from the table and walked over to a corner where they talked in animated whispers. I watched them closely, straining to hear their conversation. They appeared to be arguing about something, but I couldn't catch any words. Finally, the man shrugged and went to the back of the café where the children were playing. The woman approached me.

"Come with me. Leave your things here. My husband will look after them. My name is Katrine Silvers, and that's my husband, Aaron," she said, shaking my hand.

Katrine took a sweater from the coatrack near the front door and wrapped it around her shoulders. "Come," she beckoned me.

I followed her out the door. We walked in silence through the town, up a steep hill to Highgate Cemetery. At the eastern entrance to the graveyard, Katrine paid the admission fee for both of us and led me along the main path. We passed Karl Marx's imposing monument. There, under the leonine granite bust of the philosopher, Marx's words were chiseled in gold: WORKERS OF ALL LANDS UNITE.

The ground was muddy and soft, and my shoes kept sinking into the earth. Katrine, trudging on ahead, turned down a narrow path covered with tangled underbrush. She was a hearty walker and I hurried to keep up with her. Finally, we reached a small clearing back in the woods. Katrine marched up to a relatively new-looking headstone. She knelt down and blessed herself. I came up behind her. Carved on the headstone was the simple inscription: ERIC NORTH, 1916–1988.

"You wanted to meet Erich von Nordhausen," Katrine said. "Here he is."

I stared at the simple white stone, feeling all hope drain out of me.

"Eric North is Erich von Nordhausen?" I heard myself say.

"Yes."

I turned to her in a panic. "Are you absolutely sure? You're positive there couldn't be some mistake?"

Katrine paused. "Positive. He was my father," she said somberly.

"Oh my God . . . I had no idea. I'm so sorry."

We walked on, ignoring the light drizzle.

"Do you smoke?" Katrine said, offering me a cigarette from a pack she pulled out of her pocket.

"No thanks," I said.

She lit up and took a long drag as she stared out into the mist.

"I used to come by here every day," she said. "Sometimes twice a day. We got special permission to bury him here. My father was such a tormented man, but I loved him very much. I haven't been here in months." Her eyes teared.

"How did he die?" I asked softly.

"Heart attack. That was the official verdict, anyway. But he really died of the war. The scars of the war that never healed. He was dead a long time before his body gave out."

"Tell me about him," I asked sympathetically.

"Oh, where to begin . . ." she sighed, exhaling a long plume of smoke that vanished into the mist. "My father was born in the town of Nordhausen. He came from a very old family. My grandfather was a baron and a monarchist. I have pictures of him. He looks exactly like Franz Joseph with his mutton chops." She laughed slightly. "My father was a brilliant young man, a scholar and rather a mystic. In fact, he entertained the idea of going into the Church. But instead he became a philosopher—a devotee of Fichte. You know Johann Fichte?"

"No."

"He was a great German philosopher around the turn of the eighteenth century, much admired by Kant. But he eventually rejected Kant's theories. My father wrote a thesis on him, which brought him to the attention of Adolf Hitler." She spat out Hitler's name, as though it were poison in her mouth, then went on.

"Fichte had a theory that the German people were the *Urvolk*, as he called them—the chosen people of nature. He believed that in the relationship between states, there is only one rule: the rule of strength. And that rule is in the control of a sovereign prince, who, simply because he is mighty, is above law and personal morals and even fate itself."

"No wonder Hitler liked him."

"Yes. Herr Hitler used Fichte as a justification for his own pernicious goals. But all that is irrelevant, really," she went on. "Dad was a student at the university in Hamburg. He was having a brilliant career. And Hitler loved young aristocrats," she said with great bitterness. "That is to say, those with strong monarchist ties who were anxious to rebel against their parents and side with him. My father was young, impressionable, idealistic—perhaps too mired in academia to really understand at first what kind of monster Hitler was. Hitler was able to seduce my father with his passion for Fichte. My father told me he spent hours with Hitler, discussing the philosopher as an intellectual base for German nationalism. You see, Hitler knew just how to prey on youthful vanity. Early on, my father swore a blood oath to Hitler and then became one of his favorite pets. Like a dog, only worse. This disgusted my grandfather so much that he never spoke to his son again."

Katrine flicked her cigarette butt away and immediately lit another. "Look at me, chain-smoking. All of this makes me so sad."

"Please go on," I said.

"I have no excuses for my father. And he had none for himself, believe me. Some of us take wrong turns in life and spend the rest of the time on a road we never bargained for. That was my father . . . A few years after the war, my father moved here and changed his name from Erich Von Nordhausen to Eric North. His English was nearly perfect. He had almost no accent. He became a carpenter, of all things. It had been a hobby of his. He never studied philosophy or anything like that again. He married my mother, who was uneducated and not especially bright, but an extremely kind and understanding woman. I think he married her because he knew he could tell her the truth and she wouldn't be judgmental—which she wasn't. They had me. I'm his only child."

Just then a slight breeze ruffled Katrine's hair, dislodging her little lace cap. "God, have I still got this silly thing on?" she said, reaching up and pulling the cap off. She stuffed it in her pocket and continued her story.

"We lived a moderately comfortable life, and I grew up happily oblivious of my father's past. But then, you know, when you get older, you begin to ask questions. My father was always very evasive about his past. He said he was born in Germany and moved here after the war. That was all I really knew. Then one day, in my twenties, I was in his shop, watching him make a table. And I asked him what he had done in the war. I'll never forget that moment. He put down his hammer and stood very still for a long time. And then he burst into tears. I had never seen my father cry. It was a shock," she said with profound emotion. "It was a real shock. He sat me down there in his shop and told me the whole story. Then he took me upstairs to his bedroom, and he showed me pictures of his father and mother and even a picture of himself with Hitler."

"My God. What did you do?"

"I just listened. He told me that in 1942 he began to realize what Hitler was really about. But he denied it to himself. He said there was a plan to deport all the Jews to Mozambique. He said Hitler kept toying with that idea. Meanwhile, the death camps were beginning to operate full force. And everyone knew about them, no matter what they say now. My father knew. But he'd sworn a blood oath to this maniac, and his code of honor was just—I don't know—twisted."

"How did you feel about him after you found out?"

Her teeth clenched. "I hated him. I hated him more than you can imagine. I didn't see or speak to him for over a year. I felt tainted and soiled and ashamed that I had his blood running in my veins." She shook her head and took another long drag of her cigarette. "I started to drink, take drugs, sleep with a hundred men. I think now that I was using my father's past as an excuse to destroy myself. It was a terrible time."

Having done something of the same thing with my own father, I greatly empathized with what she was saying. I put my hand on her shoulder in sympathy and she touched me back in gratitude, continuing her story.

"Then one night I met Aaron at a friend's house. His father was a concentration camp survivor. Like my own father, he came to England after the war and didn't marry until quite late in life. Aaron and I were immediately drawn to one another. It was one of those mystical kinds of things. We spent the night together, talking about the war and our childhoods and forgiveness. Mainly forgiveness—and how it's necessary to forgive in this world, or you yourself become a victim, eaten alive by your own torment. I told him about my father."

"Was he shocked?"

"No. Quite the contrary. He was amused." Katrine forced a little smile.

"Amused?" I said incredulously.

"Really. In fact, he started laughing. He said it was so ironic that we should have come together—me, the daughter of one of Hitler's favorites, and him, the son of a concentration camp survivor. He said it was too crazy to be true. Anyway, we fell in love. I converted to Judaism. And eventually we got married. He was the one who pushed me into making up with my father."

"He sounds like a good man."

"Oh, he can be quite difficult sometimes—like all of them," she said with a conspiratorial little laugh. "But, yes, basically he's a good man. I'm lucky."

"So is he," I assured her.

She smiled. We strolled through the cemetery in silence for a time, pausing every so often to take in an interesting headstone or mausoleum.

"I envy you in a way," I said, as we ambled along one of the paths.

"Why?" Katrine asked.

"Because your father knew he had your forgiveness before he died. Mine didn't."

"What do you mean?"

"It's too long a story to go into. But my father died thinking that I despised him for something he'd done. And it wasn't true. I was going to tell him I forgave him. Actually, I was going to tell him there was nothing to forgive. It was my own narrow-mindedness and stupidity that made me so judgmental about him . . . But I never got the chance."

"I'm sure he knew you really loved him. My father said

he always knew it, even when I wasn't speaking to him. Parents understand. They do."

"Katrine, whoever killed my father robbed me not only of the best friend I had in the world but also of the most important moment of my life—the moment when I was going to tell my father that I truly understood him, that I'm truly his daughter."

"I understand," Katrine said. "Now I've told you the story of my life . . . But I think what you really want to know about is the grimoire."

I felt my heart beat faster. "Oh yes, please," I said eagerly. "Anything you can tell me."

"Welcome back," Aaron said as we entered the tearoom. "I hope you got everything straightened out?"

The table he and the children were sitting at was covered with crayons and coloring books.

"Not everything. We're going upstairs now," she said, giving him a knowing look.

"What do I do with the customers?" he said.

"There are no customers yet, my darling." Katrine walked over and patted him affectionately on the cheek. He looked up at her with a petulant expression.

"How am I supposed to get any work done?"

"You can work this afternoon. I promise. Noah . . . Rachel . . . I'd like you to meet a friend of Mummy and Daddy's."

Katrine introduced me to her children. Rachel, a blond, fresh-faced girl of nine, got up, curtsied, and shook my hand in a forthright manner. Noah, an imp of seven, ducked under the table and stuck his tongue out.

"Noah, can't you ever behave?" Katrine sighed in exasperation.

"No!" giggled the little boy, diving under his father's chair.

"See you later," Katrine said.

She led me through the kitchen and up a flight of back stairs.

"What does your husband do, Katrine?"

"He's a poet."

"I so admire poets. That's a very hard life."

"He's got a book coming out next year. Fortunately, my father left us a little money, but these days it doesn't go very far."

"How's your business?"

"What business?" Katrine shrugged. "We're off the main street, so very few people ever come here, as you may have noticed. But I love to bake, and I do a little catering to make ends meet. I sell cakes to the best teashop on the high street. I love pastries. It's the German in me, I guess."

Katrine ushered me into a cheerful but sparsely furnished bedroom, with chintz curtains and a large brass bed. She went to the closet and took down a large, tattered dress box from the top shelf. Putting it on the bed, she removed the cover. Inside was a hodgepodge of loose snapshots, documents, military medals, cards, letters, and a couple of old photograph albums. Katrine sifted through the jumble and located a picture, which she handed to me.

"That's Baron von Nordhausen," she said. "My grandfather."

I examined the thick old black-and-white photo card. "You're right. He does look like Franz Joseph. I like his whiskers."

"Dad told me Grandpapa always dressed formally for dinner, with his medals and ribbons. Here's one of my grandmother," she said, handing me a photo of an older woman in a satin evening dress and a long strand of pearls.

"She was very elegant."

"A bit stout, no?"

"But it was the fashion then."

"And here's my father," Katrine said with a mixture of pride and sadness.

I turned the faded, sepia-colored photograph toward

the light of the window. It showed a pale, ascetic-looking young man dressed in a dueling society uniform, standing stiffly in the middle of a courtyard, clutching a small bundle of books in one hand and holding a cigarette in the other, a grim, distant expression on his handsome face.

"That was taken at the university," Katrine said. "He hated being photographed, as you can see."

"He was very good-looking."

"Do you see any resemblance between us?"

I held up the photograph, comparing it to Katrine's face. "Yes, especially around the eyes."

"I take more after my mother, unfortunately. She was no beauty."

I gave the picture back to Katrine, who sighed and put it down. She continued rummaging around in the box.

"Ah . . . This is what I was looking for. Here he is with the devil," Katrine said, handing me another photograph.

I studied this picture closely. It was a snapshot of von Nordhausen, Hitler, and another young man, standing together in front of a low wall behind which a majestic view of sky and forest stretched to infinity. A German shepherd dog sat at attention at Hitler's side. Hitler, his arms crossed, was smiling at von Nordhausen as though the young man had just said something amusing. Von Nordhausen, who appeared far more relaxed in this photo, but less handsome, was smiling back at Hitler. I noted that von Nordhausen's teeth were slightly crooked and his ears stuck out a bit.

The other young man in the picture was standing off to one side with his hands sunk into his jacket pockets, his collar turned up, taking in the view. His face was shaded by a fedora, and a pipe dangled from the corner of his mouth.

"Who's that?" I pointed to him.

"Count Borzamo, the owner of the grimoire."

I immediately took an even closer look.

"I told you my father was a pet of Hitler's," Katrine con-

tinued. "Well, in 1944, my father denounced von Stauffen-
berg and the other aristocrats after the famous July
twentieth attempt on Hitler's life. He was one of the few
aristocrats to do so. Hitler then entrusted my father with a
top-secret mission. My father spoke to me about this mission only once. He told me that Hitler ordered him to go
to the Vatican to get a certain book from the pope. That
book was the grimoire belonging to Count Borzamo."

"And what was the pope doing with it?" I asked,
fascinated.

"I don't know . . . But Borzamo would know. He and my
father corresponded for a number of years."

"Is Borzamo still alive?"

"I don't know that, either. But I have his address in Italy.
It was in my father's address book. I'll give it to you."

"Do you have any of the correspondence between
them?"

"No. My father burned most of his papers before he
died. All that's left is what you see here—pictures, a family album, diplomas, citations, a few letters from friends—
nothing of any significance. Believe me, I've pored through
all of it."

"Did your father tell you anything else about the
grimoire?"

"No—except one thing."

"What was that?" I asked her, picking up the ominous
tone in her voice.

"He said that if anyone should ever come here asking
about it, I should tell them everything he told me," she
said slowly. "And above all, I should make it clear that we
didn't have it. He was adamant about that. 'Make certain
they know you don't have it,' I remember him saying over
and over."

"And has anyone else come?"

Katrine shook her head. "No. You're the first."

"So I'm right, then," I said, thinking aloud. "The real reason your father was in Rome was to get the grimoire."

"Yes, you are right. My father told me the mission was extremely complicated. He had two cover stories prepared in case he was captured. The first was that he was a priest. He knew they would break that immediately, so it was the second he concentrated on."

"And what was that?"

"When they tortured him, he gave up the names of contacts in Rome in order to make them think he was an ordinary spy. That way he never had to reveal the true purpose of his mission. He was very proud of that fact."

I got up and began pacing around the room. "And he never said why Hitler wanted the grimoire?"

"No. I honestly don't think he knew. But Borzamo might know."

"And your father never found out what happened to it?"

"No. I'm quite sure of that. He just said they confiscated it and he never saw it again or knew what became of it. I think a number of people contacted him about it after the war. But he was always very secretive about that—just as he was about his past. Imagine if the good people of Highgate had known that they had a Nazi living in their midst," Katrine said with a sardonic little laugh. "We all would have been stoned to death."

"The sins of the fathers," I said.

Katrine nodded, looking at me with deep understanding.

"And you want to hear the final irony?" she said. "The town of Nordhausen—my father's town—is where Hitler secretly manufactured the V-2 rocket in underground caves, using slave labor. The *Nibelungen*. Think of that— the death machines that decimated London," she said. "I wonder what my father thought of that."

"It seems that we're all victims of some war, in one way or another," I said. "Will you give me Count Borzamo's address?"

Katrine copied down the address from her father's tattered address book. "Here it is," she said, handing it to me. "It's near Terni, in Umbria. Do be careful, though. My father told me that Borzamo was a very, very strange man."

Katrine helped me book a flight for Rome the next morning. She made me some lunch and wished me luck. I left the little tea shop elated by the success of my mission. After walking around London a little, I took a taxi out to the airport and checked into a hotel nearby. I called Stephen to tell that I wouldn't be back for a while yet. There was no answer. I left a cryptic message on his machine, informing him that I'd arrived safely and had an interesting meeting with "our friends" as I referred to them. I didn't tell where I was going, fearing his phone was tapped.

I got undressed and took a long hot bath. When I lay down on the bed, jet lag suddenly hit me and I fell fast asleep for several hours. I woke up at three in the morning and tried phoning Stephen again. The machine picked up again. I had a fleeting pang of anxiety wondering where he could be and imagining something might have happened to him. But I quickly rationalized that Stephen was used to being in precarious situations and he was very good at taking care of himself. I couldn't afford to dwell on him at the moment. My mind was racing with thoughts of the grimoire and von Nordhausen and the mysterious Count Borzamo. I looked once more at the slip of paper on which Katrine had written his address:

Count Giovanni di Borzamo
Villa Borzamo
Borzamo, Italy

I prayed he was still alive, for I knew, instinctively, that he was the key.

Chapter 17

On the flight to Rome, my anxiety mounted as I thought about the shadowy Borzamo. I didn't know if I was more fearful of not finding him or finding him. I was haunted by the picture of him with Hitler and by Katrine's father's words that he was a very strange man. The plane landed at one in the afternoon. I stepped off the aircraft into a curtain of sweltering wet heat. A helpful young man at the airport's car rental agency supplied me with a map, tracing the best route to Borzamo in thick red pencil.

"You are going to see the famous garden?" he said, in excellent English.

"What famous garden?"

"At Villa Borzamo, of course. The Garden of the Stone Monsters, as it is called."

"Well, yes. I guess I am."

I picked up a little white sedan and headed north toward Terni. As I sped along the autostrada, I noticed a change creeping over the countryside. The unsightly skein of factories and high-rise apartment buildings gradually unraveled into an open landscape of farms and patchwork groves of olive trees, sunflowers, mustard plants, and corn. Tall, stately cypresses stood at attention over sun-baked fields dotted with bales of hay. Tiny flocks of sheep, seeking refuge from the heat, huddled bunched together in the shadows of the trees. Every once in a while, a cluttered little medieval town loomed in the distance, perched precariously on top of a steep precipice overlooking a valley. Isolated and forbidding, such towns looked like they had looked for centuries, radiating the magic and superstition of those dark times.

Three hours later, I turned off the highway and headed east, as the map indicated. Following the winding roads, I finally reached the village of Borzamo. I stopped at a café and had a cappuccino to revive myself. There, in halting Italian, I asked directions from the friendly young waiter.

"Dov'è la Villa Borzamo?" I inquired.

"Villa Borzamo? Si, si, nei boschi, nei boschi," the young man said, proceeding to fire directions at me so rapidly I had no idea what he was saying.

He took me outside to show me the route. I thanked him and drove off. Within a couple of miles, I came to the fork in the road he'd described. To the left was the edge of a dense forest. A small sign, barely visible through the foliage, read VILLA BORZAMO, with an arrow underneath. I headed off into the woods. About a quarter of a mile later, I came upon an identical sign, pointing toward a dirt road. I took the turn.

The car bounced along the bumpy path. The afternoon sun filtered through the trees, creating a soft, smoky light. Presently, the road smoothed out, leading up to a heavy black wrought-iron gate flanked by stone walls. The name BORZAMO was worked in ornate iron lettering across the top of the gate. Underneath was an iron shield bearing the Borzamo family crest, which had a serpent on it. A small sign hanging on the gate read, APERTO.

I pulled into an empty parking area to the right of the entrance. My feet sank into the soft woodland ground as I walked through the gate onto the property. About a hundred yards in front of me, outside a tiny wooden shack, I spied an old man splayed out on a rickety canvas beach chair, his head resting against the back frame. He was asleep. His shirt was open at the bottom, and the flesh of his large belly bulged out over the tops of his trousers, heaving up and down to the rhythm of his snores.

"Scusi, signore," I said, approaching him gingerly.

The old man snorted a couple of times and awoke suddenly. A pair of striking blue eyes shot out at me from his aged leather-skinned face. He was thick-featured, with a stubbly growth of beard. He rose from the chair with some effort and trudged into the shack. Seconds later, he returned with a white slip of paper, asking for the admission fee.

I hesitated. *"Uh . . . No, grazie. No biglietto,"* I said in awkward Italian. *"Voglio vedere il Conto Borzamo, per piacere."*

He stared at me and licked his lips. *"Non è possibile, signorina."*

"Ma, è molto importante," I said. *"È possibile que Lei dice the—"* I was struggling in vain with the language, so I decided to try the universal language, to wit: I opened my purse and pulled out a packet of Euros and handed it to him.

"Per piacere," I said with feeling. *"È molto importante."*

The old man raised his eyebrows with pleasure and took the money from me, pocketing it. He looked me over again.

"Exactly why do you wish to see Count Borzamo?" he said, quite unexpectedly and in beautiful English.

"Oh, you speak English!" I cried with relief.

"A bit," he shrugged.

"Look, it's very important that I speak to Count Borzamo. Is he here?"

"Count Borzamo is in Rome. Are you one of his girlfriends?"

"No," I said, flushing with embarrassment. "How old is Count Borzamo anyway?"

"Around fifty years old."

"Oh." I was deflated.

"You don't know him?" he asked me, narrowing his eyes.

I shook my head. "No. And anyway, it's not him I need to speak to. It's his father . . . I guess his father must be dead."

The old man studied me. "So it is the *old* Count Borzamo you wish to speak to."

"Yes!" I said, feeling some hope. "Is he still alive?"

"Just barely," the gatekeeper said.

"Does he live here?" I asked excitedly.

"Yes, he lives here. In the big house."

"Oh my God!" My heart was racing. "You've got to get me in to see him! Please. I'll give you anything you ask. I have a lot more cash in my purse. You can have it all."

The flicker of a smile lit up the old man's expression. "I don't know. The count sees no one these days."

"All right. Then can you get a message to him?"

"It is possible."

"Then tell him that a woman has come all the way from America to see him. It's a matter of life and death."

"May I know what it is you wish to speak to him about?"

I shook my head. "No. I must speak with him personally. Can you arrange it?"

The old man looked me up and down in a way that made me feel slightly uncomfortable.

"Yes, I think I can arrange it," he said at last. "Come with me. Ah . . ." He paused. "*Momento* . . . Wait, please."

He traipsed down to the entrance and turned over the sign, the back of which read, CHIUSO. I watched him as he closed the gate, locking it with a large old-fashioned key he extracted from his pocket. He walked back, tucking his shirt into his baggy trousers, smoothing down his thick white hair.

"Come," he said, grinning at me. "I will take you to the count."

I followed the old man up a sloping path shaded by trees and lined with underbrush. Quite suddenly, we came upon a clearing, in the middle of which was a mammoth stone elephant saddled with a howdah. The sight was so arresting that I paused and blinked my eyes. The old man took no notice. He continued along the path. Soon there was another clearing and another gargantuan statue—this time a tortoise, whose right front leg had partially sunk into the soft earth.

I ran to catch up with the old man. There were more clearings and more enormous statues—a horse, a lion, a dog, a hawk, a wild boar with a broken tusk—all beautifully carved out of dark, pitted stone, covered with spots of moss, decaying amid the unkempt greenery of the garden.

"Wait!" I cried out.

The old man halted.

"What on earth is this place?" I cried.

"It is the garden of the Borzamo family. It was created in the sixteenth century by Luigi Borzamo, who had a passion for monsters." He smiled. His teeth were large and slightly crooked. "You like it?"

"It's marvelous," I said. "So strange."

"People find it amusing," the old man said. "But I am used to it."

"Are there any others?" I asked when we reached the last one in sight.

"Yes, there are more. But they are not permitted to tourists."

"Oh, I'd love to see them. Won't you take me?"

"No," he replied curtly, and walked on.

Presently, we came to another wrought-iron gate, identical to the first. Visible in the distance was a sprawling stone manor house set on a vast expanse of wild, untended lawn. The old man took out the large key from his pocket and unlocked the gate, pushing it open so I could pass through ahead of him.

"Villa Borzamo," he muttered, closing and locking the gate behind us.

As I approached the house, I saw that it was extremely run-down. Chunks of the massive slate roof were missing. Thick cracks and chips scarred the weather-beaten stone façade. The flower gardens and low boxwood mazes in front of the villa had all gone to seed. A shabby old vintage black Mercedes-Benz was parked in the cobblestone courtyard, alongside a battered pickup truck.

The old caretaker and I walked up wide stone steps
that led to an imposing front door, its wooden frame reinforced with intricate iron hinges and large nails. Before he
could knock or ring the bell, the door was opened by an
ancient housekeeper in a long black cotton dress, a black
kerchief around her head.

"*Buona sera,*" she said, bowing slightly.

"*Buona sera,* Aldarana," the old man said.

We walked into a cool, dark, vaulted entrance hall decorated with tapestries and medieval armaments. A full suit
of armor on a pedestal stood like a sentinel beneath a life-
size oil painting of a young knight in full regalia, sitting
astride a powerful stallion.

"Luigi di Borzamo—the creator of the garden," the old
man said, pointing to the picture.

The golden-bearded young man, with a slightly curled
upper lip, had an arrogant expression and blue eyes that
pinned the viewer with a cold and penetrating gaze. I studied his cruel face for a few seconds, then followed the old
man. Our footsteps echoed on the stone floor. We walked
through a series of grand rooms crammed with cumbersome Baroque furniture and enormous, heavily varnished
paintings in need of a good cleaning. Finally, we reached a
paneled door.

"Stay here, please," the old man said.

I waited in the corridor while he slipped inside, closing
the door behind him. My heart was racing in anticipation. A few moments passed. Then I heard a low voice
call, "Enter."

Twisting the large black knob, I pushed open the heavy
door and stepped into the room. I found myself in a large
study. Two fraying red velvet couches flanked a cavernous
fireplace. The mantelpiece was a grim stone eagle embracing
the hearth with a pair of swooping wings. The walls were
covered in tooled brown morocco leather, dry and peeling
with age. A series of black-and-white etchings of snakes hung
in ornate gold frames above a desk. Family photographs in

tornished silver frames were spread over the top of a grand piano. The quiet, insulated chamber smelled of sweet tobacco. I looked around. It appeared to be empty. I wondered where the gatekeeper had gone to.

When my eyes grew accustomed to the dim light, I spied a cloud of smoke rising behind of a high-backed wing chair facing a window in the far corner of the room.

"Count Borzamo?" I said tentatively.

"Yes," said a voice from the chair.

"I . . ." I began hesitantly, clearing my throat. "My name is Beatrice O'Connell. Thank you for letting me come to see you."

"Beatrice . . . Beatrice," the voice said, pronouncing my name in Italian. "Like Dante's chaste heroine."

I drew closer to the chair. "My father named me for her," I said, craning my neck, eager to get a look at the mysterious count.

"Ah . . ." the voice sighed. "Your father was a literary man, then?"

"In a way. He was a doctor, but his hobby was book collecting."

"And book collecting is my vocation," the voice said. "Isn't that a remarkable coincidence?"

With that, the man in the chair stood up and turned around to face me, puffing on his pipe, grinning at me with a mischievous glint in his eye. I was dumbfounded. He was the old gatekeeper! He had changed out of his ragged clothes into dark trousers and a worn red velvet smoking jacket.

"You're Count Borzamo?" I said, incredulous.

"At your service."

Stepping out from behind the chair, he removed the pipe from his mouth and gave me a courtly little bow.

"Please, do sit down," he said, ushering me ahead. "Let me offer you a special little liqueur."

I sank down into one of the fraying velvet couches. As he walked over to a large library table and poured us drinks from the makeshift bar, I watched him closely, searching for some resemblance between this unkempt, fat old count and the dapper young man with Hitler and von Nordhausen in the photograph Katrine had shown me. The pipe was the only thing that linked the two of them.

"This is called limoncino," he said, handing me a cordial glass filled with a filmy yellow liquid. "It is made from the lemons at my summerhouse near Ravello. Try it. Tell me how you like it."

I took a tiny sip of the syrupy liqueur. It tasted sweet and pungent and made my mouth pucker. "It's delicious. Very strong," I said.

"Drink too much and it has the effect of absinthe," the count said, taking a long swallow. "But a little clears the head." He sat down on the opposite couch and relit his pipe, leaning back and crossing his legs. "So," he began, "tell me why you have come all the way from America to see me."

I put my drink down on the coffee table separating us and stared at him for a long moment.

"Tell me something, Count Borzamo. Do you find it amusing to masquerade as the gatekeeper?" I said, vaguely irritated at his deception.

"But, my dear girl, I am not masquerading as the gate-keeper," he protested. "I *am* the gatekeeper. That is the job I have given myself."

"Why? Can't you afford to hire someone to hand out tickets for you? Or are you afraid they'll steal the entrance fees?"

Count Borzamo laughed heartily at this suggestion. "Steal the entrance fees! Oh, that is very good! Excellent! No, the truth is that I am an old man and I tire quite easily. It relaxes me to sit in the sun and look at the people who come to see my garden—especially the young women, like yourself," he said, his eyes drifting up and down my body.

"My son lives in Rome," he went on. "My friends and enemies are all dead, so there is no more amusement there. I find the newspapers a bore. The world is so repetitive, don't you think? Reading books is a chore, since it is difficult for me to see the print. So I guard my gate. It is really the only contact I have with the outside world these days. And in any case, there is not too much else I can do . . . So I do that."

Count Borzamo suddenly seemed an entirely different person to me. His voice, his manner, everything about him, exuded an air of jaded sophistication. I perceived his simple peasant disguise as a pose he cultivated to mask a complex man with experience and taste. But there was something about this seemingly affable old libertine that made me extremely uneasy. I suspected he had a dark side lying in wait, ready to pounce on me when I least expected it.

"*Allora,*" the count continued. "Answer my question. Why have you come to see me?"

I straightened up and folded my hands primly in my lap. "I need to know about a book you once owned."

"I have owned many, many books, my dear girl. Some of them I still own."

"This is a special book. It's a grimoire attributed to Pope Honorius III."

I studied the count closely, hoping for a reaction. He showed none. His facial expression didn't change in the slightest. He merely took a sip of the limoncino.

"Continue," he said flatly.

I proceeded to recount the entire story of the grimoire and my father's murder. I revealed to the count how I'd managed to track him down through his old friend von Nordhausen's daughter. I mentioned all the principals in the drama—Antonelli, Father Morton, Schroeder, and Mr. Lovelock—offering thumbnail sketches of each one and how he was involved.

The count sat listening impassively, smoking his pipe and sipping his drink. Yet there was something about the way he looked at me that made me understand just how completely I'd captured his attention.

"So," I concluded after the long explanation, "Katrine

von Nordhausen said that if anyone could help me, you could." I paused. "Will you help me, Count Borzamo?"

The old man gazed at me, his blue eyes shining through the pipe smoke. "You would like my son," he said after a time. "He is extremely handsome. Do you like handsome men?"

I shifted in my seat, not knowing quite what to make of this question. "I suppose so," I said.

"He is—how do the English say it?—a fine, strapping young man. Fifty years old. Or thereabouts. I forget. Maybe fifty is not young to you." He laughed. "But it is young when you are my age."

"Count Borzamo, I don't mean to be rude, but are you going to help me or not?"

He didn't answer. Instead, he got up and fetched the bottle of limoncino. Returning to the couch, he sat down again and filled his glass.

"You have hardly touched your drink," he said. "May I offer you something else? Some wine, perhaps?"

"No, thank you."

"Tell me—are you married, *Beatrice*?" The count seemed to relish pronouncing my name the Italian way.

"Divorced."

"Divorced? You look quite young to be divorced. How old are you, my dear? I know it is a rude question, but I am old enough to ask rude questions."

"And I'm old enough not to answer them," I said.

"Ah, good. I admire a woman who will not reveal her age. Who was it who said, 'A woman who will tell her age will tell anything'?"

"It was probably a man. I'm thirty-two," I said.

The count seemed delighted by my response.

"Thirty-two. *'Nel mezzo del cammin di nostra vita'*—in the middle of the road of life, as your biographer, Signor Dante, wrote." He paused. "My mother was a beautiful woman. She died many years ago, as did my father. So, like you, I am an orphan now. Orphans have a bond between them, don't you think?"

"I suppose so—although I don't think of myself as an orphan."

"I was married when I was very young. It was an arrange-ment. I did not care much for my wife, but she was elegant and rich and she suited the political ambitions of my family. After the birth of my son, we lived separate lives. She would have divorced me, but in Italy we do not divorce like you Americans. Tell me, do you have a boyfriend?"

"I didn't come here to discuss my private life, Count Borzamo."

"But that is the only life worth discussing," he said, tap-ping out the ashes of his pipe into an armorial dish on the coffee table.

I was becoming a little impatient. "Count Borzamo, won't you tell me about the grimoire, please?"

He removed a small pouch of tobacco from his pocket and dug his pipe inside it. He tamped down the excess with his fingers and leaned back. "It is a very long story," he said. "Involving the entire history of my family."

"I need to know it."

"Why should I tell it to you?" He cocked his head as he lit the fresh pipe. "Give me one good reason."

I thought for a moment, wanting to choose my words carefully.

"There is no one good reason. There is simply the fact that my father is dead and that I know his death is connected in some way with this book. And if I can find out more about the book, maybe I can find out who killed him. You seem like a kind man—"

"Do I?" he said incredulously. "I am certainly not a kind man. I am a selfish old bastard!" He roared with laughter.

His guffaws turned into a hacking cough. He sipped some more of the liqueur and gradually composed himself. I had no idea what to make of him.

"Well, if you're not going to tell me anything, I suppose I should go," I said, getting up from the couch.

"No, no, per piacere, resta ancora. Stay, please!" He raised his hand to stop me.

I sat down again, prepared to listen.

"I will tell you what you want to know, on two conditions."

"What are they?"

"The first is that you will stay and have dinner with me tonight."

"And the second?"

"I will tell you that after we have dined together."

"Yes, all right. I agree."

Chapter 18

"At what hotel are you staying?" the count asked me.

Realizing I hadn't thought about that, I was suddenly embarrassed.

"Actually, I came here directly from the airport. I should make a reservation somewhere. You must know of a place?"

"I know of a very comfortable place. I shall have Aldarana show you to a room," he said with a smile.

I looked at him askance, thinking what an old lecher he was.

"Thank you. That's very kind of you," I replied in a purposely light tone. "But I'd really rather stay in a hotel."

The old count raised his eyebrows and glanced at the large bronze clock in the shape of a rhinocerous dominating the mantelpiece. When I saw that it was nearly seven, I was surprised. I had lost all track of time.

"Perhaps. But it is quite late and there is nothing nearby. And you will want to freshen up for dinner, will you not?" He looked me over when he said this, making me feel self-conscious about my appearance.

"I had no idea it was so late," I said.

A fleeting grin crossed his face. "It is always later than one thinks, as they say . . . Please, you have nothing to fear," he said, as if intuiting my nervousness. "There are twenty-seven bedrooms in this house—all of them empty. Aldarana will draw you a bath, and you may change. And then, after dinner, you can go to a hotel, if you wish."

"I better make a reservation now, don't you think?"

"That might be a bit difficult for you," the count said. "This is the high-tourist season, and most of the hotels are booked. But I am not unknown in this part of the world. If I telephone on your behalf, they will certainly find a room. Why not leave it to me?"

I felt as if I had no alternative, so I reluctantly agreed. The count rang for the housekeeper on an old-fashioned needlepoint bell pull, which hung against the wall. When she arrived, he gave her some instructions in Italian. While nodding obediently to the count, the old woman kept a critical eye on me.

"I have told Aldarana to bring your luggage up from the car. You will have my wife's old room. It has a rather nice view of the north garden. Do not worry," he added quickly. "It is in the opposite wing from mine."

I thanked him, but I was extremely wary. As I was following the old housekeeper out of the study, the count called to me.

"Beatrice," he said. "I should inform you that here in the Villa Borzamo we always dress for dinner."

I paused at the door. "I'm sorry. I didn't bring any formal clothes. I'm afraid all I have with me is a fresh blouse and a ratty old pair of jeans."

"Do not worry," the count said. "We will provide something suitable for you."

"No, I really don't think that would—"

"Please do not protest," he interrupted. "As the saying goes, 'When in Rome . . .' He smiled. "Dinner will be served at nine o'clock."

I followed the old woman back through the house, up one flight of a grand staircase and down a long corridor. We entered an enormous bedroom done up in pale blue silk damask, with magnificent gilt furniture. I was struck by the affected piety of the room. There were crucifixes everywhere—carved into the furniture, perched atop the four posters of the bed, embroidered on the silk bedspread, and woven into the fabric of the chairs. A collection of icons was propped up on the bureau, and a saccharine portrait of the Madonna hung over the bed.

The room was musty. The old housekeeper immediately opened the doors leading to a balcony in order to let in some fresh air. After she left, I poked around, opening closets and chests filled with elegant but dated women's clothes. I went into the bathroom—a cavernous Art Deco room with marble floors, a sunken tub, and antiquated, oversized plumbing fixtures. Finally, I went out onto the balcony, which over-looked an intimate, well-tended flower garden. I stood there awhile, taking in deep breaths of the gentle evening air, listening to the distant hum of cicadas. Gazing at the nearby forest, I thought about the great stone animals it contained and wondered what the other monster garden was like—the one Count Borzamo had refused to show me.

Just then, the housekeeper entered, carrying my suitcase. She set it on a painted storage chest at the foot of the bed. I walked back inside. *"Grazie,"* I said.

"Prego, signorina," the housekeeper answered. Then she asked me something in Italian. I didn't understand her. She motioned to the bathroom.

"Ah! Si, grazie!" I said, suddenly understanding that the old woman wished to run me a bath.

I was exhausted from the journey and I lay soaking in the large sunken tub for a long time, hoping to get some rest before dinner. After a time, I revived and soon I began to feel a great sense of anticipation, hoping that during the course of the evening, the mystery of the grimoire would surely be revealed to me by the old count. Then I'd be that much closer to solving my father's murder.

When I dried off and returned to the bedroom, I was amazed to see that two stylish evening dresses had been laid out for me on the bed, one in black and one in white. Alongside them was a selection of lace undergarments, four evening bags, and four pairs of identical silk evening shoes in different sizes. An assortment of precious jewels glittered on a black velvet tray.

This was like some sort of fairy tale, I thought, though I was vaguely disconcerted by the idea of dressing up for the old count in clothes that he had provided. But the dresses were very pretty and well made. Looking at myself in the mirror, my distaste was overcome by feelings of amusement. The count's parting words to me in the study, "When in Rome . . ." echoed in my ears. I thought: This is an adventure. What the hell?

A clock chimed the hour of nine as I descended the staircase for dinner. Count Borzamo, in a black tuxedo, black tie, and black velvet slippers embroidered in red with his crest, was waiting for me at the foot of the steps. Shaved, groomed, and formally dressed, the old count had managed to make himself quite presentable.

"Charming! Charming, my dear!" He extended his hand as I reached the bottom of the staircase. "I knew you would choose the white dress," he said with satisfaction.

"How did you know?"

"I was certain you would be true to your namesake in the *Divina Commedia*. Tell me, do you recall the scene in which Beatrice reproaches her beloved Dante for being unfaithful to her during her lifetime?"

"Yes, of course," I said. "And the virgins in the fields have to convince her of Dante's sincere repentance before she agrees to lead him into Paradise."

"Ah—I see you know the poem well," the count said, escorting me into a vast, candle-lit dining room, where a old servant dressed in livery was standing at attention at one end of the long rectangular dining table, set for two. "I have always found the divine Beatrice a bit of a bore, if you do not mind my saying so."

The count showed me to my place on his right and pulled out the chair for me.

"A bore—how do you mean?" I asked, as I unfurled my large white linen napkin.

"Well, imagine poor Dante," the count said, pausing before he sat down. "Here is a man who has literally been through Hell and Purgatory in order to find his beloved Beatrice—and all she can speak about when they finally see one another is what an unfaithful son-of-a-bitch he was to her on earth! I cannot imagine anything less inspiring, can you?"

"That's certainly a novel interpretation of one of the greatest books ever written," I said, laughing.

The servant pulled back the count's chair, and Borzamo sat down. Shaking out his napkin in one flick of the wrist, he tucked it into his collar and curtly instructed the man to pour the wine from the crystal decanter on the table. The count took a small sip and nodded his approval. The servant then filled my glass.

"I hope you like red wine," the count said, as I took a swallow of the velvety Burgundy. "I have rather a good wine cellar. I used to own a vineyard, but the wine was inferior, so I sold it. I cannot tolerate inferior things."

"Well, this wine is delicious," I said, drinking some more.

The count signaled to the servant to refill my glass to the top.

"What is absolutely true," the count said, continuing our discussion, "is that men and women do not think of sex in the same way." He leaned back and made a little cathedral of his hands. "For women, sex is an altar at which they worship with more or less devotion at various times in their lives, depending on their lover . . . For men, sex is simply a bath they need to take on a regular basis—and, unfortunately, not necessarily in the same tub."

I was amused by his ideas on the subject, which I thought said more about him than the current situation. Another liveried servant appeared carrying a large silver platter filled with chicken, vegetables, and roast potatoes.

He bowed slightly to me, and I helped myself to small portions of the delicious looking food. The servant then moved on to the count, who, in contrast to me, took giant helpings of everything.

"I hope you like a simple dinner," the count said.

"This is perfect," I replied.

The count used his hands to eat the chicken. His table manners left a lot to be desired, as he seemed to eat more with lust than appetite.

"A woman makes a present of her body to a man," the count continued. "And most women must wrap that present up in emotion. Otherwise it feels rather cheap."

"To her or to the man?" I inquired.

"To her, of course. The man could not care less what the present is wrapped up in, as long as he receives it!" The count laughed and laughed, pointing a chicken leg at me. "Of course, there are some women who do not feel that way. There are women who use sex as a man uses sex—as a bath. But in my experience, these women are very few. Although if you do encounter one, she can be rather dangerous."

Our eyes met across the candle flame and I quickly looked away. I was deeply embarrassed by the conversation and I wanted to change it.

"You are blushing," he said.

"Am I?"

"It is charming. American girls are reputed to be so free sexually. But you are not, I think? Am I right?"

I didn't answer him. I just kept eating, fork to mouth, fork to mouth, like an automaton, dreading what the old count was thinking. I felt his eyes on me for a long moment. Then he continued to wolf down his meal at a great rate until he'd finished.

"So," the count said at last, pushing his plate away and licking his fingers, "you wish to know about the grimoire."

"Yes, please," I said with relief. I was a little surprised as well, for under the terms of our bargain I hadn't expected him to bring up the subject until the meal was over.

The count leaned in to finger a little mound of candle wax that had dripped onto the table. He concentrated on the wax as he spoke, glancing at me occasionally out of the corner of his eye.

"To understand the grimoire, you must understand a bit about its background. The Borzamos are an ancient family. We go back many, many centuries, and we have always been great book collectors. Book collecting is more than an interest with us. It is a heritage, a birthright, a passion, which has been shared by the counts of Borzamo for hundreds and hundreds of years. It is our destiny—or *was* until that stupid son of mine was born," he said bitterly.

"Your son isn't interested in book collecting?" I asked.

"My son collects women," the count said, disgusted. "He stopped reading books when he reached puberty."

"Where is your collection, Count Borzamo? I'd love to see it."

"I am coming to that. You are an impatient young woman."

The count reached out and patted my hand. His hand, greasy from the chicken, repulsed me, though I tried not to show it. I merely pulled away with a shy smile. A flicker of malice crossed his face. Just then, the servant came in and removed my plate, replacing it with a cut-glass finger bowl. He then took the count's plate. However, instead of bringing a finger bowl, the servant left the room and returned with a large silver basin filled with water. He knelt at the count's side and held the basin up to his master. The count turned sideways in his chair, washed his hands and face, and dried himself with a linen towel the servant provided. I was fascinated by this exhibition.

"Ah!" the count said, rubbing his hands together in a gesture of contentment. "Now I am refreshed."

He instructed the servant to bring in the next course. Then he resumed his story.

"Tell me, are you familiar with the history of the Vatican Library?"

I stiffened, for now I knew I was getting close to the truth.

"Just a little," I replied. "I know that it was founded sometime in the middle of the fifteenth century—that's about all, I'm afraid."

"Not bad. It is more than most people know. The Vatican Library was really the work of two popes—Nicholas V and Sixtus IV. They must share the credit. The library was based on a collection of Latin and Greek codices—the *Bibliotheca Latina* and the *Bibliotheca Graeca*—as well as the *Bibliotheca Secreta*."

"The secret library? What's that?" I asked, intrigued.

"The old papal library, whose contents were unrecorded for many, many years. But I shall come to that . . . The Vatican Library really began to flourish in the seventeenth century. Maximilian of Bavaria donated the Palatine Library from Heidelberg around 1622. The great Latin manuscripts belonging to the dukes of Urbino and Queen Christina of Sweden were also acquired during that period. Then in the eighteenth century came the Capponiani collection, as well as the great Ottoboni library. The Borghese library, the Barberini library—so many great and famous collections came to the Vatican."

Just then the servant entered with fruit and cheese. Once again, the count helped himself to gargantuan portions of everything. I chose a single ripe peach.

"You do not like cheese?" the count said, shoving a large slice of Parmesan into his mouth.

"I'm not all that hungry, thank you. I guess I'm too riveted by your story," I replied, hoping he'd get on with it and come to the grimoire.

He grinned at me. Bits of bread and cheese had lodged between his front teeth.

"To continue, then," he said, washing the food down with large gulps of wine. "These are the collections that one has heard about: They are world famous. They form the nucleus of the Vatican Library . . . But," he went on, spearing a wedge of apple with his fruit knife, "there is another collection in that library, one which is not famous and which nobody, outside of a tiny group of people, has ever heard of." He held up the knife with the apple slice on the tip, to punctuate his point. "Indeed, the Vatican denies all knowledge of it to this very day."

"What is that collection?" I asked eagerly.

"That, my dear girl, is the Borzamo Collection!" the count cried, popping the slice of apple into his mouth.

"I don't understand. Why hasn't that collection been recognized and acknowledged along with the others?"

The count frowned slightly, as if he were searching for the correct words. "The Borzamo Collection is not—how shall I put it?—very traditional . . . It consists of only two main areas of interest." The count sipped his wine.

"What are they?"

"Pornography and black magic," he said simply.

The count gulped down the rest of his wine and licked his lips. The servant, who had been waiting by the doorway, ran to refill his glass. I peeled my peach nervously, reflecting on all the implications of this revelation. I remembered Lovelock's mentioning something of this at one of our first meetings, but decided not to say anything about that.

"So what you're saying is that the Vatican has a collection of pornography and black magic they don't admit to?" I said.

"Well, they rather wink at the collection of pornography. Many people have seen it through the ages, so it really cannot be denied. Years ago, a friend of mine visited the library and asked the curator about it. "Do you have a collection of pornography?" he said—knowing full well that they did—just to see what the poor curator would say. And the curator simply said, 'We are reputed to,' which I think is a rather good answer, as it is not, strictly speaking, a denial. However, when that same friend asked about the collection of black magic, the curator grew quite angry and said in a rather short temper, 'I think not,' and he walked off very troubled—or so my friend said."

"And these collections were given to the Church by your family?"

"In a way. The collection of pornography, certainly. It was donated by my family in the eighteenth century for the amusement of some pope or another, who was most likely a bit of a rake. By the way, the eighteenth century was a marvelous time for pornographic works, in case you are interested . . ." He studied my face for a moment. I tried to remain expressionless. I remembered Lovelock had said the exact same thing.

"And then," he continued, "as is always the case with collections, they are added to by other sources. So I am sure the collection has been enlarged quite a bit. But I am happy to say that the bulk of the pornographic collection was given to the Church by the Borzamo family," he said with mock pride.

"And what about the collection of black magic?" I asked.

"Ah," he sighed. "Now that is a slightly more complicated arrangement."

"I'm listening."

"Why don't we take our coffee in the salon?" he said, glancing at the servant.

"That dress really suits you," the count said, as we sat in the living room, watching the old servant pour coffee into two demitasse cups from a small silver pot. "Let me give it to you as a present."

"No, I couldn't possibly accept it. But thank you very much, anyway."

"Americans are such a contradiction. On the one hand you are so free and on the other so puritanical," he said, shrugging. "Why not give an old man a bit of pleasure if he wishes it? Take it, please, with my compliments. After all, I cannot wear it, and there is no one else whom I wish to have it . . . *Grazie*," he said, dismissing the servant with a wave of his hand.

The old man bowed and left the room.

"Count Borzamo, you were going to tell me about the collection of black magic," I said, trying to deflect his offer.

"So you will not accept the dress?"

"No. Please—I need to know about this collection."

The count finished his coffee in two swallows and put the cup and saucer down. He leaned back on the sofa and lit a pipe.

"I have never liked this room. It is much too big. And all my ancestors stare down at me from the walls."

I glanced around at the huge, grim-faced portraits in ornate gilt frames. "They're quite an imposing group."

"They have imposed on me a tradition that, whether I like it or not, is my birthright. You see, the Borzamos have always existed in a sort of symbiotic relationship with the Church. Ever since the Vatican Library was founded, our family has been the source of works that are—shall we say—not sanctioned by the Church but are, nevertheless, of great interest to it."

"Books of black magic," I said.

"Exactly. In the past, the Church, as you know, always made a great show of confiscating such works and burning them—along with their practitioners and creators when they could find them. But the reality is slightly different."

"And what is the reality?"

"The reality is that God and the devil—like the Church and the Borzamos, if you will—also exist in a symbiotic relationship. After all, without evil, there can be no good— there is just boredom."

"I suppose you could put it that way," I said, amused.

"Do you recall that at dinner I mentioned to you the *Bibliotheca Secreta*—the old papal library whose contents were unrecorded and which formed in part the nucleus of the Vatican Library?"

"Yes, I remember very well. Along with the *Bibliotheca Latina* and the *Bibliotheca Graeca*."

"You are a good student," the count said. "Well, eventually, that secret papal library was catalogued—by an ancestor of mine, as it happened. And there were many classical manuscripts in it, of course—great works and fragments by Plato, Aristotle, Simplicius, Apollonius, Archimedes, Aristarchus of Samos, Euclid, Herodotus, Homer, Hipparchus, Ptolemy, Hippocrates, Seneca, Tacitus, Thucydides, Pliny, Plautus, et cetera." He reeled off the names with impressive speed.

"But there were other works, which were less acceptable. Grimoires, cabalas, magical papyri, Gnostic texts, and fragments pertaining to the Eleusinian, Orphic, Phrygian, and Mithraic mysteries. These works represented occult thought and knowledge from all over the world—Egypt, Persia, China, India, as well as ancient Greece and Rome. But it was not considered seemly for the True Church to harbor such a collection, as it would appear to detract from their mission on earth. Being extremely—what is that phrase Americans use?"—he thought for a moment—"image conscious. That is right, no?"

"Image conscious. Yes."

"Being extremely image conscious, the Church was forced to hide such works. Nevertheless, they were made available to a select few for study, and they formed the nucleus of a collection which grew rapidly throughout the Middle Ages and the Renaissance."

"In other words, a collection of black magic," I said.

"Let us call it a Collection of Opposing Thought," the count said, grinning. "After all, I do not want you to think of me as the devil."

"All right—a Collection of Opposing Thought, then."

"Because a Borzamo had catalogued the original collection and knew of its existence, my family was given the honor of continuing to seek out such works, in order that the Church could remain au courant with the forces that were against it. So for the next century, the Borzamo family business was to locate heretical works—particularly those of an occult or magical nature—and bring them to the Vatican. We were well rewarded for our efforts, as you can see. All this"—he gestured expansively—"we owe to the gratitude of the Church. It gave us protection from the Inquisition and from excommunication, which was very important in those days, since persons who were excommunicated had no civil rights."

"Let me get this straight," I said. "The Church paid you and protected you so that you could find books of black magic for them?"

"Basically, that is correct. But it sounds rather sordid when you put it that way." The count caressed the bowl of his pipe with his thumb and thought for a moment. "I like to think of it more as a sacred trust. The mission of my family on this earth has been to keep the Church informed about the nefarious workings of the enemy."

"That enemy being . . .?"

"In a very small circle, the Borzamos are known as *Gli Agenti del Diavolo*—the Devil's Dealers."

"The Devil's Dealers," I said, taking a moment to digest this. "So these books are now in the Vatican Library?"

"Not now. But they were at one time."

"Where are they now?"

"During the first hundred years of the library, some of the popes were interested in reading them. Others were not. But with the fever of the Inquisition steadily rising in Europe, it was clear that the collection was in danger of being discovered. So in 1600, it was moved here, in the greatest secrecy."

"The books were kept *here*?" I said in amazement.

"That is the reason Luigi di Borzamo built the Monster Garden. The part that is not open to the public is where the collection was kept. People were very superstitious about that garden, and they would never dare to go near it."

"And"—I hardly dared ask the question—"is the collection still there?"

"No," he said decisively. "When Napoleon came to power, it was moved back to the Vatican for safekeeping. Then, after the Second World War, Pope Pius feared that the Communists would take over Italy and such a collection would be in danger of annihilation. So it was moved yet again."

"Where is it now?"

"I believe it is somewhere in America, guarded by people who fear and loathe it but who recognize its power—like an important political prisoner."

I suddenly thought: The Duarte Institute!

"You don't have any idea where in America, do you?" I asked.

"No." The count shrugged.

I suspected he was lying.

"As I say, I am retired from the family business."

"And the grimoire . . .?"

"The grimoire was part of the collection."

"So von Nordhausen got the grimoire from the Vatican Library in 1944."

"Yes."

"And when it was taken, they wanted it back."

"Yes. But for other reasons."

"What other reasons?"

"Now we come to the real story of the grimoire," the count said with a sly smile.

My mind raced as I began to put things together. "So you must know Signor Antonelli?" I said.

"Giuseppe? Of course I know him."

I was stunned. "My God! Are you the private client who was interested in purchasing the grimoire from my father?"

"Let us simply say that I was an interested party."

"He called you, didn't he? To say that he'd found it."

"He did."

"So you know who I am, don't you? You knew who I was when I came here."

The count nodded. "And I am very impressed that you found me."

I slumped back onto the couch, feeling as if the wind had been knocked out of me. I swallowed hard.

"Okay, but why did he call you, if you didn't want to buy it?"

"He needed some information. And I am the only one who could give it to him."

"What information?"

"He needed to know for certain if it was the real grimoire."

I was flushed with excitement. "You mean because of the inscription from Saint Paul?"

The count looked at me with an amused expression on his face. "You are like a dog with a bone," he said.

I ignored his remark. "Why is this particular grimoire so important? What is its secret? You know, don't you?"

The count shrugged noncommittally. I knew he was toying with me.

"All right, then," I said. "Who's the private client who wants it so badly? The Vatican?"

He continued looking at me, saying nothing. When he finally spoke, there was something dark and menacing in his voice.

"We have a bargain," the count said slowly. "I said I would tell you what you wished to know, under two conditions. You have met the first. You have had dinner with me. Now you must meet the second."

I looked at him warily. "And what's that?"

"Come with me."

The count rose from the couch. He walked over to me and offered me his hand. Reluctantly and with great trepidation, I put my hand in his and got up from my seat.

"Where are we going?" I asked.

"To the other part of the garden."

With that, he led me out into the night.

Chapter 19

The count picked up a rusty hurricane lamp that lay on the terrace at the back of the house. Lighting the wick inside, he held the lantern straight out in front of him to illuminate the way and beckoned to me. We walked across the property, down a long flight of stone steps leading to a wide expanse of lawn. The dark forest, awash with the silvery glow of the moon, loomed up ahead. It was hot and humid. The satin dress clung to my body as I walked along the grass.

We reached the thicket. The count cautioned me to watch my step as he led me along a rough little path winding through the woods. The deeper we traveled into the forest, the narrower and thornier the path became. Occasionally, the count bent down to sweep aside twigs and branches in order to clear the route for me. Despite his efforts, the pointy heels of my evening slippers kept getting caught up in the tangled underbrush, causing me to stumble occasionally. I continued on for a quarter of a mile without complaining, but I was uncomfortable and a little frightened as well.

"Where are we going?" I called out.

"Have patience, *cara Beatrice*," the count replied, looking back at me. "It is Dante who is leading you."

Finally, we reached a clearing. In the middle were four dark structures of gargantuan proportions, grouped in a wide circle. At first, they seemed to me to be nothing more than big black boulders. Then, as my eyes became accustomed to the murky light of the grove, I saw that the dark shapes were more than just monster rocks. They were huge carved statues.

With theatrical flair, the count walked around to each sculpture in turn, as I watched.

"This is the Minotaur," he said, holding up his lantern to illuminate the strange entity.

The lamp cast a delicate light on the stone—enough for me to see that towering over the count was a terrifying version of the mythical beast with a bull's head and a man's body. My eyes widened.

"And this is the Medusa," the count said, moving on.

Again, he held up his lantern, and I could make out the stone carving of the hideous Gorgon, its hair composed of snakes.

"And this is the Cyclops." He shone the light on a horrific monster with a bulging stone eye in the middle of its huge stone forehead.

The last piece of statuary, nearly twice the size of the others, appeared to be some sort of stone lizard, with great hollow eyes, a flaring hood, and gaping jaws big enough for at least three people to walk inside.

"What on God's earth is that?" I cried.

The old count stepped just inside the beast's mouth and turned to face me. His lantern glowed feebly against the immense black cavity around him. Seeing that he had my full attention, he recited some lines of poetry:

"'All set with iron teeth in ranges twain, That terrified his foes and armed him, / Appearing like the mouth of Orcus, grisly grim . . .'"

"What does it mean?" I asked.

"They are lines from *The Faerie Queene* by Spenser. They refer to the mouth of a dragon. The great dragon is Satan. Orcus is the Latin name for Hades. And this, my dear girl, is the entrance to Hell. Follow me."

I was pierced by a sharp shiver of fear. But I couldn't afford to falter now that I was so close to my goal. Shimmering like a beacon in the forefront of my mind was the knowledge that the count possessed the secret of the grimoire and that secret might lead me to my father's murderer. And besides, I rationalized to myself, although I suspected the count of incredible decadence, I basically viewed him as a harmless old man against whom I could easily defend myself if necessary. So I pressed on.

With his lantern swinging back and forth, the count led me into the dragon's mouth and down a long flight of stone steps. The farther we descended, the cooler and danker the atmosphere became, as if we were entering a crypt. At the bottom, abutting the last step, was a bronze door on which mystical symbols were modeled in low relief—pentacles, stars, crosses, numbers, snakes, astrological signs, and circles inscribed with strange writing. I recognized some of the designs from the grimoire.

The door was locked. The count asked me to hold the lantern as he removed two of the diamond-and-onyx studs from his dress shirt. He fished inside his shirt and soon produced a sizable iron key, which hung from a long gold chain around his neck. Unhooking the key, he bent down and inserted it into an ornate lock. He twisted the key this way and that until there was a resounding click. He put the key back on the chain and shoved the door open, giving it a hefty push with his shoulder. I handed him back the lantern and stood poised on the bottom stair as the count entered a black hole of a room. The darkness was so dense that it devoured the lamplight, leaving only a faint glow.

"Wait there," the count said.

I peered inside as he struck a match and lit two torches standing in tall iron receptacles on either side of the room.

"Come in," he called out when lights were blazing.

I stepped down and entered the large chamber. Deep, evenly spaced slots were cut into the jagged stone walls from floor to ceiling. Standing tall at the far end of the room was a plain black inverted cross, in front of which was a long stone bench. The air smelled foul and there was an aura of evil about the place. I was terrified and claustrophobic, imagining he might shut me in and leave me there to die. No one knew where I was. No one would ever find me.

"Welcome to the old Borzamo library," the count said. The flickering torchlight made his face look ruddy and satanic.

"The family rec room, I suppose?" I said, making a joke to alleviate my fear.

The count grinned. "It is extremely theatrical, don't you think? My ancestor Luigi had great dramatic flair, no?"

"Indeed," I said.

The count and I seemed to be circling one another. I kept my eye on the exit, ever ready to flee.

"As you can see, the room was built for the purpose of housing the collection of books. Once upon a time, these shelves were filled with the devil's literature. It is quite amusing to think of it, don't you find?"

"Fascinating. But I really want to know about one book: the grimoire."

The count paused. "I have told you. There is one more condition."

I tensed up. "And what is that?"

For the first time, I sensed the count was reticent and maybe even a little nervous. "It is a rather delicate matter," he said.

The silence in the room was so marked, it seemed to stifle the air.

"Whatever it is, I'm ready. Please." I tried to maintain a lightness of manner.

"You are not a pretty girl," he said slowly. "But you have some allure, which is more interesting."

I felt myself flush.

"And you have a young body."

I crossed my arms in front of me. "Not so young," I said.

The count stared at me lasciviously. His eyes were a lustrous black green in the firelight, like a pair of beetles.

"Take off your dress for me," he said at last.

My heart was beating so fast now I could feel it thumping in my chest.

"Why?" I asked, barely audible.

"Because I wish to see your not so young body," he said.

I swallowed hard. "Is that the condition?"

"It is the beginning of the condition."

"I—I don't want you to make love to me, Count Borzamo. I won't let you do that."

"Do not flatter yourself, my dear. I do not want to make love to you."

"What do you want?" I said warily.

"Something else."

"I don't want you to do anything, please."

The count's loud laugh reverberated throughout the chamber.

"I will not do a thing to you. *You* will do something to *me*."

"No . . . Please . . . I can't . . ."

"You can and you will," he said, easing himself down onto the stone bench, "if you consider what I am offering you in return. I know the secret of the grimoire. I am the last hope you have of ever finding it out. I will tell you this: I am certain your father was murdered for that book. I will also tell you that I am certain I know who murdered him. It seems to me that you are paying a very small price for something so very valuable to you."

"It's not a small price," I said softly. "And how can I be sure you're telling me the truth?"

"I am many things, but I am not a liar," he said. "And when you hear it, you will know it is the truth."

"If I do this *thing*"—I said the word with distaste—"that you want me to do, how can I be sure you'll live up to your part of the bargain?"

"Because I give you my word."

"Why should I take your word? I have an idea. You tell

me the secret first, and then I'll meet the second condition, whatever it is."

The count smiled and shook his head. "No."

"Why not?"

"Because what I am offering you is so much more valuable than what you can offer me. Forgive me, but it must be the way I say or not at all."

I stood staring at him for a long time. "Is it kinky?" I asked him.

He roared with laughter again. "Kinky! I love that word. I knew once a call girl in Paris named Kinky."

"Are you going to hurt me?" I asked.

"No, no, my dear girl." He paused for a beat. "You are going to hurt me."

I couldn't imagine what it was he wanted but I believed that whatever it was, it was less valuable than the information he possessed.

"I have your word?" I said after a time.

He nodded in solemn assent. "You have my word."

I took a deep breath. Slowly and deliberately, I slid the right strap of my dress off my shoulder, then the left. I pulled down the zipper in the back of the dress. The gown fell to the floor with a soft wooshing noise and lay like a white satin puddle around my ankles. Stepping over it, I stood in front of the now mesmerized count, wearing the set of white lace undergarments he had so calculatedly provided. I prayed this would be enough. But he motioned me to continue undressing. I did so with great reluctance and distaste. When I was completely nude, I lowered my head and covered my private parts with my hands as best I could, feeling the cold and abject embarrassment.

The count motioned me to come closer to him and to drop my hands to my side. I did so. Standing very straight like I was about to be shot, I faced him squarely and let the old lecher run his eyes over my naked body.

"Put the shoes back on," he said in a hoarse whisper. "Just the shoes."

I slipped my feet back into the high-heeled shoes, which were soiled from the walk. The count licked his lips and smiled in appreciation.

"Your body is very nice, my dear. You have nothing to be ashamed of," he said at last.

"Please . . . what now?" I said, dying for this ordeal to be over.

He stood up, unzipped his fly, and I jumped back in fear.

"Don't worry. I will not touch you," he said.

I watched in dread as he lowered his trousers down around his knees. He removed his baggy blue boxer shorts, with a tiny crest embroidered on the side. His dress shirt barely covered his limp penis. He turned his back to me and faced the stark inverted cross. Kneeling down on the cold floor, he hunched over the low stone bench, placing his chest on it. Arching his back, he lifted his wilted buttocks high into the air. I was so repelled by the sight I felt physically ill and squeezed my eyes shut.

"Now," I heard him say in a whisper, "spank me, my dear. Spank me as hard as you can."

I was absolutely horrified. I couldn't move.

"Come on," he said. "I am waiting."

Finally, I swallowed hard and gathered up all my courage. I walked over to the kneeling count and timidly raised my hand. I hit him once on the backside very lightly. It was like touching a reptile. Even this brief contact with his flesh made me cringe.

"Harder, my dear," he muttered.

I raised my hand again, took another deep breath, and struck him a second time.

"Harder!" he cried again.

I slapped him again, this time out of anger and humiliation. His sagging old skin rippled under the sharp blow.

"Again!" he cried.

"How many times do you want me to do this?" I said with disgust.

"Until I tell you to stop. Again! Hard!"

I struck him repeatedly, shutting my eyes, trying to block out the terrible image of him and of myself in this monstrous act. The more I hit him, the more humiliated I felt. My humiliation led to anger, which built into a pounding rhythm. The old man responded by emitting little cries of ecstasy after each whack. His hideous buttocks grew redder as I hit him over and over again, with increasing fury. I saw that the count had reached down to his penis, to masturbate as I administered the blows.

Soon the airless chamber felt like an oven, and I began to perspire. My hand was becoming sore. The count whimpered in pain and I prayed he would ask me to stop. But the harder I hit him, the more it excited him. I felt nothing but abject shame.

At last, the old man cried out one last time. He stiffened all over, then went limp. I was about to strike him again when he yelled, "*Basta!* Enough! Enough!" and keeled over onto the bench, breathing hard.

I sank to the ground, exhausted and trembling. The old count rose to his feet slowly and pulled up his undershorts and trousers, and tried to make himself presentable. He went over to my dress, picked it up from the floor, and threw it to me. I put it on immediately.

"You are a brave girl," he said as he watched me. "You must have loved your father very much."

"Yes," I replied, holding back tears. "I did."

"Come," the count said, holding out his hand to me. "We both need a drink."

The count and I sat in the library, nursing our drinks. The count smoked his pipe. I had a cigarette, which made me light-headed.

"Now, that was not so terrible, was it?" he said, puffing away and staring at me through the smoke.

"Yes, it was," I said softly.

He shrugged. "I am sorry you feel that way. Nevertheless, I am very grateful to you. It has been many years since I—"

"Please!" I interrupted him. "Just tell me about the grimoire now."

"Yes, all right, if you insist," he sighed wearily. "You have
earned the privilege."

He leaned back on the couch and made himself comfortable. He took a few sips of wine, relit his pipe and began to speak in an authoritative, professorial tone.

"The Honorius grimoire is valuable for many reasons.
First of all, it is said to contain the true spell for the raising
of the dead. Second of all, it is supposed to be the key to
the lost treasure of the Knights Templar. Historically, these
are the two reasons for which it is famous."

"Yes, I know. Mr. Lovelock explained all that. But it
seems a little farfetched that anyone would be looking for
a thirteenth-century treasure or seriously believing in a
spell for raising the dead."

"Well, as to that," the count said, "Adolf Hitler himself
was obsessed with necromancy and the occult. And the
treasure of the Knights Templar is thought by some to be
as real as King Priam's treasure in Troy—which was discovered within the last century."

"So is that it, then? You're saying my father was murdered for a spell and a goofy treasure?" I said.

The count smiled and shook his head. "No, my
dear. These are not the real reasons the grimoire is so
important."

"Why is it, then?"

"Hermann Goering was the Grand Acquisitor of the
Third Reich. His greed is legendary. He looted paintings
and treasures from every country the Reich took over. This
is well known."

"Yes . . .?"

"In the early days of the war, Goering wanted his own
international intelligence network—independent of Reichs-
führer S.S. Himmler's secret police and Admiral Canaris's
military intelligence. I knew Goering quite well. He looked
like a wild boar, a fat pig of a man, but he was very so-

phisticated, quite amusing, and rather charming, if you can believe it."

"No, I can't believe it," I said.

"No matter. Take my word for it. I was working in the Vatican as a secretary to a corrupt old prelate named Cardinal Delorio, when Goering approached me. He had a rather intriguing idea. The IOR, the Institute for Religious Works at the Vatican—actually a bank—was run by my superior, the dreaded cardinal. Delorio was a very austere man—forbidding and judgmental. Like Robespierre, he preferred to dine on red wine and bread. But more of him later.

"The three of us—Goering, Delorio, and myself—had a meeting in the winter of 1941. Goering confided to us that he did not trust either Himmler or Canaris and that he wished to have his own agents around the world. He told us that he needed the Vatican intelligence network, which of course was vast." The count paused for a reflective puff on his pipe.

I was barely able to contain myself. "Please—go on."

The count waved away a large puff of smoke and continued.

"These are memories I had long forgotten . . . In any case, Goering agreed to pay Delorio with funds he was secretly looting from rich Jews and others in the Reich. It was his habit to confiscate property whenever he felt like it. He was amassing an incredible fortune in this way. He wanted to put it into an account in Switzerland, and he asked Cardinal Delorio if he would set up such an account for him so that he would not come under suspicion by Himmler, Canaris, and especially the Fuhrer—though the chances of that were slim, as Hitler was obsessed by power and could not have cared less about money. Nevertheless, it was a precautionary measure to go through the Vatican."

The count cleared his throat and took a sip of wine. "As Delorio's secretary," he went on, "I was in charge of setting up Goering's secret account. I did it quite cleverly, if I do say so myself, using Swiss intermediaries who could not be traced to Goering or to the Reich. Rather prescient in light of recent events, no? In any case, we agreed that only the three of us would know the code names to access it. But what code names could we use? Anything well known was dangerous, and something too simple might be discovered. One evening, during the course of a rather long and drunken dinner, I had the idea of using the Vatican's copy of the Honorius grimoire as a mnemonic device."

"A mnemonic device, how?"

"In order to get access to a secret Swiss bank account, you must present a name or a number. But one name would have been too easy to discover. So in order to get into Goering's account, we decided on a series of names. In the Honorius grimoire, there is a page of names spoken by the devil—and I took this page as the key to the accounts. And as a precaution, I crossed one name out."

I knew he was telling the truth, which helped to alleviate my lingering feelings of humiliation and disgust. Indeed, the ordeal seemed to recede almost entirely as I realized the importance of what he was telling me.

"Are you saying that whoever presented these names to the bank could tap into Goering's account?"

"Precisely. But the names have to be in sequence, exactly as they appear in the grimoire, minus the one I deleted, of course. Otherwise they are of no value . . . Rather ingenious, no? We believe that the Vatican's copy of the Honorius grimoire is the only one with the inscription from Saint Paul, so it is immediately identifiable. Delorio and I called the operation 'The Devil's Account.' "

" 'The Devil's Account.' How perfect," I said sadly. "So my dear father was murdered for this terrible little book . . . For greed."

"Naturally, you are not amused. But I think it is a rather good joke, no? Who is the real devil? Goering or Satan? You see," he went on, "the book is quite unique. And with my little alteration, it seemed a safe key, as not many people will destroy an old book."

"No—just the Nazis."

The count smiled. "Yes, but they destroy only good books, and for show."

"So why did von Nordhausen have the grimoire?" I asked.

"Because he was sending it to Goering. Goering had convinced Hitler that it was something magical, something to make him immortal. He told Hitler it contained a spell for raising the dead. As I mentioned, Hitler believed deeply in the occult and, besides, he was quite mad at that point. He knew his life was in danger, so of course he was willing to try anything, especially to do with the dark arts. But Goering's real objective in getting the book was, of course, to secure the names for himself. He could not have cared less about the Fuhrer at that point."

"But he never got the book, did he?"

"No."

"So he never collected his money!"

"No, I am happy to say."

"Count Borzamo, how much would you say this account is worth today?"

"With the interest? . . . I should say Goering's fortune is worth well over a billion dollars. Perhaps more."

I exhaled fiercely and considered these things for a long moment. There was a question though.

"I don't understand. Why didn't you and Delorio just keep the money for yourselves? You had the key, after all."

"Because, quite simply, Beatrice, they would have killed us. A man like Delorio had no use for any more money than Goering had agreed to pay him for his services. And I am a terrible coward, as everybody knows. No, no, my dear girl—I did not wish to wake up one dark night with a Gestapo pistol at my head . . . I did, however, think to myself that after the war I would try to locate the grimoire. But then, as you know only too well, it vanished. Until your father received it."

I got up and walked around the room, deep in thought. Suddenly, I became aware that the Count's eyes were following me and I quickly sat down again. I couldn't bear him looking at me and I couldn't bear looking at him. The sight of him on the floor of the chamber was etched in my mind's eye. Everything about him repulsed me, but nothing moreso that what I had done. I was sorely ashamed of my own actions and wondered if they would leave a permanent stain on my psyche. He must have sensed this because he said:

"Do not worry, *cara Beatrice*, the mind has a habit of tucking away unpleasantness. I hardly remember anything about the war. And yet, I saw more terrible things in that short time than a thousand men see in a lifetime."

I wished I could believe him. "There's another thing I don't understand, Count. If only you and Goering and Cardinal Delorio knew about the book—how did all these other people find out? And who are they?"

The count nodded. "A good question, my dear. Before he died in 1948, Delorio spoke of the scheme to another member of the clergy—a man who, like himself, was a member of a secret order: an order that guards the Borzamo Collection; an order that believes in the books of black magic as if they were science manuals; an order that is convinced the world should go back to the fifteenth century and that the Inquisition is still the true law on earth."

"What order is that?"

"It is called Defensores Fidei—Defenders of the Faith."

"Defensores Fidei?" I whispered.

"Do you know of it?"

"Was this man whom Delorio told named Inigo Duarte?" I asked anxiously.

The count's eyes widened in appreciation and he toasted me with his wine. "I am impressed," he said. "So you know of the elusive Duarte, do you?"

"I know he was the founder of Defensores Fidei."

"Indeed he was. I knew him slightly when I worked at

the Vatican. He was a very strange man. He looked like a corpse. He had a greenish cast to his skin and he was emaciated. An unpleasant fellow."

"And have you ever heard of the Duarte Institute?" I asked.

The count shook his head. "No. What is that?"

"It's in upstate New York. They call it an institute for philosophical studies. I think they're connected with Defensores Fidei."

"Philosophical studies. How interesting," the count mused. "This institute . . . Have you ever been there?"

"Yes. They want my father's book collection."

"They do? That is most intriguing. So they are interested in books, are they? Well, well, well, I wonder if the Borzamo Collection could be there."

"I'm certain it is with all you've told me. And you said it was moved to America after the war."

"Yes, that is what I heard," he said nonchalantly. "But I do not keep up on these things anymore."

I knew he was lying.

"You *know* it's there, Count," I said.

"Well, it would make sense if it were there, I suppose."

"Why not admit it? You said you never lied."

He took a puff on his pipe and thought for a moment. "I like you, *cara Beatrice*. It profits me nothing to tell you all this. So let me tell you another thing. You have no idea how pernicious the Defensores Fidei are."

"Pernicious how?"

"They carry what they consider to be a moral banner. And people who are so concerned with the morality of others are far more dangerous than those of us who simply exist and accept the world as it is and has always been."

"Signor Antonelli is their dealer, then," I said, now making the connection. "They're the ones who are interested in the 'oddities,' as he called the grimoire."

"Yes, indeed, Defensores Fidei is extremely interested in black magic. They entertain a truly childlike belief in heaven and hell, and not just as abstractions but as a complete reality—angels and devils, halos and pitchforks, clouds and fires—all that sort of nonsense. It would be amusing if they were not so dangerous."

"Tell me something, Count Borzamo. What do you know about their connection to a book called the *Malleus Maleficarum*?"

He chuckled. "Ah, the *Malleus*, yes. A marvelous piece of malevolence disguised as good. And wonderfully written, I think. Filled with rich language and authoritative source material. What an amusing book it is from this vantage point in time."

"Not so amusing for the people who were tortured or died on its account, I suspect."

"Ah, no. I always think of that book as the climax to a raging fever of morality," he said, gesticulating with his pipe. "Yet it is to be admired as a document, no? So well thought out. Every contingency in witch-hunting accounted for. A really first-rate and scrupulous piece of insanity. I do not think I would have found its authors very amusing, however."

"I think the *Malleus* is connected in some way to Defensores Fidei," I said.

The count let out a gasp of laughter. "Connected?!" he cried. "My dear, the *Malleus Maleficarum* is the bible of Defensores Fidei!"

"What do you mean?"

"I mean it is the code by which they live. The reason they are so interested in books of black magic is that they believe evil truly exists and must be eradicated in an extreme way. The Defensores Fidei believe in witches and the power of witches. The *Malleus* was written to rid the earth of witches, to stamp them out. It is the hammer—literally, 'the hammer of witches.'"

"Do you think the Defensores Fidei are involved in my father's death?"

"From what you have told me, yes, I would say so. You

see the *Malleus* is their bible, but the grimoire is their gold. They will stop at nothing to get the grimoire, for with it they will have the power to make their wretched bible sacred on earth and its word law. What they want is the funds to carry on a war against modern life, which they detest and which they believe is the work of the devil. And make no mistake, they believe it is the devil himself against whom they are fighting. Anyone who knows the *Malleus* should be convinced of that . . ."

"And have you ever heard of a man named Desmond Dougherty?"

The count shook his head. "No. Who is he?"

Again, I couldn't be sure if he was lying.

"He wrote a foreword to the *Malleus*, calling it one of the great works of literature."

"Then I should say without reservation that he is a man of whom you should be extremely careful." The count took a final sip of wine. "My advice to you is this, my dear Beatrice: Find out who is the head of Defensores Fidei—and I suspect he is connected in some way to this Duarte Institute you have spoken of. Find that man, and you will have your father's murderer."

I did not spend the night at the Count's. One of his servants drove me to a little inn. I understood now why Countess Borzamo's room was filled with crucifixes and icons. She was protecting herself against the devils of this world and the next.

Chapter 20

I showered many times and in the little hotel room, and cried myself to sleep. Not only did the shame of my ordeal seem indelible, I was grieving anew for my father and angry at the terrible heritage that had contributed to his death. When I awoke the next morning, exhausted and full of anxiety, I thought about calling Stephen to tell him what the old count had revealed to me. But the sordid price of that information prevented me from phoning him. The more I thought about it, the more I doubted if, indeed, I ever would tell him about the chamber. It was too dark a secret.

However, I did want to see Stephen very badly. When I arrived back in New York, I took a taxi from Kennedy Airport straight to his apartment to surprise him. A groggy-looking Stephen cracked open the door in his jockey shorts. He started in surprise when he saw me.

"Bea! What are you doing here?"

"Oh, Stephen," I said, brushing past him. "I have so much to tell you."

Upon entering the apartment, I saw that he was not alone. A voluptuous young blond woman, clasping a handful of clothes, was making a dash for the bathroom. She slammed the door. Stephen looked at me with a pained expression and said, "Bea, you should have called."

I was literally unable to move. He walked toward me and tried to put his arms around me.

"Don't touch me!" I cried.

He bent down, swiped up a crumpled shirt from the

floor, and started getting dressed. Soon the bathroom door opened and the young woman came out, wearing a halter dress, with a large leather bag thrown over her shoulder. She headed for the door.

"Well, so long," she muttered apologetically as she left.

The door slammed behind her. Stephen and I stood staring at each other.

"Bea, I—I don't know what to say. It just kinda happened . . . I wasn't expecting you."

"Clearly," I said coldly.

We stood in silence for a few more seconds. Then he said, "So, uh, how was your trip?"

His question seemed so ludicrous under the circumstances that I burst out laughing. He stood there, looking at me. I took a few deep breaths to calm down, then walked over to the printer, pulled out the bottom tray, and retrieved the grimoire.

"What are you doing?"

"What does it look like?" I said, sliding the book into my purse. I picked up my bag and headed for the door.

"Where are you going?" he said, alarmed.

"Home."

He grabbed my arm just as I was leaving. "It didn't mean anything," he said.

I shrugged him off. "Maybe not to you."

On the way home in the taxi, my anger curdled into disappointment. Stephen was incapable of being faithful, no matter what he promised or how much he wanted to be. I understood once and for all that he could never be counted on in the way I had hoped. I really was all alone in the world. As I unlocked the front door of the house and smelled the dank interior, I was hit by a sharp pang of sorrow for all the losses of life.

Thumbing through the stack of mail on the hall table, I was stopped by a postcard with El Greco's striking portrait of Cardinal Don Fernando Niño de Guevara, a grim-looking man wearing round black spectacles, seated tensely in a chair, dressed in the scarlet regalia of his office. I knew the painting. It hung in the Metropolitan Museum of Art. I turned over the card and read the message:

"The *Roman de la Rose* is ready to be picked up at your earliest convenience. As ever, Simon Lovelock."

Absently flicking the card against my cheek, I couldn't help thinking what an odd choice that was for a card. I felt instinctively that Lovelock was trying to tell me something. But what? I tucked the card into my pocket, gathered up the rest of the mail in a little bundle, and went upstairs to the library.

Sitting at the desk, I listened to my phone messages. There were several calls including one from Father Morton, again entreating me to make a decision about my father's library; one from Detective Monahan, who said he had "nothing new to report"; and one from Signor Antonelli in Rome, who said he was calling "merely to say hello." A couple of friends had checked in, wondering how I was, and there were a number of calls from real estate brokers, who wanted to see the house.

I sorted through the rest of the mail—bills, a bank statement, catalogues, and condolence letters, which I opened, read, and tossed into a shoebox on my desk. The box was filled nearly to capacity with sympathetic cards and letters about my father's death, all of which I intended to answer by hand in due course. But not now. Now I had to concentrate on finding out who killed him.

I got a letter from one of the tonier real estate firms in the city. It read:

Dear Miss O'Connell:

> *I have a client who wishes to purchase your town house for the asking price of $6,500,000. I have tried*

*to telephone you several times at your home with-
out success. Would you be so kind as to call me at
your earliest possible convenience so we may discuss the matter?*

> *Yours sincerely,*
>
> *Edwin Moore,*
> *President, Edwin Moore Associates*

This was welcome news. Despite the boom in New York
City real estate, I never really expected to get that price.
The house needed a lot of work. I put it aside, thinking
I would call Mr. Moore the following day. I was perusing
other correspondence and bills when the phone rang. It
was Edwin Moore himself. He was very friendly and asked
if I'd received his letter. I told him that I had just finished
reading it, having only hours ago returned from Europe.
Just out of curiosity, I asked him who his client was.

"He prefers to remain anonymous for the moment,"
Moore explained. "He would very much like to see the
house first. What I can tell you is that he's a very well-to-do
old gentleman. And he has a book collection so he's particularly interested in the library. He knew of your father, of
course, and his great reputation as a bookman."

"That's very nice," I said. I'd hoped the house would go
to another bibliophile who would appreciate the wonderful room my father had created for his collection, but
serious book collectors are rare. Moore then offered his
sincere condolences to me, which was kind.

"If I could bring him around to see you and the house,
we can settle this all quickly," Moore said.

"Well, as I told you, I just got back from a trip and I'd like
to get a bit more settled, if I may. I'll call you."

"We could come tomorrow, if that's convenient."

He seemed to be pressing awfully hard and I grew wary. "I'm
very tired, Mr. Moore. May I get back to you a little later?"

"Yes, but please consider our offer firm," he went on. "By

that I mean, may I have your word that you won't take a bid from another agent? My client would never forgive me if I lost him the house."

"I haven't accepted your client's offer yet."

"No, no . . . But, of course, I just don't want you to sell it to anyone else," he said with a little laugh.

"I'll call you tomorrow," I said more firmly.

"Oh, yes. Please do. I'll be waiting."

I hung the phone up with a very uneasy feeling. I couldn't quite put my finger on what was troubling me. He was a real estate broker, after all, who wanted to make a sale. But there was something too hurried about it, too convenient. I was suspicious—perhaps not so much of the agent, but certainly of the client, whom I'd never met. Who was this rich man with a book collection?

I was startled out of my reverie by the phone. I picked it up thinking it was Moore again, and I was ready to be more curt with him. But it was Stephen.

"Bea," he began in that sheepish, little-boy voice of his. "We need to talk."

"No, we don't."

"Look, I know I fucked up. I can't say anything more. I also know you'll never forgive me. But I did want to tell you what I found out about Dougherty. He lives up in Milbern. He's a retired professor with two PhDs"—one in philosophy, one in religious studies. He's written a number of books—hagiographies, mostly. He's a widower. He's a respected member of the community and heavily involved with the Duarte Institute. I couldn't find out anything else."

"Thank you," I said.

"I can still be helpful to you, if you want me to be."

I was in a quandary. I needed Stephen to help me, but I didn't want to go back to that terrible pattern.

"I don't know."

"Did you find out anything more?"

"Yes."

"You gonna tell me?"

"Right now I'm worried about something else. Someone wants to buy the house, and he's bid the asking price, sight unseen. The broker won't tell me his name. But what if this client suspects that Dad hid the grimoire in the house?"

"How much are you asking for the house?"

"Ten million."

"That's a lot of money for a book."

"Not for this book."

"Come on, Bea. What did you find out?"

"I found out why my father died."

"Jesus. Please let me come over. I don't think it's safe for you to be alone."

"I'm fine. They don't know I have it. I don't want to see you."

There was a long pause. Finally, Stephen said, "Bea, I'm so, so sorry."

"I know. Me too."

After I hung up, I took the book out of my purse and stared at it for a long time, thinking how many lives it had cost. Its evil seemed palpable. I was almost afraid to open it and look inside for I knew that the list of names it contained unlocked a terrible treasure, soaked in blood. Very slowly and deliberately, I lifted the cover and turned the pages one by one, feeling vaguely nauseous as I did so. Then on page eighty-one, I suddenly stopped. There it was, the thing I was looking for. I was sure of it. The type changed to Gothic script, and I read the following:

Je suis Lucifer! J'ai beaucoup de noms: Alpha et Omega, Acorib, Bamulahe, Bayemon, Beelzebut, Egym, Imagnon, Madael, Magoa, Meraye, Obu, Ogia, Oriston, Penaton, Perchiram, Phaton, Ramath, Rissasoris, Rubiphaton, Satan, Satiel, Septentrion, Tetragrammaton, Tiros, Tremendum!

There was the line through Tiros. Count Borzamo's deletion. A shiver of excitement went through me. This was it:
The access code to Goering's fortune.

I stared at the names intently, committing them to my
photographic memory. I repeated them aloud. They had an
incantatory power, reinforced by their alphabetical order. I
thought to myself that if I had to destroy the book, then I,
alone, would have the code.

However, just as a precaution and also an exercise, I wrote
the names down on a piece of paper to check them against
my memory. I did well, making only one mistake, which I
corrected. When I wrote the names down, I included Count
Borzamo's crucial deletion so if that piece of paper ever did
fall into the wrong hands, the code would be wrong. Without the deletion, the code was worthless. Then I folded the
sheet of paper and put it in an envelope, which I addressed
to myself. I stamped it, then left the house, and walked to the
corner mailbox. I dropped it in. For the moment, there was
no safer place for this information than the United States
postal service.

I took a little stroll in the fresh air in order to think about
my next move. Finally, I returned to the house. Grimoire
in hand, I was climbing the stairs to my bedroom, reciting
the names in rhythm as I walked when, suddenly, a dark
figure darted out from the shadows on the landing. I was
so startled, I cried out, lost my balance for an instant, and
dropped the grimoire. I was relieved to see that it was Nellie,
who seemed every bit as frightened as I was.

"Jesus, Mary, and Joseph, Miss Beatrice!" the old housekeeper cried. "You nearly scared the living daylights out of
me! I had no idea you were here."

"Oh, thank God it's you, Nellie!" I said with relief.

"And do I have to be asking where you've been for the
past few days?"

I didn't want Nellie or anyone else to know I'd been
abroad, so I said, "With Stephen."

Nellie's eyes fastened on the grimoire, which was lying

on the landing. I quickly picked it up and tucked it under my arm out of sight.

"You could have let me know what you were up to, you wicked girl. I've been worried sick about you. The real estate agents have been calling and calling. Will you be wanting any dinner?"

"No, thanks, Nellie. I'm fine."

"Well, then, I'll be going home now, Miss Beatrice, if it's all the same to you."

As she brushed past me on the steps, she was uncharacteristically furtive. I felt she was nervous about something. "Are you all right?" I asked her.

"Yes, Miss Beatrice," she replied without looking at me.

"You sure?"

"Yes."

"Nellie, did something happen while I was gone?"

"No," she said unconvincingly.

"You didn't let anyone in this house without my permission, did you?"

She shook her head. "No."

"You swear?"

She hesitated. "I don't like to swear to things."

"You did, didn't you? Who?"

"No one."

"You're afraid to swear to me because you're lying. And you think that if you swear on a lie you'll go straight to hell."

She glared at me. "You shouldn't make light of things like that," she said.

"Nellie, do you really believe there's such a thing as hell?"

"I do," she said emphatically. "And you should too. The fires of damnation are eternal."

"Don't worry, Nellie dear. You're safe. I may not be, but you are."

"No one is safe from Satan," Nellie said with fear in her eyes. And I knew, devout Catholic that she was, that she really believed that to her core.

I tried once more to get the truth out of her.

"Nellie, are you absolutely positive you didn't let a soul into this house while I was gone?"

She couldn't look me in the eye, but she denied it again, and I knew she wasn't going to change her story, although I didn't really believe her. I was sure that she'd let in one of the real estate agents, or someone posing as a real estate agent, and that she was embarrassed to tell me about it because I had not given my permission. But even if she had, I doubt she understood the possible significance of what she had done.

"All right, Nellie," I sighed. "Go home. I'll see you tomorrow."

The first thing I did when I got to my bedroom was to hide the grimoire under my mattress. Then I lay down on the bed and closed my eyes. The next thing I knew, the telephone was ringing and it was dark outside. When I looked at the clock, it was past eleven. I'd been asleep for hours. I picked up the phone. It was Stephen.

"Bea," he began in a shaky voice. "I need to see you."

"No," I said firmly. "Anyway, I'm asleep."

"Listen to me, Cap Goldman is dead."

I shot up from my pillow. "*What?* Oh Stephen, I'm so sorry!"

"I'm coming over now, okay?"

"Okay," I relented.

Twenty minutes later Stephen arrived at the house. I let him in. He was ashen-faced.

"What happened?" I asked him.

"Another car accident," he said.

I led him to the living room where I fixed us both stiff drinks.

"How did you find out?"

"His wife called me. She knew he'd been talking to me about this big story he was working on."

"Do you think it really was an accident?"

Stephen shook his head. "No. No, I don't. He left a message on my machine this morning saying he had some interesting information for me. I—I tried to get back to him, but . . ." His voice trailed off.

"You were otherwise engaged."

He hung his head. "I guess."

"I'm sorry about your friend," I said, trying to put my bitter feelings aside.

"Yeah, thanks . . . Me too. He was a very good guy." He took a long swig of his drink. "The woman at the lodge told Marge his car went out of control into a ravine. I just don't believe it."

"No . . . They killed him."

Stephen narrowed his eyes. "Who? Who are you talking about?"

I proceeded to tell Stephen all that I had found out in London and Italy. I told him about the evil old Count Borzamo, omitting the ordeal he had put me through. As Stephen listened, his eyes grew wide with astonishment. He said he had heard of Goering's secret account, and that it was one of the great unsolved mysteries of World War II—like the theft of the Amber Room, or King Priam's treasure from Troy, which was stolen from the Reich at the end of the war and only recently turned up in Russia.

When I'd finished, Stephen looked at me skeptically and said, "So you're telling me this old Count guy just told you about the collection of black magic and the fact that the grimoire is the key to Goering's fortune—just like that? You walk in off the street and he tells you all this? Why?"

"Because he knew I had the book."

"So what? Why did he have to tell you anything about it?"

"He's old, jaded, tired of life, and . . ." I hesitated.

"And?"

"He had his price," I said simply.

Stephen narrowed his eyes. "And what was that? Not money."

"No."

"What?"

"Let's just say it was high."

He glared at me. "You slept with him, didn't you?"

I shook my head. "Not exactly."

"But it was something sexual, right?"

I didn't answer.

Stephen shot up from his chair. "Jesus! What did you do?"

I just looked at him. "If you care so much, how come you sleep with that girl when you claim to love me?"

"That's different!"

"Oh, yeah? We both used our bodies to get something we wanted. In your case it was temporary satisfaction—at least I hope so for your sake," I said sarcastically. "And in my case it was information. We both got what we needed with some unforeseen and rather unfortunate residual effects."

Stephen stepped back, as if he were appraising me differently somehow. "I want to know what he made you do."

"It's not important. I got what I wanted. So did he."

"Why won't you tell me?"

"Because it's not important," I said firmly. "What's important here is that Count Borzamo thinks that the Duarte Institute is a front for Defensores Fidei and that they might have the Vatican's collection of black magic or 'Collection of Opposing Thought' as it's called. Remember that room we saw in the basement there marked Danger—No Admittance? It could be in there. "The *Malleus* is their bible, and the grimoire is their gold." Borzamo's words. They want that grimoire so they can access Goering's secret account in Switzerland and fund their war on witches, or women—as we seem to be interchangeable in their eyes."

"You think they take the *Malleus* seriously? It's five centuries old."

"I think they take it extremely seriously. And God knows, we've seen what fanatics and fanatical doctrines can do today. I'm also beginning to think we should take it more seriously as it seems to have affected Western civilization like a hidden plague."

"Maybe that's what Cap was on to," Stephen said thoughtfully. "Maybe the so-called 'witches' are activists and feminists—the ones from Cap's clippings. After all, these are people who are traditionally in favor of things like gay rights and abortion and women in the priesthood—all of which used to be considered heresy by the Church and in some cases still are. In the old days if you believed or practiced them, you were definitely a witch."

"You know, Stephen, the worst excesses of the Inquisition didn't come in the Middle Ages, but in the Renaissance. It's when things are changing in the world in some cataclysmic way that people become the most frightened and they regress. We're in the middle of a technological Renaissance right now. There are no boundaries anymore. That makes some people very nervous. I think there's a hard-core group that really wants to go back to the Middle Ages, particularly as far as women are concerned because we've always been a traditional target. Like anti-Semitism or racism, mysogyny is the last refuge of the disappointed."

Stephen mulled this over. "Feminists as modern-day witches? Kind of a cliché. And what's the point? Why would they bother with a bunch of innocent women?"

"Witches were innocent women," I pointed out. "They were convenient targets with no power. It's the principle of the thing, don't you see? Defensores Fidei are fanatics. This is their vision. The Virgin Mary is their symbol because she's chaste. Unviolated by lust. Lust is evil. Women inspire lust. Therefore, women are evil. They really believe in the existence of evil and in the evilness of women. Isn't it interesting how so often the people who purport to be fighting evil are the evil themselves?"

"What's happened to these women, do you think?" Stephen asked.

"Well, if the men in Defensores Fidei literally believe in the Inquisition, then . . . Remember what the Inquisition did with witches?" My eyes drifted to the candle on the coffee table.

Stephen, too, was transfixed by the bright little flame.

Chapter 21

The next morning, I was awakened by the telephone. Simon Lovelock sounded anxious and insisted that I meet him at the Metropolitan Museum of Art at eleven o'clock sharp.

"Meet me in front of the portrait on the postcard," he said.

"The El Greco."

"Yes. Don't fail me." He hung up before I could ask him what this was all about.

Alarmed by his urgency, I got up immediately. The first thing I did was to take the grimoire out from under the mattress and wrap it in a book jacket from one of the books in my room. I inserted it back into the bookshelf, confident it wouldn't be noticed among the other volumes.

At eleven o'clock, I stood alone in the museum gallery, staring up at the haunting portrait of the bespectacled Cardinal Guevara when I heard a voice behind me say, "Beatrice . . . ?"

I turned around. It was Simon. He was out of breath and disheveled.

"My God, Simon . . . What's the matter? You look so upset."

"I ran all the way from the subway," he said apologetically, wiping his brow. "I didn't want to be late."

"Simon, please, what's going on? You sounded very anxious on the phone."

He turned to the picture. "Do you know this picture?"

"Yes, but I didn't know that he was called 'The Grand Inquisitor,' " I said, indicating the plaque on the gilt frame.

"His face is a fascinating study, is it not?" Lovelock said, focused on the portrait. "His expression is stern, somber, righteous. Yet his eyes are evasive. He looks down and off to the side, not addressing the viewer at all. He doesn't care about his audience, you see. As an inquisitor, he's a universe and a law unto himself . . . And note how the right hand dangles loosely over the wooden arm of the chair, while the left hand grips the armrest like a claw."

"He looks as if he's very wary of something," I said.

"Oh, he is . . . The devil. To his twisted mind, the devil is all around us, and we must be ever vigilant."

The two of us stood for some moments, transfixed by the painting. Finally, I said, "What is it, Simon? What's the matter? Tell me."

"Wait. First, here," he said, handing me a book wrapped in tissue paper. I unwrapped it. It was the *Roman de la Rose* beautifully restored. "She's all healed," he said.

"Oh, thank you, dear Simon. You have no idea how much this little book means to me."

He seemed to blush with my compliment.

"Come, let's leave the Cardinal," he said.

We strolled into the adjoining gallery, where the work of the seventeenth-century Spanish Baroque artist José de Ribera was on view.

"How deeply violent religion is," Lovelock mused, looking around at Ribera's darkly dramatic paintings of martyred saints.

I was still thinking about the Grand Inquisitor when I suddenly remembered the "G.I." in Cap Goldman's notes.

"Simon, does the 'G.I.' in Cap Goldman's notes by any chance stand for Grand Inquisitor?"

He hesitated, then gave a solemn nod. "Yes," he said softly.

"And the 'Presenters'—what are they?"

"Ribera was very influenced by my favorite painter,

Caravaggio," Lovelock went on, ignoring my question. "Caravaggio was a thief and a murderer. But he was touched by the sublime fire of creative genius. Ironic, is it not, that a man of his low and bestial character should have created some of the greatest religious works ever painted."

"Simon, please . . . Are we dealing with a modern-day inquisition?"

Lovelock stared at me gravely.

"Oh, Beatrice, I fear you're in great danger."

"I know all about the grimoire, Simon. I visited Count Borzamo in Italy."

Lovelock winced. "Yes . . . I know."

"You *know*?" I said loudly, my voice echoing in the gallery. "How do you know?"

"You're being closely watched. That's what I've come to tell you."

"By whom?"

"I'll get to that. What exactly did Count Borzamo tell you?" Lovelock said as we walked around the exhibition.

The news that I was being watched unnerved me. I tried to gather my thoughts as best I could.

"He told me about the Borzamo Collection of books of black magic," I began. "He told me about Defensores Fidei, and he said that if I found out who the head of it was, I would have my father's murderer. And," I whispered, "he told me the secret of the grimoire."

Lovelock stopped dead and pinned me with a penetrating gaze. "How badly did he abase you in exchange for this information?"

I felt my face flush with shame. "What do you mean?"

"I know him. He's a vile man, a man of no morality whatsoever—the product of centuries of corruption and inbreeding. I met him when I worked in the Vatican Library. His taste for flesh of all kinds was legendary. Borzamo is like a disease that infects everyone with which it comes into contact. That's his nature. He does nothing for free.

There's always a price. And for that information, it must have been a terrible price indeed."

"Yes," I said, lowering my eyes. "He's a truly vile man."

"I'm sorry," he said, putting a sympathetic hand on my arm. "You have great courage."

When I looked back up at him, I saw his eyes moist with tears as if he knew what I'd been through.

"Thank you for understanding, Simon."

We continued to walk around the gallery, marveling at the gruesome majesty of Ribera's tortured saints. At length, Lovelock led me back to the first gallery and the portrait of the Grand Inquisitor.

"Dear Simon," I said, as we stood before the painting once more. "Why did you bring me here?"

Simon avoided my gaze as he began to speak slowly, in a measured voice. "I want to tell you a story—the story of a little boy. When this little boy was four years old, his mother abandoned him and his father. She was pregnant at the time. Rather than have the child of her husband, whom she didn't love, she had an abortion and ran off with her lover. For a long time, the father of this little boy tried everything he could to get his wife back, even though she'd hurt him so badly. He was obsessed by her. But she wouldn't have anything to do with him. She moved away, cutting her husband and her little boy out of her life completely." Simon's voice, choked with emotion, trailed off.

"Go on," I gently urged him.

"As the years went by, the boy saw his father turn against all women, but particularly the ones who questioned or flouted the conventions of motherhood and traditional family life. He blamed these women for his wife's infidelity, for her abortion, for her leaving him, for the failure of his marriage. This blame flowered into a deep rage, and he searched for a weapon he could use against them . . . He found the *Malleus Maleficarum*, which confirmed his view that all women are essentially evil, or conduits for evil. The *Malleus* became his bible, his justification, and, ultimately, his blueprint for their destruction. Because the father was rich and brilliant, he was able to find followers who adhered to his warped vision. He had a truly satanic gift for oratory, and he united these sick people in search of a leader."

"And the boy?" I said, holding my breath, for I had now guessed his terrible secret.

"He still loved his father," Simon replied almost inaudibly. "And he either refused to see or could not fathom the extent of his father's madness. But he understood that he had to get away. So when he was of legal age, he assumed his mother's maiden name and became a Jesuit."

"Oh, Simon . . ." I said with great sympathy, for I knew he was talking about himself.

He looked at me with a pleading expression. "He wanted desperately to do good in the world in order to make up for his father's fanatical hatred. Then suddenly, unexpectedly, and even against his will, he fell in love. But that love ended tragically . . . And the little boy—now a disillusioned young man—lost his faith in the Church completely. Leaving his order, he turned to books, which were the only true friends he had ever known. He had only slight contact with his father. Then one day, he met a kind and brave woman, who seemed oddly lonely, just like himself. He found himself falling in love again. And when she unwittingly became involved in his father's nightmarish world, he could no longer close his eyes. He understood once and for all what a sick and depraved old man his father had become."

I stared at Simon. "You're Desmond Dougherty's son, aren't you? You're the son of the Grand Inquisitor."

Simon gave me a solemn nod and said, "They know everything, Beatrice."

"But who are *they*?"

"Defensores Fidei. They are so dangerous you have no idea. And they know you have the grimoire."

"How?" I was astonished. "Did you tell them?"

"No, of course not."

"Who, then? Only you and I and Stephen know I have it."

"And one other person."

"Who?" I was utterly perplexed.

"Your housekeeper."

"Nellie? No!" I gasped. But when I thought about it, I realized it was possible. "Oh my God! That's right. She saw me with it yesterday. I wondered what she was doing upstairs. She must have been searching for it all along."

Lovelock nodded.

"But surely Nellie's not in with them?" I said.

"Who do you think let them in to see your father that day?"

I felt light-headed with horror. But suddenly it all made sense. That's why she was so upset and kept begging my forgiveness. It wasn't about finding him dead, it was about having let them in to kill him.

"But Nellie adored my father. She loves me. She's like a member of our family. She couldn't have . . . She would never have conspired to kill him . . . Would she?"

"I doubt she knew what they were going to do," he said. "You still don't understand what you're up against. Your housekeeper, Detective Monahan, Father Morton, Antonelli—they're all in on it."

"Monahan too?"

"Certainly. Why do you think the investigation came to a halt?"

I felt dizzy and we sat down on one of the wooden benches in the gallery.

"I could protect you up to a point," Lovelock continued. "As long as they thought you didn't have the grimoire, you were safe. But now that they know you have it, and they suspect Borzamo told you of its value, they will stop at nothing to get it."

"They won't get it. I'll destroy it," I said angrily.

"Oh, no! You mustn't do that," Simon said.

"I'll never give it to them. Never! You think I'd willingly give them the key to all those millions? They murdered my father . . . I'll tell the police or the newspapers. There'll be an investigation. I'll go up to the institute and find out what's going on there. I'll get them. I will!"

"You don't know what you're up against. What if you tell the wrong person? Look at Monahan. Would you have suspected him?"

"No," I said thoughtfully.

"And if it's your word against his—a respected detective? Who will people believe? Don't you see? They have tentacles in too many places. You can't know whom to trust. And there's no way to prove anything. They're very crafty and they cover their tracks."

"Can't you help me, Simon? Can't we help each other? If what Borzamo says is true, if the grimoire really is the key to Goering's fortune, they'd be so powerful with it . . . But then, so would we. We could fight them."

Simon was growing agitated, and more intense. "No one can fight them. We're all powerless against them, don't you understand? How can I make you understand that? They believe they're fighting the ultimate war on earth. They're the doctors who are more dangerous than the disease. They believe that anyone who opposes them—anyone who gets in their way—is the enemy and on the side of Satan. They believe in the reality of hell more strongly than you and I believe in the reality of this bench we're sitting on! If you cross them and try to get the money yourself," he said, pointing a finger at me, "they will destroy you!"

I was silent for a long moment as I considered what he said and the vehemence of his conviction. Finally, I said, "What's my alternative?"

"Let them have the grimoire."

I bridled at this and looked at him in utter bewilderment.

"What?! So they can get their hands on the money? Simon, how can you ask me to do that? That would be like rewarding my father's killers . . . No!" I said, shaking my head, "I've got to go to Zurich and try and get the money myself. A billion dollars buys a lot of power, and power is protection. The right people will listen to me if I have enough money, believe me. That's the way of the world. And besides, this money should really be returned to the people from whom it was stolen."

Simon stared down at the wooden floor, engrossed in thought for a long time. He didn't move, but I knew he was thinking hard about what I had said.

Finally, he took a deep breath, turned to me, and said in a measured voice, "Yes, all right. That might just be possible."

For the first time, I actually felt hopeful. "You'll help me then?"

He gave me a single solemn nod. "I will. But we must be very, very careful. There's still time, so here's what you must do: Go back to your house, get the grimoire, and pack a suitcase. Then wait there for my call."

We stood up and faced one another. Gone was the reticent, ineffectual Lovelock I'd known. He seemed imbued with a new strength and conviction.

"I must hurry back to my shop now and make some arrangements. Go and do as I say."

"Just a second." I grabbed his sleeve and looked at him pleadingly. "Simon, do you know who killed my father?"

He didn't answer, but I could see from the torment streaking his face that he did. He hung his head and said at last, "Pity me, Beatrice. I am a soul divided."

He walked away, his footsteps echoing on the wooden floor. I followed him. He paused at the painting of the Grand Inquisitor. He looked at the painting, then back at me in a way that told me the answer to my question.

I understood now that my father's murderer was Desmond Dougherty, the Grand Inquisitor of Defensores Fidei, Simon Lovelock's father.

I went back home, as Simon had instructed me. I rushed upstairs to my bedroom and retrieved the grimoire from the bookshelf. I packed a bag and when I was waiting for Simon to call, I wrote down from memory the list of names from the grimoire. I checked myself against the book. My memory had not failed me. The names of the devil were branded on my mind. As I held the book in my hand, I felt more and more that it was a repository of evil. I could almost feel it move, like it had a life of its own. The more I looked at it, the more I hated it. If it ever did fall into the wrong hands, it could do untold harm. It had cost too many lives already. I made a decision. Against Simon's advice, I decided to destroy it.

I slid the metal wastebasket out from underneath my desk, and got a pack of matches from my nighttable drawer. I struck one. I picked up the grimoire and held it in my left hand, saying aloud theatrically: "Book, I commit you to the fires of hell whence you came!" I put the match to the cover. Flames quickly ignited the ancient pages. I dropped the fiery little monster into the wastebasket and watched it burn.

As I stared at the charred and smoking remains, I suddenly heard voices coming from downstairs. Terrified, I ran out of the bedroom and stood poised on the landing, listening. The voices grew louder. I peered down the staircase to see who it was. I couldn't see anyone, but I judged from the sounds that they were headed toward the library.

Clutching the banister, my heart racing, I crept downstairs and reached the second floor landing just as Nellie ushered two men inside the library. Seeing the old housekeeper, I felt a profound sense of sorrow mingled with anger at this woman who had betrayed me and my father. She glanced up and caught sight of me.

"Oh, Miss Beatrice, there's some gentlemen here to see you."

"Who?" I asked her.

Just then, a dapper, silver-haired man in a three-piece suit appeared at the library door and looked up at me. His face lit up with a smile that looked more like a frown.

"Miss O'Connell, I'm Edwin Moore. We spoke on the telephone. So very nice to meet you."

I walked down the stairs and shook his hand, trying not to show how wary I was of him.

"Mr. Moore," I said with a forced smile. "I wasn't expecting you."

He shook his head apologetically and said, "I know. Please forgive me. I did phone you this morning, but your kind housekeeper here said you were out." He glanced over at Nellie who lowered her eyes.

"I'm afraid I pestered her until she agreed to allow us to come over and take a look at the house without you," he went on in a cheerful voice. "My client just happened to be in town today and . . ." He lowered his voice, adopting a confidential air. "He's an older man, you know, and he must get back to his house in the country this afternoon. He'd very much like to meet you. I wonder, could you spare us a moment of your time?"

"I was just about to go out," I said.

"Oh, please, do come and say a quick hello," Moore implored me. "He's right here."

I had no choice but to follow him and behave as if nothing were wrong.

"What a magnificent house," Moore said as he accompanied me down the hall to the library. "My client liked it the minute he came in . . . And he's most anxious to meet you."

When we entered the library, I saw a tall, imposing figure at the far end of the room, standing sideways in a streak of sunlight with his head bowed, examining a book he had pulled from the shelf. He looked up, peered over his bifocals, and smiled. He had a round, impish face, which presented a striking contrast to his great size. His head was completely bald, and the bumpy configuration of his skull was well articulated. His neck muscles seemed to be straining against the restriction of a too-tight bow tie. His tweed suit was baggy, and he had a dithering, professorial manner.

"Miss O'Connell," Moore said, "May I present Professor Desmond Dougherty."

Though I'd already guessed who he was, icy fear shot

through me at the sound of his name. This was the man who I believed had murdered my father. I was trapped, and I knew it.

"Do forgive us, Miss O'Connell," Dougherty said, shambling across the room, holding up the large volume he was looking at in one hand. "This is a marvelous, simply marvelous, fascinating book. One wonders where on earth your father found it." He spoke with a curiously unplaceable but vaguely mid-Atlantic accent.

"Ah, yes, the Amusco," I said, trying to appear relaxed, although I felt leaden with dread.

"That's it indeed. *Anatomia del corpo humano,* by Juan Valverde de Amusco—a simply glorious, glorious book on anatomy. It's the Italian translation published in Rome in 1560. A great part of the text and the illustrations, of course, were plagiarized—and I do mean stolen with a vengeance—from poor old Vesalius, who loathed Amusco and accused him of being a thief," he said with a snicker. "There's a copy in the Vatican Library, I believe. One hasn't seen it, though."

Dougherty opened the tome and showed me a gruesome illustration of a skinless man with his raw musculature exposed, holding up the dripping hide of his own flesh in one hand and, in the other, the knife he had used to flay himself. I knew my father's small collection of rare anatomical works well. The picture had always revolted me.

"You see here?" Dougherty turned to the front pages. "Amusco dedicated it to his patron and patient, Cardinal Juan Álvarez de Toledo." He paused. "He was a Grand Inquisitor," he said with reverence.

Dougherty made a move to shake hands with me, but I backed off, pretending the large volume was in the way. His eyes narrowed for an instant as if he understood I couldn't bear to touch him.

"One doesn't know quite what to do with this book," he went on lightly, handing it over to Edwin Moore. "There," he said. "Now . . . How'dyoudo?"

Dougherty loomed over me and made another attempt to shake my hand. This time I couldn't avoid him. His hand was very large and I was struck by the strength of his grip.

"El Greco's portrait of Don Fernando Niño de Guevara. Do you know it?" he asked me. I knew then that I had been followed to the museum.

"A very distinguished picture—the sinister cardinal in his scarlet robes, with his elongated hands and his comical round black glasses. It's in the Metropolitan Museum, I believe," he said with a knowing smile.

"Yes," I said. "I believe it is."

"It's a period that greatly interests me—the Inquisition. Alas," Dougherty sighed, "like so many of the things that people do not understand or understand only superficially, it's been much maligned and misrepresented, one fears. In many ways the Inquisition was a force for good. For law and order. It solidified the power of the Church. But all that has been lost due to the excesses of a few zealous men. It's unfortunate."

Moore interjected: "Professor Dougherty, Miss O'Connell wasn't really expecting us, so perhaps we could continue the tour?"

"Oh, yes, certainly. You must forgive one. One has come to see your house, and here one is just chattering on and on like a mynah bird," Dougherty said. "Well, of course, the library's perfect, perfect! As a book collector, it is just what one needs."

My heart pounding, I nodded reflexively.

"Yes, yes," Dougherty went on. "One has a modest collection—the fruit of many years of hard labor. But it doesn't match up to this brilliant, brilliant assemblage here. Your father is a legend, of course. A legend in the trade . . ."

As Dougherty spoke, my fear increased and I could hardly focus on what he was saying. The situation was macabre. Here I was, having a polite, civilized conversation about my father with the man who had murdered him—and in the very room in which the murder had occurred! This, coupled with the fact that Dougherty's own son—traces of whose features I could see in the old man's face—was out to save me from him, gave the drama a further sense of unreality.

"One is struck," Dougherty went on breathlessly, flaring out the fingers of both hands for emphasis, "by the magnitude, the breadth, the scope—the eclecticism, if you will—of the contents. Because, you see, there seems to be no one unifying theme to the collection, and that's rare, very rare."

"My father just bought whatever appealed to him."

"And more power to him, more power to him. Knew what he liked, eh? Can't fault that in a man," Dougherty said with slight disdain. "My own collection lives in Milbern, where I live. We all live together. Quite happily sometimes and not so happily at others. But that's life, isn't it, isn't it?"

"But Professor Dougherty wants to move to New York," Moore said. "Isn't that right, Professor?"

"Oh, yes, I do, indeed I do. The winters upstate are very severe. And I'm getting on. One feels the cold of the grave creeping into one's bones year after year, and that makes the winter months so much less tolerable. One longs for the sun and the warmth of youth."

"I don't think there's much sun and warmth of youth in a New York winter," Moore chimed in.

"No, but it's not quite as dismal as the bleak of the countryside. Nothing is quite as dismal as that."

"Why don't we go upstairs?" Moore said, seeming anxious to inject a note of purpose into the darkening conversation.

I froze, for I knew that they would see the burned grimoire.

"No, no, not just yet," Dougherty said, waving at Moore blithely. "One can just picture oneself on a chilly February afternoon, seated at the desk, a log fire blazing, composing bits of this and that for posterity."

"You're a writer, Professor?" I asked, playing for time until Simon called.

"Oh, well, you know, a dabbler, a dabbler."

"Mr. Dougherty is a renowned scholar," Moore proclaimed.

"What's your field?" I asked.

"Oh, just philosophy and boring religious studies," Dougherty said evasively. "Nothing to write home about. Stodgy stuff."

"What have you written?"

"Terrible, tedious old things. Nothing that young people are interested in nowadays."

"I'm interested," I said.

"Oh, well, hagiography mostly. Lives of the saints, you know. One has written monographs on Saint Augustine, Saint Alban, Saint Francis of Assisi, Saint Catherine, Saint Teresa of Avila, Saint Mark, Saint Paul—and the Virgin Mary, of course, who is the chief saint. That sort of thing."

"What about your book on the Spanish Inquisition, which I found so fascinating?" Moore inquired.

"You wrote a book on the Inquisition?" I asked.

"The Spanish Inquisition, as distinct from the medieval Inquisition," Dougherty said. "The Spaniards were much more thorough, much more bloody. And much less forgiving."

"Forgiving?" I said.

"Well, the usual penance, fine, and imprisonment were generally not enough for the Spaniards. They burned and flayed people left, right, and center . . . Left, right, and center—that's rather a good political joke!" Dougherty guffawed. He glanced around the room again. "One is very impressed, very impressed. It's a fine house. Well maintained. My offer still stands."

"There we have it, Miss O'Connell. If I may take a shortcut here, Professor Dougherty is offering six and a half million dollars—an extremely generous sum."

"I'd like to think about it," I said.

Desmond Dougherty leaned forward. "One wonders, Miss O'Connell, if one might prevail upon you to have a little talk with me—alone," he said pointedly, glancing at Edwin Moore.

"Oh, yes, of course," Moore said. "I'll be downstairs." He walked out of the library, closing the large double doors behind him.

"Well, Miss O'Connell," Dougherty said, "we both know why one has come here, don't we?"

I was suddenly conscious of how physically small I was in comparison to Dougherty, whose presence was like an enormous shadow in the room.

"I'm afraid I don't know what you mean," I said.

"Come, come now. Coyness is attractive only in small doses." Dougherty sat down and spread himself out on the sofa, patting the cushions on either side with his hands. "One has made a generous offer."

"Yes, it's a very generous offer. But I'd like to think about it."

"Six and a half million dollars in cash this afternoon . . . Think about that. Wouldn't that be nice? Hmmm?"

My heart beat wildly as we stared at one another. Dougherty's smile suddenly vanished. He looked almost demonic.

"All right, all right. Let us not beat about the bush any further, Miss O'Connell. One wants the grimoire," Dougherty said in a voice that sounded like a growl.

I swallowed hard, trying my best not to betray any emotion. "I don't know what you're talking about."

"One had hoped to spare you any unnecessary . . . shall we say, inconvenience? But if you persist in keeping it from us, one will have to take measures."

"I can't help you," I said flatly.

He seemed genuinely puzzled, as well as angry. "You realize that by keeping it from us, you become an agent of the devil?"

I let out an inadvertent laugh and blurted, "If there's an agent of the devil here, it's not me!"

He was not amused. "As one has just pointed out, coyness

is attractive only in small doses. You have the grimoire, and it belongs to us, Miss O'Connell. Look at it this way: You would only be giving back stolen property."

"I don't have it."

"One must impress upon you that this is a crusade. We are fighting the forces of evil. You have only to look at modern life to know that the world has slipped into the devil's hands. Satan must be stopped before it's too late."

"No, *you* must be stopped before it's too late," I said, wondering how I was going to make a run for it.

As I started for the door, Dougherty reached out and grabbed my wrist. He was very strong. "One has been very patient," Dougherty said in a monotone, strengthening his grip. "One is now running out of patience."

"Let me go!" I cried, trying to get free.

"The grimoire, Miss O'Connell. Where is it?" His eyes glinted with anger.

I glared at him, feeling that my moment of revenge had come.

"You'll never get it," I said. "Because it no longer exists!"

"What have you done with it?"

At that moment, the library doors burst open. Edwin Moore stood at the entrance, holding the wastebasket. Nellie was behind him, wringing her hands.

"She's burned it!" Moore cried.

Dougherty let go of me and stood still for a long moment as rage gathered like a storm in his large body. Then, slowly and deliberately, he walked over to Moore. I held my breath as he reached down inside the basket and lifted out the burned remains of the book.

Nellie was sobbing softly. "Shut up, woman!" he barked. She fell silent immediately.

Dougherty slapped the cinders off his hands and turned to me, his eyes bulging with a maniacal anger. He was so furious he could hardly speak.

"Witch!" he thundered. "You shall pay for this!"

Pinning me with glistening black eyes, he crossed the

room in mighty strides. I shrank back, cowed by his fury. I darted behind a chair and prepared to defend myself.

"Murderer!" I cried.

With that, Dougherty raised up his enormous right hand. I attempted to duck, but he struck me with the full force of his being, delivering a stunning blow to the side of my skull. A bolt of red lightning flashed before my eyes before everything went black.

Chapter 22

I awoke to the sound of dripping water. I was lying flat on my back on a surface, which was cold and hard, like a slab. My head ached. I tried to lift up my hands but I couldn't. I was chained to something. It was dark and at first I couldn't see anything. Gradually, however, as my eyes became accustomed to the gloom, I saw that I was in a large, dank space—like a cellar. My wrists were locked into manacles attached to two chains linked to thick iron rings embedded in the stone floor. Overhead to my left, I made out a black grille with what looked like a flight of steps behind it and the faint glimmer of daylight. The entrance, I thought. My legs were free and I managed to prop myself up against the rough stone wall behind me.

Where am I? Where am I? I wondered. There was an earthy smell, like that of a root cellar. I thought, perhaps, I was somewhere in the country. The Duarte Institute was the most likely place.

The day wore on. I was hungry and thirsty and I was forced to relieve myself on the stone floor. The shackles restricted my movements so I peed through my pants, recalling with grim humor my comment to the egregious Father Morton during our first meeting: "If women could have peed from the saddle of a horse, the history of the world would have been different."

Hours passed. I tried to sleep, but mostly I just waited, wrapped up tightly in my own fear. As the light through the grille waned, the temperature dropped and I felt very cold. I was shivering and uncomfortable, humiliated that I had soiled myself. Suddenly, I heard footsteps overhead, I trembled with terror. I could hear my teeth chattering.

As the footsteps neared, the chamber became awash with flickering light and shadows. A dark figure entered, carrying a torch. He wore a long black soutane, the front of which was emblazoned with a large white cross. The torchlight illuminated his face. I recognized him as the young man behind the reception desk at the Bungalow of the Duarte Institute, at whom I'd smiled without success. He was followed by two men in similar garb. The three of them worked together efficiently. The torch bearer stood perfectly still, staring straight ahead, while his confederates unlocked my wrist manacles.

One of the men yanked me to my feet. I was weak from hunger and fatigue. Whatever energy I had left stemmed from fear. He tied my hands behind my back and pushed me hard to get me walking. We all climbed up the stone steps to the outside.

We were in the country, as I suspected. The night was cool and clear. Soft sounds of crickets and birds resonated through the woods. I took a deep breath of the fresh air, trying to get the dampness out of my lungs and regain some control of myself. The leader extinguished his torch in a vat of water outside the cellar. It made a bright, hissing sound. He strode toward a sleek black golf cart parked nearby and got in. Though it was twilight, I was able to make out some familiar stonework in the distance—a small bridge and two statues. It was then that I knew for certain that I was somewhere within the verdant grounds of the Duarte Institute.

The young man pulled the golf cart up in front of me and slammed on the brakes.

"Get in!" he commanded.

I was feeble but I managed to climb into the back of the little vehicle. One of the attendants jumped onto the seat next to me, carefully keeping his distance from me. The other man got in beside the driver. As we drove down the road, I thought what a macabre sight we made: three men in medieval garb and a haggard woman with her hands tied, careening down the road in a golf cart.

We turned a corner and there was the library ahead, standing out like a black fortress against the night sky. We pulled up to the front entrance. The driver hopped out of the cart and motioned the attendants to follow suit. One of them grabbed my arm and led me inside, marching me downstairs to the basement. We stopped in front of the black metal door marked DANGER—NO ADMITTANCE.

A small bowl filled with water rested on a pedestal to the left of the door. The young man dipped his hand in the water and blessed himself. Then he hiked up his soutane and took out a circle of keys from the pocket of his trousers. After turning three keys in three separate locks, he untied my hands, swung the door open, and pushed me inside. The door slammed behind me.

I found myself in a vast, cool room with a rough floor and no windows. Harsh fluorescent light illuminated gray slate floor-to-ceiling shelves filled with old books and manuscripts. On the right wall, some shelves had been removed to make room for an enormous television screen and an accompanying DVD player. Above the screen were rows of videotapes and DVDs in black boxes. To the left of the television was a large professional-size copy machine, a huge scanner, and two computers.

Being alone in the room, I walked over to one wall of shelves and began to examine the books, many of which looked fragile and very ancient. The more cumbersome tomes lay stacked on their sides. The smaller volumes were lined up neatly in long rows. On the bottom were mammoth black folders bursting with loose papers that peeked out over the edges.

A large brown book with a pentacle emblazoned in gold on the front it lay on top of the copier. The old binding crackled as I lifted the cover. I leafed through page after page of moons, stars, inverted crosses, and circles containing mystical symbols and occult writing. These were interspersed with Latin, Greek, and Hebrew words, as well as pyramids of upside-down numbers and intricate drawings of planets with intersecting lines.

Another book lay on the table nearby. This book was handwritten on parchment in minuscule Arabic calligraphy. I thumbed through it. Then I examined several books from the shelves. One was very ancient, consisting solely of hieroglyphics. Another was written in Hebrew; still another, in Greek. And several were printed in languages I couldn't identify. Most of them contained mystical signs or graphic artwork, reminiscent of the woodcuts in the grimoire.

Slowly, I began to understand what I was looking at: This was the long-lost Borzamo Collection of black magic!

Presently, the door creaked open and Desmond Dougherty entered the room. He was wearing a black soutane. A large gold cross was suspended from a gold chain on his chest. Illuminated by the fluorescent light, the pallor of his face and skull took on a putrid cast.

"Good evening," he said, smiling.

Feelings of revulsion welled up inside me. I was lightheaded with dread, but I managed to stand my ground, neither moving nor speaking.

"So, Miss O'Connell," he began. "We are sorry your stay with us is not as pleasant as it might have been."

Dougherty walked toward me, absently running his fingers over the spines of the books. I cringed as he neared.

"What do you think of our collection?" he inquired, stopping to admire a particular book. "It's not the whole of it, of course, but a good sampling. Quite impressive, no? Are you not excited by its power? Hmm? Do you not feel what we have here? We have the mind of the enemy right here in front of us. The contents of this room represent centuries of heresy, sorcery, and demonology . . . All Satan's tricks and wiles written down by his minions and scribes—some of them indecipherable as yet. But we are working on that," he said, holding up his index finger as if instructing me. "It is our mission . . . It is God's work," he

said piously. "Tell me, can you feel the evil in this room?
One must bless oneself before one comes in here, lest it
should infect one. The font outside is holy water."

I stood there, mesmerized by his insanity.

"One feels its dread power vibrating all around one,
even now," he went on, glaring at me. "But you feel nothing, do you, Beatrice? This is home to you," he said with a
terrible grin.

"Do you think a good man, a holy man would have
killed my father?" I asked.

"Ah! The black cat has a tongue, does she? As for your
father, he was a brave man. But unfortunately for him, a
remarkably foolish one. One didn't like doing away with a
fellow collector, but he refused to see reason."

"What reason are you talking about except the reason
of your own madness?" I said.

"*Our* madness, you say? No—it is Satan's madness. And
now it has become the world's madness. We are in a holy
war, my dear. Look around you. Surely you understand
that by now."

"I understand that you're the devil, Desmond Dougherty—you and no one else."

He heaved a mock beleaguered sigh. "Ah, if only one had
the devil's power, my dear. One could rid the earth of him
once and for all. Tell me, do you not watch television and
read the newspapers? Do you not see what is going on all
around you? The murder of innocent fetuses. Men proud of
becoming women. Women proud of becoming men. Genetic
engineering, which threatens God's work. Blasphemy, heresy, and pornographic filth all around us, sanctioned, protected, and venerated by the laws of the land! Everything is
topsy-turvy. 'The first shall be last; and the last shall be first.'
That is what the Bible says. We are living among the whited
sepulchres of sin, which indeed appear beautiful outward,
but are within full of dead men's bones! . . . O Jerusalem,
Jerusalem, thou that killest the prophets, and stonest them
which are sent unto thee, how often would I have gathered

thy children together, even as a hen gathereth her chickens under her wings, and ye would not!'"

Dougherty rolled his eyes as he spoke. He looked quite mad. "We are threatened by other religions, on the brink of Armageddon, and there is no hiding place," he continued. Lowering his voice to a hiss, he added, "This is all the work of Satan and his minions. And those of us who see it clearly have no choice but to fight back. We are doing God's work."

"Do you honestly believe that killing innocent people is God's work?" I asked him.

"*Innocent* people, you say? Witches are not innocent, just as Eve was not innocent."

"My father was innocent," I said.

"Your father would not see reason. We are not talking about him. We are talking about witches who are vile, corrupt beings, easily tempted by the devil, just as Eve was. Witches must be eradicated from the face of the Earth. Is Satan so firmly in control of your soul that you cannot even hear the word of God?"

"God? I don't see God here. What do you hope to accomplish by killing women? They're just poor, unfortunate women who happen to believe differently from you about certain issues. What purpose does it serve?"

Dougherty glared at me. "Just as a single microbe can infect an entire body, causing that body to degenerate physically and mentally, so a single witch can infect an entire population, causing that population to degenerate in spirit," he said, pointing at me.

"The Inquisition never underestimated Satan's power in that regard," he went on. "They understood what a wily one Satan is. Inquisitors traveled to little towns all over Europe, rooting out those whom you would call 'poor, unfortunate women,' but whom one would call the infection at its source."

"The Inquisition was disbanded centuries ago."

"Yes!" he said angrily. "And look what has happened to the world in the interim. Satan made great inroads during that dangerous period of inactivity. What you see around you are the fruits of his evil anarchy . . . But we are fighting back. And ultimately the Church will win."

"You don't speak for the Catholic Church, Desmond Dougherty!" I said indignantly. "If the pope ever got wind of what you and your depraved band of misogynists were doing up here at the Duarte Institute, he would excommunicate you all on the spot and have no pity on your souls!"

Dougherty paused, fingering the outer edges of the gold cross around his neck. He seemed lost in thought. Then he sighed and said, "You're right. Unfortunately, the Church has moved steadily away from its true mission on earth. As a result, it is fighting a war within itself. And it is much weakened as a result as you can see from recent times. That does not concern us. We know what the true mission is. The Church doesn't know about us, and they're not going to."

"You're going against God's word on earth, then."

"Ah, the pope, yes . . . Unfortunately, most modern-day popes have been far too moderate in their approach to the war between God and Satan. This is most lamentable, as it is the only war of lasting consequence on earth. Well-intentioned as they may be, these popes have all lost sight of the real enemy with whom they are dealing. They are fighting political battles within their ranks. And when that happens in any war, the real enemy cannot fail to prosper. We think you will agree that a weak, beclouded commander-in-chief can be far worse than no commander-in-chief at all."

"Is that how you think of the spiritual leader of Catholics on earth—as a 'beclouded commander in chief'?"

I found it slightly ironic that I should now be defending the Church I had abandoned.

"Let us just say that the Catholic Church is, at the present time, misguided. Vatican II, that disgraceful conference of libertines, was simply a harbinger of more changes to come. Dangerous changes, in our view. They are far too lenient. And so," he continued, "reluctantly, very reluctantly, we have found it necessary to take matters into our own hands. We are all fighting for the same cause, after all, but in a different way. Let us simply say that we here at the Duarte Institute are devotees of the older methods. Old-world craftsmanship, if you will—which was most durable. It simply means we are more zealous in our approach to eradicating evil."

"Why women? Why take it out on us?"

"Because women, as one has explained and as is pointed out so many times in the scripture and in the writings of other eminent ecclesiastical authorities, are universally recognized to be conduits of the devil. Their lascivious natures and unclean bodies are fertile ground for the seeds of evil. Evil flourishes in them as a crop flourishes in rich soil. The *Malleus Maleficarum* makes that quite clear."

"I believe that you're quite mad," I said.

"On the contrary," he replied matter-of-factly. "One is directed by God in this matter. It is God Himself who directs one in all matters. It is the Almighty Himself who has given one the strength and the vision to vigorously pursue His Enemy on earth."

"God is as far removed from what you're doing as good is from evil."

"Dear, dear Beatrice . . . would that one could bring you out of the darkness and into the light. One has at least spared you for the moment, because one feels that you are hiding something and one is hoping that you, Beatrice, will not prove as stubborn as your father."

How I wanted to kill him at that moment.

"You see those?" he said, indicating the copy machine and scanner. "We make copies of all our books. Scholars come from all over the world to study them so that we may learn more about Satan and his ways. This is the real purpose of the institute. If it were not for the foresight and vision of our founder, Inigo Duarte, the Borzamo Collection might have perished, and we would never know even a fragment of the stratagems and wiles of our enemy. But now, with diligence and patience, those stratagems and wiles are slowly being revealed to us. Our scholars come here to help us decipher his nefarious works . . . And upon reflection, it is one's conviction that you, being the daughter of a collector, would not have destroyed the grimoire without having first made a copy yourself."

"I assure you I didn't make a copy of the grimoire, Mr. Dougherty. I intentionally destroyed it to keep you from getting your hands on it."

"Come, come now," Dougherty coaxed. "You knew of its secret, its great value. Borzamo told you, the old fool. He should have made a copy when he had the chance, particularly as his memory is no good anymore. One cannot believe that you would have burned so important a book without some recourse to its treasure."

"Believe what you like."

"No? Truly? You made no copy? No notations hidden away somewhere? One is convinced to one's fingertips that you are holding it back from us."

"Then you can't kill me, can you?"

"Kill you? Perhaps not . . . But one has other means at one's disposal for getting the truth from witches . . . Here—one has something to show you."

Dougherty walked over to the shelf above the television. Pulling out one of the black boxes and opening it, he extracted a DVD. He slid it into the black slot of the player, picked up a remote control, and pressed a button.

While he worked, I assessed my options. Dougherty was very large, but he was old, and I wondered if there might be some way to strike at him.

The large black screen flickered for a few seconds, before the picture suddenly snapped on. A woman tied to a stake that rose from a pile of logs and kindling was screaming hysterically. I recognized her immediately as Patricia Hall, the Glenn Falls woman who had been kidnapped from the shopping mall—the one Stephen and I went to inquire about.

"Do you mind if one turns off the sound?" Dougherty said. "Screams of witches pollute one's ears."

He pressed the Mute button on the remote control. I

stared at the silent screen. A man in a black soutane, carrying a torch, lit the pile of wood in front of the stake. The flames smoldered at first and then ignited all at once. The woman tried to squirm away as the flames licked at her bare legs. Her ragged clothes soon caught fire, and she writhed in excruciating pain. Her skin seared and blackened. Her hair lit up in bright flames. Her torment was so grotesque, it seemed unreal—a special-effects concoction for some horror film.

I couldn't bear to watch. But Dougherty was transfixed. I studied his bulbous features as he stared sullenly at the screen. The cold concentration in the old man's eyes as he watched this horrific sight was the purest distillation of evil that I could ever have imagined. I thought of Simon, who could not possibly know the extent of his father's depravity.

Dougherty was so engrossed that I saw my chance. Picking up the heavy book on top of the copier, I leveled it at him, slamming it into the back of his neck. The unexpected whack caused the old man to reel. But the book was an imperfect weapon, and I was too weak to deliver an incapacitating blow. Dougherty recovered fast.

"One can see that our negotiations have failed. One's patience has run out. You are the devil's mistress!" he cried, pointing an accusatory finger at me. "And now you shall be punished!"

With that, he opened the door.

"Guards!" he called out.

Two attendants rushed inside the chamber and grabbed hold of me. Dragging me into the night, they threw me back down into my underground prison. This time, they didn't bother to shackle me to the wall. In fact, they gave me water and some bread and cheese, which I quickly devoured I was so hungry. Then they left me all alone in that dark, dank root cellar to contemplate the horrors that awaited me.

Chapter 23

I huddled against the wall for warmth. I couldn't fall asleep. I was much too frightened. My mind raced. My head ached. The chill of the cellar penetrated my bones. Gradually, however, a merciful dreamlike quality descended upon me, making my situation seem more like a nightmare from which I couldn't awake rather than a reality from which I couldn't escape.

To try and steady myself and retain some semblance of sanity, I whispered the list from the grimoire over and over again, trying to comfort myself with the idea that I as long as I had something they wanted, they wouldn't kill me. It was ironic that I was speaking the names of the devil in order to save my life. Murder me and their plan to get the fortune died along with me.

I don't know how much time passed before I saw light in the distance. It grew brighter and soon the men in black soutanes carrying torches descended down the cellar steps. Their faces were masks of indifference as they bound my hands and led me up the stone steps to the outside once more. They shoved me into the cart and drove into the forest along rough earthen paths.

The woods were black and deep and still. A crescent moon, occasionally visible through the trees, hung in a night sky flecked with lead-colored clouds. After what seemed like half a mile or so, I perceived a faint glow in the distance, which grew more intense as we approached. Suddenly emerging from the forest, we reached a clearing, in the middle of which a mighty bonfire blazed toward the night sky.

Twelve men wearing black soutanes with white satin crosses sewn on the front sat side by side one another on a long wooden bench. Behind them were five rows of benches occupied by men in plain black soutanes. Facing the company was a kind of wooden scaffold, lit by oil lamps blazing atop tall iron stands at each of the four corners.

To the right of the scaffold nearby was a giant stake embedded in a hive-shaped pile of logs and kindling, just like the pyre I'd seen in Dougherty's gruesome video. Two guards, wearing black warm-up suits and ski masks, patrolled the grounds with shotguns. Their modern terroristlike garb presented a striking contrast to the macabre medieval atmosphere of the setting.

I stumbled getting off the golf cart, sick with fear at the sight of the pyre. An attendant quickly yanked me up by the hair and shoved me onward.

"Enter the accused!" the torchbearer cried out, over the crackle of burning wood.

The assembled company turned their heads to the right in unison, their faces now fully revealed by the soaring flames. Cold-eyed and tight-lipped, the seated men stared as I was led up to the scaffold.

As I was prodded up the rickety wooden steps, I recognized the men in the first row. Father Morton was there, and Detective Monahan, Phil Burgoyne—the talk-show host, whom I'd seen on television—Edwin Moore, and seated at the far end of the grim line, Signor Antonelli, who watched me impassively, his hands resting on the hawk's-head cane.

Then Desmond Dougherty strode out of the darkness, his huge bald head gleaming like a white orb. As he walked, the large gold cross around his neck swayed from side to side across his black soutane. He was clutching a book.

"Hail to the Grand Inquisitor!" the minion announced.

The men stood up and cried: "Hail to the Grand Inquisitor!"

They reminded me of Nazis heiling Hitler.

They sat down as Dougherty mounted the scaffold. Dougherty placed the book upon a small lectern.

"All rise!" he commanded.

Once again, the men rose from their seats and stood solemnly at attention.

"Do you, Learned Judges, swear by virtue of your oath and in the name of the Lord God Almighty to keep secret all that is about to transpire here in this court?"

"We swear!" the men replied in unison.

"Be seated," Dougherty commanded them. They obeyed.

This formality seemed to me to be something they were all quite familiar with as there was a hurried, almost perfunctory air to the proceeding, as if they'd all done it many times.

Dougherty put on a pair of bifocals. Opening the book with marked reverence, he crossed himself and spoke in a sonorous voice.

"In the words of the right and true *Malleus Maleficarum*, otherwise known as *The Witches' Hammer*, an accurate and fair translation of which is here before us, we now address this august body: 'Whereas we the Grand Inquisitor, do endeavour with all our might and strive with our whole heart to preserve the Christian people entrusted to us in unity and the happiness of the Catholic faith and to keep them far removed from every plague of abominable heresy; Therefore we the aforesaid Judge to whose office it belongs, to the glory and honour of the worshipful name of Jesus Christ and for the exaltation of the Holy Orthodox Faith and for the putting down of the abomination of heresy, especially in all witches in general and each one severally of whatever condition or estate . . .' Do begin this trial. Presenter, make yourself known to this company."

Giuseppe Antonelli stood up from the ranks of the audience. Leaning on his cane to steady himself, he mounted the scaffold with effort and stood directly behind me without having made any eye contact with me whatsoever.

"Make your presentation," Dougherty said.

Antonelli placed his hand on my head. I withered at his touch.

"Stand still!" Dougherty ordered me.

I straightened up, and gritted my teeth as the old man's shaky hand rested on my scalp.

"Your Honor, Learned Men," Antonelli began in a low but clear voice. "I present Beatrice O'Connell to this court."

"In what capacity is she presented?" Dougherty demanded.

"As a defendant, Your Honor."

"Of what crimes is she accused by you?"

"The crimes of heresy and witchcraft."

"Do you yourself accuse her?"

"I myself accuse her."

"You may step down."

Antonelli slowly and carefully descended the steps of the scaffold and returned to his seat. Dougherty now addressed me directly.

"'I conjure you by the bitter tears shed on the Cross by our Savior the Lord Jesus Christ for the salvation of the world, and by the most glorious Virgin Mary, His Mother, and by all the tears which have been shed here in this world by the Saints and Elect of God, from whose eyes He has now wiped away all tears, that if you be innocent you do now shed tears, but if you be guilty that you shall by no means do so. In the name of the Father, and of the Son, and of the Holy Ghost, Amen.'"

I didn't move. I didn't say a word. Dougherty narrowed his eyes. "Bring the Holy Gospel," he ordered.

One of the minions scurried up to the scaffold, carrying a Bible. He handed it to Dougherty who ordered him to untie my hands. The young man obeyed. I rubbed my wrists where the rope had cut into my skin. Dougherty held the Bible in front of my face.

"Beatrice O'Connell," he said in a sonorous voice. "We

put to you the Question. Are you guilty of the following sins: the sin of stealing property from the Right and True Church and of willfully destroying that property though you knew it to be of value to the true Defenders of the Faith?"

I stared at him blankly for I knew that whatever I said would doom me.

"Answer me, Witch."

I remained silent.

"Are you guilty of being a fornicator and an adulteress?"

I continued to stare at him without speaking.

"The sin of using contraception?"

I said nothing, standing my ground as best I could.

"We, Desmond Dougherty, Grand Inquisitor, have, by public report and the information of credible persons, before us one accused of the sin of heresy. What is your name, accused?"

"Beatrice O'Connell," I said softly. I could feel myself trembling and about to cry.

"Beatrice O'Connell, we command you to put your right hand upon the Book of the Holy Gospel, Witch, and swear that you have committed these sins!"

I looked at the book, then back up at Desmond Dougherty and down at the judges, on whose stern faces the firelight danced demonically. Suddenly, there was a loud popping sound. A flurry of sparks flew up from the bonfire.

I don't know what came over me in that moment. But it was as if the grand hopelessness of the situation lit up in front of me. I realized I was going to die and there was nothing I could do about it. These fanatics were not interested in the truth or anything else. They would use trumped up charges as an alibi to kill me. I was terrified but I was also resigned. The image of my dear father's dead body flashed in my mind's eye and I suddenly wanted them all to know what I thought of them and their methods and this terrible tribunal.

I can't say what made me do it, because it was anything

but bravery, but I just, without thinking, raised my head and spit what little spit I had left at Desmond Dougherty.

Dougherty stepped back, startled. The company gasped in unison.

"Burn her now!" one of the men called out.

Isolated cries of "Burn her! Burn her!" swelled into a chanting chorus. Dougherty raised his right hand abruptly to silence the assembly. An even greater seriousness crept over his face.

"Stop!" he cried.

The men immediately fell silent.

"This august and learned body shall do nothing but proceed according to law," he said with civility. "Your name is Beatrice O'Connell, and since you have for many years been infected with heresy, to the great damage of your soul; and because this accusation against you has keenly wounded our hearts: We whose duty it is by reason of the office which we have received to plant the True Faith in the hearts of men and to keep away all heresy from their minds, wishing to be more certainly informed whether there is any truth in the report which has come to our ears, in order that, if it is true, we might provide a healthy and fitting remedy, will now proceed in the best way open to us to question and examine such witnesses as there are and to interrogate you on oath concerning that of which you are accused . . ."

He opened the *Malleus* and read: " 'Note that persons under a sentence of excommunication, associates and accomplices in the crime, notorious evildoers and criminals, or servants giving evidence against their masters, are admitted as witnesses in a case concerning the Faith . . . For it says: So great is the plague of heresy that, in an action involving this crime, even servants are admitted as witnesses against their masters, and any criminal evildoer may give evidence against any person whatsoever . . . And if any through damnable obstinacy stubbornly refuse to take the oath, they shall on that account be considered as heretics.' " He closed the book and removed his glasses.

"Bring forth the witnesses!" he bellowed.

Three figures wearing black hoods over their faces, only their eyes visible, appeared in the distance. I saw that one of them was a woman, wearing a blue flowered dress. Their hands tied behind their backs, they marched toward the scaffold, accompanied by a guard. Standing in the shadows, they awaited Dougherty's orders.

"Bring up the first witness," he said.

The guard escorted the woman up to the scaffold. She was placed next to Dougherty, facing me. The guard removed her hood and I gazed in horror at poor Nellie. Dougherty addressed the old woman, who, though trembling, appeared purposeful.

"Put your left hand on the Gospel and raise your right hand."

"Yes, Your Honor," she said with reverence.

Dougherty held the Bible in front of her. Nellie put her left hand on the book and timidly lifted her right hand.

"Do you swear to tell the truth, the whole truth, and nothing but the truth, so help you God?"

"I swear."

"What is your name?"

"Nellie Riley." The old woman was barely audible.

"Speak up, please," he commanded.

"Nellie Riley," she said, louder.

"Nellie Riley, are you a member of Defensores Fidei?"

"Yes."

"Do you believe in the authority of the Grand Inquisitor?"

"Yes! I affirm your authority, Your Honor," she cried fervently.

"Good, my child." Dougherty smiled. "Are you employed as a housekeeper by the accused?"

She paused. "Yes," she said, her voice cracking.

"And on the fifth day of this month, did you yourself see the accused in possession of a book which you knew to be the rightful property of Defensores Fidei and the True Church?"

"Yes," Nellie replied, avoiding my gaze.

"And did the accused subsequently burn that book in defiance of its rightful owners?"

"Yes," Nellie said.

"Nellie Riley, do you pity the accused?"

"Yes." She lowered her eyes and started to cry.

"Oh, Nellie, I forgive you," I said.

"Silence, witch!" Dougherty turned back to Nellie. "Tell us why you pity the accused?"

Nellie looked at me, her eyes glittering with tears. "Because she has abetted Satan in his war with God on earth and she is, therefore, a heretic and a witch." Contrary to her gaze, Nellie's flat patter sounded rehearsed. I knew she was just as terrified of them as I was.

Obviously pleased, Dougherty said, "You may step down."

Nellie shot me a forlorn glance as an attendant helped her down the rickety steps and led her off into the night.

"Next witness!" Dougherty bellowed.

I cannot describe the horror I felt upon seeing the man who emerged from the shadows. He gripped the banister to steady himself and mounted the steps with a slow arthritic gait. When he finally reached the top, he straightened up and stared at me with a knowing little smile. It was Count Borzamo, wearing a long black soutane with a red satin pentacle sewn on the front, his jaded old eyes as mischievous as ever.

Dougherty exhibited a marked deference toward the old man.

"Please, Sir, if you would be so kind as to state your name to this court."

"I am Count Luigi Massimo d'Este Fortunato di Borzamo, at your service," he said with a slight bow.

"This court begs you to answer some questions regarding the accused you see before you, Beatrice O'Connell. Do you know the accused?"

"We have met, yes," he said with a leer in his voice.

"Please, Sir, describe to this court the encounter that you had with the accused."

In an urbane voice laced with a hint of amusement, the Count described the scene in the cave. The sight of this man who had so abased and humiliated me filled me with fear and revulsion. I stood there, shamed and angry, as he went on to tell the assembled company in mortifying detail exactly how I had used sexual wiles to pry information out of him and get him to reveal the secret of the grimoire. Far from crediting himself as the instigator of all of this, the old Count cast himself as an innocent party who was powerless to remain in control of himself against my supernatural feminine wiles.

"And so you say that the accused performed these unnatural sexual acts upon you in order that you might come under the spell?" Dougherty thundered.

With a stiff little nod, the Count said curtly, "She did."

"Were you able to consummate the sexual act?"

"Alas, no," Borzamo said with a weary shrug.

Dougherty cleared his throat and read aloud from the book:

"Question Nine of the great *Malleus* asks whether witches can with the help of devils really and actually remove the Male Organ, or whether they only do so apparently by some glamour or illusion . . . Answer: 'There is no doubt that certain witches can do marvelous things with regard to male organs . . . through some prestige or glamour. But when it is performed by a witch, it is only a matter of glamour; although it is no illusion in the opinion of the sufferer. For his imagination can really and actually believe that something is not present since by none of his exterior sense, such as sight or touch, can he perceive that it is present.'"

He then turned to the Count and said, "And do you believe that the accused cast a glamour upon you, thus rendering you unable to function?"

The old Count curled his lip slightly and said with a hint of self-mockery, "Well, of course, that was the reason."

According to the *Malleus*, if a woman had sex with a man, she was damned as a witch for being a fornicator. If she didn't have sex with a man, she was damned as a witch for "stealing his member" and thus making him impotent. Whatever I did or didn't do, I was guilty in the eyes of this insane tribunal. It was like one of those old witch trials where the accused were "put to the test." The test was that they were immersed in water for ten minutes. If they died they were innocent. If they lived, they were declared to be witches, and subsequently burned alive.

Then Dougherty asked him the same question he had asked Nellie: "Do you pity the accused?"

"How can I not?"

"Why?"

"Because she has . . . uh . . ." He thought for a moment. "Oh, yes, because she has abetted Satan in his war with God on earth and she is, therefore, a heretic and a witch." Nellie's exact words. He had been coached, but he was rather blasé about the whole thing. "That is correct, no?"

"That is correct," Dougherty said sternly.

The old Count was obviously more amused than involved in these proceedings and his attitude irked Dougherty, but Dougherty could say nothing. It was clear to me from the deferential silence that accompanied the Count's appearance as well as from the admiring faces that gazed up at him as he testified that Borzamo, by the nature of his grand title and his family's ancient connections to this dark secret, occupied a uniquely exalted position in their ranks—greater even than that of the Grand Inquisitor himself.

"Thank you for coming here, Count Borzamo," Dougherty said with grudging reverence.

"I always do my duty," the old man said.

The old Count was then helped down from the scaffold by two attendants and escorted off the premises.

"Next witness!" Dougherty cried.

The hooded man was prodded up the scaffold. He stood

where Nellie and the Count had stood, facing me. When the guard removed the black cloth covering his head, I let out an inadvertant gasp. It was Stephen! His face was swollen and bruised, his upper lip was split, and one of his teeth was missing. His eyes were glazed and unfocused, as if he'd been drugged. The attendant untied his hands. Dougherty swore him in, then began his interrogation.

"State your name," Dougherty said.

Stephen stated his name in a barely audible voice.

"Do you know the accused, Beatrice O'Connell, who stands here before you?"

"Yes," he said weakly.

"Are you married to the accused?"

"Divorced."

"Divorce is not recognized by this court," Dougherty said with a dismissive wave of his hand. "Did you aid and abet the accused in her quest to steal and destroy the Pope Honorius grimoire, which you knew to be the property of the true Church and of Defensores Fidei?"

Stephen squinted at Dougherty in total incomprehension. I could see from his tortured face that he was not only terrified but definitely under the influence of some opiate. His gaze drifted to me and I stared hard at him, trying to communicate without words that he must not answer any question the old man put to him. But it was no use. They had gotten to him and I knew then his responses would be set.

"Yes," he said softly.

"Are you a witch and a heretic?"

"Yes," Stephen said.

"And are you aware of the punishment for such infamy?"

"Yes," Stephen said, his lips beginning to tremble.

"Stephen Carson, I put to you the Question: Are you guilty of being a fornicator and an adulterer?"

"Yes," he said.

"Have you advocated abortion?"

"Yes."

"Do you recognize these crimes as heresy?"

"Yes."

"Are you guilty of witchcraft?"

"Yes."

"Do you now repent?"

"Yes," he said, the tears streaming down his face.

"Put your right hand upon the Book of the Holy Gospel."

Stephen raised his hand with great effort and laid it on the Bible one of the attendants held out for him.

"Do you, Stephen Carson, standing your trial in person before these Lords and before the Grand Inquisitor, having touched with your hands the Holy Gospel placed before you, abjure, detest, renounce, and revoke every heresy which rears itself up against the Holy and Apostolic Church, of whatever sect or error it be?"

"I do," Stephen said, his hand trembling on the book.

"And do you also swear and promise that you will never hereafter do or say or cause to be done such crimes as you have already committed for which you are justly defamed as having committed them and of which you are held suspected?"

"I swear."

"And do you also swear that you will perform to the best of your strength whatever penance the august body imposes upon you, nor omit any part of it, so help you God and this Holy Gospel?"

"I swear."

"On your knees!" Dougherty commanded him.

Stephen sank to his knees, cowering before the old man.

Dougherty snorted his approval, then adjusted his bifocals and again read impassively:

"According to the good and great *Malleus*, 'Just as a heretic may give evidence against a heretic, so may a witch against a witch . . . We, Desmond Dougherty, Grand Inquisitor, have, by his own admission, before us one accused of the sins of witchcraft and of heresy. . . Stephen Carson, since you had for many years been infected with that heresy to the great damage of your soul, and since we wish to bring your case to a suitable conclusion and to have a clear understanding of your past state of mind, whether you were walking in the darkness or in the light, and whether or not you had fallen into the sin of heresy. Having conducted the whole process, we summoned together in council before us learned men of the theological faculty and men skilled in both the Canon and the Civil Law, knowing that, according to canonical institution, the judgment is sound which is confirmed by the opinion of many; and having on all details consulted the opinion of said learned men, and having diligently and carefully examined all the circumstances of the process: We find that you are by your own confession, made on oath before us in the court, convicted of many of the sins of witches."

Dougherty lifted up his arms to either side and said to the seated congregation, "All rise!"

The men stood up in unison.

"Learned Men, you see before you the accused, Stephen Carson. You see that he weeps and abjures his sins. Now you must decide, does he shed false tears, a common ruse of the incorrigible witch? And, by the shedding of false tears, does he remain unrepentant in his soul despite his appearance to the contrary? Is he a witch? How say you, Learned Men—yea or nay?"

I held my breath, watching the firelight flicker on the stern faces of the judges. I knew what they would say.

Then the men rumbled in unison: "Yea!"

"So be it!" Dougherty proclaimed. "Stephen Carson, I do hereby sentence you to the extreme penalty.

As the audience murmured its approval, I knew I was in a world of total insanity. The *Malleus Maleficarum*, that dismissed relic of the past, gave weight and purpose to this abominable court.

Two attendants mounted the scaffold and led Stephen

down the steps. I watched as they dragged him to the un-
lit pyre. They were going to burn him. They were really going to burn him!

"Wait!" I cried. "I'll tell you everything! But you must
promise to let him go!"

Dougherty held up his hand. The two attendants
stopped dead in their tracks. The flicker of a smile crossed
his thin pale lips, for he knew his plan had worked.

"We put to you the Question: Where is the copy?"

"You swear to let us go?"

"I swear."

"No! Put your hand on that Bible and swear."

Dougherty did as he was told. "I swear on the Bible. You
have my word as a Christian that if you tell me what I wish
to know, you will both be spared."

"You'll let us go?"

"Our hand on the Bible, as you see: We will let you go
if you tell us the truth. It must be the truth, mind you," he
said, pointing his index finger at me in an accusatory way.
"Because if we find out that it is not the truth . . . ?" He
hardly needed to finish that thought.

I didn't really believe him. But I had no choice. I had to
buy time. I thought of lying to him. But he would soon find
that out and then Stephen would surely die. So I braced
myself and said, "I wrote down the code and mailed it to
myself in a billing envelope."

Dougherty's eyes flashed with triumph. "When?"

"The day you came to my house—whenever that was. I
don't know anymore."

Dougherty nodded his head up and down with a pious
look on his face. "Good, good . . . I believe you are telling
me the truth. You have done well, Witch. And you shall be
spared until we verify your account."

With that, he motioned to the two attendants, who
continued marching Stephen to the pyre. As they tied him
to the stake, I screamed, *"No! What are you doing? No! You
swore! You promised! What are you doing?"*

Dougherty regarded me with cold condescension. "We do not make pacts with witches," he said. "And if you have lied to us about the copy, then we promise that you will suffer as slow and painful an end as any ever devised by your master, the Lord of Hell."

With that, he turned to the attendant holding a torch and cried, "Light the pyre!"

The attendant obeyed. Walking to the stake, he stabbed the kindling in several places until the dry wood crackled with flames. Wisps of smoke swirled heavenward in the gentle breeze. The crescent moon cut like a sickle into the black sky. I shut my eyes against the hideous sight, but I could not shut my ears against the sound of Stephen's agonized cries.

Chapter 24

Once again, they threw me back down into the underground prison. I remember lying there, trembling, cold, staring into the darkness in a complete state of shock. I don't know how or when but I must have fallen asleep because I suddenly awoke, sensing a presence around me. Startled, I looked up and saw a shadowy figure standing over me, eerily illuminated by the first rays of dawn filtering through the grate into the cell.

I was too frightened to move. Gradually, my eyes focused and I saw that the figure was a man in a black cowl with a large hood obscuring his face. I thought it was one of the guards come to take me away. Before I could utter a sound, the man dropped to his knees and clapped his hand over my mouth.

"SHHHH! It's me, Simon," he whispered, pulling back the hood. "Thank God you're safe."

The sight of Simon's kind, concerned face unleashed in me a torrent of emotion. I couldn't help myself. I buried my head in his chest and sobbed uncontrollably until he gently pried me away.

"We have no time to lose," he said, his voice laced with anxiety. "We've got to get you out of here."

He helped me to my feet. I was feeble, but hope gave me a shot of adrenaline and I was able to steady myself. He pulled out a bundle from under his cloak and shook it out. It was a black soutane.

"Here, put this on," he said, helping me pull the habit over my head.

When I was dressed, I stood facing him. "They killed Stephen," I said. "Burned him."

Simon winced. "I know. He's not the first."

"It's just like the Inquisition," I said.

"Yes."

With that, he draped his cloak around me and pulled the hood over my head to obscure my face.

"Follow me," he ordered.

I trailed closely behind Simon as he climbed the steps. Just before he lifted the grate leading to the outside, he turned to me and said, "Are you strong enough to make a run for it if we have to?"

"I don't know. Hope so."

"Pray."

We stepped up to the outside into a chilly, lemon-colored dawn.

"Now listen to me closely," Simon began. "Fold your hands in front of you and keep your head down. We'll walk together side by side along the path. Whatever you do, don't make a sound, and don't run. I'm going to try to walk us into the woods. No matter what happens, don't stop for anything. Just keep going. Promise me?"

I swallowed hard, my mouth dry in fearful anticipation.

"I promise."

We walked on in silence through the tranquil grounds, whose idyllic beauty, heightened by the soft warbling of birds and the mild rustling of the trees, belied the terrible secret of the place. I kept my eyes firmly on the dewy path in front of me. My heart beat wildly.

In moments that seemed like hours, we reached a large clearing, beyond which were dense woods. Hazy rays of early-morning sunshine filtered through the trees. We veered off the path onto the rough, grassy terrain, studded with rocks. We finally reached the woods and started walking faster and faster. Soon, we were trotting along at a clip. I did my best to keep up with Simon, who constantly looked behind to see how I was doing. I was growing weak and winded as we navigated our way through the tall pine trees. I slowed down to catch my breath. Simon doubled back and grabbed my hand, pulling me forward.

"Keep going!" he urged me. "Don't stop!"

Simon dragged me through the woods until we came to barbed-wire fencing.

"Wait here," he said, letting go of my hand.

I sank to the ground, exhausted, as Simon walked up and down the fencing searching for the opening in the barbed wire. He had gone quite far away, almost out of my sight, when I suddenly saw two men in black, with rifles, stalking through the trees. I quickly ducked out of sight, burrowing under a clump of bushes, where I stayed hidden.

The next thing I knew I heard shouting, then raised voices. I crawled through the underbrush and peered through the branches to try and see what was happening. I caught sight of the two men. One of them was tying Simon's hands behind his back. The other was poking at the underbrush, undoubtedly looking for me.

The first man marched Simon back toward the compound. The other man continued to hunt for me in the surrounding woods. I held my breath and lay very still under the bushes. He came within feet of me; so close I could hear him breathing. Then, abruptly, he uttered an exasperated cry and moved away, following the others.

When I was sure he was gone, I scrambled out of the bushes and started running for the place where they had captured Simon. I found the opening in the fence where the barbed wire had been snipped.

Throwing aside my cape and lifting up the soutane, I managed to climb through the jagged opening. When I stood up on the other side, my legs were scratched, but I was free! Free and infused with a new burst of energy. My one thought was of Simon and of what they would to him for having helped me escape. I ran straight ahead until I reached the road where I heard a car behind me. As I turned to flag it down and it slowed, I suddenly imagined, for one terrible moment, that it was someone from the Duarte Institute come to capture me again. But it wasn't. It was a middle-aged woman in a big old station wagon. She rolled down her window.

"You okay?" she asked.

"Could you take me to the police station, please?"

"You poor child. Get in!"

I got into the car. The woman, who was dressed in riding clothes, gunned the motor and we sped off.

"What happened, dear? Are you all right?"

I didn't want to engage her, so I said simply, "I just need to see a policeman."

I'm sure she suspected the worst because she kept giving me sympathetic glances. But whatever awful things she suspected, they weren't a patch on what had actually occurred.

Forrest Whiting, chief of the Milbern police, sat behind his desk, jotting down notes on a legal pad, as I recounted my nightmare journey through the Duarte Institute and the hellish event I'd witnessed there. Clearly skeptical of my grisly, improbable-sounding tale, he and two younger police officers flashed each other incredulous looks as I spoke. I struggled to maintain my composure, yet convey to them the sense of urgency I felt for Simon's safety.

"I didn't know whether to come here or not," I said in conclusion and almost at my wit's end. "I don't even know whether you might be part of it. But because Simon Lovelock is in such danger, I had to take the chance. Please help me."

Whiting, a fatherly man with an amiable expression, raised his eyebrows, leaned forward, and looked at me with what I can only describe as perplexed pity.

"When you say I might be part of it . . . ? Part of what exactly?"

"That's what I'm trying to tell you. It's a vast conspiracy

of powerful men. An Inquisition . . . A modern-day inquisition. Believe me, I know how crazy it sounds. But other things have sounded crazy and just look at the world today. I swear to you it's true. You can't believe the men who are involved in this thing. Powerful, important men!"

"Like who?" he asked in a skeptical tone of voice.

"There's Father Morton, Phil Burgoyne—"

"Phil Burgoyne?" he interrupted. "The talk-show guy on TV?"

"Yes! I know it sounds mad. But they're all part of it. They're all torturers and murderers! And they burned Stephen alive right in front of me . . ." I said, breaking down into tears.

One of the officers handed me a tissue. Whiting waited until I had calmed down.

"And you say Desmond Dougherty is the head of this inquisition? The, uh—what'd you call him?"

"The Grand Inquisitor."

"Right, the Grand Inquisitor," he said mockingly, making a note on the legal pad. He glanced up at one of the officers and said, "Deak, how do you spell 'inquisitor'?"

The officer let out a slight guffaw.

"Never mind," Whiting said.

Finishing his notations, the chief sighed, leaned back in his chair, and toyed with the pencil, rolling it between his thumb and index finger. He stared at me as though trying to size me up.

"Well, now, Miss O'Connell, that's quite some story," he began slowly. "And I feel obliged to tell you that I know Professor Dougherty personally. Not well, of course. But he's lived up here for many years. He's a real solid citizen, the Prof is. Very well thought of by folks around here. I know he's a bigwig in the institute and he does a lot of work there."

Whiting paused, absently stroking his cheek with the pencil eraser.

"What you have to understand," he continued, "is that

the Duarte Institute is kind of a feather in our caps, so to speak. People come from all over the world to visit it and study there. Scholars, you know, and other important people. There's a lot of prestige attached to it. And they do a good deal of business in the town here. They're a nice bunch of people. Pay their taxes and their bills on time, keep to themselves. Always friendly when you meet 'em . . . We've never had any complaints."

"I don't care what they appear to be!" I interrupted him. "I'm telling you what they *are*! They're murderers, fanatics! They burn innocent men and women. If you dig up those grounds, God knows what you'll find . . . You'll find Stephen . . ." I said, unable to hold back fresh tears.

Whiting motioned to one of the officers to bring me some water. The officer filled a paper cup from the water cooler in the corner and handed it to me. I drank it down and thanked him.

"I'm sorry," I said. "We don't have much time. I told you my friend Simon is there. And there's no telling what they'll do to him if they know he helped me escape. Please . . . We've got to go there now while there's still time. I beg you."

Whiting tossed his pencil on the desk and threw up his hands in a gesture of resignation. "Okay," he sighed. "I'll take you on over there . . . Deacon, order us a car."

The police car turned into the entrance to the Duarte Institute and headed up the winding trail. I sat in back next to Chief Whiting. The two officers sat up front. As we reached the white gravel road leading to the high wooden fence surrounding the property, I felt a rush of fear the like of which I had never known. As we drove, I recalled the last time I'd seen that gate and the sprawling farm beyond. I'd been with Stephen. I closed my eyes and took a few deep breaths to calm down.

The gate clicked open, and we drove on through, cruising slowly past the imposing nineteenth-century barn with its gleaming copper roof and rooster weather vane, past the bucolic pastures and grazing animals, into the wooded grounds on the road leading to the Bungalow.

"You know, I'd forgotten . . . this is some spread they have here," Chief Whiting remarked admiringly, staring out the window. "Over three thousand acres . . . Oh, to be a rich man," he added wistfully.

"Hey, get a load of that little guy in the bushes," one of the officers said, pointing to the stone statue of Pan peeking out of the trees.

Finally, we pulled into the circular driveway and stopped in front of the limestone Bungalow. The officer driving the car got out and stretched. Deacon, the other officer, opened my door and helped me out. I was so shaky I could hardly stand. Hunger, shock, and exhaustion were taking their toll.

As Whiting and I climbed the steps, the double doors to the entrance swung open and Father Morton appeared, looking fresh-faced and alert. The sight of the portly cleric so repelled and terrified me that I reeled slightly. Whiting had to steady me.

"Dear Miss O'Connell," Morton cried with an unctuous smile. "How lovely to see you, my dear!"

He extended his hands toward me, but I stepped back.

"Keep away from me!" I said. "Where's Simon Lovelock?"

Morton then looked at Chief Whiting in apparent bewilderment.

"I, uh, don't quite understand, Officer. What is all this about?"

"Good day to you, sir, I'm Forrest Whiting, chief of the Milbern police."

"Father Morton. I'm pleased to meet you, Chief Whiting," he said shaking hands.

Whiting cleared his throat. "We need to come in and talk to you, if we can."

"Yes, yes, of course. Please do come in," Morton said

solicitously. "Anything we can do to help the police. Beatrice, my dear, you look unwell. May we get you some water?"

I didn't reply. I couldn't bear to look at him. I just marched on, staying close to Chief Whiting as Morton led us into the building, then on through the large entrance hall to the pristine white dining room where Stephen and I had lunched with him during our visit. Morton planted himself in a wooden armchair at the head of the refectory table and motioned the others to be seated on the benches. Folding his hands on the table and leaning in with a look of great concern, he addressed the chief of police.

"Now," Morton said, "what exactly is going on here?"

"Well, that's kinda what we want to ask you," Chief Whiting replied.

As Whiting repeated a short version of my story, Father Morton's face gathered a theatrical look of astonishment. When the chief had finished, Father Morton rested his elbows on the table, propped up his chin with the tips of his fingers, and considered for a long moment.

"I'm afraid I really am at a loss for words," he said then pinned me with a hard gaze. "Beatrice, my dear, is this your idea of a joke?"

"You know what I saw last night. You and Dougherty . . . You're all murderers. Where is Simon Lovelock?"

Morton shook his head from side to side with wide, disbelieving eyes, which he occasionally cast at Chief Whiting.

"I really don't know what to say. What on God's earth has led you to dream up these terrible, terrible accusations, Beatrice? I can't even begin to fathom it. You have a very macabre imagination, my dear."

"Where's Desmond Dougherty?" I asked him.

"I have no idea where Professor Dougherty is at the present time. In his own house, I would suppose. He doesn't live at the institute, you know."

"What about Signor Antonelli and Phil Burgoyne?" I said.

"Phil Burgoyne? The talk-show host? I'm afraid I don't know him. And I don't know that I'd care to. His views are a bit too conservative for my tastes."

I turned helplessly to Chief Whiting. "He's lying. Can't you see he's lying?"

Morton, too, addressed the chief. "Honestly, I'm very fond of this young woman. But I have absolutely no idea how to react to this . . ." He paused for effect. "This insanity," he said. "The child is obviously distraught and, though I'm loath to say it, a bit deranged."

Whiting was clearly at a loss and I understood exactly why. I knew full well how implausible my story sounded, particularly weighed against Morton's measured and clever rebuttal. Who would take my word against the word of such an eminent man?

"Well, listen, Father," Whiting said. "Would you mind if we had a look around? We don't have a search warrant, but, uh—"

"The Milbern Police don't need a search warrant to look around this property, Chief Whiting. We have nothing to hide. Look anywhere you wish. The grounds and the buildings are all open to you. I'll accompany you myself, take you anywhere you wish to go."

I knew the moment he made this offer that they had swept their path clean and that Simon was probably no longer there. We walked through all the buildings. Then Father Morton summoned the miniature golf carts and took us around the property. But I knew it was meaningless.

None of the open fields he led us to contained the slightest evidence of the grisly ceremony. They had covered their crime well. I kept on the lookout for the root cellar, thinking they might hold Simon a captive there where they had held me. But the grounds were far too extensive and twisty and I could make no differentiations in the myriad paths of the verdant landscape.

Father Morton was overly solicitous with Chief Whiting and infuriatingly smug with me. Whenever he knew we were unobserved, he narrowed his eyes and flashed me a threatening stare. I confess I was terrified.

After a couple of hours, everyone was exhausted. Father Morton offered us lunch and Whiting gratefully accepted. I hated to eat their food but I knew I had to keep up my strength. At one point, I feared they might try to poison me so I asked to switch plates with Chief Whiting. This elicited an incredulous look on Whiting's part and he glanced at Father Morton, who gave him a sad smile, as if to say, "Pity the poor child." But I knew he understood how perfectly I was playing into his hands.

When we'd finished the meal, Father Morton pushed back from the table and said, "Now, my dear Beatrice, I know only too well how the death of your father has grieved you."

Whiting perked up. "Your father died recently?"

"My father was murdered . . . By *them*!" I said, pointing an accusatory finger at Morton.

Morton shook his head over and over. "There, there, my child. Grief does such strange things to people. This is all nothing more than a delusion—a hideous dream of yours. You must look to God and have faith that He will help you in this most terrible hour of need."

The sight of Morton's bulky frame and simpering countenance filled me with revulsion. "Where is Simon Lovelock?" I demanded.

"I'm afraid I don't know this person to whom you refer. Who is this man?"

"He is Desmond Dougherty's son. And you have him."

"Well, if you say so, my dear," Morton said. Then he turned to Whiting in an aside that I overheard. "Professor Dougherty has no children. I fear she is confused. I think the best course of action would be to get her to a clinic."

Whiting nodded. I knew he wasn't one of them, but he certainly didn't believe me—not against the pastor of St. Xavier's Church. The situation was hopeless.

Outside, I was herded back into the squad car while Whiting and Morton conferred together in hushed tones on the steps of the Bungalow. I could just imagine the sympathetic offers of assistance Morton was proffering on my behalf under the guise of great concern. The two men kept glancing over in my direction. It was painfully clear Whiting believed Morton and thought I was deranged. I had to change my tactics because now I was afraid he might try and lock me up.

"Don't hesitate to call upon me if there's anything I can do," Morton said as the two men parted. "I'm very fond of the dear child, and she's been through a great ordeal. I believe she and her father were extremely close." They shook hands.

Whiting got into the car and slammed the door.

"Okay, Deak, let's get outta here," he said with an aggravated sigh. He turned to me. "You satisfied?"

"I guess I have to be," I said disconsolately.

"Listen, I know you don't believe it, but that guy is on your side, honey. He really is."

"You think so?"

"I sure as heck do. He just now told me about your dad and the terrible thing that happened to him. He said there was no telling how it had affected you—how a trauma like that would affect anyone . . . Listen, I have a daughter myself, and if something like that happened to me, she'd go bananas."

I swallowed hard, ever mindful of my new goal.

"Maybe you're right. Maybe I dreamed it."

We drove in silence for a few minutes.

"There's just one thing, though," Whiting said after a time. "How did you get up here? You have a car?"

"No. I—uh—I don't know how I got here. Maybe I took the bus."

"'Cause I got a daughter just around your age and if anything happened to her . . . Hell, I'm gonna take you to the hospital and have 'em check you over."

"Oh, no! No, I'm fine, I really am. I just need to go home."

"Do you have someone there to look after you?"

I assured him I had friends and I would be all right. He looked at me with great concern.

"Look, Sweetheart, you can't go around making crazy accusations against people. Particularly not distinguished and important people. Now, we'll go the hospital and get you checked out. Then you can go home."

Chief Whiting ordered Deacon to take us to the Milbern Clinic, where I was examined by an attending physician. He treated the cuts on my legs and gave me a shot. I freshened up. They let me go.

The story of how I'd lost my father obviously touched Whiting deeply and he took pity on me. They didn't charge me at the clinic and Whiting loaned me the money for a bus ticket back to New York out of his own pocket. He even gave me twenty dollars extra, all of which I promised to return. He and Officer Deacon drove me to the bus station.

"We all go through rough times in this life," he said, pressing the ticket and the money into my hand. "You've had more than your share, what with your dad and all. But you have to understand, Sweetheart, we live in a world where folks can get into a heck of lot of trouble if people start slinging mud at them. It's a darn dangerous thing to do, and I hope you've learned your lesson."

"Thank you. I have."

His expression mellowed. "Go home now. Get some rest. You'll feel better with a good night's sleep."

"You want to know the thing that shocks me most in today's world?" I asked him as I boarded the bus.

"What's that?"

"Kindness . . . You're a very kind man, Chief Whiting."

The compliment seemed to both touch and embarrass him.

"Don't you get yourself into any more trouble, Miss O'Connell," he said gruffly, pointing a finger at me. "Next time, people may not be so understanding."

Chapter 25

I sat alone near the back of the half-empty Greyhound bus as it sped south down the Taconic Parkway toward Manhattan. I was utterly drained and at a loss. I couldn't go home. They'd be waiting for me there, and waiting for the letter. I couldn't go to Stephen's because they'd surely be watching his apartment as well. And my recent experience with the police had taught me the futility of going to the authorities. Besides, Detective Monahan was a key conspirator. God help me if I ever crossed his path again.

I briefly thought about going to the FBI. But there again, how likely would they be to take my puny word against so eminent a group as the board of directors of the Duarte Institute? And even if I somehow miraculously succeeded in convincing them to at least look into Stephen's case, they would require time. Time was one thing I didn't have. I was convinced that Simon's life was at stake, as well as my own.

Finally, I was so overcome by profound fatigue that I could no longer think. Lulled by the hum of the engine and the steady motion of the bus, I leaned back, closed my eyes, and instantly fell asleep. I awoke to a dusky Manhattan skyline looming in the distance. As the bus crawled its way through the outskirts of the city, I stared out the window, once again trying to formulate a plan.

Simon was now paramount in my mind. Was he still alive? And if so, where had they taken him? How could I get to him? I knew I had no chance of saving him all by myself. The members of Defensores Fidei were far too ~~powerful~~ ful, and there were too many of them in ~~his~~

places. I figured that my best bet was to try and get to Zurich as quickly as possible—before they did. Goering's vast
fortune would give me the means to hire protection while
I launched my own investigation. Yes, that was it! I had to
get to Zurich. But I couldn't go home to retrieve my passport because they would be watching.

In the midst of these ruminations, I was suddenly aware
that one of the passengers—a thin young man in a black
suit with pale, pockmarked skin—was staring at me. The
moment we made eye contact, he quickly turned away
and faced front. A little arrow of fear pierced my heart. I
was sure that he was following me.

Now I had to figure out where I was going to go when I
got off that bus. I couldn't risk putting any of my friends in
jeopardy. Plus, they might think I was crazy, unhinged by
my father's death.

Then it hit me. There was one person in the world who
might believe me simply by instinct—a person who lived
outside the law herself: Sister Marleu, the old Santería *madrina*. Who better than a witch to help a witch? I thought
with a grim chuckle.

By the time the bus pulled into the terminal, I'd made
up my mind to go seek Sister Marleu's help.

I purposely remained seated until all the other passengers had filed out of the bus, keeping a particular eye on
the young man who had been looking at me. He got off,
and after the last person had disembarked, I walked down
the aisle and cautiously left the bus myself. The gritty bus
station was bustling with travelers. I scanned the crowd for
the pockmarked man in the black suit. He was nowhere in
sight and I knew my paranoia had gotten the better of me
after all. He was just another passenger.

Outside in the night, I had trouble finding a taxi so
started walking uptown. As I walked, I thought what a
big risk I was taking going to seek the help of a woman I
barely knew. But there seemed to be no alternative. I also
thought of Luis Díaz. If Sister Marleu wouldn't help me,

maybe I could go to him. Finally, I saw a free cab and ran to catch it. I got in and gave the cabbie the address of the shop. The cabbie seemed surprised.

"You sure you wanta go to that neighborhood this time anight, girly?" he asked me, squinting at me in the rear-view mirror.

"I'm sure," I said. "Just hurry, please."

He shrugged and gunned the engine. The meter clicked away. We drove to Harlem and pulled into the block where Sister Marleu's little shop was located. I paid the fare and noticed that after I got out, the cabbie locked all his doors and sped away.

The block was dark, except for a dim streetlight on the corner. I descended the short flight of stairs leading to the shop, only to discover that the place was closed. A small sign that read CERRADO hung in the window.

I peered through the glass pane and detected faint light from within. I started pounding on the door hoping that Sister Marleu was inside but simply not open for business. I prayed she would answer, but there was no response.

Running up the steps to the street, I dashed into a little convenience store a few doors down. The woman behind the counter was arranging packs of cigarettes in a display.

"Sister Marleu," I said breathlessly. "Do you know how I can get in touch with her?"

The woman looked up at me blankly. *"Qué?"*

"Sister Marleu, Marlooo," I said pointing my finger toward the shop, trying to make her understand.

"Ah, Marloo! *Si, si. Al lado. Al lado*," she said. I didn't understand what she was trying to tell me.

"Is she there? Does she live there?" I asked, frustrated with my inability to communicate with the woman.

"Qué?" the woman grimaced.

Just then, a fresh-faced teenage girl with her hair in rollers came forward from the back of the store, carrying two Coke bottles, a bag of corn chips, and a box of detergent. She put the items on the counter and pulled out some money. As the woman behind the counter rang up her purchases, I tried to strike up a conversation.

"Hi," I said.

The girl turned and looked me up and down suspiciously without replying.

"I wonder, can you help me?"

"What you want?" she said, shifting her weight from one leg to the other as she waited for her change.

"You speak Spanish?"

"Yeah," she said as though it was a stupid question.

"Then could you do me favor and ask her if she knows whether Sister Marleu lives next door in her shop?"

The girl acted like it was no big deal. "Yeah, sure." She turned to the woman behind the counter. *"Quiere saber si Sister Marloo vive al lado? En la tienda?"*

"Sí, sí. Ella vive ahí," the woman said as she placed the items in a bag.

"Yeah, she does," the girl said.

"Could you ask her if she's there now? The shop is closed."

"Esta ahi ahora?"

The woman shrugged. *"Qué se yo?"*

"She says, 'How would I know?'"

"Oh," I said, deflated.

"Casi siempre esta ahi. Escondiendose," the woman volunteered.

The girl snickered.

"What did she say?" I asked.

"She says almost always she's there—hiding."

Back on the street, I decided to try my luck once more. But as I approached the little shop, I glanced across the street and thought I saw the pockmarked man I'd seen on the bus. The darkness made it hard to tell if it really was him or not, but whoever it was stood across the street on alert, looking all around, as if he were sniffing for game. I quickly ran down the flight of steps and ducked out of sight.

I tapped lightly on the door, fearing he might hear me.

Still no answer. I sneaked up the steps for a quick look to
see if he was still there. He was nowhere in sight. I was too
terrified to make a run for it. And besides, I had nowhere to
go. I huddled beside the door of the shop and kept tapping
softly, hoping that if Sister Marleu was inside, she'd eventually hear me.

A few moments passed and then, unexpectedly, the
door cracked open. The curtain of red beads rustled and
Sister Marleu appeared above me, holding a candle. A
faint reddish light glowed behind her.

"What do you want?" she said.

I stood up.

"Do you remember me? I'm Beatrice O'Connell. I came
here with Luis Díaz."

"Oh, yes," she purred. "Sister remembers you very well."

"I'm being followed. Can I come inside?" I said with
urgency.

She held the beaded curtain aside so I could pass, locking the door behind me. Once again, I found myself standing in that magical little place, filled with jars, bottles, and
amulets. The short, plump woman held the candle up to
my face and leaned in so close that I could feel her breath
on my skin. She looked deep into my eyes and said, "Yes,
you have trouble. Big trouble . . . "

"That's right. I need your help."

"You have changed," she said with a knowing air.

"Yes . . . Yes, I have."

"Trouble has made you change. Trouble makes us all
change. Sister likes you better now."

"This man is following me. I think he's going to kidnap
me or kill me. If he asks them at the bodega, he's going to
find out I'm here."

Marleu waved her free hand dismissively. "Do not think
about him. He is a goat in the lion's den . . . Come, come,"
she motioned. "Sit with me."

Marleu guided me to a chair at the back of the room
and bid me to sit down. She sat down on a chair and faced

me, holding the candle up to my face as I spoke. Weak and tiny as it was, the candle flame gave the place an eerie glow.

"Now," the old woman began, "tell me why you have come to Sister."

I swallowed hard in an effort to collect my thoughts, barely knowing where to begin. Then I told her about the grimoire, and my father's murder, and Defensores Fidei, and my discovery of their old and dangerous secret. I told her about the *Malleus*, describing it to her as a lawbook for witch-hunters. I was afraid to tell her details about the Inquisition I had witnessed, fearing that she, like Chief Whiting and the Milbern police, would simply scoff at my story. But as I related the events in a halting manner, she listened with great interest and when I faltered, she encouraged me to go on.

I was in the middle of telling her all about Simon, how he rescued me and was then captured, when she suddenly stiffened and went on alert. She raised her index finger to her lips and said a sharp, "Shhh!"

I too heard a noise that sounded like a door handle rattling.

"That's him!" I whispered in alarm.

"Stay here," Sister Marleu said calmly, rising from her chair. She stood very still, her black eyes gleaming in the candlelight. She blew the candle out and we waited.

I hardly breathed as I heard the front door open and the swish of the beaded curtains parting. The shadowy figure of a man holding a gun was visible in the faint light.

"Beatrice," he called out in an eerie, singsong voice. "I know you're in here . . . You can't escape from us . . ."

With that, he saw Sister Marleu, standing, facing him with a defiant look on her face. Tossing her head around, so that her black snake-like braids swung from side to side, she let out a demonic howl. As he focused and aimed his gun at her, I leapt to my feet and gave her a mighty shove with all the strength I had left, which pushed her aside and sent her crashing into one of the souvenir-laden tables.

But at least she was out of harm's way. I just stood there, paralyzed with fear, expecting a shot to ring out. Instead, all I heard was a kind of whooshing sound, followed by a hideous little cry, then a raspy gurgle, then silence.

Sister Marleu, a plump little woman, chuckled softly as she struggled to her feet. I was still too frightened to move.

"You are a brave girl. Sister is grateful."

She struck a match and lit several candles this time. I looked over at the beaded curtain. Two squat young men with round, chocolate-colored faces reminiscent of Sister Marleu's were standing over a body. They wore rolled-up shirtsleeves and jeans, and each held a commando knife. The blade of one knife was bloody. The pale pockmarked man in black was lying on the floor in a growing pool of blood. His eyes were wide and glassy. His throat had been slit from ear to ear. I couldn't bear to look at him.

"Meet my sons, Alfredo and Manuel," Sister Marleu announced proudly, flashing the brilliant, toothy grin I remembered from our first meeting. "My sons are my lions. They look after me. I do not open my door without my lions nearby . . . In this business, they have their work cut out for them, believe me."

"El cabron esta muerto, Mama. Viva Chango!" one of the young men said.

"What does that mean?" I asked.

"It means, 'The goat is dead. Praise to Chango,'" Sister Marleu replied. "You come now . . . Sister will make you tea, and you will tell Sister how she can help you."

Marleu led me through a narrow corridor at the back of the shop into a small kitchen parlor. Plants and herbs, in pots and dried in sheafs were crowded inside the gaping mouth of a big old-fashioned rolltop desk. A kettle and two copper pots simmered atop the gas burners of a large black stove. On a table next to the stove were several bottles containing murky liquids of varying hues and consistencies, along with a collection of ladles, measuring cups, and spoons. A row of glass jars filled with colored powders lined the sill of a calico-curtained window that faced out onto a brick wall. Sister Marleu directed me to sit down on a fraying tufted armchair while she prepared the tea.

I watched the little woman snip a variety of herbs into a china teapot and pour hot water over them, after which she added a teaspoon of greenish powder from one of the jars and a shot of brown liquid from a bottle. Then she lifted up the pot in both hands, jiggled it around so the water sloshed from side to side, and put it down again, letting the brew steep for a minute or two. Pouring two cupfuls, she handed one to me.

Still unnerved by the killing, I took a cautious sip, prepared to be revolted. Much to my surprise, however, the concoction tasted delicious. After a few more swallows, I felt a soothing warmth sweep over me.

"This is wonderful," I said, as she refilled my cup. "What's in it?"

"Tranquility and energy . . . mixed," Marleu said, playfully rubbing the thumb and index finger of her left hand together in a circular motion.

"Is this where you make the potions for your shop?" I asked her.

"This is where dreams come true . . . Nightmares too," she responded. "You are in search of a nightmare, I think."

"It's more like a nightmare's in search of me," I replied. "And there's no hope of it ending unless you help me. Even then . . ."

"So, tell Marloo your desire."

I explained the situation in detail. She stared at me in that intense way of hers so that I felt her mind was penetrating mine, curling around it, almost like a snake.

"What I need is protection so I can go home, get my passport and credit cards, and a few things so I can go to Zurich. I know they're watching the house. Watching for me and for the mail. I can't go there alone."

"You must not go there at all," Sister Marleu said, narrowing her eyes.

"But I have to get to Zurich and I need money and my passport."

Sister Marleu held up her hand. "You will tell Marloo where your house is and where to find those things. Marloo will send someone."

I shook my head. "No, I should go with them. I can't let you put someone else in danger. And, believe me, the danger is unimaginable."

A flicker of a smile crossed the old woman's lips. "You will write down for Sister the address of your house and where you have put those things. Marloo will send someone good."

I had a feeling this strange old woman was unafraid of danger, no doubt because she lived with it on a daily basis. She handed me pen and paper and I did as she directed.

"We keep a spare key in the garden, under the plant stand by the back door," I told her. "I hope it's still there. Otherwise whoever you send will have to break in and maybe get caught by the police."

Marleu laughed. "We are used to the police," she said.

I gave her back the piece of paper with all the instructions on it. She left the room and shortly after that I drifted off to sleep. Sometime later, I awoke with a start. The room was dark. For a moment, I wondered where I was. But I felt much better as if I'd had a good night's sleep. The light flicked on and there was Sister Marleu standing in front of me handing me a beat-up brown wallet.

"Have a nice rest?" she asked me as if she already knew the answer.

"Yes, very. Thank you. What's this?" I said, taking the wallet.

"It is from the pocket of your dead friend."

Feelings of revulsion still did not prevent me from eagerly opening the billfold to examine its contents. Not surprisingly, there was no identification—nothing to mark this would-be assassin if he got caught or died in the act,

I thought. There was only a hundred fifty-odd dollars in cash, the receipt for the bus ticket, and a thin scrap of yellow paper with some numbers scrawled on it.

I sat in the chair, absently fingering the slip of paper as I watched Marleu brewing her potions at the stove. This strange little woman did indeed have a potent aura of mystery about her, which prevailed in spite of her theatrics, not because of them. Díaz had been right: She had real power. Maybe she really *was* a witch, I thought with some amusement, which would have been a grand irony considering the present circumstances.

I examined the numbers once more. And then it hit me. I asked Sister Marleu if I could use her telephone. Engrossed in her potions, she grunted an assent. I punched out the numbers. Shortly, the phone started ringing—a European staccato double-ring.

"Baur-au-Lac Hotel. Guten Tag," said a cheery female operator's voice.

"Where am I calling?" I asked.

"You are calling the Baur-au-Lac Hotel in Zurich, Switzerland, madame. How may I help you?" Her tone was most obliging.

Zurich! They either had the code or were waiting for someone to send it to them, I thought. I took a chance.

"Um—Mr. Desmond Dougherty, please," I said, expectantly.

There was a brief pause. Then the operator said, "One moment, please. I will connect you."

After several short rings, a groggy voice answered the phone.

"Yes?"

I waited, not daring to speak.

"Hello . . . ? Who . . . Who is this?"

I knew that voice. "Simon!" I cried. "Simon! It's me, Beatrice! Are you all right? Can you talk?"

"Beatrice . . ." He sounded drugged. "Where are you? How did you find me?"

"Never mind that now," I said urgently. "Are you all right?"

I heard him breathing heavily, struggling to speak. "Yes . . . Where are you?"

"I'm in New York. I'm safe."

"No . . . ! No . . ." he said with growing anxiety. "Not safe . . . They sent someone to kidnap you—"

I cut him off. "Don't worry. He's been dealt with. I'm okay."

"Thank God. Can't talk long . . ." he said, obviously fading.

"Did they get the code?"

"Yes . . . But it's wrong . . ."

"I know . . . It's one word off. I did that as a precaution. Only I know the word."

"They won't stop until they get you." He was breathing very hard. "I can't help you. In two days, my father is taking me to a clinic in Davos . . ."

"Why?"

"Going to give me shock treatments."

"Where in Davos? What clinic?" He didn't answer. "Simon! Are you there?"

"Dr. Friedrich," he said at last. "Wilhelm Friedrich."

"Simon, I'm on my way. Don't give up, whatever you do."

"Too late . . ."

I heard a commotion at the other end of the line. It sounded as if the phone had dropped.

"Simon! Simon! Are you there?"

A long silence followed in which I sensed that someone was listening on the other end—and it wasn't Simon. I just knew it was Dougherty so I hung up.

Sister Marleu turned to me. "More trouble," she said, as if it were a fact.

"Very big trouble, I'm afraid. I have to get to Switzerland as fast as possible."

"You will," Marleu said.

While Sister Marleu went about her business, funneling potions into glass vials and sealing them with cork stoppers, I thought about the evil Desmond Dougherty, who wanted to incapacitate his own son and eventually kill me in order to get his hands on a great fortune. There was no doubt in my mind that Dougherty deserved to die. He was responsible for the torture and murder of countless innocents, my father and Stephen included. In control of a vast fortune, there was no telling how many more would die or be infected by his misogyny.

But could I kill him, monster that he was? Was I capable of such an act, even if the intended victim so richly deserved it?

I tried to rationalize the thought by telling myself that it wouldn't be a murder so much as the execution of a deranged and demonic criminal. But who was I to be an executioner? I didn't know if I had the stomach for it.

Sometime later, in the midst of my ruminations, we heard voices at the front of the shop. Marleu left the room but soon returned holding my passport and credit cards in her hand.

"Was there trouble?" I asked her.

"There is always trouble, as you know," Marleu said matter-of-factly. "But it is over."

Marleu ambled over to the desk and stooped down, extracting a key from the pocket of her shift. Unlocking the bottom drawer, she pulled it all the way out, brought it over to me, and placed it on the table next to my chair. The drawer was filled with cash—bundles of ragged hundreds, fifties, and twenties, bound with rubber bands.

My eyes widened. "There's a fortune here."

"Take more than you will need," she said.

"I'll pay you back, I promise," I said, taking out a brick of hundreds and one of fifties.

Marleu fetched me a small duffel bag for the money.

"Where did you get all this money from?" I asked her.

"The believers are very generous," she said.

"Some must be drug dealers," I joked. Marleu didn't laugh. She threw two more bricks of hundreds in the bag and replaced the drawer in its niche.

"You will need something else too," she said.

"What?"

"A weapon," she said, as if she'd been reading my mind.

"I don't know, Sister . . . I doubt I'm capable."

"Marloo sees many things. Marloo sees the future. You will need a weapon. A woman's weapon."

"What's a woman's weapon?" I asked.

"Poison," she said.

Chapter 26

S ister Marleu supplied me with a small suitcase filled with warm clothes and two items that were far more important: a vial of poison and a hypodermic syringe. The poison, she informed me, was odorless, colorless, and untraceable. It could be used on food or put into the syringe and injected into the body. Either way, the result was fast and deadly.

I took the plane to London and later an afternoon flight to Zurich. I changed money at the airport and hired a car to drive me up through the Alps to Davos. The driver, a glum but courteous older man, bowed slightly, took the suitcase from me and escorted me to a roomy black sedan parked nearby. He informed me the trip would take around three hours.

Scattered lights from distant towns and villages twinkled across the horizon as the car traveled through the crisp Alpine night. We wound our way up into the dense black mountains, where the road narrowed significantly. I asked the driver if he knew of a good hotel in Davos.

"Ja," he grunted, without further elaboration.

"Take me there, please."

It was close to one in the morning when we reached the dark, sleepy little village. The car pulled up in front of a small hotel with a gingerbread façade, just off the main street.

"Schweizerhof," the driver announced.

I got out of the car and stretched, breathing in the fresh, clean mountain air while the driver took my suitcase into the lobby. I followed him inside and after he had kindly roused someone at the desk to help me, I thanked him, paid him in cash, and sent him back on his way to Zurich.

The lobby of the Schweizerhof was decorated with sturdy, unpretentious wooden furniture and a few touches of folksy bric-a-brac—a Swiss horn, some cow harnesses, and, in a high recessed space on the back wall of the enclosed reception area, a row of colorful antique beer steins. I gave the man at the desk my passport and he checked me in.

"Do you know a Dr. Wilhelm Friedrich?" I asked him.

"Dr. Friedrich, ja." The man nodded.

"He runs a clinic here?"

"A clinic, *ja.*"

He reached to the right of the front desk, where the keys of unoccupied rooms dangled on little hooks above cubicles for mail. Two keys remained, and he plucked one down.

"Second floor. Very quiet, but no view. It's all right?" he asked tentatively in his Swiss-German accent.

"That's very nice, thank you."

He walked out from behind the desk, picked up my bag, and led me to the elevator.

"There are many tourists in Davos just now," he said as the elevator door opened. "A big conference. All the hotels are nearly filled."

"Where is Dr. Friedrich's clinic?" I asked as I followed him.

"Above the village," he said, pointing his index finger upward. "You must take the cable car."

"Can I go tonight?"

He smiled and shook his head. "No, no. Closed. Seven o'clock tomorrow it will start again."

The elevator stopped. The man led me down a narrow corridor to my room. Thanking him, I went inside and immediately drew myself a hot bath. It was close to three in the morning by the time I fell into bed, exhausted.

The next morning, I had a quick breakfast and immediately set out for Dr. Friedrich's clinic. The neat little village of Davos was picturesque and compact. Everything was within walking distance. I hurried past the decorative

shops on the main street, taking note of the pretty church
and a small café next door, where people were sitting outside, drinking coffee and reading the newspapers. What
a lovely, pleasant village, I thought. It was so difficult to
imagine that in the midst of this fairy-tale setting, there was
such evil.

I came to the station, bought my ticket, and waited.
Gradually, the little waiting area filled up with tourists,
hikers, and locals. After about twenty minutes, a clanging
bell heralded the arrival of the cable car. I walked toward
the platform with the other passengers. A steel gate barred
us from going outside right away. In the near distance, I
saw the cab, with windows running the length of the sides,
gliding down the mountain on heavy steel cables, its white
metal exterior gleaming in the morning sunshine. The
bulky conveyance bumped to a halt. The doors slid open
and a few people got out. When the last of them had disembarked, the steel gate swung open to allow the new passengers to get on.

Taking my cue from those around me, I shoved my way
onto the spacious but seatless cab and grabbed hold of one
of the leather straps hanging from the ceiling. In a few minutes, the automatic doors slammed shut. The cab shuddered
slightly, clanking as it disengaged from its harbor. Suddenly,
we were airborne. As we traveled up the mountain, I admired
the breathtaking view. The majestic Alps were all around us,
studded with thick shawls of pine trees.

After about fifteen minutes, we reached the top. The
doors slid open, and the eager crowd piled out and quickly
dispersed, showing scant regard for courtesy. I left the station and looked around. To my left was a restaurant. Some
distance ahead of the restaurant, up a gently sloping hill,
was a tall gate made of thin wrought-iron bars shaped like
arrows, pointing to the sky. I walked up to the gate to get a
better look. Visible through the bars at some distance away
was a sprawling two-story building in the style of a chalet
that looked like a grand old luxury hotel. I assumed that this

was Dr. Friedrich's clinic, though no sign was posted. The gate was locked, and there was no buzzer.

I walked back down the hill and went inside the restaurant to inquire how to get in. A fresh-faced young man, dressed in lederhosen, knee socks, and a Tyrolean hat with a feather, was polishing glasses in front of the bar. He looked sexless in the cunning little folk costume.

"Bitte," I began. "Do you speak English?"

"A little," said the young man in a thick accent. His voice was unusually high-pitched. "But I am sorry, but we are closed."

"No, I just want to ask you a question. Is that Dr. Friedrich's clinic up there behind the gate?"

"It is a clinic, *ja.*"

"How do get in?"

"Ja, I think for this you must have the appointment or they do not let you come. When you have the appointment, then they are sending someone down here to meet you."

"How do I make an appointment?"

He shrugged.

"Have you ever been inside?" I asked him.

"I? *Nein!*" he said, laughing and pointing at his chest as though the thought amused him. "It is for the very rich people."

The young man suddenly fumbled and dropped the glass he was holding. It didn't break, but when he leaned down to pick it up, his hat fell off, revealing a long blond ponytail. It was only then that I realized that he was not a young man at all, but a young woman!

I stared in surprise as she straightened up, stuffed her hair back into her hat, and continued on about her business.

"Is that the costume of the restaurant?" I asked her.

The young woman nodded. *"Ja,* the costume. All of the boys, they wear the lederhosen, and the girls, they wear the dirndls. But my brother is sick, so I am taking his position for two days. This is his costume. You understand?"

"Yes, thank you."

I walked outside again and took another look around. I concluded that if Simon were there in the clinic, it would be very difficult to sneak in, much less try and get him out. And I had to assume that Dr. Wilhelm Friedrich—whoever he was—was a member of Defensores Fidei, and therefore not exactly ready to help me in any way.

There was only one thing to do. I had to confront Dougherty directly and try and make a deal with him. I had something he wanted, and he had Simon. A deal was the only hope I had of saving Simon—if it wasn't too late already. Of course, I had to be very careful, for I knew that if Dougherty managed to grab me first and got me somewhere where I was helpless, he would surely use Simon or more physically persuasive means to force me to give him the correct code. Then he'd have the fortune and Simon and me all just where he wanted us—in the palm of his evil hand. I took the cable car back down to the village.

As I walked, the image of the young woman wearing lederhosen kept flashing through my mind. I passed a shop window that had a similar outfit on display. I went into the shop and tried on the ensemble—socks, breeches, shirt, and hat. I stuffed my hair into the hat and pulled it down low over my brow. The wide-legged, loose-fitting short pants, and the thick high socks hid my legs. Only my knees peeked out. The loose white shirtsleeves covered my arms, and the bib covered my breasts. I really could have passed for a boy, like the girl in the restaurant. I bought the outfit and headed back to the hotel. The concierge greeted me at the front desk.

"Miss O'Connell, good day!" he said cheerfully. "You have found the clinic?"

"Yes, thank you . . . I need to call there in fact. Is there a phone down here I can use?"

"Just over there," he said, pointing to a booth at the far corner of the lobby. "Tell the operator and she will connect you."

The hotel operator put me through to the clinic. A smooth male voice answered the phone.

"Friedrich Clinic, *guten tag.*"

I swallowed hard and said, "Mr. Simon Lovelock, please."

There was a brief pause. "I am sorry. There is no one here by that name."

"Then . . . Mr. Desmond Dougherty, please."

There was another pause and then the receptionist said, "One moment, please."

They were there! Simon and Dougherty were there. I gripped the receiver tightly as the call was being transferred. There were several staccato rings, then a weak voice answered, "Hello?"

"Simon?!" I cried. "It's Beatrice. Are you okay?"

"Where are you?"

"I'm here, in Davos. I'm going to get you out of that clinic."

"No! Don't come here! It isn't safe!"

"I know. But I have plan. I want to talk to your father."

"God, no, Beatrice. Don't do this, please!"

"I'm going to do it. Let me talk to him."

"He's not here."

"Where is he?"

"With Friedrich."

"Simon, what have they done to you?"

He hesitated. "It's not what they've done. It's what they're going to do."

"Oh my God . . . You've got to get out of there. Can't you escape?"

Simon gave a weak chuckle. "No. If I could have, I would have by now."

"Well, I'm going to get you out of there. You'll see. When is your father coming back?"

"You know he'll kill you if he gets the chance," Simon said. "I don't know why he doesn't kill me. Perhaps he will . . ."

"He won't kill either of us as long as I have what he wants. Simon, listen to me . . . Are you strong enough to walk?"

"Barely."

"Simon, you've got to fight! When is your father coming back?"

"Soon now. Any moment," he said.

"I'm going to ring back in fifteen minutes."

"Don't do this. Leave. Just leave and hide."

"Fifteen minutes," I said, hanging up.

When I called back fifteen minutes later, I heard that dreadful, thundering voice I would never forget.

"Hello," Dougherty said.

I hesitated out of fear more than anything else.

"Hello?" he repeated sharply.

"Professor Dougherty," I began, trying to keep my tone firm and measured. There was no response. "This is Beatrice O'Connell speaking."

"Yes, I know. Where are you?"

"Never mind that just now," I said, feeling my heart racing. "I have a proposal I want to make to you."

"I'm listening."

I swallowed hard. My mouth was very dry. I spoke slowly and deliberately in order remain calm.

"I know you've been to the bank and discovered that the code on the paper is inaccurate."

"My son has informed you of that, has he?"

I ignored this comment. "I also know that you have your son there with you against his will."

Silence. I could hear him breathing hard on the other end of the line—in a rage, I suspected.

I went on: "You want the code. I want Simon. Are you willing to trade Simon for the code?"

"I am," he said without hesitation.

"Good." I chose my words carefully. "I'm here in Davos. Meet me at one o'clock at the little café next to the church on the main street . . . With Simon. I'll have a car waiting there and the three of us will drive to Zurich and go to the bank tomorrow. I'll go with you myself and give you the correct code so you can get the money. Then I'll take Simon home to New York with me."

A very long silence ensued. Finally, he said, "One o'clock," and hung up the phone.

I arranged for a car with the concierge, and asked him to instruct the driver to meet me at the café at one sharp.

"Meyer's at one o'clock," the concierge said, jotting it down in his book. "He will be there."

I told him I was checking out and asked him to prepare my bill. Then I went upstairs to my room where I removed the hypodermic needle and the vial of poison from the suitcase. I carefully filled the syringe with the lethal yellow liquid, placed it gingerly on the table, and stood staring at it for a very long time, wondering if I could go through with my plan.

Could I kill Dougherty?

The rationalization was there: He would surely kill me or have me killed and hurt Simon if I didn't get to him first. He was a serial killer himself. He had killed Stephen before my very eyes and in the most excruciating way. So he deserved to die. But could I do it?

I knew one other thing for sure: If Dougherty got his hands on the fortune, he would do untold harm. Armed with that kind of money, he could buy anything, including an acquittal if they did catch him.

So again I asked myself: Could I go through with it?

The plan I had in my mind was very imperfect and very strange. I had to administer the poison quickly, stealthily, so he wouldn't even know what had happened to him. I trusted Sister Marleu, who had assured me that it was a speedy death.

I packed my suitcase and dressed up in the boy's costume I had just bought. Wearing sunglasses, armed with the syringe in my pocket, I went down to the lobby to settle my bill. At first the concierge didn't recognize me. He addressed me in German and when I took off my sunglasses and hat, he roared with laughter.

"Ah! I thought you were a boy! The girls, they wear dirndls, not lederhosen," he said with a wink. "You have bought the wrong costume."

"American girls are different," I said, winking back at him. "The car is arranged?"

"One o'clock, Meyer's Café."

"He may have to wait."

"Ja, ja. No problem."

I paid the bill and gave him a nice tip. When I tucked my hair back under the hat and put on the sunglasses, the concierge said with a laugh, "You want to fool all the people of Davos to think you are a boy?"

"No. Just one."

I arrived at the station a little before noon. Riding up the mountain in the crowded car, I concentrated on the view as I fingered the syringe in my pocket. I tried to spur myself on and comfort myself with the notion that this was an execution rather than a murder. But I still wondered if, when the time came and assuming I got my opportunity, I would be capable of the act. I don't think any of us really knows what we're capable of until we're put to the test. My test was coming. I'd know soon enough.

I waited near the station, keeping my eyes in the direction of the clinic. They had to take the cable car down. It was the only way. Time dragged on and it grew close to twelve-thirty. The cable cars came and went, always full of people. For one anxious moment, I wondered if I'd missed them—if they'd gone ahead. But no, I thought. They would have needed time to get ready. They were still there. They would come.

Suddenly, in the distance, I saw three men walking to the station from the direction of the clinic. I pulled my hat low over my brow and eyed them as they made their way down the road. I immediately recognized Dougherty and Simon, but not the third man, who was wearing a dapper tweed jacket, tan melton trousers, and a loden-green felt hat.

Oh Christ, I thought, who the hell is he? And what if he comes with them?

Dougherty gripped Simon's arm, guiding him down the

sloping hill toward the station. Simon looked very pale and thin. He was having difficulty walking.

This third man, whoever he was, supported Simon on the other side. He was a tall, sandy-haired man with rugged Nordic features and the leathery complexion of a sportsman. He pulled a pipe from his breast pocket and they all three stopped for a moment while he lit it.

They resumed walking and got quite close to me when the stranger let Simon go. He walked over and put his hand on Dougherty's shoulder and the two men exchanged a few hushed words while Simon stood staring into space. He looked as if he'd been drugged. At one point, the men broke into laughter and though I couldn't hear exactly what was said, I caught Dougherty say the name, "Wilhelm." I assumed that the man was Dr. Wilhelm Friedrich, the head of the clinic.

I now worried that Friedrich might accompany them down in the car. Then I'd have to change my plan completely. To my profound relief, however, Dougherty and Friedrich shook hands at the station and, after Friedrich gave Simon a little pat on the shoulder, he turned and walked up the hill toward the clinic, puffing on his pipe.

Dougherty pulled Simon into the station and bought their tickets. I followed at a good distance, careful to keep out of sight. Concealing myself behind a group of boisterous tourists, I waited on the platform, watching the two of them intently. Finally, the cab lurched into its dock at the station and came to a halt. The incoming passengers disembarked and the gate opened, allowing the embarking passengers to move forward. The car was packed.

Once we were all inside, I stood with my back to Dougherty and Simon, who were off to one side. Simon leaned against the window, looking as if he might pass out. Dougherty whispered in his ear as the cab lurched forward, then glided down the mountain.

As we descended, I edged my way closer to Dougherty, who seemed entranced by the view. He was wearing a heavy tweed jacket and twill pants. I was nervous that the needle would not penetrate the material. I would have to go for the bare skin at the back of his neck, despite the risk.

After about fifteen minutes, the little station loomed ahead. I was very near to Dougherty now—almost within striking distance. I carefully pulled the syringe out of my pocket and positioned the hypodermic between the third and index fingers of my right hand, pressing lightly on the pump with my thumb. I kept it low and out of sight. Dougherty, his back to me, was still looking out the window. I glanced around. No one was paying the slightest attention to me. They were all either talking or admiring the view.

Then, suddenly, without warning, Dougherty pivoted around and looked right at me. I froze. But the blank expression on his face told me he hadn't recognized me. He blinked and stared past me, seemingly preoccupied. The cable car lurched and came to a halt. People started crowding forward as the doors slid open. Dougherty took Simon's arm and held him back to avoid the crush. They were right in front of me now. As Dougherty held Simon and navigated his way out of the car, I raised my hand and stabbed him with the hypodermic needle, pumping the poison into the back of his neck.

Dougherty cried out in pain and grabbed the back of his neck with his hand, turning to see what had hit him. I backed away. This time he did recognize me.

"Witch!" he cried:

He lunged for me. I saw that giant body lurching toward me in a terrible fury, like a great wave about to crash down on me. I couldn't move. He was just about to reach me when he suddenly dropped down to his knees and fell face forward on the cabin floor. His body jerked in spasms as he groaned.

I gathered my wits about me just in time to yell, "Heart attack! This man's having a heart attack!"

A commotion began as people rushed in to see him convulsed on the floor in the throes of death.

Simon was dazed. He seemed to have no idea what was happening. I grabbed hold of his arm and quickly pulled him off the cable car before the crowd became too big for us to move. We hurried out of the station into the street. I propped Simon up and we managed to walk the short distance to Meyer's Café where the car from the hotel was waiting. The driver helped me get Simon into the backseat and I climbed in beside him.

"Zurich," I said to the driver.

"Jawohl," he said, and gunned the engine. We were off.

In the car on the way to Zurich, Simon slept. When we got to the hotel that night, I explained to Simon that his father had suffered a fatal heart attack. He seemed unable to entirely comprehend it, but he was able to tell me that Friedrich had given him drugs and that the plan had been to kill us both after I gave his father the real code.

I knew then that I was right in doing what I did. But still, I cried. Simon cried with me.

I thought that perhaps one day I would tell him the truth. Not now.

Chapter 27

Two days later, I was standing in front of a dung-colored six-story 1920's building on the Bahnhofstrasse in Zurich. The discreet gold plaque near the entrance read: UNITED SWISS BANK. Tucked under my arm was that day's International Herald Tribune in which a small headline on the inside read: FATAL HEART ATTACK STRIKES AMERICAN PROFESSOR ON DAVOS CABLE CAR.

I walked into the foyer and told the receptionist I'd come for my appointment with Carl Haemmerli, the bank's president. Presently, Herr Haemmerli, a tall, white-haired man, impeccably dressed, came down personally to meet me. Speaking English with only the faintest trace of an accent, he was extremely correct in his manner. He accompanied me to an old-fashioned elevator and we got in. He pushed a button, and the brass gate clicked shut.

At the top floor, Herr Haemmerli escorted me into his spare office, where we sat down.

"Now," Haemmerli began, "will you give me the name or number under which the account is to be accessed?"

I opened my purse and handed him a slip of paper.

"I'm not sure this is exactly right," I said.

Haemmerli looked at me sternly. "It must be *exactly* right," he said, making no mention of Dougherty's failed attempt to get at the funds or of anything else, for that matter.

I studied Haemmerli's expression as he opened the piece of paper. On it was the list of names from the grimoire, which I had written down from memory, minus the name Tiros, which was Borzamo's crucial deletion.

He had no reaction as he read the list. His face remained impassive. If, indeed, he knew what he was looking at, he didn't betray any emotion at all. The Swiss banker's legendary discretion, I thought. Presently, Haemmerli excused himself and rose from his chair.

"One moment, please," he said.

As I sat there, I wondered if the code was indeed correct . . . And not only if I had gotten it right. Did the treasure really exist? Or was it all a grand hoax, right from the beginning? Maybe there was no fortune. Or maybe it had long since been claimed by God knows who. What a gruesome irony that would have been: All those lives lost for nothing. Like so much of history, it too was a waste.

But then I thought, what if it is right? What if my memory has served me well, this treasure really does exist, and then what? Goering's fortune would be mine. But not mine really . . . It belonged to others who had paid so more for it than I. I thought with some amusement, what if I donated the money to every cause that the Nazis and Defensores Fidei would detest. It would be one of history's most expensive jokes—the haters financing a war against hatred.

One thing I knew for certain was that I had to expose Defensores Fidei. Now that his father was dead, Simon had no fear of telling all that he knew. Between us, we'd agreed to go to the FBI and every authority we could think of to launch an investigation. The Milbern property was a killing field. There was enough evidence there to convict everyone.

In the meantime, I'd hire enough protection for us both in case Defensores Fidei got any ideas about revenge. But somehow, I doubted that they would. Insane causes need an insane leader, and Desmond Dougherty was mercifully dead.

As I waited and waited, I thought about my father and wondered what he would think of his daughter now. I had killed a man. And yet I felt my father was watching over me, forgiving me.

I thought about Simon. I loved him, wounded bird that

he was, though it would never be a romantic love. It was a courtly love. I referred to Simon affectionately as "my true and faithful knight," without revealing to him that I was the one who slayed the dragon! I could never ever tell him the truth about how his father had really died. Another secret I would always have to keep to myself. Simon had said to me the day after we got to Zurich: "I have lived so long under the shadow of evil that I have forgotten how to love . . ." I hoped that was not the case.

As I was thinking about all these things and about Stephen and how much he would have enjoyed this moment whatever its outcome, Herr Haemmerli entered the room and interrupted my reverie. This very correct and humorless man stood before me and handed back the paper I'd given him. I held my breath.

"Miss O'Connell," he said in a crisp, businesslike tone, on his face a banker's tight smile. "If you will please come this way . . . I would like to have you meet some of my colleagues and explain to you the services we offer our clients."